RESURRECTION

A fine red mist seeped up and out from every bone fragment, drifting over the skeleton and drawing together the bits and pieces of dust and bone.

Malcolm watched in horrified fascination as the bones of the skeleton grew together, as the mist solidified and became flesh, as full red lips grew out from the skull, as the eyelids formed over the empty sockets and then filled out as the eyes grew beneath them. The eyes opened and shone with a mad red light. The lips parted, and a pink tongue drifted obscenely over the pointed fangs. . . .

A cold hand shot forward and caught Malcolm by the throat. . . .

BLOOD
OF THE
IMPALER

Jeffrey Sackett

BANTAM BOOKS
NEW YORK · TORONTO · LONDON · SYDNEY · AUCKLAND

BLOOD OF THE IMPALER
A Bantam Book / October 1989

ISBN 0-553-28183-6

Published simultaneously in the United States and Canada

Bantam Books are published by Bantam Books, a division
of Bantam Doubleday Dell Publishing Group, Inc. Its trade-
mark, consisting of the words "Bantam Books" and the
portrayal of a rooster, is Registered in U.S. Patent and
Trademark Office and in other countries. Marca Registrada.
Bantam Books, 666 Fifth Avenue, New York, New York 10103.

PRINTED IN THE UNITED STATES OF AMERICA

O   0 9 8 7 6 5 4 3 2 1

*This novel is for my brother Gary,
with whom I used to stay up late
on school nights to watch* Shock Theater
when we were children.

Author's Note

The historical events referred to in this novel have been presented as accurately as possible, with due allowance, of course, for artistic license. The Balkans in the fifteenth century was a rather tumultuous place, and the sequence of historical events is still a hotly debated topic, so I have chosen to follow a chronology which fits my general plot needs. I have taken some liberties with Balkan geography as well, for the same reason. I hope that this will not upset the observant reader too severely. (And I wish to extend a word of thanks to John Prehn for his research assistance.)

Any reader unable to distinguish between the historical and fictional elements of the plot is urged to seek professional help as quickly as possible.

Readers intimately familiar with Bram Stoker's *Dracula* may be chagrined by what appear to be errors in references to character names. To you I can only say, Read on. The text explains it all. Those readers who have only seen the Dracula movies or the stage play upon which so many of them were based may be confused by the character references. This is understandable, because the films take the names of Stoker's characters and jumble them up and switch them around for reasons I have never understood. (For example, the Langella version of the story contained a character named Mina Van Helsing. Mina Van Helsing?! I mean, I ask you!) To such readers, the English teacher in me responds, Read the book, dammit! Don't just sit there in front of the television set!

A word about Vlad IV, also known as *Vlad Tepes*, Vlad

the Impaler: he ruled the Rumanian province of Wallachia as voivode (a Rumanian title of nobility, usually rendered into English as "prince," though "count" will do well enough) from 1456 until his overthrow in 1462, and then again briefly in 1476, the year of his death. In the course of his brief rule he adopted and discarded religions as one might change clothes, betrayed every ally he ever had, and according to some estimates killed one-quarter of the population of his own realm, which makes him proportionally a greater mass murderer than Hitler or Stalin. He acquired a reputation for savage brutality unique even in that savage, brutal age, his most famous act being the simultaneous execution of thirty thousand captive enemy soldiers by impalement, i.e., a stake driven up through the anus and out the mouth.

He was not a nice fellow.

"Wallachia" is pronounced "Vallakhia" and is spelled in a variety of ways. The Rumanian nickname "Tepes" is pronounced "Tsepesh." Vlad's other nickname is sufficiently well known to make any explanation of pronunciation unnecessary.

Enough said. I have to go now and hang some fresh garlic on the windows.

J.S.

Out cam the thick, thick blud, out cam the thin,
Out cam the bonny heart's blud til there wass non within.
Mither, Mither, mak me bed, mak for me a windin' sheet.
Wrap me up in a cloak o' gold and see if I ca' sleep...

—SCOTTISH BALLAD

MEPHISTOPHILIS: Now, Faustus, ask what thou wilt.
FAUSTUS: First will I question thee about Hell.
   Tell me, where is this place that men call Hell?
MEPH.   Under the heavens.
FAUST.   Aye, but whereabouts?
MEPH.   Within the bowels of these elements,
   Where we are tortured and remain forever.
   Hell hath no limits, nor is circumscribed
   In one self place, for where we are is Hell,
   And where Hell is there must we ever be.
   And, to be short, when all the world dissolves
   And every creature shall be purified,
   All places shall be Hell that are not Heaven.
FAUST.   I think Hell's a fable.
MEPH.   Aye, think so,
   Till experience change thy mind.

—CHRISTOPHER MARLOWE, *Doctor
Faustus*, Act II, scene i

... for the blood is the life...
—*Deuteronomy* 12:23

Prologue

Death dreams drifted through his dead mind.

He lay in the darkness, only vaguely aware of the sound of the waves as they crashed against the hull of the ship. He was still and silent. His chest did not rise and fall with breathing, for he did not breathe. His cold white hands lay folded upon his stomach and his head rested upon a layer of his native earth. The red fire of his eyes, burning in the darkness of night, had dimmed with the sunrise, and now they stared ahead of him at the inside of the lid of the box. His empty eyes did not see and did not move, as he dreamed the dreams of the dead.

He was in great danger. If they caught him now as he lay helpless in the wooden crate, no power on earth or in hell could protect his heart from the wooden stake. They had been chasing him for weeks, following him all the way from the English coast to the mouth of the Danube. He was in danger of true death, and his motionless body seemed almost tense with the knowledge.

The beast in him predominated at such times, the cunning jungle animal which was ever listening, ever alert to danger. His dead human brain slept the sleep of death, but his animal soul heard and knew. He heard the sounds of leather boots on the deck above him, the cries of the gulls, the raucous laughter of the storm-hardened seamen as they raised and lowered sails.

Time passed as the sun traveled in its slow circuit, and still he slept. He felt the soft thud of the hull against the mooring post, and he heard voices drifting down to the hold from the deck above him.

1

"This is the *Czarina Catherine*?" asked a voice with a middle-European accent and an aged tremor.

"Can't ye bludy read? 'Course it is," was the reply.

"Good, good. And you are maybe the Captain Donelson?"

"Aye, I be Donelson. 'oo the bludy 'ell are you?"

"I am Hildesheim, Herr Captain, Immanuel Hildesheim."

"'oo...?" A pause, and then, "Oh, right. 'ildes'eim. We got that bludy box, and you can 'ave it and be damned wiv it."

"I have here the...ah...the invoice..."

"Aye, aye, keep your bludy hinvoice. Jus' get this bludy thing off my ship."

"There is a problem, Herr Captain?"

"No, no problem, not if you think makin' me crew all prayerful and skittish ain't a problem. I expects to lose a man or two in foul weather, but this voyage I've lost three, and never a day or night's been stormin'. No rain, no snow, nuthin' but a damned cold fog what wrapped us up of a night and blew us on like 'ell's own breath."

"*Ja, ja*...but..."

"And I makes good progress of a day on this ship, but never sailed so bludy fast and gone so bludy far so damned bludy quick, and me crew blames that bludy box. I even 'ad a man jump ship in Gibraltar, and I hain't never 'ad a man jump ship afore. So you're 'ildes'eim, and I'm to deliver the box to you, so take the damned thing and the 'ell with ye both."

He drifted back and forth between the world of sunlight and the world of shadows, between the land of the living and the realm of the dead. As part of him moved through the murky otherworld, part of him heard the grappling chains being affixed to the box. He felt himself being hoisted upward from the hold and swung over to be lowered onto a cart which waited on the dock. He felt the rumble of wooden wheels on cobblestones and heard Hildesheim whistling as he drove the team of horses.

More time passed, and at last it was drawing close to sunset. He did not know this with his thoughts, but he felt it in his ancient bones, in his infernal blood. He was growing hungry.

"Herr Hildesheim?" he heard a voice say.

"*Ja*, I am Hildesheim."

"My name is Petrof Skinsky. I believe that—"

"*Ja, ja,* Herr Skinsky, of course. I have expected you long time ago." A pause. "Skinsky, Skinsky. You are maybe the Skinsky who works the Slovak crews on the upper Danube, *ja?*"

"*Da,* I am that Skinsky. You have a—"

"You be careful, Herr Skinsky. The Slovaks, they slit your throat for a *groschen, ja?*"

"I know my men, Herr Hildesheim. You have a box to deliver to me?"

"*Ja,* is in the warehouse out back. Wait, I get the papers..."

The sun touched the tips of the distant Carpathian Mountains.

When he awakened, it was not slowly or with confused distraction as living humans awakened. His hands suddenly flexed as his serpentine tongue flicked hungrily against the tips of his fangs. He sensed the movement of the sun closer to the horizon, and his dead body was infused with a sudden, horrible semblance of life. His eyes shone crimson in the darkness of the box, and he laughed softly. He did not wish to disturb the nails which had so tightly secured his temporary home, so he dissolved into mist and seeped out through the narrow, almost imperceptible space between the box and the lid.

Skinsky and Hildesheim were talking in the office, and when they walked back to the warehouse neither thought it unusual for the sunset to have brought fog. It was November, and the moist air drifting in from the Black Sea often mingled with the colder air from the snow-laden lands of the Danube valley to produce such mists.

They did not notice that the fog waited motionless until they had entered the warehouse and were not outside to see it move slowly out onto the dark street where it coalesced into the figure of a tall man, clothed in black. The only things interrupting his darkness were the patches of white at his temples, the iron gray of his drooping mustache, the cadaverous hue of his waxen flesh, and the hellfire which burned in his unearthly eyes.

He walked slowly along the streets of the port town of Galatz, listening to the sounds coming from the taverns and the houses. His gaze shifted rapidly back and forth, and his tongue eagerly licked his cold lips. At such times, when the hunger was upon him and the hunt was underway, his movements were like those of a carnivorous animal.

A prostitute stood near the dim signpost of a tavern, and he walked toward her. "'*Nacht'n, Min Herr,*" she said drunkenly in her gutter Balkan German. "*Such'st en Freund fürm Aben'?*" She was young in years, no more than twenty, but excessive drinking and the diseases incumbent upon her profession had aged her, and the bloom had long since faded from her sallow cheeks. He stopped walking a few yards away, and she tried to sway her hips provocatively as she came to him, but she had drunk too much to do more than stumble. "*Ik heiss' Lara,*" she slurred. "*Wa' heiss'n Sie, Min Herr?*" He did not respond to her words. "*Such'st een Kuh für de fickend? Mein'st b'reit, Liblin . . .*"

He smiled coldly as his eyes bored into hers. At first she attempted to feign a seductive smile, but then she felt herself drained of strength by the inhuman power of those eyes, and she neither cried out nor offered resistance as he grabbed her by the hair, pulled back her head, and sank his fangs into her throat.

He drank deeply and long, for he was very, very hungry. He had taken a few crew members on the long voyage from the coast of England to the mouth of the Danube, but he had forced himself to go without food for a few nights. The crew of a ship the size of the *Czarina Catherine* was not large, and he did not wish to repeat his arrogantly confident gluttony of the previous year. Then, when he had sailed on the *Demeter* from Varna to Whitby, the ship had been tempest-tossed into port with a dead crew and a dead captain whose hands were tied to the wheel.

There was no need to draw such attention again. Not when he was fleeing and in danger, for the first time in four hundred years, in true danger of being destroyed.

He drained the woman of every drop of blood, and he felt much better as he let the corpse drop onto the wooden platform before the tavern. As a rule, he disliked turning to such people for his sustenance, for the dregs of human society held no appeal for him. He preferred the highborn or at least the well-bred, for he had been a nobleman, a prince, in those distant days when he had been alive. His greatest joy was in degrading the pure, profaning the sacred, destroying the well-beloved. To destroy the outcast and the unwanted was not particularly satisfying. Still, blood was blood. He dared not take the time to be selective, for he was being pursued.

He turned and walked back toward the warehouse, but he did not enter. The arrangements had all been made through intermediaries, even as Skinsky himself was an intermediary between Hildesheim and the Szgany, even as Hildesheim had been an intermediary between Donelson and Skinsky. Everything, including the impending meeting with Skinsky, had been arranged by letter and telegram. He was to meet his agent in the graveyard of the Petruskirche, St. Peter's Church, as soon as he had accepted delivery of the box which held all that remained of the supply of Rumanian soil.

Fifty boxes of earth, he thought angrily, though with grudging admiration for the old man who led his enemies. Fifty boxes of earth shipped to England not one year ago. And now he had only one left. He had shipped a few to Varna in an attempt to throw them off his trail, and the rest had been rendered useless to him, sealed forever with bits of sacred wafer, of consecrated host.

He stood in the shadows and waited. The half-moon floated in a starless, cloudy sky, and only the quiet gnawing of nocturnal rodents and the ubiquitous sounds of insects disturbed the silence of the graveyard.

It was an hour before dawn when his agent arrived, and he stepped forward from the shadows into the dim moonlight. "Herr Skinsky," he said.

Skinsky peered at him through the darkness. "Is that you, Voivode?"

"I am here," he replied. "Is everything in order?"

"Yes, Voivode," Skinsky replied, looking around nervously. "The Jew Hildesheim has delivered the box to me, and I have it in my warehouse near the wharves."

"Is it secure?"

"Oh, yes, Voivode, quite secure."

"Excellent," he said with satisfaction. "And the other arrangements?"

"I have carried out your instructions to the letter, Voivode. At dawn, my Slovak boatmen will get the key to the warehouse from my man Riasanovsky, and will load the box onto one of my barges. They will ferry it up the Danube to the junction with the Siretul River, where they will transfer it to your Szgany servants."

"And you have made it clear to them that you will not be there when they embark?"

"Yes, Voivode."

"And you have spoken of this to no one?"

"No, Voivode." He paused. "But those Gypsy Szgany, I do not think they can be trusted, Voivode. Once they have taken the box from my Slovaks, they may dump it in the river to avoid the hard poling upstream."

"My Szgany are faithful servants," he replied. "They have served . . . my people for centuries, and they know what fate awaits them if they disobey."

"Yes, Voivode." He paused again. "And may I ask what further services you require of me? You said I would not be here in the morning when my Slovaks load the barge . . ."

"That is correct," he said, walking up to his agent. "You have another task to perform, a very important task." He reached out and grabbed Skinsky by the collar. "You must bleed, Skinsky, and you must die." Before the man could react to the swift movement, the Voivode closed his teeth upon Skinsky's throat and ripped it open.

Petrof Skinsky tried to scream, but the blood pouring from his throat turned the sound into a frenzied gurgle as he stumbled backward, clutching madly at the huge gash. Skinsky fell to his knees and then pitched forward onto his face.

The Voivode gazed down impassively at the bleeding body as it twitched and quivered in its death throes. "This must not be my fate," he muttered. I have cheated true death for four centuries. I will not, I *must* not end as a pile of rotting dust and bone. My heart must *not* be host to the wooden stake of the executioner. I must defeat them, destroy them, survive, triumph. I must!

He smiled in the darkness, amused at his own thoughts. What is this, Voivode? Are you nervous, Lord of Wallachia? You, who waged war upon the Ottoman Turks, are you now afraid of the miserable cattle who pursue you? Do you fear them, that aged German, that American barbarian, those effete Englishmen, that pathetic woman?

He walked quickly from the churchyard toward the wharves. He did not need to know precisely where Skinsky's warehouse was to be found, for his nostrils could smell the inviting warmth of his native soil. When he reached the warehouse, he dissolved again into mist and seeped through the doorway and then through the space between the box and the lid. Once inside, again safe upon the earth of his homeland, he resumed his physical form.

And then he slept and dreamed the dreams of the dead.

He heard the liquid sounds of the Slovak tongue when he awakened with the next sunset, but he steeled himself to remain within the box until the sun had again completed its circuit. He needed the Slovaks to ferry him to the mouth of the Siretul River, and he dared do nothing that might cause them to jettison their cargo with the dawn. He lay silent and motionless in his conscious state, and the hunger gnawed at him. I must have blood, he thought, and then told himself, no, no, tomorrow night, wait until tomorrow night.

Dawn. He slept. He dreamed.

Dusk. He awakened.

He gnashed his teeth angrily when he heard that the boatmen were still speaking Slovak, which meant that he was still on the Danube. Again he steeled himself against his hunger, again he lay motionless through the long night as his self-imposed famine gnawed at him. The hours passed slowly, torturously, and he was on the verge of losing control when dawn broke and he fell back into his death dreams.

At last, when his empty eyes again moved with the setting of the sun and he listened to the voices from without, the words he heard were in the language of the Szgany.

He seeped out as mist to find himself on an old barge, surrounded by his Szgany Gypsies, the terrified and obedient servants of his many years of mastery. He solidified in their midst, and they dropped their barge poles onto the deck and fell to their knees. He looked from face to face. "Where is Kurda?" he asked imperiously.

"He . . . he is dead, V . . . Voivode," said a young Szgany. "He died last week. I am his son, Miklos."

He nodded. "And you command here?"

The young man bowed his head. "*You* command here, Voivode."

He nodded, smiling. "Then my needs are known to you, Miklos Kurdescu."

The Gypsy scurried over to the rear of the barge and returned with a burlap bag. He undid the rope and then took the immobile body of a seven-year-old boy from the bag. He held the child out as if it were an offering to a bloodthirsty deity.

He did not take the child from the Szgany. He smelled

the blood but saw no signs of life. "If you know of me from your father, Miklos Kurdescu, you know that I am like unto the serpent, which does not devour the dead. If this child is dead, he is of no use to me, and one of you must serve in his stead." He could hear the frightened intakes of breath as he spoke these words. "Does the child still live?"

"Yes, Voivode," Miklos replied, praying in his terror that the bag had not suffocated the child, praying that he had not failed in his first service to the dark lord who had ruled his people for centuries.

"Then rouse him," said the Voivode.

Miklos knelt down by the edge of the barge and took a few handfuls of water to splash on the child's face. In a few moments the little boy began to squirm and whine. Miklos and the other Szgany emitted audible sighs of relief as he again held the child out to the dark lord.

He took the child in his dead hands and waited for the eyes to open. He smiled and spoke softly to the semiconscious little boy, seeming to coo soothingly. Then he placed his mouth over the unlined white throat and began almost gently to drink. The child moved his little hands slowly for a few moments as the life was sucked out of him. Slowly his eyes grew blank and empty, and the boy fell still. The fresh young blood of an innocent child, the Voivode thought. So sweet, so sweet. When the body was cold and bloodless, he tossed it callously into the gently rolling waves of the Siretul River.

He looked at the Szgany. If they had been horrified or repulsed by what he had just done, they did not allow it to be seen on their faces. "Return to your task," he commanded, and they quickly picked up the barge poles and began again to push the barge on its long upstream journey toward the junction of the Siretul and Somesul rivers. He turned to Miklos as the other Szgany labored against the current. "Miklos Kurdescu. Come here."

The young Szgany came closer to him and swallowed nervously. "Yes, Voivode?"

"Do you know what must be done?"

"We . . . we are to take the barge up the Siretul to the Somesul and then to the Bishta River, and we are then to go up the Bishta to the last dock, thirty kilometers from Oradea. Then we are to load the . . . cargo onto a cart and take it to your castle."

"Correct," he said. "There is more. Listen carefully."

The Szgany glanced over their shoulders at Miklos as he listened and nodded. They avoided looking at the eyes of the demon as they burned red in the darkness of the Carpathian night, for to look too deeply into the eyes of the devil would be to lose one's soul. They continued to lean their weight against the ends of the barge poles, and the barge made its way slowly upstream through the pitch-darkness.

All through the night the Voivode stood at the bow of the barge, an unearthly captain of a stygian vessel. He looked behind him at the black river that wound its way back into the darkness of the Balkan night, and he could almost sense his enemies drawing closer to him. He knew that they were still far away, but his cold lips grew narrow and tense with the knowledge that each passing minute reduced the distance between them, reduced his already precarious margin of safety. "Faster," he ordered, and the Szgany strained at the poles in their effort to obey. He summoned his powers over the elements and called up a cold, biting wind to beat against the current of the river and aid him in his flight.

Is this fear? he wondered. It has been so long since I have feared . . .

When dawn approached, he again dissolved into mist and seeped back into the box. This would be the last day, he thought as he slipped into his death dreams. Within an hour the barge would leave the Somesul for the Bishta, and the Szgany would begin the arduous last stage of the journey. The dock nearest the border city of Oradea should be reached early in the afternoon, and thus he would be home by sunset.

Home, he thought as his eyes grew empty and his cold hands grew still. Home, where I will be safe again. Home to hundreds of hiding places. Home to my wives and my noble coffin. Home to my grave.

The sun was high in the heavens when he stirred slightly in his undead sleep. He had a fleeting vision of the bearded, heavyset old man creeping quietly through the crypt of his ancestral home, and he saw him throwing back the lid of coffin after coffin. He heard silent screams of agony echoing from the distance as the stakes were driven through the hearts of the women who had been with him through all the long centuries since they had been killed by the Turks. He heard Magda's mind screaming "Voivode! Voivode!" as the wood invaded her body, heard Katarina and Simone shrieking as they were reduced to dust.

He lay in cold, mute, impotent fury. *To lie here helpless as they invade my home and massacre my wives! Helpless, defenseless, weak! Damn them! Damn them all!*

He awakened as the sun's rim kissed the turrets of his castle ruins. He felt himself being tossed and jostled roughly within the box as the cart sped along the pitted dirt road. He heard the cries of his Szgany as they whipped their horses for more speed, and he heard the almost deafening pounding of hooves upon the roadway. And then, drawing closer with each moment, he heard the sound of gunfire.

They had found him.

"No!" he screamed. *"No!"* *In my own land, surrounded by my own people, not one mile from my castle, not one minute to sunset, and they are upon me!*

It must not be thus! I will not have it thus!

He sent out a silent command to the wolf packs that dwelt in the crags, summoning them to his aid. The sudden chorus of howls and snarls mingled with the gunfire and the shouts of his Gypsies as the battle was joined on the cold Carpathian road. He hissed in anger and his red eyes blazed as the sun began to sink behind the mountains.

"Damn you, Van Helsing," he whispered...

"...In the midst of this I could see that Jonathan on the one side of the ring of men, and Quincey on the other, were forcing a way to the cart; it was evident that they were bent on finishing their task before the sun should set. Nothing seemed to stop or even to hinder them. Neither the leveled weapons nor flashing knives of the Gypsies in front, nor the howling of the wolves behind, appeared to even attract their attention. Jonathan's impetuosity, and the manifest singleness of his purpose, seemed to overawe those in front of him; instinctively they cowered aside and let him pass. In an instant he had jumped upon the cart, and, with a strength which seemed incredible, raised the great chest, and flung it over the wheel to the ground. In the meantime, Mr. Morris had had to use force to pass through his side of the ring of Szgany. As Jonathan, with desperate energy, attacked one end of the chest, attempting to pry off the lid with his great Kukri knife, Mr. Morris attacked the other frantically with his bowie. Under the efforts of both men the lid began to

yield; the nails drew with a quick screeching sound, and the top of the box was thrown back.

"By this time the Gypsies, seeing themselves covered by the Winchesters, and at the mercy of Lord Godalming and Dr. Seward, had given in and made no further resistance. The sun was almost down on the mountaintops, and the shadows of the whole group fell long upon the snow. I saw the Count lying within the box upon the earth, some of which the rude falling from the cart had scattered over him. He was deathly pale, just like a waxen image, and the red eyes glared with the horrible vindictive look which I knew too well.

"As I looked, the eyes saw the sinking sun, and the look of hate in them turned to triumph.

"But, on the instant, came the sweep and flash of Jonathan's great knife. I shrieked as I saw it shear through the throat; whilst at the same moment Mr. Morris's bowie knife plunged into the heart.

"It was like a miracle; but before our very eyes, and almost in the drawing of a breath, the whole body crumbled into dust and passed from our sight."

Bram Stoker, *Dracula*

I

BLOOD RELATIONS

... visiting the iniquity of the fathers upon the children unto the third and fourth generation of them that hate me...

—Exodus 20:5

Chapter One

"Malcolm?" Rachel Rowland pounded insistently upon the bedroom door. "Malcolm! Get up and get dressed. It's after six o'clock in the evening. Father Henley will be here for dinner any minute." She waited a moment and then pounded again. "Malcolm! If you don't get up, I'm going to come in there and get you up!"

She heard a muffled and annoyed, "Okay, okay!" from within and frowned to herself. *He has a lot of nerve, sleeping all day.* "Why don't you get a normal, respectable job and get a decent, healthy night's sleep? Working all night, playing until the early hours of the morning, and then spending all day in bed... it just isn't proper, Malcolm!"

The bedroom door swung open and Malcolm Harker gazed at his older sister through bleary eyes. "Sis, get off my case, will you?"

"Don't you take that tone of voice with—" He slammed the door in her face and she began to pound on it again. "Malcolm!"

"All right, I'll be right down. Just go away!"

Rachel sniffed and harrumphed and then walked down the stairs to the dining room. Her husband, Daniel, was standing at the bar, and he looked over at her placidly as she marched into the room. "Prince Charming awake?" he asked.

"Spoiled brat," she muttered. "Yes, I suppose so."

Daniel Rowland shook his head. "How old is he now, twenty-six?"

"Twenty-seven," she muttered as she walked around the dining table, inspecting the place settings for the tenth time.

"Twenty-seven," he mused. "Why, when I was twenty-seven, I'd already made my first big killing in the market.

Had a Mercedes when I was twenty-seven. Had a few CDs, a mutual fund, and a good stock portfolio, all before I was thirty."

She nodded. "I just don't understand that boy. He seems to have absolutely no ambition whatsoever. If he doesn't get himself straightened out, I don't know what's going to..." She paused at the sound of a slow shuffle at the doorway. "Oh, hello, Grandfather. Have a nice nap?"

"Couldn't sleep," old Quincy muttered as he walked slowly into the dining room, leaning heavily upon his cane. He shuffled over to the table and sat down awkwardly at the head. "Malcolm was having nightmares again. Kept talking in his sleep."

"I don't wonder," Daniel observed as he uncorked a bottle of wine and placed it in the middle of the table. "All those misfits and malcontents he's always hanging around with at that bar where he works..."

"Not that bottle, Danny," Rachel said. "That's the dessert wine. Open the white for dinner."

"White? Fish or fowl?"

"Cornish hens," she muttered as she marched into the kitchen.

"Oh, well," he sighed. Daniel Rowland was not overly fond of poultry—strictly a meat-and-potatoes man. "But he should cultivate a few respectable friends," he continued as he corked the bottle and began to uncork another. "Why, when I was his age, I had friends and contacts in all branches of industry..." A mutter from the old man interrupted him. "What was that, Grandfather?"

"I said I'd be content if the boy would just go to church," old Quincy repeated in the soft voice which, though weak and trembling with advanced age, was still precise and dignified. Though the family patriarch had lived in the United States for over eighty of his more than ninety years, he still retained some small vestige of his English accent. He sighed as he absentmindedly reached up to smooth back the hair which his bald head had discarded decades ago. "I wish I was strong enough to go," he said. "I've taken the sacrament every Sunday since I was a child. It bothers me, not going to church."

"Oh, Grandfather, don't be silly," Rachel said. "Father Henley or Father Langstone can come to the house to give you communion."

"Not the same," he insisted.

"Besides, you can't expect to hop out of a hospital bed and go running off to church. When you get your strength back, you'll be able to go."

"What makes you think I'll be getting my strength back?" Quincy asked with annoyance, the wrinkles in his face made all the more prominent by his frown. "I'm not immortal, you know, and I've already gone beyond my three score years and ten."

"And I'm sure you have many years left," Rachel insisted, not quite truthfully. Though the doctors had claimed that the prostate operation had been routine and successful, the ordeal had weakened the old man considerably, and he appeared to be slower of movement and wearier with each passing day.

Quincy glowered at his granddaughter as she picked up a perfectly clean fork and began to wipe it with a spare napkin. "Omniscient now, are we?" he asked.

"Now, Grandfather, don't get in one of your moods," she said briskly as Quincy continued to glower. "Don't forget, we have company this evening."

"How old are you now, Rachel?" Quincy asked, watching as she inspected the table obsessively. Rachel was austere and prim, the potential attractiveness of her high cheeked, narrow face and thin, aristocratic nose offset by the penetrating, judgmental, constantly disapproving eyes and the holier-than-thou demeanor. Her short brown hair was pleasantly styled and her clothing was always the latest in fashion, but there was nothing even remotely feminine about her. She was too cold, too hard, too humorless.

"Hm?"

"I asked how old you are."

"I'll be forty in December," she replied. "You know that."

The old man nodded. "That makes you sixty-five."

Rachel looked over at him. "Whatever are you talking about?"

"Twenty-five and forty make sixty-five," he muttered. "You've been acting like a forty-year-old since you were fifteen."

Rachel turned her head in her grandfather's direction and stared at him silently for a moment, her brusque austerity seeming to be softened by some unspoken sorrow as her face was briefly suffused with an uncharacteristic vulnerability. She swallowed hard before responding, "Yes, I suppose I have. Fifteen was a difficult age for me."

She continued to stare at him, and the old man sighed. "Now, Rachel, you know I didn't mean to say. . ."

"I know what you meant," she snapped, hard and unyielding once again. "And you know what I mean."

"And I know what you both mean," Daniel offered, not understanding at all. "Adolescence is a difficult time of life for everyone."

Quincy looked at his granddaughter and sighed once again. "Harder for some people than for others."

"Stop it, Grandfather," Rachel sniffed. "Be of some help to me, will you? Try to make Malcolm behave himself."

"Yes, really," Daniel Rowland agreed, his irritatingly precise little mustache twitching with disapproval above his fat lips. "The boy's attitude is absolutely disgraceful. Now, I know that my own good fortune had an element of luck involved in it, but it was hard work and farsighted investments which made me what I am today." He patted his ample belly arrogantly, not taking the time to reflect that a man who marries a wealthy woman and then takes up residence in her grandfather's house is at best a dim reflection of Horatio Alger. "If that boy doesn't start planning for his future, he isn't likely to have one. Why, when I was his age. . ."

"You owned a fleet of ships and were happily ripping off most of Central America," Malcolm said as he ambled wearily into the dining room. "We've heard it all before, Danny." He walked over to his grandfather and smiled as he kissed him on the cheek. "Hiya, Gramps," he said cheerfully. "How's it going?"

Old Quincy smiled affectionately. "Afternoon, Malcolm. I'm glad you got up to join us."

Malcolm laughed as he sat down beside his grandfather. "Rachel didn't give me much choice."

"I certainly did not!" his sister remarked as she strode back into the room, carrying a large bowl filled with salad. "It's simply disgraceful, sleeping until this time of day."

"Sis, I work until three in the morning," he reminded her.

"Well, you shouldn't!" she snorted. "You should have a regular, decent job."

"I'm a bartender! That's regular!"

"Oh, Malcolm," she said with exasperation, "that's no

kind of job for a college graduate! And even if it's regular, it certainly isn't decent!"

"She's got a point there, Malcolm," Daniel agreed. "Why, when I was your age—"

"You were selling impure baby formula in Nigeria. Yeah, I know."

Daniel grew red in the face. "Just a moment, here, young man! I don't think there's any call for that tone of voice!"

"Hey, listen," Malcolm said angrily, "why don't you two just stop this mother-father crap you're always laying on me! You're my sister and brother-in-law, that's all! If you want to play parent, have a kid, but get off my back!"

"Malcolm!" Rachel snapped. "You will *not* speak to Daniel in that manner!"

"Sis," Malcolm said, "why don't you go take a flying..." His imprecation was cut off by knocking on the front door.

"That will be Father Henley," Rachel said, smoothing back her hair and arranging her skirt. "Now, Malcolm, you behave yourself."

"Yeah, yeah," he muttered. The parish priest coming over for dinner, he thought glumly. That's just great.

Rachel opened the door and smiled cheerfully. "Hello, Father. So nice that you could join us!"

"Thank you, Rachel," Father Henley said as he removed his hat and handed it to her. "I'm grateful for the invitation." He looked past her into the dining room. "Is Malcolm here?" he asked quietly.

"Yes," she whispered. "He's just gotten up. Isn't that disgraceful?"

"Well, the boy works nights," he said casually as he walked into the dining room, and went directly over to old Quincy, his hand extended eagerly. "Hello, Mr. Harker. I'm so glad to see you looking well!"

"Father." Quincy nodded, shaking his hand. "Good to see you."

"You're looking quite a bit better than you were the last time I saw you... three weeks ago, wasn't it...?"

"Yes, about that."

The priest gave Daniel's hand a perfunctory shake and then sat down beside the old man. "They seemed to be treating you quite well over at St. John's. It's quite a modern hospital."

"It is that," Quincy replied, already growing bored with the conversation. "Damned prostate!"

"Well, you pulled through with flying colors." Father Henley smiled. "Sorry I haven't come over to see you sooner, but..."

Quincy waved away the apology. "Father Langstone's been over almost every other day. He's a nice young fellow."

"Yes, he is," Father Henley agreed. As senior rector of Saint Thomas's Episcopal Church in Forest Hills Gardens, Henley had long ago delegated tedious home vistations to his subordinate. Except, of course, under a circumstance such as this, involving the soul of a young man who seemed on the verge of abandoning the faith. He glanced over at Malcolm, wondering how to begin, how to broach the topic of Malcolm's recent absenting of himself from services.

"I was sorry to hear about Mrs. Phipps," Rachel said, breaking into his thoughts as she fluttered about the table, checking and straightening the place settings. "I suppose we should have gone to her funeral, but we just couldn't get away."

"How old was the poor woman?" Daniel asked.

"Eighty-one," Henley replied, "and not sick a day in her life until her heart gave out."

Daniel nodded. "Eighty-one. Well, she had a long life, and a happy one."

Quincy harrumphed. "Long life," he muttered, winking at Malcolm. "She was a spring chicken."

Malcolm smiled.

"It was a lovely funeral," Henley added.

"No funeral is lovely, and every funeral is a waste of money," Quincy said. "Now, you listen to me, Father. I've told Rachel and Malcolm this a hundred times, but I just don't trust either of them to remember it, so you make sure they do. When I die, I don't want any money wasted on a fancy funeral. I don't want a viewing, I don't want one of those cement-lined steel coffins, and I don't want lines of people filing by me, telling each other how good I look. When I go, I want to go quickly and with no fuss. Just have me put in the cheapest coffin you can buy, and plant me as soon as possible."

"Now, Grandfather..." Rachel began.

"I'm serious, girl!" Quincy said sternly. "Money is something which should be spent on the living, not on the dead."

He wagged his finger at the priest. "You remember, you hear? When I die, just put me in a box and bury me. No viewing, no fuss." He laughed grimly. "I've outlived all my friends anyway. Why waste money on a funeral no one would attend?"

"Will I see you at mass on Sunday?" Henley asked, changing the subject.

Quincy shook his head. "I'm getting too old to get out much."

"Well, that's understandable. I can come over once a week to hear your confession and administer the sacrament." He turned to Malcolm and said, smiling under reprovingly raised eyebrows, "I haven't seen you at church lately either, Mal. Have you been ill?"

I really don't want to have this conversation, Malcolm thought, but he said, "No, Father. It's just that . . . well, I work late each night"—he ignored his sister's skeptical snort—"and it's awfully hard for me to get up on Sunday mornings. I'm sure you know what I mean."

"Of course I do." The priest smiled. "That's why we have mass in the afternoon as well." He continued smiling at Malcolm, which made the young man very uncomfortable.

"Yeah, well," he muttered, "I should go in the afternoon, I guess . . ."

"You certainly should!" Rachel said emphatically. "It's terrible, allowing yourself to become remiss in your religious obligations!"

"I agree," Daniel said, pouring a glass of wine for each of the people present. "Why, when I was your age, I went to church each and every Sunday of the year, and on all the holidays, too."

Quincy tapped his fork lightly against his glass and said softly, "The boy said he'll go in the afternoon. Leave him be."

"All I was trying to—" Rachel began.

"Leave him be," Quincy repeated. Rachel was too obedient to argue with him, and she began to serve the salad.

Henley's brow furrowed slightly as he continued to look at Malcolm. The young man's color was not good; he looked wan and ill. His eyes seemed tired and somewhat pained. As Malcolm reached up to scratch his scalp beneath his thick black hair, Henley noticed that his long, thin fingers were trembling. "Are you sure you've been feeling well lately, Malcolm?" Henley asked. "You look a little under the weather."

"Just the job and the hours," Malcolm muttered.

Henley nodded. "I imagine you get home rather late each night."

"Each morning, you mean," Rachel said disapprovingly.

"Yeah," Malcolm replied to the priest, ignoring his sister. "I start working at about eight and I get off at . . . well, whenever the place closes, usually about three."

"And you sleep until six in the evening?" the priest asked.

"Oh, he wouldn't have to, if he'd come right home," Rachel snapped knowingly. "But after work he goes off running around with his friend Jerry, looking for easy women!"

Malcolm rubbed his still-bleary eyes. "Rachel, will you shut the hell up?"

Daniel frowned at him. "Don't speak to your sister that way!"

Quincy coughed loudly, his standard means of getting attention. All eyes turned to him as he said quietly, "Rachel, get the meat. Daniel, go with her and carve it out in the kitchen."

"Now, Grandfather—" Rachel began.

"Rachel, get the meat!" he repeated sternly. "Daniel, go with her and carve it out in the kitchen!" After exchanging annoyed glances, his granddaughter and her husband rose from the table and left the room. As the door to the kitchen swung shut, the old man turned to the priest and said, "Thank the Lord I'm not Malcolm. I think I'd have shot both of them years ago."

Malcolm smiled, gratified at his grandfather's affectionate, if hyperbolical, defense. "Thanks, Gramps."

Quincy took a sip of his wine. "You will go to church, though, won't you?"

Malcolm patted the old man on the arm. "Sure I will, Gramps. This Sunday afternoon, for sure."

Quincy nodded and smiled. He turned to Father Henley and said, "Malcolm is keeping company with a charming young lady, by the way."

"Oh, isn't that nice!" Henley said, genuinely pleased.

"We're not . . . I mean, it isn't serious," Malcolm said quickly. "In fact, I don't even know if we're going to see each other again."

"It looked serious to me last week when you brought her home to meet us," Quincy said.

"Well, last week was last week."

Rachel and Daniel returned a few moments later with the roast, and the rest of the meal was spent pleasantly enough. Henley nodded and smiled as Rachel spoke critically about most of the people she knew and as Daniel reminded everyone how successful he was. The priest strove to repress his laughter whenever old Quincy would make some caustic remark to his granddaughter and her husband. Malcolm said nothing throughout the meal. He looked disinterestedly at his food, pushed it around his plate with his fork, and eventually rose from the table, leaving the food uneaten. "I gotta get ready for work."

"Okay, boy," Quincy said as he downed a glass of wine.

"Bye, Father. Good to see you."

"Good-bye, Mal. See you in church." The priest smiled.

"Malcolm!" Rachel snapped. "You haven't touched your food!"

"Not hungry," he said over his shoulder, and bounded up the stairs.

It's funny, he thought as he showered. I felt like shit when I woke up, didn't eat a thing, and now I feel a hundred percent better. Must be the screwy hours. I hate to admit it, but maybe Rachel's right. Maybe it does something to your system, staying up so late and then sleeping through the afternoon. Maybe I should try to get another job.

He stepped out of the shower and began to shave. Another job. Out of the question. His brief experience down on Wall Street had taught him that he was just not cut out for a nine-to-five job. He did not seem able to function properly that early in the morning. There are day people, and there are night people, and you cannot change what you are. Malcolm was wide-awake at three in the morning, and always dead tired at three in the afternoon.

He splashed on some after-shave and pulled on a gray turtleneck sweater. Maybe that's why Jerry and I get along so well, he reflected. Jerry's always ready to party all night. He never gets tired.

Well, I hope he's in a partying mood tonight. After last night, I need a little fun, a little something to lift my spirits.

Finished dressing and not wishing to have to make any further good-byes, he walked quietly down the stairs and left the house. Thank God! he thought with relief. Any more conversation with Henley and Rachel and Daniel, and he . . . well, he *might* very well have been tempted to shoot somebody. As he walked the short distance from Granville Place in the Gardens to Ascan Avenue, he felt just a bit guilty about his grandfather and the priest. Go to church! He had absolutely no intention of going to church, this coming Sunday or any other time. If nothing else, he had reached intellectual discretion. Superstitious nonsense, all of it. He knew it upset his grandfather, and he felt some affection for Father Henley, but one had to be true to one's beliefs.

As he rounded the corner and walked down Ascan Avenue toward Queens Boulevard, he tried to shake off any hint of depression or unease. Gonna be a good night, he thought. Me'n Jerry'll spend six or seven easy hours mixing drinks and flirting with the women at the Strand, and then either we'll have some fun with a couple of them or we'll go someplace else and find some women there.

Everything will be okay tonight, he thought confidently. Last night was a fluke, nothing but a fluke. Happens to every guy once in a while, just as Holly said.

Holly. . . I guess I won't be seeing Holly anymore. She probably thinks I'm a fag or something now.

He turned left at the huge Roman Catholic church which stretched for an entire block along Queens Boulevard, and in a few minutes he was at the Strand, where he and his friend Jerry tended bar. The Strand had been named rather self-consciously after the famous street in London. It was a restaurant and after dark, a somewhat sedate but still acceptably funky disco and singles' bar frequented by affluent young adults. This accounted for both the classy atmosphere and the inordinately high prices.

This was fine with Malcolm and Jerry. The higher the prices, the higher the tips.

Malcolm entered to find Jerry Herman already behind the long, horseshoe-shaped bar. "Hey, Mal," Jerry called out. "'Bout time you showed up!"

"Why, am I late?" he asked.

"Nah, it's only eight o'clock. But I was getting bored. This place is dead tonight."

"It's only Tuesday, Jerry," Malcolm reminded him. "It'll be nice and quiet."

"Who likes it nice and quiet?" Jerry asked. "The busier the better, I always say. Makes the time go faster and brings in a lot more good-looking women. And speaking of which, how did things go with Holly last night?"

Malcolm flushed slightly. "Great, Jerry, just great." Horrible, he thought. So damned embarrassing.

"Lucky son of a bitch," Jerry muttered in mock despondency. "I don't know what she sees in you. She'd be a lot better off with a stud like me."

Malcolm laughed in spite of himself. "Oh, yeah, really?"

"Sure," he said, nodding. "I can go nonstop for two hours with only a fifteen-minute bathroom, smoke, and bourbon break."

"Gee, you're my hero, Jer," Malcolm said, still laughing.

"Herman! Harker!" the voice of their boss boomed from the kitchen at the end of the room. "Get your asses in here and help me unload these kegs!"

"I'll do it, Mal," Jerry said, nodding toward the door. "You got company."

Malcolm turned around and swallowed hard, suddenly very nervous and ill at ease as Holly Larsen closed the door behind her.

The hours passed quickly for Jerry, no doubt. He scampered back and forth along his side of the bar with his usual speed and cheerful efficiency, living up to his self-proclaimed reputation as the only bartender in New York who could work, flirt, think, and make proper change simultaneously. Jerry's somewhat broad and acne-scarred face set above a body too skinny to be fashionably thin had never deterred him from his pursuit of the fair sex, nor had it impeded his lotharial success. He was funny enough, friendly enough, and eager enough to counterbalance any physical shortcomings.

It had never been so with Malcolm. Strikingly handsome in an ascetic, almost aristocratic manner, he had never needed to develop the suave manner and false good cheer which might have made his night so much easier on him, and on Holly as well. She had seated herself squarely on the center stool on Malcolm's end of the bar, taking no offense at his cold and aloof attitude. She knew that his behavior was born of embarrassment, so she remained where she was as the hours passed, carefully nursing a few ginger ales as the night passed into the early morning, patiently waiting for him to stop acting like a child.

Malcolm had been able to avoid speaking to her during

the busiest time of the night, but by two o'clock too few customers remained in the Strand for him to ignore her any longer. Steeling himself for an unpleasant conversation, he walked over to her and said, "Hi. Still here?"

"Hi, yourself," she replied. "Of course I am."

He nodded and tried to think of something to say. "You waiting for somebody?" Good grief! he thought. What a stupid thing to ask!

"Yup," she said, nodding. "I'm waiting for you to grow up."

He looked down at his feet before speaking again, thus making himself unconsciously, boyishly, innocently adorable, and she struggled to hide her affectionate amusement. "Look, Holly, about last night . . ."

"Honestly, Malcolm," she said laughing, not unkindly, "you are so stupid."

He blushed slightly and then smiled. "Yeah?"

"Yeah," she said. "You don't have to worry about some asinine 'superstud' image with me, Mal. What happened last night happens to every guy once in a while. It's not a big deal, and it certainly doesn't matter to me."

"Really?" he asked, liking her enormously.

"Of course," she replied. "I mean, I could just as easily interpret the whole thing as meaning that I'm not attractive or exciting, right? It could be a reflection on me, not you, right?"

He laughed. "Holly, that would be ridiculous!" Absurd, absolutely absurd, he thought as he looked at her. Her eyes were hazel, soft, warm, deep, inviting eyes. She had hair the color of burgundy wine, hair that cascaded down around her shoulders in curly ringlets, and flawless skin the color of ivory. Her figure was slender, her legs long. She combined pristine beauty with lusty earthiness, a dual heritage from her Norwegian and Irish ancestors. "You're gorgeous, Holly," he whispered.

"Hmm, tell me more," she said, and leaned forward to kiss him, relishing the compliment that might have sounded false and cloying coming from anyone else.

Malcolm felt a familiar stirring in his loins, and he called over his shoulder, "Hey, Jer, I think I'll leave early, if it's okay with the boss." To Holly he said, "Don't go away, please! I'll be back in a minute." He kissed her again and then walked quickly away. As Malcolm Harker rushed back to the kitchen to let the owner know that he was leaving, Holly Larsen whipped a compact from her purse and gave herself a quick once-over. *Lookin' good,* she thought to herself. *I hope he's okay tonight. It doesn't matter to me if it happens once in a while . . . they say it happens to every guy once in a while . . . but I don't want anything to mess up this relationship.*

Jerry Herman walked toward her from the other end of the bar, waving a greeting. She smiled at him and said, "Hiya, sailor. Buy me a drink?"

"Cute, Holly," he said, grinning. "Real cute. So, it's your fault that I'm gonna have to tend this bar all by myself tonight!"

"You can handle it," she said, amused by his feigned rebuke. "The place is emptying out."

"Yeah, I know, I know." He nodded. Then, as if the thought had just occurred to him, he said, "Hey, how's Marlene? I haven't seen her for weeks. How's she doing?"

Holly laughed. "She still doesn't want anything to do with you, if that's what you're asking."

He blushed slightly and grinned again. "Really? I thought maybe she might have sort of missed me, just a little bit."

"She says that you're an octopus, Jerry. Lots of hands, and all of them all over her all the time."

He shrugged. "So I'm enthusiastic."

"I don't think that's quite the description she would choose," she chuckled.

He shrugged again. "C'est la vie."

"C'est la guerre, more likely," Malcolm said as he approached them. "You think of women as enemy territory to be conquered, Jer."

"Ah, yes," his friend replied, tapping his fingers contemplatively against his lips, "the thrill of combat."

"Come on," Holly said to Malcolm as she slid off the barstool. "Let's go before Jerry starts to make me ill."

Jerry Herman watched as Malcolm held the door open and he and Holly left the Strand. He shook his head, muttering, "You got it bad, buddy boy," as he emptied a tray of clean glasses and placed them into the overhead glass rack. *You're too romantic, Mal,* he thought, *too unrealistic when it comes to women. You think everything is like in the movies. Holly's a fine-looking woman, and real nice, all right, but don't kid yourself into thinking that her feelings for you have nothing to do with your family's bank account. It's the old* story. The guy is after the body and the girl is after the wallet.

"C'est la guerre," he said aloud, "c'est la guerre, c'est la guerre . . ."

Jerry's cynicism would have outraged both Malcolm and Holly, had they been privy to his thoughts. True, Malcolm was not immune to Holly's physical beauty, which was considerable, and the joint motives of love and lust mingled in him without distinction; but overriding both of these urges was the simple fact that he *liked* her, that he enjoyed being with her, that, until the previous evening at any rate, he felt comfortable with her. It was true that Malcolm sowed his wild oats with the recklessness characteristic of young men, and that he had initially regarded Holly as just another warm furrow to be ploughed, but his feelings for her had very quickly grown deeper and more meaningful.

For her part, Holly Larsen was neither the self-serving gold digger Jerry assumed her to be nor the wide-eyed, selfless innocent of Malcolm's fantasies. She knew that Malcolm Harker came from a wealthy family, and she would have been a fool not to have been pleased by that fact; but her own career as a real estate agent in a time of booming prices had persuaded her that she did not need to be taken care of by Malcolm or any man. Only twenty-six, she already possessed a good and growing stock portfolio, a number of bank accounts, and a co-op apartment in the better part of Forest Hills. She was not wealthy, of course; but she had every reason to believe that she would be, five or ten years down the road.

So the wealth of the Harker family, while pleasant, was not what made Malcolm attractive to her. He was simply so utterly different, so totally outside the range of her experiences with men. Holly had lived in New York City for only five years, but she had gone through her share of urban playboys, pseudosophisticates, perpetual adolescents, and upon occasion, closet queens. Social relationships had seemed much less complicated—or at least the men had been more honest and unpretentious—in the small town of New York State's Finger Lakes region where she had been born and raised, but Holly had adjusted to the urban social scene easily enough. She had shed some element of her rural naïveté while pursuing her business degree in college, and by the time she met

Malcolm she was close to being as hard and unfeeling as her environment; and New York City can be a cold town.

But that all changed when she went to a party given by her coworker Marlene and there met Marlene's friend Jerry Herman and Jerry's friend Malcolm Harker. He was, as the saying goes, tall, dark, and handsome, and she had allowed herself to be drawn to him by his physical attractiveness, all the while suspecting that he was as big a jerk as the other men she had been meeting lately. She had not hopped into bed with him at the first opportunity, for Holly was too intelligent and too cautious to be promiscuous in an age of frightening sexual diseases; but she realized very soon that Malcolm was unique, and she found herself wanting him very badly, physically, emotionally, romantically.

She wondered, as they walked along Queens Boulevard toward her apartment, making small talk, just when it was that his uniqueness had first become evident to her. Perhaps it was when he told her that he had graduated from Columbia with a major in European history and a minor in classical languages—and had gone on to do graduate work in both areas before dropping out, bored and impatient with the restrictions of formal study. It had struck her as so odd that in a time of self-centered ambition, with everyone in her generation obsessed with money and wealth and upward mobility, that someone such as Malcolm would spend his college years reading Cicero and Plato and Xenophon, or studying Bismarck and Disraeli and Lenin. She understood, of course, when she learned of his family's wealth. She realized Malcolm's job at the Strand was just a way of killing time and having fun, that he had never felt the kind of economic pressure which she had felt, that he had always been able to pursue his academic interests without ever having to worry about earning a living, that while she and her peers had been studying accounting and management and business law, he had been studying German and French, Latin and Greek, philosophy · ¹ isto-ry, literature and music and art.

He fascinated her.

And when they began seeing each other, Malcolm did not take her to bars and dance clubs. He took her to Ingmar Bergman film festivals, to the opera, to museums. And two weeks before, as they sat upon a blanket on a grassy knoll in Forest Park, drinking wine as he read to her from the poetry of Lord Byron, two thoughts had occurred to her. The first was that the afternoon's activity would have been embarrassingly corny with anyone else, but with Malcolm it was ineffably romantic. The second, which almost took her by surprise, was that she had fallen for Malcolm Harker. She had fallen hard.

They turned from Queens Boulevard and walked down Austin Street toward the charming old building where Holly lived. They mounted the stairs to the second floor and went to the door of her apartment. As she inserted the key into the lock, Malcolm kissed the back of her neck and whispered in her ear as his hands reached around and moved gently over her breasts. She closed her eyes and leaned her head back, allowing Malcolm's hands and mouth to express his need. She opened the door, they entered, then she closed and locked it behind them.

Three hours later she lay quietly in his arms upon her bed, listening to his heartbeat as the first rays of the morning sun began to drift into the room through the open shades. "Malcolm," she said softly.

"Hmm?" he replied curtly.

"It really doesn't matter. Honest to God it doesn't. It happens to..."

"Yeah, yeah, I know," he said irritably. "It happens to every guy once in a while. But two nights in a row?"

She leaned up upon her elbows. "Listen, Mal, you just make it happen again by worrying about it. It doesn't mean anything, not a damn thing. The psychiatrists call it performance anxiety. Nobody feels like making love all the time, no matter what the movies try to tell us. So you didn't really feel like it last night, and worrying about last night messed us up for tonight." She kissed him lightly. "Just don't worry about it."

"Yeah, yeah, I know," he said, his tone indicating dismissal, not agreement. "Maybe I ought to see a doctor."

She yawned, saying, "Oh, don't be silly! You don't need a doctor for something like this! It's very common and very unimportant."

"It's not just this," he muttered. "I think I need a checkup or something."

"Why?" she asked. "Are you feeling ill?"

"Not ill, exactly," he said, sighing. "I've just been feeling...I don't know, funny. I never have much of an appetite. I feel weak and listless all the time. I can't seem to sleep at night..."

"You're never home at night. You work at night."

"Yeah, but not every night, and I don't go out and do things every night when I'm off. When I go to bed, I just toss and turn. I can't seem to fall asleep until morning half the time, and when I wake up, I feel like shit for hours."

Holly sighed. She had never been the type of person who enjoyed reviewing personal problems with friends, and she was not particularly interested in Malcolm's sleeping habits. Part of her was hoping that he would snap out of this malaise, part of her was worrying that he might have some sort of sexual problem, and part of her, though her conscious mind denied it, was reluctant to continue a relationship with a crippled libido. What she said was, "Okay, so you have insomnia, and you can't stand your sister's cooking, and you're suffering from performance anxiety." She forced a laugh. "If that's all that's bothering you, you're a lot better off than most people."

They were silent for a long while, and then he asked, "Do you think something's wrong with me?"

"Yeah," she muttered sleepily. "You think too much. That's the problem with you intellectual types. You spend so much time thinking about life that you can't live."

He considered this for a moment and then said, "Holly?"

"Ummm?" she asked.

"Okay if I close the blinds? The sunlight hurts my eyes."

"Yeah, sure, go ahead," she said indistinctly, and then a slight contraction in her nether regions was followed by a moist trickle of warmth. "Ah, shit," she muttered.

"Get your period?" he asked distantly as he rose from the bed to block out the sunlight.

"Yeah. It's due, and I felt it coming all day. 'Scuse me for a minute." As she went to the bathroom, she wondered, that's odd. How did he know? I didn't tell him.

Malcolm lay back down upon the bed, too self-absorbed to ask himself the same question. Had he taken the time to think it over, he might have realized that he had smelled the blood.

Chapter Two

At four o'clock the following afternoon, Jerry Herman knocked loudly on the door of the Harkers' house. He waited patiently, reasoning that whoever was home needed some time to get to the door. Jerry had come from a long line of apartment building dwellers, and he assumed that anyone who lived in a house this large probably spent their leisure time in the library or the conservatory or the aviary or in some other unusual room far from the front door.

He knocked again and waited longer, and at last Rachel opened the door and said, "Yes . . . ? Oh, it's you."

"Afternoon, Mrs. Rowland," he said, grinning.

"It's almost evening," she snapped. "What do you want?"

"Is Malcolm in?"

She appraised him critically for a moment and then pulled the door open wider. "Yes, he's upstairs sleeping. Why don't you go and wake him up?"

"I hate to disturb him," he said untruthfully as he walked past her into the foyer.

"Feel free," she said. "Still asleep at four in the afternoon! I've never heard of such a thing! At least you seem to get up at a decent hour."

"Yeah, I've been up since noon," he said, ignoring the daggers her eyes shot at him. He walked toward the staircase and stopped as he noticed old Quincy sitting in his easy chair in the large sitting room to the left of the stairs. "Hi, Mr. Harker," he called out.

The old man raised his rheumy eyes from his newspaper and squinted in the direction of the voice. Then he smiled and said, "Hello, Jerry. How are you today?"

"Fine, just fine. And yourself?"

32

"I can't complain, boy. I think Malcolm is still sleeping."

"Well, I'll go and see," Jerry said, and started up the stairs.

"Malcolm is going to mass this Sunday afternoon. Why don't you come along with him?"

Jerry smiled, slightly perplexed. "Well, uh, maybe I will. We'll see." As he continued up the stairs toward Malcolm's room, he wondered if the old man was losing his memory. He was reasonably certain that Quincy knew that Jerry was Jewish, but old folks sometimes have a hard time remembering their own names, let alone the religions of their grandchildren's friends.

Rachel watched him disappear around the corner just past the landing and sniffed disapprovingly at her grandfather. "I don't see why you have to be so friendly to that person," she huffed.

"He's Malcolm's friend," Quincy muttered distractedly, returning to his *Times*. "Never hurt anyone to be civil."

"He's a bad influence on Malcolm," she insisted.

"I don't think anyone is an influence on Malcolm, for good or ill."

"And he's nothing but a middle-class oaf, to boot!"

Quincy looked at his granddaughter over the rim of his bifocals. "Don't try to be a snob, Rachel," he said seriously. "You can't afford to be, not with your background."

Her jaw dropped open at his raising of the unspoken topic. "Wh . . . whatever are you . . . ?"

"The boy may be a middle-class oaf, but I'll wager his father was never hanged for murder, not to mention . . . well, the other thing."

She trembled angrily, considered a stinging retort, considered reminding him that her father was also his son, but then thought the better of it and marched away in a huff, muttering to herself. Quincy watched her leave and then, shaking his head sadly, returned to his newspaper.

Upstairs, Jerry pushed Malcolm's bedroom door open softly and leaned his head into the room. "Mal?" he whispered. "Mal? Are you awake?"

He saw a huddled mass beneath heavy blankets stir on the bed in the dark room and heard a hoarse voice say, "Go away, goddamn it. Leave me in peace."

"Mal, it's me, Jerry." He did not enter, but neither did he withdraw.

After a moment, Malcolm said, "Come on in, Jer." He sat up in his bed and rubbed his eyes. "Sorry. I thought you were Rachel or Daniel."

"Hey, thanks a lot." Jerry laughed and walked over to the window and opened one of the venetian blinds, allowing the late afternoon sun to illuminate the room. "I wanted to know if you'd like to catch a movie before work. They're showing the new Woody Allen at the Midway." He paused and frowned. "Hey, you look like shit!"

"Thanks," Malcolm muttered as he climbed out of bed and went over to examine himself in the mirror above his bureau. His eyes were bloodshot and his skin chalky white. His customarily thin face seemed somehow haggard and slightly emaciated. "God, I look like I just came down from a five-day binge."

Jerry sat down on the edge of the bed and grinned at him. "I guess Holly really knows how to party!"

He glared at him. "What was that supposed to mean?"

"Hey, nothing, man," Jerry said quickly, startled at Malcolm's anger. "I was just kidding. I mean, I thought that since you were with her last night, the two of you probably drank too much or smoked too much or something, that's all. What's bugging you, anyway?"

Malcolm sighed and sat down on the bed beside his friend. "Jerry, can you keep something to yourself?"

"Sure. I'm as tight-lipped as they come. What's the matter?"

"I'm not kidding, because if you ever told anybody about this, I'd kill you!"

"Don't worry about it, Mal," he said sincerely. "I won't tell a soul."

Malcolm sighed again. "The last two times I was with Holly, I . . . well, I couldn't . . . I mean, when we started making out and stuff, I . . . well, you know, I just couldn't . . ."

"You couldn't get it up?" Jerry asked simply.

Malcolm grimaced. "You've got a delicate touch, Jer."

"Okay, so what's the big deal?" he asked. "Happens to everybody."

Malcolm looked over at him. "Ever happen to you?"

"Of course it has!"

This surprised him. He had expected a vehement denial. "No kidding?"

"No kidding." Jerry paused. "Of course, I'd kill *you* if you ever told anybody I said that!"

Malcolm laughed, slightly relieved at having someone in whom to confide. "You got a deal. So you don't think I should worry about it?"

"Nah, course not! If you can figure out why it's been happening, fine. If not, forget about it." Jerry grinned. "Or why it hasn't been happening, actually."

"Holly says it's performance anxiety," Malcolm said as he began to dress.

"Probably right." Jerry nodded. "Hey, aren't you gonna take a shower?"

"Took one before I went to sleep," Malcolm muttered. "Anyway, I don't know if I can just forget about it."

"Well, it's like riding a bike or rolling off a log. Get right back up into the saddle."

Malcolm shook his head and smiled. "You're confusing your similes, Jer."

"Huh?"

"But I know what you mean. Problem is, I've probably convinced myself that . . . well, that Holly and I won't . . . well . . ."

"No, no, you dope, not with Holly." Jerry laughed. "You find another chick, get it on with her, show yourself that you've still got what it takes, feel silly about worrying about being impotent, and then everything'll be okay with you next time you're with Holly."

Malcolm shook his head. "I don't know, Jerry. Things just seem different with Holly. I mean, I feel different when I'm with her than when I'm with other girls. I don't think I'd want to . . . I don't know, I feel like I'd be cheating on her or something."

"What are you talking about? You two engaged or something?" Malcolm shook his head and Jerry smiled with exasperation. "Well, you're a little too old to be going steady!"

Malcolm felt himself being swayed. "Holly would be awful mad. Hurt, I mean."

"Malcolm, will you grow up! You don't tell her about it, for Pete's sake. You just do it!"

"Maybe," Malcolm muttered as he stepped into his loafers and brushed his hair. "Maybe. But I'm not the kind of guy who just picks girls up and ends up in bed with them. I mean, don't think I haven't tried!" He laughed softly and

Jerry smiled again. "But I've just never had that kind of, well, social talent."

Jerry appraised his friend with amusement. Mal, old buddy, he thought to himself, if I had your looks, your poise, and your family's money, I wouldn't be able to get out of bed often enough to change the sheets!

"What I mean," Malcolm went on, "is that it would take me a while to develop the kind of relationship with a girl which would—"

"Malcolm, will you cut it out?" Jerry said, shaking his head. "Who's talking about a relationship? We're just talking about getting you laid, that's all!"

"Yes, but I'm trying to tell you that it isn't all that easy for me. I don't know the kind of girls who are that willing on the spur of the moment."

With an expansive flourish, Jerry pulled a tattered, compact address book from his back pocket. "Leave that part of it to me. Where's your phone?"

Malcolm looked away from the mirror and tossed his brush onto the bureau. "A little black book? Jerry, you've got to be kidding!"

"Hey, there's a lot to be said for tradition. Where's your...?" He looked around the room and saw a telephone lying on the floor beside the bed, half-covered with discarded, soiled clothing. "Here we are," he muttered, picking up the phone and placing it on his lap, after which he began to turn through the worn pages of his address book. "Let's see, let's see... Vanessa, Vanessa, where is Vanessa?"

Malcolm sat down on the edge of the bed opposite Jerry, shaking his head and grinning with bemusement. "I feel like I'm in an old rerun of *Dobie Gillis.*"

Jerry ignored him as he dialed the phone number and then waited for the call to be answered. After a few moments he said, "Swen? Howya doin', man. This is Jerry, Vanessa's friend. Is she home? Thanks." He waited for a moment more, then said, "Hiya, kid, it's me, Jerry. Listen, are you still involved in that whatchamacallit thing you were... Yeah, yeah, I know, I'm sorry... No, of course not, I'm not making fun... Sure... Sure... Yeah, I'm sure that Leon Trotsky was the true prophet of the masses..."

"Great," Malcolm muttered. "A Trotskyite. Just what I need."

"... Yeah... Yeah... Sure... No rest until final victory... I know, I know... Listen, Vanessa, I'm calling because I have a friend who sort of feels the same way you do about... Yeah... Yeah... I know, I know... He thinks Stalin was a son of a bitch, too... Sure... Well, if you're not doing anything right now, we could... Yeah, yeah, great. We'll see you in about a half hour or so." Jerry hung up the phone. Turning to Malcolm, he said, "Now let me tell you a few things about Vanessa...."

"A Trotskyite, Jerry? A Trotskyite, for Christ's sake!"

"So she's odd," he said defensively. "The important thing is that she says she thinks of having sex as a revolutionary act, like striking a blow against the bourgeois order or something like that. You'll have no problem getting her into bed, believe me, I promise you. *Everybody* gets it on with Vanessa. It's like shaking hands to her. Believe me, I know it for a fact."

Malcolm considered this. "You've made it with her?"

"*Everybody's* made it with her."

"And you didn't have any trouble getting her into bed?"

"*Nobody* has any trouble getting her into bed."

"Well... I don't know..."

"Malcolm," Jerry said, reaching over and placing his hand on his friend's arm, "trust me, okay?"

When Malcolm awakened, the pain in his side and in his jaw almost sent him sinking back into unconsciousness. The first thing he noticed as his mind cleared was that his head and neck were encumbered by a brace of some sort, and that long strips of thick bandages were girdling his midsection. He tried to clear his vision only to find that his left eye had swollen shut. He looked up groggily and saw Jerry Herman staring down at him with concern. "Wh... what... ?" he rasped.

"Take it easy, Mal," Jerry said. "Just take it easy. You're okay, basically. You have a couple of bruised ribs and loose teeth, and your neck's gonna be sore for a while, but other than that you're okay."

"Wh... where am I?" he asked with obvious difficulty.

"In St. John's Hospital. The doctor says you should stay here overnight, but your sister says she's coming over to take you home."

"My sister... Rachel... ?"

"Yeah, I called her up. I hope that's okay. I mean, I

figured that your family ought to know where you are. She's gonna be here soon with one of those private ambulances."

"What happened... what happened to me?" Malcolm asked, his voice a strained whisper.

"Don't you remember?"

He tried to shake his head but found that the neck brace prevented him from doing so. "No," he whispered.

"What *do* you remember, Mal?" Jerry asked. Neither he nor Malcolm noticed Rachel as she entered the room behind them, her face frozen in its customary half-smile, half-grimace, with just a hint of concern in her eyes.

"I remember... I remember talking to... to that girl..."

"Vanessa, yeah, right. Do you remember Swen, her roommate's boyfriend?"

"Swen...?"

"Yeah, great big blond guy, big muscleman-type guy. Do you remember me and him sitting down and having a few beers while you went into the bedroom with Vanessa?"

"Yes... yes, I think so."

"Okay, good. What else do you remember?"

"I remember... going into the bedroom and... and getting undressed while she was getting undressed... and we kissed... and I started feeling her a little, you know?"

"Yeah, yeah, and then what?"

"I don't know... it's all so foggy."

"Try to remember," Jerry prompted. He did not turn to see Rachel covering her open mouth in outraged shock at what she was hearing.

"We lay down on the bed... I started kissing her all over... and she was... she was, you know, kissing me all over." He shut his eyes tight. "I don't know, Jerry, I just can't remember. I think I was starting to get excited..." He furrowed his brow painfully. "I can't remember, Jerry, I just can't remember. Can't you tell me anything? How the hell did I wind up here?"

"I'm not sure what happened, not all of it, anyway," Jerry said. "All I know is, I was sitting there shooting the breeze with Swen, and I heard Vanessa scream. We ran into the bedroom and found you pulling back her head by the hair, trying to bite her throat out."

Malcolm stared at him dumbly through his one fully opened eye. "Wh... what!"

"Yeah, honest to God, man! There was blood all over the

place. You must have bitten her pretty bad. She was punching at you and kicking at you and you just kept trying to get at her neck."

"I ... I don't believe it!"

"I didn't believe it either, man!" Jerry nodded. "You were really acting nuts. When Swen pulled you off her, you tried to bite him, too, and he started using you like a punching bag, but you just kept coming back at him." He paused. "That was pretty stupid, Mal. I mean, the guy's gotta be three times your size."

"Get out of here!" Rachel screamed.

Jerry spun around just in time to deflect the large, heavy purse that was swinging toward him. He jumped to his feet and stepped back from the bed.

"You little bastard!" Rachel yelled. "Taking my brother to see a woman of that type!"

"Hey," Jerry said, "take it easy! I didn't do anything. He's the one who started the trouble!"

Rachel began swinging the purse at him again, driving him toward the door. An orderly came forward, prepared to intervene, but Jerry managed to get out the door, which swung shut behind him. "Jesus!" he muttered. He pushed the door open slightly and looked back in. "Malcolm!" he called out quickly, "I'll come by and see you in a couple of days!" He allowed the door to close again before Rachel, screaming like a banshee, reached it.

"Hell of a day," Jerry muttered to himself as he left the hospital. "Guess I might as well forget the movie." He waited patiently at a bus stop and then rode the bus up the boulevard to Forest Hills. He got off near Continental Avenue and walked into the Strand, a good hour before he had to report to work.

Holly Larsen was already there, drinking a soda and tapping her fingernails on the bar top. "Shit," he said to himself aloud.

She looked up at the unintelligible mutter and smiled slightly. "Hi, Jerry. Where's Mal?"

"Uh ... well, I don't know."

"I called his house, but nobody's answering. I mean, I guess his grandfather is home, but I didn't let it ring too long. I didn't want to make the old guy get ..." She paused as she noted the odd expression on Jerry's face. "Hey, what's the matter?"

"Oh, uh, nothing," he replied, very unconvincingly.

She became suddenly alarmed. "Jerry, what's going on? Has something happened to Malcolm?" Jerry sputtered and muttered and she slid off the barstool and approached him worriedly. "Jerry, dammit, what's happened?"

"Well, I don't know if I should tell you. I mean, maybe Mal'd want to tell you. I mean—"

"Tell me what!" she cried. "Is he hurt? Was he in an accident?"

Handling this real good, Jer, he said to himself. You didn't have to say anything; all you had to do was act cool and ordinary, and everything'd be fine. Now she's half-hysterical and you either have to lie through your teeth or tell her the truth. Or at least part of the truth.

"Jerry, you better start talking and pretty damn fast, or I'm gonna scratch your eyes out!" she said angrily.

He took only a few minutes to outline the events of the day, the reasons for his part in them, and the results of their brief if unfortunate adventure. He had expected her to be angry at him, but he had not expected her to assume a look of pained concern. "You had a lot of nerve, Jerry," she said.

"I know," he replied, a bit surprised that this was the extent of her ire. "I was just trying to help. I mean, it was all my idea, not his. Don't hold it against him."

"Why the hell not?" she sniffed, though she knew that she would have felt angrier had she not felt so worried. "Am I supposed to accept it, even if I don't like it?" She shook her head. "I hope he's not having a breakdown or something. If he can't even remember what happened..."

"If so, it's a hell of a breakdown! I mean, you can't imagine what he looked like in there! He was like really nuts, you know?"

She shook her head again. "No, your perception is flawed."

"Huh?"

"You must have misunderstood what was happening. I know Malcolm. He wouldn't act that way."

"Hey, Holly, I know what I saw!"

"Maybe she tried to knock him out and rob him or something," she mused, ignoring Jerry. "Maybe he was defending himself against her. You can't tell. What you just told me can't be true."

"But if he's having a breakdown..."

"No, that was a silly thought. Breakdowns don't just happen," she said with certainty. "They build up over long periods of time and are detectable before they occur. Okay, we've been having a little trouble in bed the last few nights. That's normal, common. Doesn't mean anything." She looked at Jerry. "You're mistaken, Jerry. There has to be an explanation for what happened."

The clarity of the events was already blurring sufficiently in his memory for Jerry to begin to doubt them. "You think so?" he asked. "Maybe so. Maybe it was just a fight and it just kind of looked like... maybe so... Vanessa *is* a little strange."

Holly picked up her purse from the bar and asked, "Where is he? St. John's?"

"Probably home by now, or on his way at least. Rachel came to get him. The doctor said he should stay for observation, but she wouldn't hear of it."

Holly nodded. "What about the police?"

"What about 'em? What are you talking about?"

"Well, aren't they going to prevent his release from the hospital? Doesn't he have to be placed in custody or something?"

Jerry laughed. "Oh, I understand. Listen, Holly, the cops have nothing to do with this. Vanessa didn't report this to them."

She frowned. "Are you sure? I mean, what you just described to me sounded like a pretty serious assault. If anybody did that to me, I sure as hell would—"

"You're not Vanessa," Jerry interrupted. "Vanessa is a revolutionary nut, you know? I think she was born ten years too late. She should have been a Weatherman in the sixties, blowing up draft boards and stuff like that. She isn't gonna go running to the cops."

Holly considered this. "You sure?"

"Absolutely."

"Good," she said, walking toward the door of the Strand. "I'm going over to his house to see him."

Jerry coughed nervously. "You gonna tell him that I told you what happened?"

"Sure I am," she replied. "Why not?"

Jerry nodded. "Well, I guess that's okay. I mean, if you aren't mad at him, I guess he can't be mad at me."

"What makes you think I'm not mad at him?" she asked. "For that matter, what makes you think I'm not mad at you?

And what makes you think that I give a shit whether he gets mad at you or not?"

Jerry grimaced and then whined, "Hey, Holly, I was just trying to help, you know? I was trying to help both of you."

"I think I can live without your kind of help," she said as she opened the door.

"I don't think Rachel's gonna let you in to see him," Jerry called after her.

"Screw Rachel!" she shot back, allowing the door to swing shut behind her.

Jerry reflected briefly on the shrieking harpy who had driven him from the emergency room. "Better you than me, kid," he muttered.

Chapter Three

Rachel refused to admit Holly that day, the next day, and the day after, but on the third day following Malcolm's injury, old Quincy answered the door when Holly knocked and was busily greeting her and ushering her in before Rachel could interpose herself between them.

"Come in, child, come in!" Quincy said, taking her by the arm and pushing Rachel out of the way with his bony shoulder. "I'm glad you've come. Malcolm has been very depressed. Seeing you should cheer him up some."

"Thank you, Mr. Harker," Holly said, shooting Rachel an angry glance. "I've been coming by every day, but Rachel didn't seem to think that Mal was strong enough for visitors."

"Really!" Quincy said, feigning surprise, though he had known about it all along. "Is that so! Well, be that as it may, he's certainly strong enough now. You just go right on up. His room is the third one on the left."

"Grandfather, I hardly think it's proper to—"

"Oh, be quiet, Rachel!" he said. "I hardly think that a boy in bed with three bruised ribs and a neck brace is going to be either in the mood or the condition to misbehave!" He grunted with irritation. "Now, just go on up and have a nice visit," he said to Holly, smiling.

As Holly began to mount the stairs, Rachel came to the foot and placing her arms akimbo, called up, "You keep that bedroom door open, young lady, do you hear me?" Holly ignored her and proceeded on up to Malcolm's room.

She knocked first and, receiving no response, pushed the door open and walked in softly. Malcolm was lying on his bed in a terrible state, bruised and battered, pallid and haggard, and some small element of Holly's anger and hurt dissolved into pity. She had entered the room with every intention of taking him to task for his actions, but he looked so forlorn that she felt her resolve weakening. She knelt down beside the bed and touched his thin, sweaty hand. "Malcolm? Are you awake?"

Malcolm opened his eyes and seemed to take a few moments to focus them. "H . . . Holly!" he said weakly.

"Hi," she said, trying to sound cold.

"I, uh . . . I got hurt," he said needlessly, not knowing what else to say to her.

"I know," she said, her words clipped and precise. "Jerry told me what happened."

"Everything?" he gulped.

"Yes, everything, from start to finish." Her eyes were unsympathetic and accusatory.

"That stupid son of a bitch," he muttered, and then he sighed. "Holly, I'm sorry, I really am. I guess I just wasn't thinking straight when I let Jerry talk me into going to . . . well, into . . ."

"Uh-huh," she said, nodding. "So it's all Jerry's fault, right?"

He lowered his eyes. "Of course not. It's all my fault, really, I guess."

"I guess so," she agreed mercilessly. "You know, Malcolm, if you don't want an exclusive relationship here, I can relate to that. We can both see other people."

"Holly, I don't want to see anybody else, honestly I don't! I was just trying to . . . well, make things better between us, that's all."

"I see," she said, pretending understanding. "Sleeping with other women is designed to improve our relationship. That's a very interesting concept, Mal."

He sighed loudly and then groaned as a stabbing pain radiated outward from one of his bruised ribs. "Oh, shit, Holly. I'm really sorry. I don't know what else I can say."

Holly Larsen tried not to forgive him—and lost the struggle. She laughed softly. "Malcolm, you look so unbelievably pathetic!"

He grinned at her weakly. "Feel sorry for me?"

"Not in the least," she said, smiling, "but I'm considering giving you another chance." She paused. "What about the rest of it? The fight, I mean. What happened?"

"I can't remember a thing about it," he said morosely, "not a damn thing. All I know is what Jerry told me, and I . . . well, what he said happened . . . I don't know, Holly, I just can't understand . . ."

"It's simple," she said, rising from her knees and sitting down on the side of the bed. "Jerry is usually half-drunk, so he didn't know what he saw. Malcolm, don't give yourself anything silly to worry about. Just rest up and get better."

He sat up slowly and painfully in bed, trying his best to smile at her. "I'm not as bad off as I look, actually. My ribs are killing me, but my neck's okay. This brace is coming off tomorrow. And the swelling on my face has gone down a lot."

Her eyebrows raised in surprise as she surveyed his still-swollen eye and cheek. "God, you must have been a mess if you're better now!" She laughed, and he laughed slightly also until the discomfort in his side stopped him. "Have you been out of bed at all?"

"Of course I have. I'm not crippled, you know. Just wound up fighting somebody four times my size, that's all." He grabbed her hand and kissed it. "I'm so happy to see you, Holly!"

Then you should have come to me instead of to that slut, she thought. What she *said* was, "You know, that sister of yours turned me away at the door three days in a row."

"Rachel!" he said, growing angry. "I swear to God, someday I'm going to . . . !"

"Someday you're going to be all better and then this whole silly week will be just an embarrassing memory. In fact," she said, a hint of anger creeping back into her voice, "I'm looking forward to giving you a hard time about this someday."

He smiled and yawned, saying, "Sounds good to me." He yawned again sleepily. "I'm sorry, Holly. The doctor gave me a painkiller and it makes me drowsy." He lay back down.

"That's okay," she said softly. "Just go to sleep. You really look like you need it."

"Haven't been eating right, I guess," he muttered, his eyes closing against his will. "But I'm okay. I can stay up and talk for a while . . ."

"I wouldn't bet on it," she said, smiling. "Just sleep.

Sleep and rest. I can wait until you're better to yell at you some more." He seemed to drift off almost immediately, and Holly left the room, closing the door softly behind her.

As she descended the stairs, she heard Rachel saying coldly, "Miss Larsen, I wish to speak with you for a few moments, if you please."

Holly sighed, realizing that she had to attempt to establish some sort of amicable relationship with this woman, and not wishing in the slightest to do so. "Sure, Rachel," she said as cheerfully as possible. Rachel turned from the bottom of the stairway and walked into the sitting room. Holly followed her, willing herself to project an image of unruffled calm and poise, no matter what was to come.

"I don't believe that you have met my husband, Daniel," Rachel said in her hostile, rapid-fire voice. "Miss Larsen, Mr. Rowland. Miss Larsen is the young woman with whom Malcolm has been associating of late." Rachel's disapproval and dislike seemed to drip from her words.

"Hello, Daniel," Holly said amicably, extending her hand and walking forward toward him. "It's nice to meet you."

"Miss Larsen," he said, nodding, not moving to take her hand.

Okay, if that's the way you two want it, she thought angrily. "What can I do for you?" she asked Rachel.

"For one thing, you can stop attempting to see my brother," the older woman replied.

Holly emitted a curt laugh, stunned at the presumption. "Is that so!"

"Yes," Rachel said matter-of-factly. "Quite frankly, I don't think it would be in either of your best interests to pursue this friendship of yours."

"Really! Well, quite frankly, I don't think my relationship with Mal is any of your goddamned business!" Holly began to flush, angry not only at the other woman's words, but also at the way in which she managed to make the word "friendship" sound obscene.

"Young lady," Daniel said coldly, "I'll thank you to keep a civil tongue in your head when addressing my wife!"

"Then tell your wife to mind her own business!" Holly said as she turned to walk out.

"Are you aware of the fact," Rachel called after her, "that

our father, Malcolm's and mine, was hanged for murder twenty years ago?"

This stopped Holly in her tracks. "What are you talking about?"

Rachel laughed humorlessly. "Ah, I thought that might interest you. Yes, Abraham Harker, our father, was convicted of murder in Kansas and executed for the crime."

"So?" she asked angrily. "So what?"

"Isn't it obvious?" Rachel said. "Certain forms of insanity are hereditary, and can be triggered by improper associations and experiences. Our family is an old one, and we must guard ourselves very carefully lest we become involved with persons of unsavory characteristics. In Malcolm's case, his recent behavior, it seems to me, is a result of his relationship with you and his friendship with that Barry person."

"Jerry," Holly corrected her. "And I'm not going to bother arguing with you about something this stupid." She turned again to leave.

"It is quite serious, Miss Larsen," Rachel said firmly, again stopping her before she left the sitting room. "For us, only religious devotion can serve to repress the bad strain, the bad blood, as it were. You, I take it, are not particularly religious?"

"My religious beliefs are my own concern!" she snapped.

"So." Rachel nodded, as if Holly's response had confirmed her suspicions. "I'm afraid, Miss Larsen, that if you and Malcolm continue to see each other, it will have a terrible effect upon him. And if, God forbid, you two should marry, I shudder to think what your offspring would be like." She said all of this in a largely expressionless monotone.

"Okay, listen up, lady, and listen good!" Holly said heatedly. "Point one: the only kind of insanity which can be hereditary is a type of schizophrenia which comes from a chemical imbalance, so any notion of insanity running in a family is superstitious nonsense. Point two: I don't care one bit what Mal's father was like or what he did. It doesn't mean anything to me at all. Point three: I draw a very clear line between being religious, like lots of nice, kind, friendly people are, and being an overbearing, narrow-minded, pompous, parochial, ignorant ass, which is what you are. And," she shouted over Rachel's and Daniel's voices as they began to speak angrily, "point four: I love Malcolm, and I think he loves me, and if you don't like it, you can just go ... go ... well, I don't know what," she huffed, "but you can just go do it!"

"Rachel. Daniel. Leave me with the child," old Quincy said as he shuffled into the room, his sudden appearance silencing all of them for a moment.

"Now just a moment, Grandfather," Rachel began.

"Don't argue with me," Quincy said sternly. "Just go about your business and leave me with the child." Rachel and her husband stormed out of the room, casting Holly one last angry look. Quincy turned to her and smiled. "Don't let them bother you, my dear. Neither my granddaughter nor her husband have ever developed the, ah, social graces, shall we say."

She smiled at the old man and blushed slightly, embarrassed at her own flare of temper. "I'm sorry if we disturbed you, Mr. Harker," she said. "I really am. I just came by to see if Mal was okay, and they started ... well, why go into it. I'm just sorry, that's all."

"Think nothing of it. It's not important." Quincy paused and looked up and down appraisingly with that innocent presumptiveness acceptable only in the very old and the very young. "I'm gratified to see that my taste in ladies has been handed down to my grandson. I know Rachel thinks that Malcolm isn't safe in the same room with you, but I have to say that if I were seventy years younger"—and his rheumy old eyes twinkled—"you wouldn't be safe in the same room with me!"

She blushed but could not keep herself from laughing. "Mr. Harker! Please!"

"I'm well into my nineties, my dear," he said, smiling. "That gives me the right to say anything I want." He chuckled. "How else do you think I keep Rachel at bay?"

Holly shook her head. "I don't know why she doesn't like me. I've never done anything to her, and I ... well, I'm very, very fond of Malcolm."

"I think that Rachel takes after her mother, Cynthia," he said, shuffling over to the large cut-glass decanter on the table and pouring her unbidden a glass of sherry. She did not really want it, but she was reluctant to offend the old man by refusing his hospitality, so she accepted it as he handed it to her. Then he said, "Cynthia, my son Abraham's wife, was as stiff as a starched shirt and just about as stimulating. I never did understand why he married her."

Holly waited for a moment before speaking so she could choose her words carefully. "Mr. Harker, I don't mean to be nosy, but what Rachel just said a moment ago . . . I mean . . ."

"About my son, Abe?" He nodded sadly. "Yes, that was true. He killed a man in the Midwest, and they hanged him for it." The old man sighed and shook his head. "The poor boy. He was lost to us, lost to God. Just lost, period."

She felt simultaneously sad and uncomfortable. "I'm very sorry, Mr. Harker."

"Ah, well"—he shrugged—"it wasn't his fault, not really. He just couldn't control himself."

"His temper, you mean?"

He ignored the question. "Malcolm never knew his father. Abe died when Malcolm was only about four, I think, four or five, and his father hadn't been living here at home for a good long while before that. Over a year, I think."

"Was he a salesman or something?"

"No." Old Quincy shook his head. "Just a ne'er-do-well, a drifter. He and Cynthia never really got along too well. She was as straight as an arrow, and just about as much fun, and Abe was . . . well, at times Abe was a lively fellow. Oil and water, those two."

"What happened to Malcolm's mother?"

"She died." Quincy sat down heavily in the easy chair. "Cancer, a few years later. You know, Holly, you have to understand that Rachel sort of raised the boy. I know it doesn't excuse her behavior, but it does explain it to some degree."

"I understand." Holly smiled. "I'll try to get along with her."

"Yes, well, now," he said, suddenly all businesslike. "I think you're a charming young lady, and I'm pleased to see that Malcolm is keeping company with you, but there is one thing you must understand: This is a religious family, a very religious family. I don't know what your own beliefs are, and I certainly would not presume to question you about them, but I sincerely hope that a full participation in the life of the church will be part of whatever life you and Malcolm make with each other." He noticed that she was beginning to blush and he hastened to add, "Please don't take offense at what I'm saying, Holly. I know that some people seem to think that when a man hits ninety he is entitled to say anything that comes into his head, but—despite my teasing you just now—I've never agreed with that. I certainly don't want to offend you."

"Oh, no, Mr. Harker, it isn't that at all," she replied. "It's just that...well, Malcolm and I have only been seeing each other for a few months. I think it would be a little premature to begin talking about...well, about our life together."

"Of course, of course, I understand," he said. "But I was not really speaking about that. I was speaking about religious devotion. Now I know that Rachel sounds a bit daft with her gibberish about hereditary insanity and all that, but I can't help but feel that a bit more Bible and a bit less booze might have saved my son, Abraham, from his sorry end."

Holly felt so warmly toward the old man that she decided to reassure him. "Well, I'm not really a regular churchgoer or anything, but I believe in God and all that. I mean, I wouldn't have any objection to going to church with Mal, if we...well, if we...well, you know."

"Marry?" he finished for her, his eyes twinkling once again. "You can say it, my dear. It isn't foul language, you know."

She laughed. "No, I know it isn't."

"Malcolm and I are going to mass tomorrow afternoon. I'm sure he would like it if you were to come with us. Are you Episcopalian?"

"No," she said. "I'm a Methodist. Sort of, I guess."

"Well, that's fine. My mother was a Methodist, until she married my father, that is." He smiled at her. "Please don't think me pushy, but it would make my old heart glad."

She returned his smile. "Oh, I'd love to come along. I've never been to an Episcopal service before"—I haven't been to any church in years, as a matter of fact, she thought—"but I've heard that they're very beautiful."

"I think they are," he said, nodding, "but of course I've grown up with them. Well, we'll see you at twelve noon, then?" He began to struggle to rise from the chair.

"I'll be here," she said, "and please don't trouble yourself to get up, Mr. Harker. I can let myself out." On an impulse she leaned over and kissed him on the cheek.

"My, my!" He laughed. "That was the most fun I've had in years!"

She laughed along with him, finding him utterly charming and delightful as only the serene elderly can be. "I'll see you tomorrow. Good-bye, Mr. Harker."

"Good-bye, my dear," he said, watching as she walked out into the foyer and left the house.

Rachel Rowland was in the room in an instant. "I heard that, Grandfather! What on earth is the matter with you? That girl isn't acceptable, not acceptable at all!"

"Oh, hush up, Rachel," he grumbled. "I know what I'm doing."

"But she isn't right for him! She isn't what he needs!"

Quincy shook his head. "I don't agree. I think I made a mistake with Abraham, forcing him to marry that prune of a woman. I think it was that more than . . . more than the other thing which led to his downfall. I think Malcolm needs someone lively and in love with life."

"Oh, Grandfather, for pity's sake!"

"Rachel, leave me be!" he snapped. "I've had crosses enough to bear in my life. I don't need you adding to the weight with your constant harping!"

She drew herself up, a portrait of affronted dignity. "As you say, Grandfather. But believe me, it will take more than a pretty smile and a 'love for life' to counterbalance 'the other thing,' as you call it!" She spun around on her heel and marched from the room.

"I know, Rachel," he muttered. "I know that full well." And then he began to pray.

Holly Larsen knocked on the Harker door at five minutes to twelve the next day, a clear and beautiful Sunday in May. She had taken care to dress in an attractive but not flashy manner, even to the extent of wearing a hat that matched her purse and shoes. She rarely wore hats but had fished around in her closet until she found an appropriate ensemble. She knew that no matter what she wore, it would make a bad impression upon Rachel and Daniel, but she did not care. She wanted old Quincy Harker to like her, and she reasoned that proper attire for church was a step in that direction.

It was Malcolm who opened the door and admitted her, smiling at her warmly, kissing her lightly, and saying, "Holly, I'm so sorry about this. I had no idea Gramps was gonna pressure you into going to church with us."

"He didn't pressure me at all, Mal," she said cheerfully.

"He just invited me along, that's all. And I thought it was a sweet thing for him to do."

"Well, that's good," he said, unconvinced.

"You look a lot better than yesterday," she observed, noting that the neck brace was off and the swelling on his face was somewhat reduced. "Your color's better, too."

"Yeah, I feel better," he agreed.

She frowned at him with mock austerity. "Maybe this will teach you to behave yourself!"

"Oh, it has," he said, laughing. "It has. Let me gather up Gramps and then we can go. The mass starts at twelve-fifteen."

"Aren't your sister and brother-in-law going?" Say no, she wished.

"No," he complied to her great relief. "They go to the nine-o'clock service." He led her into the sitting room and said, "Holly's here, Gramps. You ready to go? You sure you feel up to it?"

"Certainly, certainly," the old man said. He was standing in the dining room, helping himself to a glass of sherry. "Just fortifying myself for one of Father Henley's sermons," he said, grinning at Holly.

"Father Henley tends to be rather long-winded," Malcolm confided to her. "Nice fellow, though."

"I'm sure he is," she said. Quincy walked over to them, offered her his arm, and they departed.

Fortunately, the church was just around the corner on Ascan Avenue. It was abundantly clear that the old man could not have managed a longer walk. As it was, this short distance taxed him considerably. He was flushed and winded by the time they reached the church and seated themselves in the front pew, Quincy sliding in first, Holly following, and Malcolm sitting beside her. Quincy Harker always sat in the front pew when he attended church. As the oldest member of the parish, he had an unspoken right to it, so that the priest could come down to him and administer the sacrament rather than having him struggle up the steps to the altar rail and then kneel down upon stiff knees.

He made quiet conversation with Holly until the organist began the prelude, and then they and the other people in attendance fell into a contemplative silence. Holly paged through the *Book of Common Prayer* and then gazed up at the stained-glass windows.

And Malcolm was becoming terribly, terribly uncomfortable. It's almost summertime, he thought. Why the hell don't they turn on the air-conditioning? It's hot as a blast furnace in here. He looked around and noticed that some of the women in the pews were pulling their scarves and stoles around their necks, and then in a brief silence between the end of the postlude and the priest's invocation he heard the faint hum of the air-conditioning unit. Maybe I'm getting feverish, he thought. Maybe it wasn't such a good idea to get out today.

"In the name of the Father and of the Son and of the Holy Spirit," the priest chanted, making the sign of the cross.

"Amen," the congregation sang.

Malcolm began to feel dizzy, slightly nauseated. The air conditioner must be broke, he thought. I feel as if I'm sitting in a steam bath. Beads of perspiration welled up on his forehead and trickled down his cheeks.

He found that by closing his eyes and breathing deeply he could master the growing nausea. The sounds of the service became blurred and indistinct in his ears, and he rose and sat mechanically as he heard other people doing it. Only on occasion did some familiar sound or phrase penetrate his self-imposed isolation.

"Kyrie eleison, Christos eleison, kyrie eleison . . ."

Better go back to the doctor, he thought. I really don't feel at all well. He opened his eyes for a moment and a wave of nausea swept over him. He struggled to repress it but felt the telltale pressure of sour air beginning to force its way up from his stomach. No, no! he ordered himself. Not here, not in church, not with Holly here, not when it means so much to Gramps for me to have come today. He managed to press down the threatening flow.

"Praise God from Whom all blessings flow . . ."

"Malcolm," he heard a voice whisper, and he snapped his eyes open. Father Henley's smiling face was close to his own, and the priest said, "Your sister told me that you've had an accident. Are you all right?"

Malcolm looked around, noting that the collection plates were being passed and that Henley had taken advantage of the brief hiatus in the service to step down from the altar and speak with him. He looked back at the priest and tried to smile. "Yes. Well, no, not really. I feel a bit feverish, actually."

"Well, don't bother coming up to the railing. When I bring the elements down to your grandfather, I'll administer them to you also. No need to tax yourself."

Malcolm was enormously relieved. "Thank you, Father, thank you very much. I don't know if..." Henley noted that the collection plates were being carried forward, and he winked at Malcolm and returned to his place at the altar.

Malcolm looked over at the wall and saw to his chagrin that the top of one of the windows was open and that sunlight was streaming in upon him, bathing him in its unpleasant warmth. No wonder I'm so dizzy and sick to my stomach, he thought. I've been getting a damned tan, sitting here. He looked ahead of him and saw that Henley was consecrating the elements. Not much longer now, he thought, and I can get out of here. He wiped his brow and tried not to feel sick.

"The same night in which our Lord Jesus was betrayed, He took bread and brake it, and gave it to His disciples..."

Must be my imagination, Malcolm thought, but the people in here today don't seem to have bathed very well. The smell of unwashed body odor was beginning to reach his nostrils, and it was a few moments before he realized that he was the source of the smell. Oh, great, he thought, just great. Holly'll love this! He was sweating so profusely that his trousers were damp against his legs. Hurry up, Father, will you? he thought desperately.

"After the same manner also He took the cup when He had supped..."

He began to feel the nausea rising in him again, and he struggled again to force it back. Maybe I should have eaten breakfast, he thought. Maybe I'm just hungry. But he knew that this was not the case. He had been eating in a careless, desultory manner for days, eating because he knew he must, but deriving neither pleasure nor satisfaction from it.

Henley came forward carrying a silver chalice, followed by an acolyte carrying a silver tray that held the wafers. He walked over to Quincy and placed a wafer in his mouth, saying softly, "The body of Christ." He waited a moment and then tipped the lip of the chalice as he placed it against the old man's mouth and said, "The blood of Christ." He moved sideways and looked at Holly questioningly. Not knowing if it was proper for her to partake, she shook her head.

Henley then moved to Malcolm and took a wafer from the tray. Malcolm opened his mouth as the priest placed the wafer on his tongue, saying, "The body of Christ."

What is this, cinnamon? Malcolm thought. Communion

wafers were always bland, unleavened bread, but this tasted a bit spicy. Very spicy.

Horribly spicy!

The wafer seemed to be burning his tongue and his eyes went wide with pain. When the priest tipped the chalice to his mouth, he drank deeply of the wine, hoping to quench the fire. The wine rolled over his tongue and slid down his throat. It was like drinking molten lead, and it burned its way down his gullet and seemed to set fire to his stomach and chest.

Malcolm jumped to his feet, knocking Father Henley down, and then, clutching his throat and stomach, he ran screaming from the church.

Chapter Four

Malcolm did not return home that afternoon nor that evening nor that night. Holly remained in the Harker home for a few hours, anxiously awaiting him, then took her leave after exacting from Quincy his promise to contact her the minute Malcolm showed up. The old man was averse to telling untruths, but he agreed nonetheless, knowing full well that when and if his grandson returned, they had much to discuss before anyone would be told that Malcolm was home.

Quincy waited up for Malcolm that night, and he dozed sporadically in his easy chair all the next day. It was not until nearly ten o'clock on Monday night that Malcolm dragged himself into the large Victorian house and walked unsteadily toward the stairs. His grandfather watched him enter, noting with sorrow and anxiety the chalky-white face, the eyes red from weeping and weariness, and the slight bend to the young man's back, a bend expressive of sorrow and confusion.

"Malcolm," he said softly. His grandson turned slowly when he heard his name called. He looked at his grandfather and made no reply. "Are you all right, boy?"

Malcolm nodded slowly. "Yes. Much better now, thank you."

"Where have you been?" Quincy asked kindly and with concern.

Malcolm shook his head. "I don't know. I honestly don't know. In Forest Park, I think." He paused. "Yes, I was in Forest Park. I remember the band shell."

Quincy nodded, understanding the boy's disorientation. "How is your stomach, your throat? Still hurt?"

"No, they're okay," Malcolm replied. "The pain passed pretty quickly, I think." He walked away from the stairs and approached his grandfather. "I'm sorry, Gramps. I don't know

56

what happened, I don't know what's wrong with me. I just feel so ill all the time, and the communion service... I don't know. Please forgive me."

The old man held out his hand affectionately and Malcolm took it. "It's all right, boy, it's all right."

"Was Holly upset?"

"Sure she was. She's worried about you."

"I'd better call her," he mused. "She probably thinks she's getting involved with a mental case or something."

Quincy sighed. "She's a fine young woman."

"Yeah, she is," Malcolm agreed. "I'll go call her up—"

"Wait, boy. Not yet," Quincy said, rising shakily to his feet. "We have to talk for a little while."

Malcolm's face assumed a slightly pained expression. "Gee, Gramps, can't it wait until later? I really want to take a shower and try to pull myself together a bit."

"You don't need a shower, boy," Quincy said, shuffling toward the stairs. "Just come on with me up to my bedroom. I have a few things I want to show you."

Malcolm did not move, saying, "Honest, Gramps, I'd really rather this wait until—"

"Malcolm," Quincy interrupted him, "there are some things you must know. This is vitally important to you. Please come with me."

Malcolm sighed and followed after him, walking up the stairs as slowly as Quincy. It would be hard to say for whom the trudge up the steps posed the greater difficulty—the ninety-two-year-old man or his twenty-seven-year-old grandson. Both took each step as if it were a summit to be scaled, a hardship to be endured. "Wafer and wine burned you, didn't they, boy," Quincy commented, breathing heavily from his exertions.

"Yeah," Malcolm replied. "Must be I'm getting an ulcer or something."

Quincy laughed grimly. "Wish it were an ulcer, I do indeed." Before Malcolm could comment on this cryptic remark, Quincy said, "Sunlight hurts your eyes, doesn't it. Tired all day, energetic all night. No appetite."

They reached the landing and Malcolm frowned slightly. "Yeah. How'd you know? I never discussed it with you, Gramps. Did Holly tell you?"

He shook his head as he opened the door to his bedroom. "Didn't have to, boy. I know just what you're experiencing. Your father went through it. So did I, at a much younger age."

"No kidding!" The sudden, terrible thought that he was suffering from a hereditary disease drifted into his mind, and he asked, "What is it? I mean, is it a nerve disease or something?"

"No." Quincy laughed humorlessly. "It isn't a nerve disease." He motioned Malcolm into a chair that stood beside the large window of the bedroom, and then he shuffled over to his closet and began to search around on the floor. "Come here, boy. Pull this box out for me."

Malcolm had just seated himself, and now he pulled himself wearily to his feet and went over to the closet. He knelt down and grasped the sides of a square wooden box the size of an orange crate and pulled it out with difficulty. It was not particularly heavy, but it was too heavy for him to manage comfortably. "Put it up on the table there," Quincy requested, motioning to the marble-top table beside the chair.

When he had done this, Malcolm fell into the chair and wiped his brow. "I feel so weak!" he sighed.

"I know, boy," Quincy said sadly. "I know." He opened the wooden box and began taking out old notebooks and sheaves of bound paper, yellowed and frail looking. They smelled of age and dust. He tossed a few on the table and handed Malcolm a few others. Then he looked at Malcolm contemplatively and said, "Boy, I have something to tell you that you won't want to hear. You won't even believe it at first, but it's true, nevertheless."

Malcolm began to feel panicky. "Gramps, if I've inherited some sort of illness or something—"

"It isn't an illness, boy," he interrupted. "It's worse than an illness, much worse than an illness. Religion is its only cure. No, not cure. Controller. It can't be cured. It can only be controlled." He paused. "You've heard Rachel talk about inheriting bad blood and all that, haven't you?"

Malcolm felt suddenly relieved as he began to suspect that his grandfather was going to begin saying the same sort of nonsense that his sister always said, about hereditary insanity and improper associations, and he laughed. "God, Gramps, you scared the hell out of me!"

Quincy's eyebrows rose. "What do you mean, boy?"

"If this is all building up to your telling me that Rachel is right and that I've inherited insanity from my father, then please just forget it. That's nonsense, all nonsense."

Quincy nodded. "If that were all I had to say, you would be right. But it isn't insanity we're talking about here. It's something much worse than insanity."

Malcolm's heart sank. God, he thought, it is a disease. "Okay, go on," he said. "You say that you had the same problem I'm having. What is it?" He waited expectantly.

Quincy looked down for a few moments, as if to collect his thoughts, or perhaps to marshal his strength. Then he said, "You've never read any sensationalist literature. I know that, because we've never allowed any of it in the house."

Malcolm could not repress a smile at his grandfather's conviction that keeping something out of the house could effectively shield his family from it. "I haven't read much," he admitted. "I never cared for it, really. So what?"

"And yet," Quincy went on, "you have seen films and watched television and so forth, so you know something about that type of entertainment."

"Of course. So?"

Quincy paused. "Have you ever heard the name Dracula?"

"Of course I have. Everybody has. He's a famous monster in movies and books." Malcolm began to rise from the chair, saying, "Listen, Gramps, I really feel like I need a shower—"

"Sit down, boy," the old man said, tossing him one of the books he had taken from the box and sitting down on the bed. "Turn to the last page of this book. Read the first paragraph aloud."

Malcolm examined the book in a cursory fashion. It was an old copy of *Dracula* by Bram Stoker. "Listen, Gramps—"

"Malcolm, please," the old man insisted. "Just open to the last page and read the first paragraph aloud."

He waited patiently and Malcolm, sighing, complied. He flipped to the last page and read, "'Note: Seven years ago we all went through the flames; and the happiness of some of us since then is, we think, well worth the pain we endured. It is an added joy to Mina and to me that our boy's birthday is the same day as that on which Quincey Morris died. His mother holds, I know, the secret belief that some of our brave friend's spirit has passed into him. His bundle of names links all our little band of men together; but we call him Quincey.'" He looked at his grandfather. "What . . . ?"

"Read the name at the bottom, the name in capital letters as if to indicate a signature."

Malcolm looked back at the page. "'Jonathan Harker,'" he read.

The old man nodded. "My father. Your great-grandfather. The woman named there, Mina—Wilhemina, actually—was my mother, your great-grandmother. And I, of course, am the little boy he mentions, Quincey Harker. Quincey Abraham John Arthur Harker." He rubbed his old eyes wearily. "I dropped the 'e' when I was in my teens. I thought it made the name seem somehow effeminate."

"Gramps," Malcolm said gently, "I hate to argue with you about anything, but this is a novel. This is fiction."

Quincy nodded understandingly and said, "Turn to the very first page, before the title. Read what is written there."

Malcolm did as he was bidden and squinted in an attempt to read the somewhat odd and antique handwriting. "'My dear friend Jonathan,'" he read. "'Accept this first edition in the hopes that there will be others to increase its value, and also accept my thanks for making the records of your little band available to me. Your devoted friend, Bram Stoker.'" Malcolm frowned, growing angry, "Hey, Gramps, if this is supposed to be funny..."

"Do you see me laughing, boy?" his grandfather asked him. "Am I trying to keep from smiling?" He sighed. "Everyone assumed then that it was a novel. Everyone still does. But it isn't a novel. It's a written record, a record of fact, of real events and the tragedies of real people."

Malcolm did not quite know what to say or how to react. He kept waiting for his grandfather to start to chuckle or to slap him on the shoulder and laugh, but old Quincy merely sat and looked at him sadly. "Gramps, you can't be serious about this book! It's a fairy tale!"

"No, a demon tale, boy," he muttered. "Now turn to page two hundred and seventy-three. Be careful with it. The page is worn and delicate from years of use. I've read and reread that page thousands of times." He waited as Malcolm searched through the page numbers. "There's a section marked in pencil. Read it to yourself."

Malcolm found the designated page and allowed his eyes to move over the lines:

The moonlight was so bright that through the thick yellow blind the room was light enough to see. On the bed beside the window lay Jonathan Harker, his face flushed and breathing heavily as though in a stupor. Kneeling on the near edge of the bed facing outward was the white-clad figure of his wife. By her side stood a tall, thin man clad in black. His face was turned from us, but the instant we saw we all recognized the Count. With his left hand he held both Mrs. Harker's hands, keeping them away with her arms at full tension. His right hand gripped her by the back of the neck, forcing her face down upon his bosom. Her white night-dress was smeared with blood, and a thin stream trickled down the man's bare breast. The attitude of the two had a terrible resemblance to a child forcing a kitten's nose into a saucer of milk to compel it to drink.

Malcolm looked up and Quincy said, "That was when he infected my mother."

A moment of uneasy silence preceded Malcolm's response. "Gramps, you've got to be kidding! This is absurd!"

"Turn two pages, to the next section marked with pencil. Read it to yourself. Read what he told her." Malcolm turned a few pages, found the marked section, and read:

And so you, like the others, would play your brains against mine. You would help these men to hunt me and frustrate me in my designs! You know now, and they know in part already, and will know in full before long, what it is to cross my path. They should have kept their energies for use closer to home. Whilst they played wits against me—against me who commanded nations, and intrigued for them, and fought for them, hundreds of years before you were born—I was countermining them. And you, their best beloved one, are now to me flesh of my flesh, blood of my blood, kin of my kin...

Malcolm threw the book down angrily. "Goddamn it, Grandfather, I'm not going to read any more of this garbage. Are you trying to tell me that I'm not feeling well because I've inherited... I mean, that I'm infected... I mean..."

"Dracula's blood flows in your veins," his sister Rachel's

voice said from the doorway. "And in mine and in our grandfather's, and it was in our father's as well. We are all his bastards." Rachel walked in slowly and sat down on the bed beside Quincy. She looked at her grandfather and asked, "Has he read the diary yet?"

"No," he shook his head. "Not yet."

Rachel turned to her brother and continued, "You must read it, all of it, from cover to cover. Our great-grandmother's diary."

Malcolm stared at his sister in disbelief. "Rachel, don't try to tell me that you believe all this crap! Good God, I mean, you of all people! You're so straight-laced and religious and conventional . . ."

"Of course I am," she replied softly. "I have to be, and so do you." She sat down on the edge of the bed, and Malcolm noticed that her eyes, usually narrow, cold, and radiating unrelenting puritanical propriety, seemed somehow soft and moist. He found himself wondering if his sister had been weeping. No, that's impossible, he thought. I've never seen her cry, not once.

"When I was a teenager," she said, "I was . . . well, I was as bad as you are."

"I'm not . . ."

She cut him off. "Please, Malcolm, just listen to me. I was almost sixteen when Grandfather told me the truth about our family. He could see that I was heading down the wrong road, that the blood was struggling to assert its power over me, just . . . just as it had over our poor father. And when I realized that what he had told me was true, I also realized that I had to make a decision, just as you have to now." She leaned forward, took his hands in hers, and squeezed them earnestly. "Don't you see, Malcolm? The only way any of us can keep the power of the blood submerged is by living upright, moral lives, by devoting ourselves to God, by partaking of the sacrament . . ."

"Oh, come on, Rachel, cut it out," he hissed angrily through clenched teeth.

Rachel closed her eyes and sighed. "Malcolm, haven't you ever wondered why Daniel and I don't have any children?"

He shrugged. "Not really. I suppose I just assumed you didn't want any."

"Daniel doesn't," she nodded. "He never has. That's one

of the reasons I married him." She paused. "And I've seen to it that I can never have any."

"What are you talking about?" he demanded.

"I didn't want to have to live alone my whole life, but I just would not pass this . . . this *plague* on to another generation of Harkers. So I married a man who had no interest in being a father, and I took steps to insure that I would never become a mother."

He stared at her. "You mean you . . . you had some kind of surgery? You had yourself sterilized, because of this crazy story?" She nodded sadly. Malcolm looked from his sister to his grandfather and said, "No offense, but I think you're both nuts!"

"Sit down, Malcolm," Quincy said. "We aren't finished."

"Well, I am," he replied heatedly. "This is the stupidest thing I've ever heard in my whole life!"

Rachel's voice was tired and sad. "You must read Mina Harker's diary. Not the part that was published. The rest of it, the later sections."

"Listen, Sis," he shouted, "I've seen my share of vampire movies, you know? I know that when the vampire gets killed, which he always does—even Dracula—then the people he's bitten are okay. They heal or something. The things you two are telling me don't even make sense as a vampire story!"

"Malcolm, listen to me," Quincy said patiently. "Stories are stories, movies are movies, and facts are facts. We are discussing facts here, not fiction."

Rachel took one of the other old books from the table and dropped it into Malcolm's lap. "This is the diary of our great-grandmother, things she wrote subsequent to the materials published in the book. Read this carefully, from start to finish."

"It will explain everything," Quincy added.

Malcolm looked at his grandfather hard and long before he said, "Gramps, I'll read this as a courtesy, because I love you. But don't think that I'm going to take any of this as being anything more than goddamned, superstitious bullshit."

"Don't blaspheme, Malcolm," Rachel said.

"What's the matter, Sis?" he asked sarcastically. "Vulgar language brings out the Dracula blood?"

"And don't be flippant. This isn't funny."

"Well, it seems awfully funny to me," he snapped. "I'll

look through this junk later. Right now I'm going to take a shower." He rose and left the room.

Rachel watched him go and then muttered, "He doesn't believe us."

"Of course not," Quincy responded. "Did you believe it, when first I told you of this?"

"No," she shook her head. "I didn't. Of course I didn't. On the surface, the story simply isn't believable."

"I had always hoped that after three generations the blood would be so diluted that... well, I had hoped that neither you nor Malcolm ever need be told." He emitted a soft, bitter laugh. "I wouldn't have told you, Rachel, if you hadn't been such a rambunctious young girl. I could see what was happening to you. It terrified me, especially after what happened to my son."

She smiled at him sadly. "I've done what had to be done, Grandfather. And don't think my life has been a pleasant one for it."

"You believed me, at least. Malcolm's reaction is like his father's. Abraham didn't believe me either."

Rachel sighed. "Perhaps our father simply didn't care."

Malcolm Harker huddled in the shadows of the doorway on the side of Austin Street opposite Holly Larsen's apartment house, watching with a peculiar mixture of sorrow and fury as she drew nigh her doorway. Her arm was entwined in that of a blond man of medium height and athletic build, someone unknown to Malcolm. His lips pressed together tightly, growing white and cold, as he watched Holly lean forward and kiss the stranger deeply upon the mouth.

"'It doesn't matter,' she said," Malcolm muttered. "She told me it doesn't matter, and so she dumps me and starts seeing someone else the first chance she gets." He hissed as he drew in a breath. "Bitch!" he whispered. "Goddamn bitch!"

Holly's voice carried to him softly through the cold night air, unintelligible yet softly seductive words drifting to his ears. She turned and entered her building and the stranger began to walk away, heading down the street toward Continental Avenue. After a moment's pause Malcolm leaned out of the doorway, looked right, looked left, and then began quietly to follow him.

The stranger walked to the subway station on the corner

of Continental and Queens, pausing to smoke a cigarette on the street before descending the stairs to the train. Malcolm passed by him, not looking at him, not drawing attention to himself, and proceeded down the stairs. He turned to the left when he reached the bottom and hid in the doorway of the men's room. He drummed his fingers nervously against the grimy tiles and waited.

A few minutes later he heard the footsteps of his rival as he walked easily down the steps. The stranger walked directly past Malcolm, not suspecting anything, unaware of the danger until Malcolm jumped out from the doorway. He wrapped his right forearm around the stranger's throat, pulled it back with his left hand, throttled him, crushed his windpipe, and left him lying on the dirty, gray cement floor, trying with pathetic futility to draw breath into his lungs. The stranger died in a few moments, but by then Malcolm was already up the stairs and back on Continental Avenue.

He walked casually toward Holly's apartment. The only people he passed on his brief journey were a stumbling, disheveled couple who were quite obviously enraptured by their own narcotic preoccupations and a young black man who was waiting impatiently for the bus.

He opened the front door of the co-op apartment building and rang Holly's bell. A few moments passed, and then he heard her voice, fuzzy through the intercom, ask, "Who is it?"

"Telegram, Miss Larsen," he said, laughing.

"Malcolm? Is that you?"

"Yeah, Holly. Let me in, will you?"

"Do you know what time it is!"

"Yeah. I'm sorry I'm coming over so late, but this is important."

"What could be so important that you'd come over here this time of night?"

"Just let me in, Holly, just for a few minutes. I have something very important to show you."

There was a pause and then the buzzer sounded, unlocking the interior door that led into the lobby of the building. Malcolm pushed it open and ran up the stairs toward Holly's apartment. He knocked softly on the door and waited for her to open it. When she finally did, he was a bit surprised at her appearance. Her burgundy hair was up in curlers and there was a film of white grease covering her face. Guess you don't think you have to worry about what you look like when you see me, he thought bitterly. "Hi," he said.

"Okay, Mal, come on in, but just for a few minutes," she said. "I've had a hard day."

And a hard night, no doubt, he thought, following her into the apartment and closing the door behind him. "How are you?" he asked.

Holly placed her balled fists upon her hips, and without a hint of friendliness she said, "Mal, what do you want? What are you doing here?"

He drew closer to her and smiled. "I want to show you something," he said.

"Well? Go ahead." She was impatient and uninterested.

"Watch," he whispered. He drew close to her, and moving much too rapidly for her to stop him, he reached behind her and grabbed her hair in his right hand. A gasp escaped her lips as he wrenched her head backward, sending curlers bouncing onto the floor.

"We're going to have a new type of relationship, honey." He smiled, then leaned forward, opening his mouth and then closing it upon the smooth white skin just below her left ear. He could sense her beginning to scream, but before she could utter a sound he had closed his teeth upon her and pulled her head back forcefully, tearing open her throat.

The blood spurted horribly as if from an unblocked fountain, and Malcolm pressed his mouth down upon the wound, relishing the bitter warmth of the thick liquid as it flowed over his tongue. With every drop of blood he drank he felt stronger, healthier, more vibrant, more alive. He drank cheerfully as the struggling woman grew weaker and weaker, at last hanging limp in his arms.

And then Malcolm heard a sound, a sucking sound, very close to his ears, and he realized with a start that he was not the only one who was drinking from Holly's neck. He had not noticed it until that instant, but there were two other arms wrapped around her limp form. He looked up and stared in wonder into the face that seemed simultaneously to withdraw from the other side of Holly's throat to stare at him. Standing beside him, his red eyes shining in the darkness, his lips red with blood, the collar of his cape pulled high, was Bela Lugosi.

Malcolm sat up in bed.

"Goddamn it," he said aloud. Stupid nightmare! First

time in weeks it looks like I'm going to get some decent sleep and I have a goddamn stupid nightmare! "Thanks a lot, Gramps!" he muttered as he reached over and switched on the lamp upon his night table. Goddamn stupid stories! Curse of Dracula! Christ!

He picked up the book he had been reading on and off for the past few weeks and opened it, intending both to get his mind off the conversation he had had with his grandfather and sister and to read himself to sleep. The book was a collection of the letters of the ancient Roman essayist Pliny, and Malcolm paged through it until he found the section in which Pliny describes the eruption of Vesuvius. Malcolm always found that section oddly relaxing.

His eyes drifted up from the book, and he noticed with irritation that the box that he had dragged out of the closet for his grandfather earlier, the box that contained the dusty old collection of papers as well as the supposed first edition of *Dracula*, was now sitting on the floor beside his bureau. "Oh, Rachel, give me a break, will you?" he muttered. Sneaking that thing into my room while I'm asleep! Come on!

He got up from the bed and walked over to the box, uncertain whether to carry it back to his grandfather's room or leave it outside for the trash collector. Can't do that, he thought to himself. As stupid as this all is, there's probably stuff in here that is important to Gramps. He decided, just on principle, to move the box from his room out into the hallway. Let Rachel put it away somewhere, he thought. He bent down to pick up the box. He had lifted it up halfway from the floor when the bottom of the box broke and bundles of paper dropped onto the carpet. "Damn!" he muttered.

Most of the papers in the box seemed to have been tied together, therefore making his task of picking them up easier than it might have been. There seemed to be three bound piles of papers, a number of loose sheets that appeared to be letters, and the old edition of Stoker's novel that he had seen previously.

Malcolm's curiosity got the better of his annoyance, and he untied one of the bound piles. The pile of papers had a plain cover sheet, and when he removed it, he saw the words, "Dracula: a romance by Bram Stoker." The words were handwritten in a script with something of a self-conscious flourish. Malcolm flipped through the hundreds of pages that rested beneath the first page and found that each was written in the same hand. "The original manuscript?" he whispered aloud. "Is that possible? This must be worth a fortune!" He turned a few pages until he came to the first chapter, then opened the first edition to the same place in order to compare them. In the printed first edition he read:

Chapter 1
Jonathan Harker's Journal
(Kept in shorthand.)

3 May. Bistritz. Left Munich at 8:35 P.M., on 1st May, arriving at Vienna early next morning; should have arrived at 6:46, but train was an hour late...

Malcolm looked from the printed book to the manuscript, and he frowned at what he saw.

Chapter 1
Jonathan Harker's Journal
(Kept in shorthand.)

Bistritz
3 May. ~~Oradea~~. - Left Munich at 8:35 P.M., on 1st May, arriving at Vienna early next morning; should have arrived at 6:46, but train was hour late...

Odd, he thought. The printed book says the entry was written in a place called Bistritz, but it seems as if the original manuscript used the name of a different place, Oradea, and was then changed. Could have been a revision, of course. Stoker must have written the book and then changed things around. I'm sure all writers do that.

He looked over at the two other bound piles of paper, and sitting down on the floor beside the broken box, he picked them up. He untied one of them and saw that it was a pile of papers of different sizes and consistencies. A cursory glance through the pile revealed a variety of different handwritings and some typed pages. He looked at the first page and read the following:

Whitby, June 3, 1896

My dear Mr. Stoker:

As you requested, Mina and I have arranged
all of the personal memoirs and records that are at
our disposal in the proper and appropriate order.
Mina has made a transcription for you both of my
own journal, which I kept in shorthand, and of the
phonographic records maintained by Professor Van
Helsing and our friend Jack...

Malcolm turned to the first full page of writing and read
it quickly. There was no heading, no title. Just the plainly
handwritten words:

3 May. Oradea. - Left Munich at 8:35 P.M., on 1st
May, arriving at Vienna early next morning; should
have arrived at 6:46, but train was hour late...

His eyes moved from the book to the manuscript to the third
pile of papers.

Bistritz.

Bistritz.
~~Oradea~~.

Oradea.

Malcolm frowned again, perplexed, and then he understood what he was looking at. He felt a sinking feeling in his
chest as his eyes moved from the pile of papers to the
manuscript to the book, from what must have been the
original documents to what must have been the working
manuscript that contained revisions to the final printed form.
A change in place names, Malcolm thought. And a change in
the names of people as well? Possibly, quite possibly. He
flipped through the manuscript to search for names, then
searched through the printed book until he found the same
places. Then he swallowed hard as he felt his heart jump.

The names had been changed.

Not all of them, but enough of them. John Stewart had
become John Seward. Arthur Wellesley, the Duke of Wellington,
had become Arthur Holmwood, Lord Godalming. And though

the name Abraham Van Helsing had been left intact, this
German professor had suddenly become Dutch.

Malcolm knew that only one logical reason explained
why the author or the editor would have made such changes.
The emotional aspect of his personality rejected the explanation absolutely. The logical, rational side of Malcolm Harker
could not avoid the obvious conclusions.

A chill ran up his spine as he began slowly and carefully
to read and compare the first printed edition with the manuscript and the source papers. When he had finished this task,
he moved without stopping to the final set of documents, the
old book that purported to be the diary of his great-grandmother,
Wilhelmina Murray Harker.

Neither his grandfather nor his sister disturbed him as
he read, and the rising and the setting of the sun went
unnoticed. As the hours passed, he read without rest and
without nourishment; and if at any time it struck him as odd
or significant that he felt better after sunset than he felt after
sunrise, that despite his hunger he had little interest in
conventional food, he did not pause for reflection. Only once
did he stop reading, and that was to lean back and mutter,
"God help me!" in hushed, trembling tones.

Chapter Five

Mina Harker's Journal

28 September, 1896. - Jonathan is better today, though Jack
has told me privately that the instances of recovery from
consumption are depressingly few. But still I shall act in my
poor dear's presence as if his full recovery were in sight, as if
all were well with the world.

I know that we all face the same fate in the end, and that
though it will be a crushing sorrow to me if Jonathan dies, I
have nonetheless been privileged to love and be loved by a
great and good gentleman, and thus must not allow myself to
grow bitter. And yet I cannot keep from asking why he was
spared in our battle with the Count only to fall victim to the
prosaic scythe of so common a reaper as this disease. The
Professor says that we must not question the infinite wisdom
of God, and he is of course correct. And yet, still I wonder
and still I ask, and still I pray for Jonathan's recovery. I do
believe I would gladly die in exchange for the opportunity
once again to see him robust and strong and quick, once
again to see that warm and happy smile. I have never said
this to him, nor shall I ever, but his aspect today is depressingly
similar to his aspect as it was when first I saw him again after
his escape from the castle and his subsequent stay in hospital
in Europe. Oh, the poor, dear man! Give him leave to stay
with me, dear Lord! Please!

3 October. - How fortunate we are—Jonathan, little Quincey,
and I—to have so steadfast a friend as Jack Stewart. He is as
an uncle to our little boy, as are Arthur and the Professor, but
Jack comes daily to visit with Jonathan and to spend precious

time with Quincey. My sweet little boy so desperately needs
a father, and Jonathan is simply too weak to play with him
and talk with him. This makes Jack's daily visits so important
to us!

I know that Arthur and the Professor would do the same
if they were here, but of course they are not. No Duke of
Wellington could remain here in England in ease and comfort
while such trouble is brewing in South Africa, and so Arthur
has gone to the Cape Colony to serve his Queen. "My
great-grandfather did not shrink from Waterloo," he told us
before his departure, "nor shall I shrink from whatever
warfare to which the Crown calls me." Such a brave man!
Braver even than the great Duke, for he faced only Napo-
leon, while Arthur has faced the devil himself.

And the Professor is too old now for much traveling. He
lives in a pleasant cottage not far from Rostock in Mecklenburg,
enjoying the retirement he so greatly deserves. He has
written that he shall visit us soon, no later than the end of
November, and hopes to be able to stay past the new year, "if
you will have me," he asks. If we will have him! Sweet,
beloved old man! What would I or Jonathan or any of us be,
had not Professor Van Helsing come to open our eyes to what
was happening to us?

28 October. - I am greatly disturbed by the behavior of my
son. Quincey has always seemed a bit headstrong, even in
infancy, and Jonathan and I always joked that the child had
inherited some of Quincey Morris's brashness and brave
impetuosity, but little Quincey has never before been rude to
his elders.

The child has not been eating properly. When he was an
infant, he ate poorly, so his recent problems did not surprise
me at first. I remember how much difficulty he had in taking
the breast, how his little teeth bit and nipped and caused me
to bleed so that he could not get the milk, and I remember
how great a dislike he evidenced when we introduced him to
solid food. But the past few years have seen no reluctance on
his part to eat heartily and healthily, like any strong and
normal six-year-old.

And then yesterday he would not eat his mutton, and
Quincey has always loved mutton! I coaxed and then demanded,
but he would have none of it. He pushed his plate away so
forcefully that it fell from the table and broke upon the floor,

the gravy staining the carpet and a good set of china now ruined. I must admit that I most likely grew too angry and spoke to the child too sharply, but it was the look in his eyes that startled and unnerved me. For a moment it seemed as if a stranger were sitting at the table and staring at me, a look of hostility and resentment suffusing his face. I blush to admit that I began to weep, and my tears made him again my little Quincey, and he ran to me and embraced me and begged me to forgive him.

I am being foolish, I know; but for an instant, I was frightened of my own son! I have mentioned none of this to Jonathan, of course.

Perhaps the child is ill. I pray that he is not, for I am growing weak and worn from caring for Jonathan and could not abide yet another charge of ministration.

How cold and cruel and selfish that sentence reads! Do I begrudge my beloved the attention he needs in his illness? Would I account myself ill-used were I to have to nurse my own darling boy back to health? Never, never! They are my life, my husband and my son, they are my very life! I fear that I am in dire need of rest. My nerves are frayed and threaten to shatter.

12 November. - Mr. Stoker has come and gone, and how greatly conversing with him has lifted poor Jonathan's spirits. The book, the "romance," as Mr. Stoker calls it with a twinkle in his eye, will be published early next year, and the publisher has great hopes for its success. Our financial situation is not yet desperate, but though neither Jonathan nor I ever discuss the problem, it may become so presently, so that we dare to hope the publisher to be correct in his projections.

Mr. Stoker came to tell us that the revisions and changes have all been made, and he told us that he plans to return the papers of our little band as soon as possible. My Jonathan, ever the bibliophile, asked if we might have the manuscript as well, and Mr. Stoker has promised to see if that is possible.

I must admit that I cared for Mr. Stoker not one whit when first I met him, but I have come to feel great affection for him in the past year. Jonathan says that I merely mistrust anyone so intimate with the life of the popular theatre, and the Professor jokes that I suffer from a dislike of the Irish so common to the English petite bourgeoisie. They are in all likelihood correct, for my mistrust and dislike have been conquered by Mr. Stoker's charm, courtesy, and consideration.

He explained to us the changes he made in the text in accordance with the wishes of our friends. Jack fears that his professional reputation may be compromised by a public association with so bizarre a tale, and so John Stewart shall become "John Seward" in the book, even as his hospital shall not be St. Anselm's, but rather simply "Seward's Sanitorium." In like manner, Arthur told us that he had no desire to explain to his peers in the House of Lords the role he played in what must appear to be the cold-blooded murder of a Rumanian nobleman, and so the Duke of Wellington shall become Lord Godalming. He assumes that the Lords will reject out of hand any reference to vampires, and he is correct, of course. Would we have believed, had we not seen, had we not suffered?

Mr. Stoker himself does not fully believe our tale. This is evident from his reaction to the Professor's request, a request to which he acceded willingly but with a clear sense of confusion. He had expected that the Professor would wish his name changed also, but the Professor told him that he had no concern for his professional reputation and no fear that he might be called upon to explain his actions. But he did say he feared that the book might become popular, and that if it does, it may lead the curious to seek out the sites of the events and thus perhaps unwittingly unleash more of these creatures upon the modern world. I have never been able to bring myself to ask if the Count, in his undeath of four centuries, created only three others in his native land like unto himself, but it is the terrible possibility that other undead creatures prowl the Carpathians that impelled the Professor to make his request. Mr. Stoker agreed as a matter of courtesy, and so he has changed the names of the towns and cities in central Europe to conform to a false geography.

The Professor also told him that he was too old to undertake upon another quest such as the one upon which we all embarked seven years ago, and so he wished his identity to be hidden from those who might seek him out for help, even if Mr. Stoker chooses not to hide his name. So Professor Van Helsing of Rostack in Germany shall be Professor Van Helsing of Rotterdam in the Netherlands.

Our names, of course, Jonathan and mine, shall remain

unchanged, in accordance with the agreement. It is a small price to pay in exchange for fifty percent of the royalties.

Mr. Stoker sees no need to change the names of those who did not survive, and so our dear friend Quincey Morris shall remain himself, as shall the brave lunatic Renfield, and our friend Lucy.

Lucy. I have not thought of her for years. Lucy. Poor Lucy.

20 November. - I am so worried about little Quincey! Jack cannot fathom his behavior, and all he has been able to suggest is that we wait until the Professor arrives next week and has the opportunity to observe the child. He has been restless at night and so terribly lethargic during the day, and each mealtime has become a battle of wills between us. The boy simply refuses to eat! At first I feared that his lethargy bespoke the presence of the same disease that afflicts my husband, but Jack assures me that consumption is not a contagious disease.

And yet I fear, yet I fear. Dear God, if it be Thy will that Jonathan be taken from me, I pray that I do not live to bury my son!

28 November. - I wept with joy when Professor Van Helsing stepped from the train today at the station in Whitby. So much love radiates from that old, weary face, and I felt his aged frame tremble with emotion as I embraced him, my dearest friend, my protector, my shield.

He has spoken with little Quincey at length and has watched the child in play and at rest, and he has shaken his head and said that he cannot begin a diagnosis until he has had more time to observe and contemplate. I know that I was unrealistic in my hope that the Professor would be able to look at Quincey and understand immediately what is wrong with him. My memory of all that the Professor knew and said and did during that horrible year after Jonathan went off to Transylvania has made me think our dear old friend omniscient. He is not, of course, and a diagnosis will take time. And he has told us that the problem may be nothing more than a silly mood of childhood, which may be passed by and forgotten with time.

I pray that he is correct, and I feel a stirring of hope and a growth of ease just from his very presence. Dear, strong, wise Professor Van Helsing!

6 December. - I am writing only to distract my thoughts and still my heart and keep my trembling hand occupied as we await the arrival of the police. My little boy has disappeared. My dear, sweet little Quincey is missing.

17 December. - Eleven days since I entered my son's room to find his bed empty, eleven days such as I hope I shall never suffer through again. Though the boy is again beneath our roof, he is bound by a strait-waistcoat from Jack's hospital, and we must wait until morning for the priest.

It is not over. We all thought that it had ended on that dusty Transylvanian road seven years ago, but it is not over, and I am polluted, I am unclean, I am the carrier of a plague, infecting my own darling little boy with my filth.

I cannot write more. I know that I must set the story down, but I cannot do so now. Now I must weep and I must pray, and I must go as a child for comfort to Professor Van Helsing, whose heart, too, seems to be breaking from the conclusions he has drawn.

I shall set down the words when the torment in my mind eases. Now I cannot write more.

18 December. - Jack has given me a sleeping draught, but his estimation of the amount required to calm the engine of my nerves has fallen short of my need, and so I cannot sleep. I shall strive to keep the pen in my hand, for I must set this all down. Even now the sun is rising, and the priest may arrive soon, so I shall not waste time. I know not what the final outcome of this may be, but a record must be made.

Twelve days ago, as Jack and the Professor were enjoying late-night brandy and cigars (Jonathan having already fallen asleep in his bed), I went to look in on Quincey as I do every night, as I am certain all mothers do with all children, only to find his bed empty and his window open. I must have lapsed into shock, for when at last I rushed from the room to fetch the others, I was drenched and frozen from the snow that the wind was hurling through the window.

Jack and the Professor came at once to search the child's room, and I must have been babbling hysterically about kidnappers, for the Professor shook me roughly and forced me to examine the scene carefully. I know that the gentle old man would not have been so brusque had my condition not demanded it. "Look, Madam Mina, look!" he said. "The latch on the window is still affixed to its mate, and it has been broken off on the inside. And see the ground below the window, see the one set of small footprints in the snow." He shook his head and frowned. "The child runs away, my dear lady. He is not kidnapped."

"But why would he do such a thing?" I wept. "We have worked so hard to make a good home for him!"

"I do not know, Madam Mina," the Professor said, "and there will be time enough to discover the reason once we find him."

And so we sent for the police and they searched the grounds and found nothing. Quincey's footprints led to the main road through Whitby and then disappeared, buried beneath the still-falling snow. No trace was found of my dear little boy, not in Whitby and not in the surrounding countryside.

With each passing day my hopes sank lower and lower, and my despair and sorrow grew. Jonathan was so devastated by Quincey's disappearance that his health began to fail, and I overheard Jack tell the Professor that he might not survive the ordeal.

It seemed as if my life were falling apart around me, and were it not for the sedatives that Jack gave me, I think I would have gone mad. Telegrams announcing the child's disappearance were sent to police forces throughout the realm, and the Professor insisted upon paying for notices in each and every newspaper and periodical published in England. I tried to thank him for his help, but my tears were so fast and heavy that the words would not come, and he took me gently by the hands and smiled down into my face, saying, "Madam Mina, years ago I put my very life at risk for you. Do you think I would not begrudge a few pounds for the little child who bear my name and the names of all whom I love?" I could not speak to respond, and so I merely wept.

It was at last Mr. Stoker who found my little boy. Our literary associate is, of course, the business manager of Mr. Henry Irving, whom I have never had the pleasure of seeing on stage but who is a thespian of some repute. Mr. Irving has apparently spent many hours observing the behavior of prisoners and lunatics so as to improve his representation of such characters on the stage, and one result of this practice is that he has established friendships with hospital administrators throughout the realm. He heard of our trouble from Mr. Stoker, and when he learned of a little boy who had been remanded to a lunatic asylum in Hempstead, he mentioned it to Mr. Stoker, who then made inquiries. The little boy had been found killing and eating a cat in an alleyway in Hempstead town, which action resulted in his being put into the asylum. The child told the arresting constable that his name was Quincey.

Desperate hope seemed to overcome us all when we received Mr. Stoker's telegram, and we departed Whitby for Hempstead almost immediately. Poor Jonathan insisted upon rising from his sickbed and accompanying us despite my earnest entreaties, the Professor's advice, and Jack's orders to the contrary. The poor man refused to stay at home while we went to Hempstead, and so he came along, supported by a cane and Jack's strong arm, coughing and shivering in the midst of the cold wind and snow.

As we sat in the private compartment on the train which was carrying us south, the Professor turned to me and said, "Madam Mina, I had hoped never again to see Hempstead." It was only then, only when I heard those words, that I fully realized that we were on our way to the site of tragedy and sorrow. I looked over at Jack and saw from the look on his face that he, too, had been thinking of the past, thinking of Lucy Westenra, whom he had courted in vain and who had fallen victim to the monstrous evil of the Count.

I of course had not accompanied them on that terrible night, but I have heard it described in frightening detail. It was Lucy's supposed illness, her "acute anemia," which had prompted Jack to send for Professor Van Helsing in the first place, and we all had assumed that her subsequent death was the result of her affliction. Indeed it was, but her affliction was Count Dracula, not acute anemia. It was not an easy task for the Professor to persuade Jack and Quincey Morris and Arthur that Lucy had become so foul and unholy a creature as a vampire, but they could not deny the evidence of their own eyes when they saw her, undead, returning to her grave; and it was in the graveyard in Hempstead, in the Westenra family crypt, that the Professor and Jack read prayers as Arthur drove the wooden stake into poor Lucy's heart.

I do believe that not one of us ever wished again to visit Hempstead; and yet there we were, Professor Van Helsing,

John Stewart, Jonathan Harker, Mina Harker, all again on our way to that town. Thank God the Duke of Wellington is in South Africa, for were he here in England, he would of course have come with us, and the memory of that night and his holy if horrible deed would have distressed him greatly.

We reached Hempstead after dark and went immediately to the lunatic asylum that Mr. Stoker mentioned in his telegram. My heart seemed almost to fail when we arrived there only to be told that the child, who we all assumed was my little Quincey, had escaped from his overseers. The man in charge of the institution, a Dr. MacKenzie, was quite upset and understandably embarrassed when he told us that they had not kept a careful watch on the child, and under other circumstances I might have been charitable and understanding. I fear that I was not so on that night. I was in the midst of a bitter, frenzied recrimination of poor Dr. MacKenzie, a reaction to the sudden dashing of my hopes that I would be able immediately to embrace my little boy, when the Professor interrupted me by making a request for a hand torch. The calm and unruffled tone of his request startled me into silence, and I remained in that state as Dr. MacKenzie left the room and returned a few minutes later with a lantern. The Professor thanked him and then ushered us all out and back into the cab that we had kept waiting. When Jack asked him where we were going, the Professor said darkly, "To where the child might be, to where I pray the child is not."

The priest has arrived! I see the coach pulling up to our door even now, and I hear Jack and Professor Van Helsing talking to each other downstairs as they go to greet him. I must interrupt this entry.

(*later.*) - With the departure of the priest comes some hope, but I have lived so long with hope frustrated that I dare not wax complacent. This evening will tell. For now, I must return to my record and bring the story up to date.

"To where the child might be, to where I pray the child is not," Professor Van Helsing had answered Jack. The three of us looked at each other in confusion as the cabman closed the door and asked us for our destination. It was the Professor who answered, "The graveyard of the Church of St. Mary."

I gasped and trembled when he spoke the words, for it is there that poor Lucy was laid to rest eight years ago. Jonathan leaned forward and coughed as he said, "Professor, what does this mean?"

"It may mean that I am a foolish old man," he replied, "who can no longer distinguish between logic and fear. It may mean nothing. I speak no more until I am seeing for myself what there is to see or is not to see." And he refused to say another word.

The last time I had been to the graveyard in Hempstead was on the day of Lucy's funeral, and I had forgotten how cold and dismal and windswept it was. All graveyards are cold, to be sure; but perhaps the season and my mood combined to make this one an epitome of desolation. As the cab pulled to a stop, the Professor said to me, "Madam Mina, you should remain here. Jack and I are enough to see."

"To see what, Professor?" I said, weeping. "Is my child in that graveyard? Is my child dead? Does all of this have something to do with Lucy or"—my tongue faltered as I struggled to say the name—"or Count Dracula?"

"Jonathan cannot go walking in this weather," the Professor said, not answering my question, "and he cannot be left alone."

"I will be fine," my brave dear objected, knowing that I was determined to go with them, knowing that he would be more hindrance than help. "Take Mina with you, Professor. Do not forget what she has been through. Do not forget how strong she is."

These words brought a tear to the old man's eye, and he smiled at me. "Yes, such a fool is Van Helsing, that he forget the courage that battle demons. Come, Madam Mina, come." We left Jonathan with the cabdriver and entered the graveyard.

I have heard that in London and Manchester the authorities have begun enclosing graveyards with fences and locks to guard against vandalism, but I am thankful that Hempstead, like Whitby, has not yet had that particular plague of the end of this century visited upon it. The stone wall which surrounded the old parish church and the place of burial was interrupted in its circuit by a slate walkway, and we were thus able to enter the hallowed grounds without difficulty. Professor Van Helsing stopped before going in among the tombstones, and he said very, very softly to us, "Listen to me with care, my friends. If the child is here, he will not wish to return with us, he will run if he see and hear us. So we must be quiet, very quiet, as is the mouse of the church. You, my dear

Madam Mina, you above all must not cry out to him if you
see him, for if he see you and he run, we may never again
have the chance to find him." He paused, looking from me to
Jack. "You must promise me this thing."

"I shall do what you say," Jack replied in a whisper.

"As shall I," I replied in tones similarly hushed. "In this
as in all things, I trust you with my life and shall heed
whatever injunctions you issue."

He took my hands and raised them to his lips to kiss. "If
the boy is here, I shall go to his left, and you, friend Jack, to
his right. Madam Mina, you will approach from the front.
Between us we shall trap him."

He spoke as if we were tracking an animal, but I knew
the affection he had for the child and so I took no offense at
his words. Jack and I followed behind him as he went in
among the stones. The moonlight was bright enough for us to
see clearly, and the Professor lowered the wick in the lantern
as we went farther into the graveyard. And then, oh! such a
sad and pitiful sight awaited us when we reached the Westenra
mausoleum!

There was my little boy, my sweet, darling little Quincey,
frozen and half-naked, swinging from the iron bars on the
door of the crypt as a monkey, kicking against the heavy wood
and iron as if he were attempting to break down the door. He
was wailing softly and sounded for all the world like a sick,
frightened infant. It took every ounce of strength I could
muster not to cry out and run to him, but I steeled myself to
silence and immobility. Then the Professor nodded to Jack
and they each began to walk carefully toward either side of
the mausoleum. When they were in position, the Professor
signaled me with his hand and the three of us rushed at my
poor little boy.

It was as the Professor had feared, for when Quincey
heard my footsteps and turned his head to see me approaching,
he dropped from the iron bars and ran. The Professor stopped
him, but his weak old hands could not keep their grip, and
Quincey broke free and fled in the other direction. Then Jack
grabbed him and held him fast.

My poor little boy struggled madly against Jack's grip,
but his child's strength was of course no match for that of a
grown man in the summer of his years, and I dared to hope at
that moment that all we needed to do was return to Whitby
and begin whatever sort of treatment the Professor would

decide appropriate; but it was not to be so. Professor Van Helsing, rubbing his eyes and sighing, said to Jack, "My friend, I must ask you two questions, neither one happy or welcome. First, I know that when you are in London, you come here to Hempstead and place flowers on Lucy's coffin in this crypt. This much you write me in your letters."

"Yes," Jack replied, somewhat puzzled and struggling to restrain my little boy. "What of it?"

"I know that Miss Lucy die and her mother die, and there is no family, and you and our friend the Duke are the mourners and the loved ones, and you have access to the grave all those years ago. The key to the crypt. You carry it with you on your chain of keys?"

Jack paused before replying, "Yes."

The Professor nodded. "May I have it, please?"

Jack's face seemed in the pale moonlight to grow itself as pale as the cold orb that floated above us amid the clouds. "Professor, what are you saying?"

Professor Van Helsing shook his head. "I say nothing, I imply nothing, I fear all and I suspect all."

We stood in odd silence before the Westenra mausoleum for what seemed an eternity. It was I who broke the silence by asking, "Professor, my dearest friend and guardian, are you trying to tell us that Lucy is not truly dead? Are you saying that she is somehow striving to control my Quincey?"

The dear old man seemed about to weep as he replied, "Madam Mina, I have pray that you are spared this. I have pray that my apprehensions are the foolish meanderings of a foolish old mind. But think back, sweet lady, think back to those horrible days. The Count, did he not make you drink his blood? Did he not pollute you with his own demonic uncleanliness? And is that blood not still coursing through your veins?" He stopped speaking, as if unable to state the final question.

I stated it for him. "And is that blood not even now in the body of the child who grew in my womb?"

He lowered his eyes and then bowed his head, not needing to respond.

I felt the world begin to spin around me and I reached out and took Jack's arm for support. He did not take my hand, for he was still clutching the frenzied child, but he exclaimed, "This is impossible, Professor! When we killed the monster, the curse was lifted! Do you not remember that when you touched Mina's forehead with the consecrated host, it burned her? Do you not remember Quincey Morris's dying words on that twilight road as he saw the scar fade from her skin the moment that the Count's body was reduced to dust?"

"Yes," the Professor responded, nodding sadly, "the power of the Count cease with his death. But the blood remain, the blood remain. And the blood is the life."

"But why do you wish to enter the crypt?" Jack asked.

The Professor sighed. "Why does the child wish to enter the crypt?"

Jack looked down at little Quincey, who was still struggling like a captive animal against his grip. "Yes, indeed," he muttered. "Why is he so determined? Why is he so mad with the desire to break through that barrier?"

"Why did he run away at all?" I asked in my turn. I turned to the Professor. "Do you suspect that Lucy is still . . . still . . ." I did not complete my question, for to have asked if poor Lucy was still alive would have been a blasphemous travesty.

"I know not, Madam Mina," the Professor replied, "I know not. But the child flee from the warmth and security of his home, he suffer through the cold and the darkness, to come to this place. He make to enter this crypt. We must not allow him to do so, but we must do so, we must do so. We must see what he wish to see."

"If," Jack began, his voice trembling, "if Lucy . . . if Lucy is . . . if . . ."

"I know your thoughts, my friend," the Professor said. "We are not here armed against the undead. We have no crucifix, we have no garlic, we have no consecrated host, no stake, no holy water. But think, friend Jack, think! Is it not night? Is the sun not set? If Lucy be still the foul creature the Count make her, will she not be absent from her grave? Will not the coffin be empty?"

"Then why enter the crypt?" Jack cried.

The Professor sighed yet again, his aged frame heaving from the emotions he felt but dared not as yet express. "Why does the child seek to enter the crypt?"

Jack paused for a moment, and then, after wrapping his arm around my little boy's waist, thrust his free hand into the pocket of his trousers and pulled forth his key chain. He winnowed out the key to the crypt and held it out to the

Professor. "Here," he said, his voice breaking. "Go in and see what is to be seen. I cannot. I cannot."

"But I can," I said. "Jack, I charge you to stay and guard my child, and if need be to flee from this place with him, if the Professor and I find..." and again I could not finish my words.

"But no, Madam Mina!" the Professor said as he took the key from Jack's hand. "Within may be nothing, and within may be... may be..."

"Professor Van Helsing," I began, striving to sound strong and resolute in the midst of my fear and my sorrow, "do you remember that night, many years ago, when I stood alone at night within the sanctified circle in the hills of Transylvania, alone, my old friend, when the three brides of the vampire approached me? Did I then shrink with fear? When the Count broke into my room, immobilized my husband, and then forced me to drink his own foul, satanic blood, did my heart stop from fear? Am I so weak and so frail that whatever is within that crypt will frighten me to death?" He looked at me in silence, his old, tired eyes filled with love and compassion, and I said, "Open the door, Professor, unlock the bars and let us enter. If my dear child is at risk, if some unnatural danger threatens him, then shall I fight against it as would a lioness in defense of her cub!"

The Professor nodded. "So be it, Madam Mina." He turned and unlocked the iron bars that covered the wooden door of the crypt. Then he raised the wick on the lantern and holding it high, pushed open the door and entered the burial chamber. I followed behind him, trying in vain to ignore the frenzied cries of my dear Quincey, who, seeing that the barrier that had kept him from his goal was now removed, increased his struggle against Jack's unrelenting grip.

I will not deny that a thrill of terror struck me as I stepped across the threshold into the tomb, for all the horror of that most horrible year of 1889 seemed to rush back into my mind as I watched the Professor take a small penknife from his pocket and begin to draw it across the rusty line between the coffin and the lid, attempting thus to loosen the natural cement that had sealed the sarcophagus. He worked slowly and methodically, and when he was done, he motioned me to approach, saying, "Madam Mina, I am too old and too weak to move this alone. I must ask that you assist me, but I must warn you that the remains of a friend seven years dead will not be a pleasant sight. Help this old man push, but keep closed the eyes."

I stood beside him at the head of the coffin, and together we pushed the heavy lid downward two feet. I fought myself to close my eyes, but I failed in my struggle against myself and caught a glimpse of the remains of my poor, dear, murdered friend Lucy Westenra, her golden hair still long and luxuriant upon the grinning skull. I fell back away from the coffin, for within the coffin the unmentionable reek of human decay had been mingling for seven years with the stench of rotting garlic, and the odor was overwhelming and unbearable.

Professor Van Helsing, as a medical man of course no stranger to such things, held the lantern close as he gazed into the coffin. I thought I heard him sigh as he said, "All is well, Madam Mina, all is well—with Miss Lucy, in any event. The stake is still through her ribs. The body decay, so the soul is free."

"Then why—" I began, but my question was cut short by the sound of Jack's voice crying, "Quincey, Quincey, no, no!" and I feared that the child had escaped to flee into the night. Escaped he had indeed; but he ran into the crypt and rushing past me, jumped onto the coffin, screaming, "Mother, Mother!"

"I am here, my darling!" I cried, but he ignored me as he tried to crawl into the coffin. The Professor pulled him away, but the mad child, weeping and screaming, began to gnaw at his own arm, and I was desolated by the sight.

Jack ran into the crypt just behind the child, and he grabbed him once again. Jack began to say something, but he looked inadvertently into the coffin and saw the remains of the woman whom he had loved with such devotion, and in that instant doubtless his mind conjured up the memory of her death and her undeath, the memory of that night when the stake was pounded into her flesh. "My God..." he muttered, weeping bitterly. "My God...my God..."

Professor Van Helsing's voice was strong and commanding as he said curtly, "Jack, take the boy outside immediately. Madam Mina, accompany them." The sound of his voice seemed both to brace Jack against his own sorrowful memories and to restore my self-control, and we left the crypt, dragging little Quincey with us back out into the cold moonlight. We waited as we heard the sound of stone grinding against stone as the Professor, leaning his weight against the bottom of the lid, pushed it back into place.

We returned to the waiting cab, and Jonathan . . . The child is screaming again. I must go.

20 December. - All day and all night without sleep, without rest, standing watch over my tortured child, feeling the weight of my own guilt, my own pollution, pressing down upon me. And now, with the sunrise, the child sleeps, praise be to our good Lord, the child sleeps; and I cannot, for when I close my eyes and slip into dreams, the face of the Count floats before my mind's eye, that grinning, cruel, horrible face, and I taste the blood upon my lips and feel my face pressed against his chest, and I feel his cold, undead skin, and I hear him calling me flesh of his flesh and blood of his blood, and I awaken screaming from the vision.

So I return to this journal and write, for if I do not somehow occupy myself, I fear that I shall sleep, and I fear sleep as I fear the very fires of hell.

We returned to Whitby by the morning train, and though both Jack and I pressed the Professor to reveal his thoughts to us, he kept his counsel and remained sunk in deep, silent thought.

When at last we were back in the warmth and security of our home, and Jack had fetched a strait-waistcoat with which to restrain the child, and Jonathan (against all medical advice) had braced himself with a snifter of brandy, the Professor seated us all in the drawing room and said, "My dearest friends, I must share with you what I am thinking, what I am fearing."

"A part of that I can surmise," my Jonathan said. He coughed terribly and then continued, "When the Count forced our dear Mina to drink from his foul stream, he placed into her body a plague which did not lose its unnatural power with his own destruction; and she"—he paused, reaching out to grasp my hand and squeeze it so as to show me that he loved me and held me in no way accountable for what had happened—"and she passed it on to our son."

"Yes," Professor Van Helsing said softly, "and the blood of the Count strive even now to control the boy, to impel him onward to acts so unnatural that we cannot begin to understand them. The blood is powerful, more powerful than we ever imagine. It may even now have the power to create beings like the Count, it may even now have the power to restore the dead to undeath."

"And so," I said, weeping afresh, my body shaking with sorrow and dread, "and so, I am damned and my innocent little boy is damned, and we have not defeated the Count. He reaches out, not only from beyond his grave, but even from beyond the end of his own undeath, to destroy us."

"But no, Madam Mina!" the Professor said adamantly. "I do not believe that the power of the devil is greater than the power of God. I cannot accept so blasphemous a proposition!"

"And so . . . ?" Jack asked. "What can be done? Our lives have been ruined by this creature, Professor. Our Lucy dead, Quincey Morris dead, our friend Arthur desolate and alone, I desolate and alone, Mina carrying this curse within her very body, and now this poor child cursed!"

"It is the blood of Count Dracula which carry this plague," Professor Van Helsing said firmly. "And what is the antidote to any poison? It is the substance which destroy its power. The antidote to the blood of the Count is the blood of the Lord."

I was so greatly distressed that I could not understand his meaning. "Professor," I said, "you must speak to me in simple terms, for I am weak with sorrow and ill with grief."

"The sacrament," he said simply. "The consecrated wine, the blood of Christ. It must overcome the evil blood." The Professor took my hands in his and spoke to me and Jonathan in a voice serious but strong. "My dear friends, I am a son of the Church of Rome, which I believe to be the church of the apostles, and you know as well as I that the centuries have not seen our two churches friends. But the teaching of my church is that the signature of the true church rest in the apostolic succession, in the handing down of authority and power from the apostles to their successors, down through the ages. My church tell me that you of the Church of England are heretics; and yet your bishops and priests stand in the apostolic succession, from Augustine in the seventh century to your Archbishop of Canterbury today. And so when your priests are ordained, it is a valid ordination; and when your priests consecrate the bread and wine, it is a valid consecration; and so we must obtain consecrated wine from ¬ne of your priests, and we must force little Quincey to drink t. For only the blood of Christ can counteract the blood of he vampire."

I hear a coach on the stones before the house...

It is time! It is time! Father Gordon has returned! I must
pause in my narrative. I pray God that when I resume my
writing, I shall be weeping with joy and not with sorrow.

21 December. - Praise be to the Lord God of heaven and
earth, Who in His infinite mercy has smiled upon His poor,
miserable children.

I must bring this record to a close, for I am liquid with
weariness and believe that I can sleep at last.

I have told of the events of the past fifteen days, and the
horrible theory that Professor Van Helsing proposed to us.
Neither I nor Jonathan wished to believe him, and Jack
seemed to grow angry at the thought of the Count's continuing vengeance, but we all knew that the Professor spoke the
truth.

And so we waited as the message was sent to Father
Gordon at St. Cuthbert's, and so I sat and wrote this record
as we awaited his arrival, and so Father Gordon listened with
a skepticism that turned to anger and at last to horror as I
pleaded and Jonathan begged and Jack demanded and the
Professor argued, and in the end he believed our strange tale
and returned to his parish church to fetch consecrated wine.
It was in the small hours of the morning that Father Gordon
returned, bearing with him the silver cruet that contained
the ineffable sanctity.

I cannot bring myself to detail the misery of my little
darling as Jack and Professor Van Helsing struggled to hold
him still and Father Gordon poured the sacred liquid down
his throat; I cannot describe in detail the agonized shrieks
and the terrified screams that burst from those tiny lips, for I
had placed my hands over my ears so as to block out the
sounds and at last fled the room, for I could not bear it,
could not bear it. The attempt at purification went on and on
and as I knelt in prayer in the drawing room, I shuddered
each time my boy's screams lapsed into silence, for I knew
that this rest they were giving him was but a brief hiatus, a
time allowed for the holy blood to do battle with the satanic
blood; and then, after a time, the screaming would begin
again, and my heart would break.

I made no note of the time, but the sun was rising when
I heard my boy laugh. I rose from my stiff, aching knees and
rushed to the bedroom, and the sight that greeted me filled

ny heart with such thankful joy that I felt for a moment as if
he relief which was flooding me would cause me to swoon.
Little Quincey was sitting upon his father's lap, looking very
red and ill, but very happy. Father Gordon, Jack, and the
Professor were standing in watchful silence, smiling down at
hem, and at last the Professor turned to me and said, "The
child is ours again, Madam Mina. The consecrated wine has
overcome the power of darkness, and the child is again the
pure innocent whom we all love so dearly."

I walked forward unsteadily and embraced my child,
weeping freely as his little arms wound around my neck and
he said, "Mother!"

Enough. Enough. I must rest, I must sleep.

25 December. - How joyous a Christmas, how good a Yule! My
little child is himself again, my Jonathan seems almost stronger
for the struggle of these past few weeks, Jack and the
Professor are sharing our holidays, and all seems right with
the world!

I know that I shall never forget the dire warning that
Professor Van Helsing gave me two days ago. The blood of
the Count still flows in my veins, and in my Quincey's veins,
and shall flow in the veins of my grandchildren and their own
children down through the centuries; but we are a religious
family, and I have every trust that my descendants shall
follow in our footsteps in this regard.

Is it an accident, a coincidence, that Jonathan's illness
caused me to neglect the first communion of little Quincey,
which should have come at his sixth birthday, and that as he
approached his seventh year the power of the Count's blood
began to assert itself? That was my error, my fault, my sin,
and I shall never allow myself to forget it. I shall see to it that
Quincey takes the sacrament weekly, and when he comes of
age, when he is old enough to understand, I shall explain to
him this entire horrible situation, and I know that he will
understand and will guard against the unholy blood for the
rest of his life, and he will raise his own children to do the
same. And for all that, this burden is not so great, for should
not all Christians partake of the sacrament?

And so my universe is brighter this morn. If only my
dear Jonathan would heal, would grow stronger, then I would
be content. I would be content.

*   *   *

18 February, 1897. - The romance has been published, and Mr. Stoker is quite excited about the sales thus far. We expect our first share of the royalties within the fortnight, and it will be greatly welcome, for our funds are almost depleted. Jonathan is frantic with worry as the debts pile up and the bank statement shrinks.

30 May. - How can such sweetness mingle with such bitterness? How can relief and grief stand so close and embrace each other so

II

CHILDREN
OF THE
NIGHT

Graves at my command
Have waked their sleepers,
Op'd, and let 'em forth,
By my so potent art.

—*The Tempest*,
Act V, scene i

Chapter Six

Holly Larsen and Jerry Herman were sitting at a table in the Strand with Malcolm, staring at him with blank, expressionless looks. Neither of them knew quite what to say in response to his unexpected and thoroughly bizarre discourse. He had spread numerous sheets of old, yellowed paper out on the table, and he was pointing excitedly from one to the other and to the book he held in his hand, a new paperback copy of *Dracula* by Bram Stoker.

"And it just explains so *much*!" he was saying. "I mean, take Van Helsing, for example. Lots of Germans are named van instead of von... look at Beethoven, Ludwig van Beethoven... so nobody ever thought that he was German, not Dutch. Think about it, think about it! If anybody ever tried to check this book out, look into its historicity, they'd have been thrown completely off the track by all the changed names and places."

"Mal..." Jerry tried to interrupt.

"So Stoker got the credit and my great-grandparents got fifty percent of the royalties. No wonder my family is well-off! Can you imagine what fifty percent of the royalties from *Dracula* must have amounted to over the life of the copyright? My God, it must have been millions over the years!"

"Malcolm..." Holly began.

"The only names he didn't change... other than Mina's and Jonathan's, that was part of the deal... were the names of people who died. And who would have known or cared about a lunatic like Renfield? When word reached Texas that Quincey Morris had been shot to death, who would have given it a second thought? Can you imagine how many Texans died of gunshot wounds in the 1880s?"

"Malcolm, hold on a minute," Jerry said.

"Lucy Westenra had no family, neither did John Hawkins, Jonathan Harker's employer, so using their names wouldn't have caused any stir." Malcolm paused and took a sip from his glass of burgundy. "But I'm getting off the subject. You see, the whole point here is that . . . well, as everybody knows, when you get bitten by a vampire you get infected somehow, and eventually, when you die, you become a vampire yourself."

"Yeah, everybody knows that," Jerry agreed, his sarcasm going unnoticed by Malcolm. Not so Holly, who poked him in the ribs with her elbow.

"But sometimes a vampire also makes his victim drink *his* blood, and that has a different kind of effect. That's what happened to my great-grandmother. She was forced to drink the vampire's blood, and that's a different kind of infection. She began to take on Dracula's characteristics for as long as he was still alive . . . well, not alive, but you know what I mean. As soon as he was done away with by Quincey Morris and my great-grandfather, the curse seemed to vanish from her. The burn scar on her forehead, made when Van Helsing touched her with the consecrated host, disappeared." Malcolm paused for dramatic effect. "But the point is that the polluted blood was still in her system, and it was passed on to my grandfather, my father, and Rachel and me. Van Helsing told my great-grandparents that it was a permanent element of evil in our systems and could only be counteracted by a constant infusion of sanctity, by a regular taking of the sacrament in church."

"Malcolm . . ." Holly began to say gently.

"That's why Grandfather was so worried about my not going to church anymore. He was afraid that the polluted blood would gain dominance. According to him and the diary, that's why I can't sleep at night, that's why sunlight hurts my eyes and I never have any appetite." He looked at Holly. "That's why you and I haven't been good together these last few times. Vampires' desires are not sexual."

"Honey," she said, "you don't take any of this stuff seriously, do you? I mean, really!"

He rubbed his eyes. "I don't know, I don't know. It all seemed so stupid when Gramps and Rachel were talking about it, but after I read the papers, it all seemed to make sense."

"Mal," Jerry said, laughing, "I wish you could listen to

yourself. I mean, you're talking about being cursed with the blood of Dracula, for crying out loud!"

"I know, I know, it sounds absurd," he agreed. "I hope that it is all nonsense. But God, Jerry, can you think of any other explanation for what's been happening to me?"

"So what's been happening to you?" his friend asked. "You have insomnia, you're off your feed, and you couldn't get it up a couple of times. So what?" He shook his head, laughing again. "I really don't think that if you went to a doctor and described those symptoms, he would shake his head and say"—and Jerry's voice shifted into a very bad imitation of Bela Lugosi's—" 'We are dealing here with the curse of the Undead!' "

Malcolm did not laugh. "So explain what happened in that place you took me to."

This sobered Jerry up and he became a bit defensive. "Hey, I don't know what happened in there. You and that Swedish gorilla got into a fight, that's all."

"Jerry, you told me that the girl was bleeding from the neck and that I was trying to get at her, and I don't remember anything about it."

"Okay, okay," Jerry said hotly, "so you're a fucking nut case, okay? You belong in a rubber room or something, but don't give me any of this vampire shit!"

"Jerry!" Holly said sharply. "Don't say things like that! Can't you see how upset he is?"

"He may be right, Holly," Malcolm said. "I hope he's right. I'd almost be relieved if I were just having a breakdown or something like that."

"Well, you're not having a breakdown and you're not turning into a vampire!" Holly said emphatically. "Mal, honey, I'm not even going to bother trying to make you see how silly this whole thing is. If you ask me, your grandfather . . . and I like him, don't get me wrong . . . is a senile old man who doesn't know what he's talking about. And this sounds to me like your sister is going along with it just as a way of breaking us up. She doesn't like me, you know!"

"I know," he agreed, "and she's a jerk, I know that, too. But . . ."

"No buts about it, man," Jerry said. "Listen to her, will you? This is crazy, Malcolm! Absolutely nuts!"

"You can't believe any of it, Mal," Holly added. "It isn't even worth talking about."

"Look, I didn't call you two up and ask you to meet me here just to argue about it," he said firmly but without rancor. "I know it sounds ridiculous, and I know there are probably a hundred other explanations for what's been happening to me... though I can't think of one that would explain what happened when I took communion last Sunday."

"You have an ulcer," Jerry muttered.

"Maybe so," Malcolm said, nodding. "And maybe not. In any event, I have a plan. I have to prove to myself either that it's true or that it isn't. I have to know, one way or another."

"It isn't true," Holly and Jerry said in unison, after which they exchanged amused glances.

"Well, there's one way to find out," Malcolm went on. "It's the original text of Stoker's book *Dracula*. He names people and places and all that in the book. I'm going to England as soon as I can arrange it, and I'm going to see if the places he mentions exist. I'm going to see if there really is a town called Whitby and a house called Carfax Abbey. I'm going to check records and archives and see if there ever was an asylum run by a doctor named John Stewart, see if there ever was a mental patient named Renfield. I'm going to see if a German professor named Van Helsing ever visited England..." He paused and looked off into space. "Abraham Van Helsing," he muttered. "My father's name was Abraham. I'd always assumed he was named after Lincoln or something like that, but maybe..."

"Malcolm, listen to me for a minute—" Jerry began, but Malcolm cut him off as he returned to the description of his plan.

"I'm going to check to see if there ever was a Duke of Wellington whose fiancée, Lucy Westenra, died of acute anemia, if there ever was a man named John Hawkins, Esq., who arranged a real estate purchase for a Rumanian nobleman—"

"Damn it, Malcolm, will you listen to me?" Jerry said forcefully. "You're talking about spending an awful lot of money just to prove the falsehood of something that a ten-year-old kid would know isn't true!"

"And besides," Holly added, "there's a better, cheaper way to go about it, if you're determined to do it."

"What do you mean?" Malcolm asked.

"What do you know about research procedures and sources in England? Nothing, not one thing. You—"

"I've done extensive historical research, you know," he said a bit defensively. "I mean, I did get a degree in classics, after all!"

"Sure, fine, so you know your way around the New York Public Library," Holly responded. "Malcolm, if you want to do research about all of this nonsense, then you should hire people in England to do it for you, not go there and try to do it yourself!"

"Of course, man!" Jerry agreed. "With the amount of money you'd be spending on airfare and hotels and all that, you could hire a whole team of researchers." He paused. "And besides, you could probably look up most of that stuff right here. I mean, the New York libraries have books and maps!"

Malcolm shook his head adamantly. "No, Jerry, no to both objections. I have to do this myself. I can't hire anyone else to do it, and I can't rely on local information."

"Oh, Malcolm, why not?" Holly asked with exasperation.

Malcolm seemed to lapse into pensiveness as he said, "I can't really explain it. Last night, as I was reading my great-grandmother's diary, the idea just sort of came to me, and it just seemed to make perfect sense."

"How can such a half-assed idea make perfect sense?" Jerry asked.

"It just does," Malcolm insisted, and then smiled. "I even dreamed about it, dreamed about searching for the truth, dreamed about being in England . . ."

"Well, I've dreamed about that myself often enough," Holly muttered. "I think everybody dreams about going to Europe."

"I'm glad to hear you say that," Malcolm said, looking from Holly to Jerry. "I want the two of you to come with me."

"Are you nuts!" Jerry exclaimed. "I can't afford to go to Europe!"

"Don't worry about money," Malcolm reassured him. "I've discussed this idea with Gramps, told him what I want to do and why, and he thought it was a great idea. He's agreed to pay for all three of us. He'll foot the whole bill." He turned to Holly. "Can you come?"

"I think so," she said, suddenly very pleased with the idea. "I haven't taken a vacation in two years, so I'm sure there won't be any problem at work." Visions of Harrods department store and the boutiques and shops along Carnaby

Street and King's Road began to drift through her mind. A European vacation with Malcolm! London, Stratford-upon-Avon, Windsor Castle! The pubs, the antique shops, the theaters! What a delightful idea!

And, she noted as an afterthought, absolutely free. My favorite price!

"I don't have to ask you if you can make it, Jerry," Malcolm said to his friend. "You and I were planning to go to the Bahamas together this month anyway. I know you can take off, and it won't cost you a cent."

As visions of English shops were drifting through Holly's mind, visions of brown, nubile women in string bikinis were vanishing from Jerry's. "Oh, well," he sighed. "Sure. What the hell, why not."

"There's one more thing I want to do . . . I have to do," Malcolm said seriously. "And if the idea doesn't sit well with either of you, I'll understand. I don't want to force anybody to do anything they don't want to do."

"What is it?" Holly asked.

Malcolm, with a melodramatic flourish, held up the paperback copy of *Dracula*. "I picked this up today at Waldenbooks on Continental Avenue. I wanted to have a copy for reference, one I could write in and stuff like that."

"Of course," Jerry said, sounding a bit tried and bored.

"Listen to this," Malcolm said, flipping through the book, searching for a specific part. He found it and began to read aloud to his friends:

> Arthur took the stake and the hammer, and when once his mind was set on action, his hands never trembled nor even quivered. Van Helsing opened his missal and began to read, and Quincey and I followed as best we could. Arthur placed the point over the heart, and as I looked, I could see its dint in the white flesh. Then he struck with all his might.
>
> The Thing in the coffin writhed; and a hideous, bloodcurdling screech came from the opened red lips. The body shook and quivered and twisted in wild contortions; the sharp white teeth champed together until the lips were cut and the mouth was smeared with a crimson foam. And then the writh-

ing and the quivering of the body became less.
Finally it lay still. The terrible task was over.

"Yeah, creepy," Jerry said. "What about it?"

Malcolm paused before speaking. "That's how the book
describes the death of a woman named Lucy Westenra.
According to the book, she was my great-grandmother's best
friend. She was killed by Dracula, turned into a vampire after
death, and had a stake driven through her heart by the guy
she was going to marry, a nobleman named the Duke of
Wellington, though Stoker calls him Lord Godalmung."

"That's what the novel says," Holly said pointedly.

"That's what the book says," Malcolm corrected her. "I
can't call it a novel until I know for sure that it's all fiction."

"Okay, okay," Jerry said impatiently. "So you're gonna
look for her grave, right? See if she really existed?"

"I'm going to open her grave," Malcolm said. "I'm going
to look at her remains. According to the book, after they
drove the stake through her heart, they cut off her head and
stuffed her mouth with garlic, then placed a piece of consecrated host on her stomach. If we open her grave and find a
stake or a severed skull . . . well, then, I'll know for sure."

"Mal," Jerry said, laughing, "you know you can't go
around digging people up! It's against the law!"

"No digging involved," he said. "The book says she was
put in a mausoleum."

"Well, whatever," Jerry said. "You still can't go around
messing with dead bodies, even real old ones. You'll get
arrested."

"I know, I know," Malcolm said, nodding. "That's why
we'll leave it for last. If there's no Whitby, no Carfax Abbey,
no Dr. Stewart's asylum, no Renfield, no Van Helsing, we'll
just forget about her. But let me be clear on this point: If the
other stuff checks out, then we go to Hempstead and look for
her grave. And if we find it, we open it. Agreed?"

Holly leaned forward on her forearms and looked him
straight in the eye. "Malcolm, I'm going to agree to all of
this, for one simple reason. Do you know what the reason is?"

He smiled a bit sheepishly. "Because you love me?"

"Not at all," she replied, not smiling. "I do love you, you
know that. But there are limits to anything, and this nonsense of yours is pushing it. No, Mal, I'll agree to this for the
simple reason that I'm certain that we'll go to England,

investigate this, and not find a damned thing. This whole idea
is just so stupid!"

"But what about these documents?" Malcolm asked. "If
there's no truth to any of this, why does my grandfather have
all this stuff?"

"Maybe," Jerry answered, "just maybe your great-
grandfather was a book collector and he bought Stoker's
manuscript at an auction or something. Maybe he even knew
Stoker and got the manuscript and stuff from him. Maybe all
of this handwritten stuff is a private joke by your grandfather!
Maybe somebody copied over parts of the book for . . . I don't
know, some kind of fraud or hoax or something. There are lots
of maybes here, Mal, and 'maybe my best friend is turning
into a vampire' is not very high on the list."

"Right," Holly agreed. "So I'll agree with everything you
want, I'll even agree to opening Lucy Westenra's grave,
because I'm certain that she never existed. If by some bizarre
coincidence your great-grandparents had the same names as a
couple of characters in the novel, well, then, all it is, is a
bizarre coincidence."

"What about the other names?" Malcolm asked heatedly.

"What about them? All you've told us is that there are
two different sets of names for some of the characters, and the
same names for some of the others. So what? That doesn't
mean anything. I mean, really, Mal! The Duke of Wellington?
Come on!" She put her arms around his neck and smiled at
him, her eyes laughing at him and mocking his foolishness
and fear. "I'll agree to anything you want, because it won't
mean a thing. It's fiction, Malcolm, just fiction."

"I'll second that," Jerry said, raising his glass of beer to
his lips.

"Fine," Malcolm said, nodding. "Just so long as it's
understood that if the rest of it checks out, we look for Lucy's
grave and open it." He sipped again from the glass of burgundy.

Jerry glanced over at Holly, his eyes twinkling and a
smile struggling to emerge on the corners of his mouth.
"Hey, uh, Mal, I thought you guys didn't drink . . . wine."

"That's not funny, Jerry," Holly snapped.

Malcolm did not reply. He was gazing pensively at the
glass of wine that he was holding, noticing with curious
dispassion that it was the color of blood. "Stupid thing to pop
into my head," he muttered.

"What, honey?" Holly asked.

"Nothing, nothing," he replied. "Let's go to a travel agent and get things moving. We'd better arrange for a rental car also. I've never driven on the left-hand side of the road before, but lots of people do it, so it can't be all that difficult."

"Hey, if it is, you can always turn into a bat and—"

"Jerry!" Holly shouted.

"Sorry." Jerry sniffed and took another swig of beer. Curse of the vampire! he thought. Good grief!

By Saturday all the necessary preparations had been made, and late Sunday evening they boarded the plane at Kennedy Airport and were on their way to England.

Chapter Seven

Under other circumstances, Malcolm would have been fascinated by the sights and sounds of London and its environs. The country was dripping with history, and a young man of Malcolm's deep interest in the past—in particular Europe's past—would have delighted in it; under other circumstances, of course.

Under other circumstances, Holly would have spent many a carefree hour wandering through Harrod's enormous store, would have browsed through a multitude of quaint little shops, examined the wares of the swarms of street vendors along King's Road and Carnaby Street.

Under other circumstances, Jerry would have flitted happily from pub to pub, and if he was lucky, female to female, exulting in the varieties of ales, bitters, and lagers, seeing if the carefully cultivated social presence he had developed over the years had any effect upon the leggy girls with their multicolored hair.

Under other circumstances, all of this might have been the case. But after allowing for a few hours of jet-lag-induced sleep, Malcolm had badgered his friends into joining him in the archives and dusty old stacks of the huge British Library, seeking clues and verifications of the places and people mentioned in Stoker's book.

Holly remained convinced that the entire problem rested in Malcolm's extreme sensitivity and trustfulness, coupled with a particularly active imagination. She cursed his family inwardly for having stuffed his mind full of foolish old stories, and she was certain that as soon as he realized that none of the people mentioned in either the altered or unaltered text ever really existed, he would calm down, begin to enjoy

102

himself, and start acting like his old self again. Jerry con-
curred wholeheartedly, and he somewhat testily resented
each hour spent in libraries instead of pubs, in archives
instead of discotheques.

And all the while, as Malcolm dragged them with him
along the motorways of England from place to place and city
to village, the verifications of Stoker's text began to accumu-
late with depressing, frightening regularity. Malcolm had
starred or underlined passage after passage in the altered,
"corrected," paperback editions of *Dracula* that he had purchased in Forest Hills, and as he and his companions searched
through the tax records, the obituaries, the ordnance survey
maps, the dusty old ledgers and property registries, a terrible
fact began to emerge: Bram Stoker's book was not a work of
fiction.

In the county archives in Exeter, they found a copy of
the partnership agreement between John Hawkins and Jonathan
Harker, dated two months after the latter's return from his
business trip to Eastern Europe.

In the *Times* index they found an obituary for Arthur
Wellesley, the seventh Duke of Wellington, who died fighting
in the Boer War in South Africa in 1898.

In the index to the *Journal of the British Philosophical
Society* they found a listing for an article entitled *Über
Metaphysische Ganzheit,* "Concerning Metaphysical Unity,"
published in 1899, written by Abraham Xavier Klemens Van
Helsing, translated by Dr. John Stewart.

In the tax records housed in the British Library, they
found a record of import duties paid by the shipping firm of
Carter, Patterson and Company on fifty boxes of soil. The
point of origin was listed as the Hapsburg Empire, that
sprawling realm which in 1889 included the province of
Transylvania.

In the Hall of Records they found a death certificate for
one Richard Michael Renfield, place of death: St. Anselm's
Asylum, Whitby, Yorkshire; cause of death: "misadventure";
attending physician: Dr. John Stewart. At first Malcolm was
confused by the signature on the certificate, for Stewart had
written the words "body embalmed" in parentheses after his
name. Death certificates did not provide space for any record
of the disposition of the body, but Stewart seemed to want it
recorded and known that Renfield had been embalmed before burial.

And then Malcolm understood, and he swallowed hard as he stared at the words on the death certificate. Embalming in late-nineteenth-century England was an expensive procedure, not a commonplace one. Under ordinary circumstances, the body of a penniless lunatic would not be embalmed.

Unless the attending physician had reason to want to make very, very certain that no blood remained in the corpse when it was buried.

Van Helsing, Wellington, Hawkins, Renfield, Carter and Patterson. Real. All real.

And yet, their research yielded no reference to a place called Carfax Abbey, and no record at all of a young woman named Lucy Westenra. Malcolm, half-wishing to be proven wrong and half-determined to be proven right, speculated that the death record of Lucy might have been suppressed, and that the Carfax estate might have been called by another name. When Malcolm insisted upon driving north from London to the town of Whitby in Yorkshire, Holly and Jerry objected in the strongest possible manner. "What's the goddamned point, man?" Jerry asked with exasperation. "If there was any truth to all this bullshit, don't you think the name of Dracula's estate would have been recorded somewhere?"

"Yes, I do," Malcolm replied. "That's why we have to go to Whitby. The record of the sale might only have been filed locally. And besides, we know from the book that the estate was originally called Quatre Face because of its shape, and Carfax was a local name. Maybe it's listed somewhere as Quatre Face or something else entirely. In any event, the information would more likely be in Whitby than in London."

"This is absurd!" Jerry said. "If there's no mention made of the place in any of the records we've checked, then it doesn't exist, period! I think we should just forget this whole stupid idea of yours and just try to enjoy the last week we have here!"

The emphatic tenor of his words might have had a greater effect had they not been driving into the Yorkshire town of Whitby as he said them. The drive from London to the coastal town set on the central coast of one of England's northernmost provinces, only shortly removed from the border of Scotland, had taken them but a day. This was a result of Malcolm's frenzied driving and the fact that he had ushered them out of the London bed-and-breakfast well before dawn.

By the time the sun rose they were past Oxford, and at Whitby by midafternoon.

The land office of the town doubled as the local constabulary, so there was no need to worry about closing hours once Malcolm explained that he was researching his family's past. Unlike many peoples in other countries, the British are sympathetic to Americans of Anglo-Saxon stock who are seeking information about their forebears. The police officer politely sent them downstairs to the room in which local archives were stored, and the clerk who was about to lock it up politely invited them to browse about to their hearts' content. He was unable to give them any information himself, having never heard of Carfax Abbey or Quatre Face. He apologized profusely, and Holly and Jerry told him sincerely that he need not do so.

As Malcolm began poring over ledgers and newspaper files, Holly motioned to Jerry and whispered, "Let's go upstairs for a minute, okay?"

"Sure," he replied, glancing at Malcolm. His friend was too engrossed in his search to notice when they left.

They mounted the stairs and walked out onto the cobblestone street where the Yorkshire wind, damp and a bit cold even in early June, made Holly shiver. "Jerry," she said earnestly, "I don't like the way this is working out at all. He's getting much too worked up over the whole thing."

"Yeah, I know," Jerry agreed. "He's starting to act weird . . . I mean, weirder than usual. Did you see the way he looked at me when I argued with him about driving up here? I've never seen him get so angry. I think that if I'd insisted, he would have hit me or something."

Holly shook her head. "You're his best friend, Jer. He wouldn't have done anything like that. But I'm not talking about how he's acting, not about how obsessed he seems, anyway."

"Okay, so what are you talking about?"

"Well," she said, frowning slightly, "I figured that he'd find out right away that the book is fictional, but he keeps turning up things that bear it out. And we've been helping him do it, which doesn't make me feel—"

"Oh, come on!" Jerry interrupted. "Don't tell me you're starting to think there's something *to* all this crap!"

"Of course not!" she said with annoyance. "Lots of novels use real people's names and real places and all that. But listen, let's just suppose that Mal's great-grandfather knew all the people in the book, and that the writer, Stoker, knew them, too. Stoker might very well have written the book as sort of a fun thing for his friends, sort of an in-joke. I mean, he wrote the book to make money, sure; but if you were going to write a novel and you thought that your friends would get a kick out of being in it, wouldn't you use their names?"

Jerry nodded thoughtfully. "You know, that makes sense! So, of course everything checks out against facts. That's a great thought, Holly!"

"No, it isn't," she said seriously. "If what I just said is true . . . and we know at least that Stoker did know Jonathan Harker, from the inscription in the first edition Mal's grandfather has . . . then the more research we do the more evidence Malcolm will find to prove that the book is a record of fact. If that happens, then nothing we say or do is going to make any difference. He's going to end up convincing himself that it's the truth, and I don't think he's in any shape psychologically to resist a delusion like that."

Jerry understood her concern, and he placed his hand gently on her arm. "I really wouldn't worry about that. No matter how much local color Stoker used, no matter how many real people—friends of his, even—the story is still all make-believe. Mal's got to realize that eventually. In fact, the longer he's away from his family, the better. They're the ones who dumped this load of shit on him in the first place."

"Maybe we should tell . . ." She stopped. "Is that Malcolm?" They both listened hard for a moment to the faint voice calling their names from the basement of the building. Distance made it almost impossible to hear actual words, but even so they realized that Malcolm was shouting. They went back inside and walked quickly down the stairs to the archives room.

Malcolm was sitting at a table, papers spread out haphazardly before him, gazing at one with undisguised absorption, almost happiness, as if he had become so devoted to the task of proving the truthfulness of Bram Stoker's account that he had forgotten what such proof portended for him. "Come here!" he said excitedly. "Look at this!"

He tossed the sheaf of papers to Holly, who caught it and looked at it uncomprehendingly. "What is it?"

"It's a bill of sale, a transfer of ownership! It says on the bottom of the form . . . there"—he jabbed at the page—"that there are three copies: one to be filed, one for the buyer, and one for the seller."

Jerry looked over Holly's shoulder and squinted at the faded writing. "Hey, Mal, this isn't for Carfax. This is for someplace called the Davignon Estate."

"Of course it is, of course it is!" he exclaimed. "That's why we couldn't find any record of Carfax or Quatre Face anywhere. That wasn't the real name, the legal, official name of the property!"

Holly tossed the papers back onto the table. "So how do you know it's Carfax? I mean, good Lord, Mal!"

"Malcolm," Jerry said seriously, "you have to get hold of yourself. You're starting to rave."

"Don't you understand!" Malcolm shouted. "Carfax, Quatre Face, four faces—these were local nicknames! It's like . . . well, I don't know . . . like calling some buildings the Twin Towers instead of the World Trade Center, or, ah, calling the Capitol Building 'the Hill.' Everybody knows what it means, but you won't find it on any official documents!"

"Okay, so if it's a local nickname, how come the people here have never heard of it?" Holly asked.

"This is why," he said, holding out an old edition of the local newspaper. "The whole area was devastated by German bombs during the Blitz . . . you know, World War Two."

"I understood the reference," Holly said dryly.

"The point is, when the Germans were trying to bomb England out of the war, they concentrated a lot of their missions on *ports*, and Whitby is a *port*! In the process of trying to destroy Whitby, they blew up Carfax! That's why nobody's ever heard of the name! If you're fifty years old, like those cops seem to be, you'd have been an infant during the war!"

"Mal, why are you calling it Carfax?" Jerry said, a hint of exasperated anger creeping into his voice. "I mean, look at your logic, man! What it comes down to is that you're calling it Carfax simply because it isn't called Carfax. That's nuts!"

"Oh, for Christ's sake, Jerry, look at the goddamn bill of sale, will you!" He grabbed it from the tabletop. "Look here, right here. Who was the agent for the sale? What does it say?"

Jerry looked down at the page that Malcolm was holding. "Okay, so it says John Hawkins. So what? So Hawkins was a successful solicitor and he did some work up here. Again, so what?"

Malcolm paused. "So look at the name of the witness to the buyer's signature. Look at it!"

Jerry looked again. "Okay, your great-grandfather. Mal, we already knew that Jonathan Harker worked for John Hawkins. That still doesn't mean—"

"Look at the buyer's signature. Look carefully."

Holly and Jerry took turns trying to decipher the almost illegible letters. "Looks like an abbreviation," Holly said at last.

"Yeah," Jerry agreed. "Just letters. But none of them is a *D*."

"Okay, okay," Malcolm said as if he were speaking to a couple of unusually slow children. "What are the letters?"

"They're . . ." Holly began, squinting at the scrawl, "they're . . . WL . . . WAL . . . WOI . . . I think."

"Will Walwoi?" Jerry said, trying to make auditory sense of the letters. "Will Walwoi? You're trying to tell me that you can get the name Dracula out of Will Walwoi!"

"Damn it, Jerry, that was his name, his real name!" Malcolm shouted.

"Good thing he changed it," Jerry mused. "Who could take a vampire named Will Walwoi seriously?"

"Jerry . . . !"

"*Will Walwoi, Prince of Darkness! Curse of Will Walwoi! Will Walwoi Meets the Wolfman! Abbott and Costello Meet Will Walwoi!*" Jerry began to laugh. "Can you imagine Bela Lugosi saying, 'Good eeevening. I am Will Walwoi!'" At this, Holly started to giggle.

Malcolm's jaw clenched as he grew red in the face. "Will you two shut up!" They did, startled into compliance by the sudden intensity of his anger. "Listen to me, both of you! In languages that use the Roman alphabet for writing, the letters *U, V,* and *W* are often interchanged. This *W* is a *V*."

"Okay," Jerry said, starting to laugh again, "so it's Vill Valvoi, Prince of Darkness."

"This isn't funny, goddamn it!" Malcolm shouted.

Jerry quieted down and listened, trying not to think of other amusing movie titles, knowing that this was a matter of deadly seriousness to his friend.

"The *W* is a *V*," Malcolm went on. "You've read the

book, like I asked you to. Where did Dracula come from? What was his title?"

"The *novel*," Holly said, "calls him a Transylvanian count."

"Right, as far as it goes," Malcolm said, still red in the face from his anger. "But the word 'count' is an English title, or maybe it's French. The point is that it isn't Rumanian. What was his Rumanian title? What was the Rumanian name for his province, not where he lived when my great-grandfather met him—"

"Your great-grandfather did *not* meet him!" Holly said.

"—but the province he ruled historically, back in the fifteenth century," he said, ignoring her objection.

"Mal, who the hell knows?" Jerry said. "I didn't memorize the fucking book, you know!"

Malcolm glowered at him. "He was called Vlad Tepes, which means Vlad the Impaler, when he ruled the province of Wallachia as prince, or in Rumanian, voivode." He jabbed his forefinger hard on the signature. "WlWalWoi. Vlad of Wallachia, Voivode."

Holly shook her head. "I really think you're reaching here, Malcolm."

"Oh, come on, Holly! Admit it! It's proof positive! This guy's father was called the Dragon by his people, and he was called the Little Dragon, Dracula. But his name, his real name, was Voivode Vlad of Wallachia." Malcolm sat down heavily at the table. "This clinches it. Dracula bought Carfax Abbey through my great-grandfather and Mr. Hawkins, shipped boxes of native soil to England through Carter, Patterson and Company. It's all real. Van Helsing, Stewart, Wellington, Carfax . . . it's all true!"

Jerry looked at Holly. "Tell him what you told me outside."

Malcolm looked up excitedly. "Tell me what?"

Holly repeated her theory and Malcolm listened attentively, skeptical at first, but becoming increasingly thoughtful as she pressed her point with insistence. She concluded her argument by saying, "You have to admit that it would make a lot more sense than all of this supernatural stuff, wouldn't it?"

He nodded, not convinced but desperate to be convinced. "It's possible . . . it's possible . . ."

"Of course it's possible," Jerry said casually, as if it were obvious to even the most benighted intellect. "I mean, the alternative is impossible, so this must be the truth."

Malcolm continued to nod his head but then said firmly, "There's one way to settle it once and for all. I told you what I was going to do if everything else checked out as real."

Jerry moaned as Holly said, "Malcolm, you are *not* going to start opening people's graves looking for wooden stakes!"

"Holly, I have to—"

"No! I'm putting my foot down here!" she said petulantly. "Jerry and I have gone along with you this far, but this is it! This is the end!"

"She's right, Mal," Jerry added. "We've checked the obits and all that stuff, and there's no reference to Lucy Westenra anyway."

"So we go to Hempstead and look for her grave," Malcolm said.

"No, Malcolm!" Holly said. "I've just about had it with this nonsense! We've driven all the hell over the place ever since we got here; my eyes are probably damaged from reading all these faded old documents; I've inhaled enough dust to make me feel like a coal miner. Enough, Malcolm! Enough!"

His eyes narrowed as he stared at her, and she felt herself shivering slightly. There was a coldness about his look, something unfamiliar and alien, and when he spoke, his voice was hard and bitter. "You promised me," he said. "You both promised me. I have to find out the truth, and I don't want to have to do it alone. You say that you're my friends, and yet... and yet..." He paused and looked from Holly to Jerry. "You promised me, both of you."

Holly looked to Jerry for support, but she saw that he, too, had been nonplussed by the strangeness of Malcolm's aspect. She turned back to Malcolm and said, "I didn't mean to yell at you, honest I didn't. I know how upset you are, and... well..." She stopped speaking and looked again to Jerry.

"Look, uh, Mal," Jerry said tentatively, "how about this: We go to Hempstead tomorrow and look around the graveyard. If we don't find the grave, we go back to London and party like crazy for the week we have left. Will that satisfy you?"

Malcolm nodded slowly. "And if we do find the grave?"

Neither of his friends replied.

"And if we do find the grave?" he repeated. "Remember

what I said back in New York. If we find Lucy Westenra's grave, we open it up and examine her remains. Right?"

Again, no response.

"Right?" he said again, slowly and forcefully.

Jerry nodded. "Yeah, sure. Sure, Mal, sure."

Malcolm looked at Holly.

After a moment she said, "Okay, Malcolm."

He nodded. "Good." Then something of the customary melancholy warmth returned to his face, and he smiled as if slightly ashamed of his attitude of a moment before. "You have to bear with me. This whole thing is eating me up inside."

Holly was relieved at the sudden disappearance of the stranger, and she smiled as she squeezed his hand. "You know what I think?"

"What?" he asked.

"I think we'll leave here bright and early and get back to southern England by the afternoon. We'll go to Hempstead, find the churchyard, look around, and not find a thing. It's one thing to write a book using your friends' names just for a laugh and using real places and all that, and it's something else entirely to use the name of a real person as a murder victim. Believe me, Malcolm, there just simply was no Lucy Westenra."

"Couldn't have been," Jerry agreed.

Malcolm considered their statements. "You both seem pretty certain."

"I *am* certain," Holly said confidently. "Aren't you, Jerry?"

"Not a doubt in my mind," he replied.

"I hope you're right," Malcolm said, nodding softly.

Jerry laughed. "Of course we're right, Mal, and by this time tomorrow, not only are you going to realize how silly this whole thing has been, but Holly and I are going to be making you the butt of more jokes than you'll be able to count!"

They left Whitby the next morning with the dawn. By four in the afternoon they had reached Hempstead. By four-fifteen they had found the old churchyard.

At four-thirty they were standing silently before the Westenra mausoleum.

Malcolm Harker gazed out the window of the room he had taken in the King Edward Hotel in Hempstead, watching as the sun sank slowly down toward the distant hills. He did not hear the gentle tap on the door, and thus he did not turn to see Holly Larsen enter his room. "Malcolm?" she asked. "Can I come in for a minute?" He did not respond. He was staring at the ruddy orb pensively, silently. "Malcolm?" she repeated. "Are you okay?"

He spun around quickly as if startled, startling her in turn with the rapid motion. He gazed at her for a moment and then smiled. "Oh, Holly. I'm sorry. I didn't hear you come in."

She moved farther into the room and closed the door behind her. "I think we have to talk, Mal."

He nodded. "Yes, we do. I've been thinking this whole thing over, and I have a few ideas I'd like to run by you."

"That's not what I mean, Malcolm," she interrupted. "I'm not interested in this nutty fantasy of yours, and I'm starting to wonder if . . . well, if maybe . . ."

He sighed. "If maybe we shouldn't see each other anymore, once we're back in the States?" She assented with her silence, and he walked over to the bed and sat down, not looking at her. "I can't say I blame you. There's no reason in the world why anyone would want to stay with someone who has the kind of problem I might have."

"Damn it, Malcolm!" she said angrily. "You don't understand at all, not at all! Your only problem is that you believe this stupid horror story, and that's what I'm concerned about!" She sat down beside him and took his hand in hers. "Listen, Mal, I'm not really sure that we should break up. It's just that I've had just about as much of this nonsense as I intend to take, you know? You have to get yourself together, Malcolm, you really do."

Malcolm nodded. "I know I do, I know I do." Then, changing the subject, he asked, "Where's Jerry?"

"Out hitting the pubs. He's fed up, Mal."

He sniffed. "Great friend."

"He *is* a great friend," she insisted with an adamance she did not truly feel. Were the truth to be known, she had not quite forgiven Jerry for leading Malcolm into the ill-fated tryst with Vanessa; but Jerry's skepticism and common sense were allies in her struggle against Malcolm's delusions, and so she defended him. "You've gotten so wrapped up in this crazy idea that you've forgotten how this looks to me and Jerry. Malcolm, this is nuts."

He looked over at her and then nodded as he squeezed

her hand. "Maybe so. We'll know tonight, one way or the other."

Holly gritted her teeth and sighed. "Malcolm, you are *not* going to break into someone's grave!"

"I have to."

"You *can't!*"

He rose to his feet and began to pace back and forth, saying, "Listen to me, Holly, listen to me carefully. A lot of very strange ideas have been popping into my head ever since we found Lucy's grave, ideas so weird that they almost scare me, but the ideas keep coming anyway, and the more I think them over, the more sense they make."

Holly sighed and lay back on the bed. "Oh, Malcolm!" she muttered, her voice laced with pity and disgust.

"Holly, just listen to me, okay?"

She sighed again. "Okay, okay."

"Let's say, just for discussion purposes, just for the sake of argument, that Dracula was somehow able to alter the composition of his blood, make it both static and also somehow regenerative. . . ."

"Malcolm," she said wearily, "don't try to make a foolish superstition sound scientific by phrasing it nicely. It's still all nonsense, and deep down inside, you know that it is."

"Listen, listen!" he said. "Let's just suppose that his own blood held the key to . . . well, to what Van Helsing called Undeath, in some chemical manner we can't understand."

"Uh-huh," she said with growing irritation.

"Let's say that there's a chemical reaction of some sort, and that human blood, real, living human blood, is the catalyst necessary for the reaction to occur. Wouldn't that explain everything? Wouldn't that explain why he lived on for centuries, why he had to drink blood from living people?"

She sat up in the bed and sighed, resigned to the conversation. "Okay, let's examine that idea for a minute. How does that explain how people killed by Dracula, drained dry by him to the point of death, became vampires after they died?"

"Maybe he forced them to drink his blood also. If it's the altered blood that enabled him to return from death, maybe he gave them his blood after drinking from theirs."

She shook her head. "It doesn't say that in the book."

"Of course not," he replied. "No one ever saw Dracula attack his victims. Maybe each night that he drank from Lucy

Westenra, he gave her some of his blood in exchange." He paused. "In fact, why should we assume that what he did to Mina Harker was an isolated incident? Maybe it was, you know, standard operating procedure!"

"Okay," Holly said. "So if the presence of the blood in the system makes the corpse... I don't know, wake up or something, then why didn't your great-grandmother become a vampire? Why didn't your father rise from his grave, looking for blood?"

"Because this is America in the twentieth century, not England in the nineteenth. When a person dies he or she is embalmed. The blood is drained from the body and replaced with embalming fluid. They didn't do that to Lucy Westenra. They didn't do that to the women in Dracula's castle, the ones that Van Helsing destroyed just before the final attack on the Count." He paused again, his eyebrows knitting and his eyes blazing with furious thought. "Don't you see? The power, the real power, is in the blood. It's in the blood!"

"Okay, fine," she said, too tired to argue about it.

"Second thought," he went on. "If Dracula was the only vampire who ever existed, except for his victims, and if he became a vampire by some sort of conscious alchemical process, doesn't it stand to reason that the process is reversible? I mean, aren't most chemical processes reversible?"

"No," she answered simply.

He ignored her objection. "If it could be done, it can be undone, I'm certain of that. There must be a way to counteract the influence of his blood, some way besides taking communion." He paused and thought for a moment. "I know I'm sort of rambling, but the idea is sound."

"The idea is anything but sound, Malcolm," she said. "Don't misunderstand me here; there are no such things as vampires. But if there were, there wouldn't be any sort of scientific explanation of them."

"Okay, so there isn't a scientific explanation, there isn't any sort of rational explanation. The important fact remains that the power is in the blood, and there must be some way to figure out why the blood is so powerful." He looked at her seriously. "That brings me to my third idea."

"Go on," she sighed.

"Later on, when the town is asleep, we're going to go and check out Lucy Westenra's coffin. Maybe we'll just find the remains of a dead person."

"First logical thing you've—"

"But maybe we'll find more. Maybe we'll find a stake sticking out of her ribs. Maybe we'll see that her head was cut off, like it says in the book."

"Yeah, sure. Maybe."

"If the blood in my veins is Dracula's blood, then it was this blood, my blood, that turned her into a vampire in the first place. It was the presence of this blood in her body that caused her to rise from death and become a vampire. If it did it once, it can do it twice."

She stared at him uncomprehendingly for a moment, and then her eyes went wide as his meaning became clear to her. *"What?"*

"Of course!" he said excitedly. "What do you, I, or anyone know about vampirism, except the stuff we read in legends? Nothing, nothing at all! If I want to understand what's been happening to me, and more importantly, if I want to figure out what to do about it, who better for me to question than a real, honest-to-God vampire?"

She continued to stare at him, and then she began to laugh uncontrollably. "Oh, Mal, this is too much! This is too much!"

"I'm not kidding, Holly," he muttered darkly.

"I know you're not," she said through her laughter. "That's what makes it so funny!"

He jumped from the bed and went over to the closet, where he took out a black leather carry-on bag he had brought with him on the plane. "While you and Jerry were in the antique shop, I went out and bought this stuff." He emptied the contents of the bag onto the bed: crowbars, a hammer, a flashlight, a whisk broom, and a small silver crucifix. "I'm in deadly earnest, Holly. If we just find an old skeleton, I'll be the happiest guy in the world. But—and I'm not just saying this—if we find evidence that she had been a vampire a century ago, I'm going to try to bring her back to question her."

"Uh-huh, sure," Holly said, trying not to start laughing again. "Will you be insulted if I tell you that I'm not the slightest bit worried about that possibility?"

"Of course not. I hope that this is all foolishness. I want to feel stupid more than anything else I've ever wanted in my life. I really want to be shown up for a paranoid asshole, I really do."

"Well," she muttered, "you're gonna get your wish."

He either ignored her response or did not hear it. He gazed out the window at the setting sun and said, more to himself than to her, "If it works, we'll be in danger. You will be, anyway. I doubt that Lucy could do anything to me, with my blood already polluted." He turned to her. "You may have to keep a firm hold on the crucifix, Holly. With the crosses and the garlic we should be able to control her, we should be able to force her to obey us. . . ."

Holly sprang from the bed. "I'm going out to find Jerry and have a few drinks." Her voice was angry and impatient.

"Wait a minute," Malcolm said. "I'll come with you."

"Don't!" She shouted. "Please don't. Just stay here and, and . . . I don't know, sharpen stakes or something!" Then, relenting slightly, she said, "I'll be back in an hour or so, and then we'll go break into the mausoleum. We'll probably end up in jail, but when I make a promise, I keep it." Her eyes narrowed as she glared at him. "But I'm warning you, Malcolm. This is it, you understand? This is it!"

She slammed the door behind her, and as she strode angrily down the corridor, she thought, Great, just great. I finally find a guy who isn't a jerk and he turns out to be a nut! I mean, *vampires*, for Christ's sake!

In the hotel room, Malcolm turned back to the window and watched as the sun vanished behind the hills. "It will all be over soon, Holly," he whispered. "Tonight we'll either know that it's all myth, or we'll have a vampire to interrogate." He remembered the narrative he had read in his great-grandmother's diary. I wonder if that's what my grandfather was trying to do when he was a child, when he tried to break into Lucy's tomb. I wonder if he had an instinctive urge to resurrect her.

He frowned at his own thoughts. What a strange thought! Why on earth would a six-year-old child have an idea like that?

Malcolm Harker did not pause to wonder why that same idea had so unexpectedly occurred to him.

Chapter Eight

The fog drifted about their feet as they stood in the shadows near the crypt in the old churchyard. Malcolm was calm, but it was the calmness of the still air before a thunderstorm.

"Malcolm," Holly whispered, "I want to go home!"

He shook his head slowly, without looking at her. "Either it's all true or it's all false, the evidence we've uncovered notwithstanding. If it's all nonsense, then nothing is lost, no one is hurt, and everything is okay. If—God help me—if it's true, then I'll be safe, and I'll be able to protect you. She would want true human blood, not mine."

"Oh, Malcolm!" Holly sighed.

He stopped and stood contemplatively before the rusted iron gate whose bars covered the cracked wooden door. Then he dropped down to one knee and began to rummage around in the black bag as his companion rubbed her arms against the cold, damp night air and looked around nervously. "What if somebody sees us?" she whispered. "We could get arrested!"

"Shhh," he replied, taking a flashlight, a crowbar, and a hammer from the bag.

"I'm serious," she said. "I mean, nobody'd believe the story that you—"

"Shhh!" he repeated emphatically, shooting her an impatient frown. He rose to his feet and inserted the crowbar between the two iron slats that formed the nexus of the gate frame and the heavy inlaid lock. He grabbed hold of the end of the crowbar with both hands, and after bracing himself against the wall of the tomb with his left foot, he gave a mighty pull. The rusted old lock snapped, and the iron gate

117

swung open as bits of brown metallic dust splintered off and
fell from the long unused hinges.

They stood for a long while, staring at the wooden door
with the long warped crack that extended from top to bottom
on the right side. At last she said, "Please, *please* let's get
away from here! I'm scared!"

Her words seemed to awaken him from some private
reverie and he snapped his head in her direction. "I thought
you didn't believe in any of this."

"I don't," she replied, just a bit defensively.

"Well, then, what are you afraid of?"

"I'm afraid of getting arrested!" she said. "I'm afraid of
meeting some nut prowling around here at night! Can't we
leave, please?"

He turned away from her, not responding to her request.
He pushed gently on the wooden door and felt it give
slightly. Then he raised his foot and kicked against it, sending
it flying open and leaving a section of crumbling wood lying
beside it on the damp stone floor of the crypt. "Wait out
here," he muttered as he stepped over the threshold into
the darkness of the interior.

"Are you kidding?" she whispered. "I'm not standing out
here all by myself in the middle of the—"

"All right, all right," he said testily. "Come in if you want
to. But just be quiet." His last words were spoken more
harshly than he had intended them, and he smiled at her,
saying, "I'm sorry. I'm just a little jumpy."

His smile was forced and impatient, but she chose to
accept the apology. "Sure," she smiled back. "It's okay." She
waited until he had switched on the flashlight and then she,
too, entered.

The air was musty and dank. It was obvious from the
condition of the exterior and the layers of dust in the interior
that the crypt had neither been cared for nor visited for
many, many years. This did not surprise him, for he knew
that the grave that they had sought was occupied by a young
woman who had died shortly after the demise of her widowed
mother. There were no relatives, no family to care for the
burial place. There had been friends, of course, but they
were all long since dead and buried themselves.

Malcolm and Holly quietly entered the sepulcher. He
moved the flashlight beam about slowly, resting it for a
moment upon the brass plaque that had been affixed to the

side of one of the three antique lead coffins. "Her mother," he muttered. He moved the beam to the left and illuminated a similar plaque on a similar sarcophagus. "Her father," he said. "She must be here," and he swung the light quickly over to the third coffin. Holly Larsen did not move from her spot as he walked over and read the third plaque. "This is it," he whispered. "Try to close the door."

"Close the door! Whatever for?" she asked.

"We don't want to be interrupted, do we?" He began to work the tip of the crowbar in between the heavy lid of the sarcophagus and the main body of the lead casket.

"Well, I wouldn't mind being interrupted," she replied. "I don't even want to be here! This is the craziest—"

"Will you shut up!" he said angrily. "You didn't have to come here tonight, you didn't have to come to England at all! If you're not going to be of any help to me, then get the hell out!" He paused, glaring at her. "I mean it!"

"Okay, okay," she said, angry at his ingratitude. "I'll try to close the goddamn door." She turned back to the doorway and reached out to pull shut the iron gate. After she had done so, she pushed what was left of the wooden door shut from within. "There. Happy now?" she spat.

"Thrilled," he muttered, and resumed his efforts. He was able to force the crowbar into the narrow space easily, and then, taking the hammer, he pounded against the flat end of the crowbar and drove it deeper into the gap, thus lifting the lid slightly from the coffin. Malcolm took three more crowbars from the black bag and repeated his actions at the other end of the coffin and then on the other side as well. "Lid isn't as heavy as it looks," he said aloud to himself. "Of course not. Mina and Van Helsing were able to move it all by themselves while Stewart was waiting outside, holding on to Gramps."

"What?" Holly asked.

"Nothing, nothing. Just get out of the way." She stepped back toward the corner of the room and watched in nervous silence as he leaned his weight against the side of the coffin lid and pushed with all his might. The lid slipped with a screeching, crunching sound across the edges of the leaden box and then crashed loudly onto the floor.

Malcolm stepped back from the coffin and reached down for the flashlight. He picked it up and shined it into the sarcophagus. Holly waited for him to say something, and her heart raced as he stood motionless, staring downward. She did not move forward and look herself. An endlessly long moment passed in total silence, and then she heard him whisper, "God damn it! God *damn* it!" His voice bespoke fear and fury.

She forced herself to walk forward, forced her eyes to remain open as she leaned over and looked down into the coffin, but she knew before looking what it was that he had seen.

It was all there, just as he had described it to her, just as he had imagined it must be, just as the book had told him it would be. The long strands of brittle yellow hair still clung to the decayed skull of what had once been a beautiful, vibrant young woman. The skeleton was in an advanced state of decomposition, but the bones of the hands still wore the rings and bracelets that had been placed upon them before burial a century before, and the hands still rested folded upon the faded, crumbling, yellowed linen that had been the woman's burial gown.

The skull and the vertebrae were not connected to each other, for the head had been severed from the body. That had not been the cause of death, of course. Holly and Malcolm both knew how she had died, they both knew who had killed her. The decapitation had occurred after death, was one of the precautions taken by those who loved her, who wished to make certain that her death would be both blessed and final, who had acted, not out of malice, but out of devotion.

The fresh garlic with which they had stuffed her dead mouth had long since rotted away to nothing, but not before it had imparted its pungent aroma to the interior of the coffin. The consecrated communion wafer that her friends had placed upon her stomach had likewise fallen victim to the passage of time. But Malcolm knew and Holly knew that both substances had once been there, both of them, the garlic and the wafer. They knew this as surely as they understood why her decayed skeletal rib cage still held, in the spot beneath which her young heart had once beat, a wooden stake.

"My God!" he said between clenched teeth. "My God, my God!"

Holly grabbed him firmly by the shoulder. "Malcolm, let's get out of here, right now, Malcolm, right now!"

"It's true," he said darkly. "It's all true."

"This doesn't prove a damn thing, Malcolm!"

"Doesn't it?" he asked, sarcastic through his misery.

"No!" she said emphatically. "All it proves is that she really lived and really died, and..."

"Yes, and what?" he asked angrily. "And what? That after her death someone opened her coffin and for no reason whatsoever cut off her head and pounded a wooden stake through her heart? Do you think that was customary funeral procedure in Victorian England?"

"Of course not," she replied. "But it doesn't prove anything about *her*, either! All it proves is that people back then were very superstitious—"

"Oh, stop it, Holly!" he snapped. "We're talking about a suburb of London, not some primitive backwoods! Civilized, educated people did this, and they wouldn't have done it if there hadn't been a damn good reason." He paused. "And you know the reason for it as well as I do."

"Stop it!" she said harshly, shaking him by one shoulder. "You're letting this get to you, letting your imagination run away with your common sense. This doesn't prove anything! Think about it, for pity's sake! It doesn't actually prove anything!"

"It proves that the story is true."

"It does not!" she insisted. "Okay, it proves that somebody did a little research, stuff like that. But it doesn't prove anything about her, and it certainly doesn't prove anything about *you!*"

He seemed to calm down slightly, and she allowed herself a brief hope that her words had made sense to him. That hope died when he turned to her and said, "You know what I'm going to do now. I think you'd better go. I don't really know if you would be safe."

Her nervousness and fear and his obstinacy combined to make her angry. "Don't be ridiculous," she said. "I'm not going anywhere. I'm not going to stand outside in a graveyard all by myself in the middle of the night, for one thing, and I'm certainly not going to leave you in here all alone with your morbid fantasies getting out of control." She folded her arms imperiously across her chest, her gesture and tone conveying irritated and impatient condescension. "Go ahead, get on with it. Get this nonsense over with. Do what you think you have to do, and then when nothing happens and you feel like a jackass, we can get out of here and go back to the hotel." She waited a moment and then repeated, "Well? Go ahead!"

He stared up at her for a moment and then whispered, "You have no idea how much I want to feel like a jackass about this. You have no idea."

The sorrowful honesty of his tone prompted in her an urge to embrace and comfort him, but she repressed it. She reasoned that she could help him best by maintaining an annoyed skepticism, so she said, "Stop wasting time. Get on with it!"

He turned from her and gazed back down at the moldy skeleton. Without taking his eyes from it, he reached into the bag and drew forth a whisk broom and a bottle of vinegar. He poured the vinegar freely over the teeth and jaws of the skull so as to wash away any vestigial remains of the garlic, and then he deftly flicked the whisk broom over the faded linen that still encumbered the pelvic bones, thus making certain that no tiny bits of the consecrated wafer remained upon the surface of the funeral gown.

He watched and waited for a few moments as the vinegar dripped down from the teeth and spread out over the bottom of the coffin. Then, slowly and almost reverently, he took the skull in his hands and moved it a few inches downward toward the body, aligning its base with the tip of the spinal column. He paused, breathing heavily. Then he grasped the wooden stake by its protruding end and withdrew it from between the ribs.

"Well?" Holly, yawning, said sarcastically. "Is she ready to go out dancing with us, or what?" Her yawn was improvised, for effect.

"Shut up," he muttered. He reached into the black bag once again and felt around for a few moments. Then he took out a small penknife and a small metal crucifix. He tossed the crucifix to her and said, "Stand by the door. Block it."

"Oh, for Pete's sake!"

"Don't argue with me!" he said, his voice strangely even and controlled. "Just do it!" As she complied, he opened the penknife and made a small incision in his forearm. The blood welled up from the cut, and when it began to flow freely, he leaned his arm into the coffin and allowed the blood to drip onto the teeth of the skull. In a few moments the bones were running with red streams.

He stepped back and wrapped a handkerchief around his

small but stinging wound, and then he waited. And Holly waited. She felt as if she could hear her own heartbeat echoing from the walls of the crypt as the long minutes passed. Then she stepped forward and looked down into the coffin. "See?" She laughed harshly. "I told you. This is all nonsense, and your grandfather is nuts. Now let's go back to the hotel."

He frowned as he gazed down at the motionless skull. "I don't understand this," he muttered. "I don't understand this at all. If what I was told is true, something should have happened."

"But nothing did!" she said cheerfully as she began to lead him by the arm back toward the door of the chamber. "I mean, of course nothing happened! You've just been acting silly, that's all." She poked him playfully in the ribs. "And you know it, don't you! I'll bet you feel like a grade-A jerk just about now."

He forced himself to smile at her. "Yeah, maybe so, sort of. I guess so." He placed his hands upon the cracked wooden door and began to pull it open, then froze in place. "What was that?"

"What was what?" she asked calmly.

"Listen!" Neither of them moved. Even their breathing was hushed.

Almost imperceptibly at first but then increasingly louder, a hissing sound was coming from the coffin.

Malcolm walked slowly and unsteadily toward the sound, his hands trembling so violently that he was scarcely able to keep a grip on the flashlight.

Holly remained at the door, willing her legs to move and follow him, failing in the attempt, clutching the crucifix to her breast. "W...wait..." she stammered. "Don't...don't look..."

He ignored her. He leaned over and gazed down into the coffin, muttering an unintelligible prayer when he saw the fine red mist seeping up and out from every bone fragment, drifting over the skeleton and seeming to draw together the bits and pieces of dust and bone. He watched with horrified fascination as the bones of the skeleton grew together, as the mist solidified into a yellowish liquid that itself began to form flesh, as full red lips grew downward from the skull and covered the grinning teeth, as the eyelids grew over the empty sockets and then filled out as the eyes formed beneath them, as the eyes opened and shined with a mad, red light, as the lips parted and a pink tongue drifted obscenely over the pointed fangs, as a low inhuman laugh reached his ears at the same moment that a hand reached up and grabbed him by the throat.

Holly fainted as the creature in the coffin crawled out, never releasing Malcolm from its dead grip. The aged, decaying linen of her burial gown clung to her voluptuous form, bizarrely accentuating the pallid flesh by draping it with faded yellow cloth. Her flesh was not white as might be the skin of a delicate and sheltered woman; rather, it was the cold, lifeless color of a corpse. Her teeth champed together horribly as she hissed and laughed and drew him closer. There was the stench of death about her, and as her mouth drew nigh him, he could feel her breath upon his face, breath reeking of rot and disease, breath like unto the stagnant air of a slaughterhouse.

Malcolm was strangely calm. He thought himself at first to be in shock, or paralyzed with fear, but he rapidly realized that what he felt was merely resignation, despair, and a hint of morose confidence. So now I know the truth, he thought sadly. Now I know.

The thing which had just crawled out of the coffin brought her smiling lips closer to his throat, but something, *something* in his eyes distracted her, unnerved her, halted her, froze her in place despite her overwhelming hunger. "Who...?" she rasped. "Who...?"

"You know," he said quietly.

She continued to stare at him as she shook her head. "No," she said hoarsely.

"Yes," he whispered. "Look at my eyes. Taste the blood I have given you. Tell me who I am."

She backed away from him, fear and confusion suffusing her face. "But you...you are not...you are someone else." She paused, staring at him. "And yet...and yet..." She heard a moan coming from behind Malcolm, and she looked to see Holly, as yet only semiconscious, struggling to awaken from her faint. The confused, fearful look shifted in an instant to one of lustful animal appetite and she crouched slightly, as if readying to spring upon the defenseless woman. Holly opened her eyes and looked groggily over toward Malcolm, and when she realized what she was seeing, she leaped to her feet, screaming, clutching the crucifix to her breast with trembling hands.

Malcolm stepped in front of the creature and said, "No!"

She looked up at him furiously. "I must feed!" she hissed.

"Not from this woman," he said.

She backed away from him farther into the shadows of the rear of the crypt, well out of range of the flashlight beam that shined upon the wall nearest him. He had dropped the light when she grabbed him, and it remained where it had fallen. "Who are you?" she demanded, her tone mingling anger and dread, her red eyes glowing in the darkness. "Why have you come to me?"

"I have not merely come to you," he said sadly. "I removed the stake that had been driven through your heart."

"A stake!" she screamed. "Who dared to do such a thing!"

"He who loved you best," he replied. Was it his imagination, or did an almost human light pass briefly over her eyes as he spoke those words? If it did, it passed almost instantly. "I pulled the stake from your chest and washed the garlic from your mouth. I gave you my own blood, to bring you back. You have lain in decay and death for a century."

"Time has no meaning to us," she spat, "and if you have indeed done what you say, do not expect my thanks!"

"I do not expect your thanks," he said simply.

She moved out of the shadows, closer to the flashlight beam, though still out of its range. "Why have you done this?" she asked angrily.

"I need your help. I have questions. I need answers, information."

She stepped back into the darkness and laughed bitterly. "You need my help? You need *my* help! What help can I render to you or to anyone?"

"Listen to me. I will explain."

"I must feed!" she shrieked.

"You will hear me out," he repeated, "and then perhaps I will allow you to draw sustenance from me."

Another bitter laugh. "Your blood is like unto *his* blood. You can give me no nourishment, even as I can do you no harm."

"You begin to understand," he sighed. "Now, listen . . ."

Holly stared ahead of her, terrified and fascinated, as Malcolm related to the creature the events of the past few weeks. He spoke calmly and intelligently, mentioning every detail, omitting nothing of importance, seeming calm and unruffled, as if he felt comfortable talking with her, as if now, facing the reality of his situation with the full light of knowledge, he was no longer worried or upset. He was standing in a tomb, conversing with a vampire, and he was acting as if it were the most natural thing in the world.

Holly shook her head in wonder at his attitude and demeanor. How can he be so calm? Why isn't he frightened? Why isn't he running, screaming, from this tomb? Why is he acting as if he feels so totally at ease, almost as if he has known this creature for years?

And then she remembered something that Malcolm had forced her to read, something from Mina Harker's later diary.

When little Quincey Harker had run away from home and had finally been captured at the door to this very tomb, he had been seeking entrance for reasons that neither Mina Harker nor Jonathan Harker nor Abraham Van Helsing nor John Stewart could fathom. And when Van Helsing and Mina had entered and had opened the grave to make certain that Lucy Westenra was still blissfully dead, the child had broken free of John Stewart's grip and had run into the tomb, had jumped onto the open coffin, screaming, "Mother! Mother!"

Holly Larsen shuddered and her blood ran cold. She realized what the child had meant by his frenzied cry. He had not been pleading for maternal protection, had not been crying out for Mina Harker to help him.

He had not been speaking to Mina Harker at all.

Chapter Nine

As Malcolm Harker finished his narrative, the creature remained silent, attentive but impatient. The white points of her elongated canine teeth glinted slightly in the dull glow of the misdirected flashlight. At last Malcolm fell silent and stood waiting for her to respond.

"A pretty tale," she hissed, "for all the interest it is to me. Now tell your little friend with the crucifix to stand away from the door and let me pass. I must feed."

"I told you," Malcolm said, "that if you need blood you can drink from me. I cannot allow you to leave this place."

"But I cannot stay," she replied. "I have no need of your blood, for it gives me nothing which I do not already have."

"It gave you life," he pointed out.

A horrible laugh burst from her dead mouth and echoed through the tomb. "Life! Life! This is not life, you little fool! If you know as much as you say, then you must know what you have done to me! I was *dead*, I was truly, blissfully *dead*! I was free of the pain, free of the needs, free of this life in death, and you, you selfish idiot, you wrenched me from my peace!"

Malcolm would not be swayed. "Nonetheless, you may not leave this place. You may drink from me, but—"

"Are you deaf as well?" the creature screamed. She walked toward him menacingly. "I have no need of you. Your blood is not what I need."

Malcolm reached out and grabbed her by the arm, saying, "Stop! I will not allow you to injure anyone." He released her arm almost immediately, shivering slightly. Her flesh was hard and cold, like the skin of a swamp reptile. "I have questions—"

"I have hunger!" She glanced at Holly and then turned back to Malcolm. "Tell her to stand aside!"

"No!" he said firmly. "If you wish your peace, your repose, I can return it to you. When the sun rises, I can give you back your death."

"You fool!" she spat. "Do you understand nothing? No one cursed as I am willingly submits to the stake! You have returned me to this, you have given me back my hell, and I shall keep it! The need drives me, the hunger drives me, the evil drives me!"

"I need your help—"

"Be damned, you and your needs! I have my own needs!"

He paused thoughtfully. Then he said, "Very well. What can I give you to gain your help? What can I do for you to make you willing to answer my questions?"

She began to hiss her reply, but then her face went suddenly blank. She stood motionless, her red eyes clouding over and fixing on a nothingness in the distance, as if she were hearing something that neither Malcolm nor Holly could hear. A few silent moments passed, and then her gaze focused upon Malcolm, and she smiled at him, an odd, mocking smile. "Mina and Jonathan married, did they? How sweet. Your great-grandparents! And their son is living yet, and he was named after my old friend Quincey Morris. Remarkable!"

"Tell me what you want," Malcolm repeated.

She rasped a laugh. "Very well, little Harker. I want your friend to stand aside and let me pass. I will feed, and then I will return here before dawn and speak with you."

Malcolm shook his head once again. "I cannot allow you to infect anyone else. I need information from you because I want to end this thing, not spread it."

"The choice is yours," she said, laughing. "You can keep me here until dawn if you wish to. You have the power, with your crucifix and your, ah, rather commendable willpower. If that is your choice, I will be at your mercy with the sunrise, and you can return me to true death." She paused and her red eyes narrowed wickedly. "But keep in mind, my dear boy, that I and I alone can cure you. I and I alone can rid you of the plague which you carry in your body. And I shall do nothing to help you if you do not let me pass."

Malcolm stared at her, half of his mind disbelieving what

she had just said and the other half needing to believe it desperately. "You know how to cure me?" he whispered.

"Yes," she hissed. "An even trade, a fair exchange. Your freedom for my own. And I am not a fool, Malcolm Harker, so do not delude yourself into thinking that you can entrap me here with the sunrise and then dispatch me at your leisure. I shall make provisions for my rest elsewhere."

He looked at her long and hard before asking, "How do I know that I can trust you?"

She shrugged. "Why should you not?"

"That isn't an answer," he responded, shaking his head.

"No," she said softly, "I suppose it isn't. Perhaps I feel an inclination to help you because you are Dracula's bastard descendant, even as I am his morganatic wife. Or perhaps it should suffice to say that I am bound by the limitations of my own being. I cannot enter a building unless invited to, for example. If my exit from this place is made possible by your willing acquiescence, then I am bound by the terms of the agreement to which I willingly adhere."

He shook his head again. "I've read a good deal about you creatures, and I've never heard of anything like that."

"Live and learn, little Harker," she replied, mockery in her voice.

Malcolm continued to stare at her. Then, without taking his eyes from her, he cocked his head in Holly's direction and said, "Stand away from the door."

Holly was certain that she had not heard him correctly. "Wh . . . what?"

"Let her out, Holly," Malcolm said firmly. "Stand away from the door and let her out."

Holly Larsen's mouth dropped open with astonishment and disgust. "Malcolm! You can't! You can't! She's going to go out there and attack someone, kill someone! You can't go along with this! It's . . . it's inhuman!"

"Inhuman!" Lucy chuckled. "You are the only human being in this room, or had you not noticed that?"

"That's not true!" Holly said angrily, her anger momentarily transcending her amazement and terror. "Malcolm is sick, he's ill, he's—"

"He is Dracula's bastard," Lucy said evenly. "From what he has told me, the Count's blood is strong in him, stronger than it is in his grandfather, stronger perhaps than it was in his father. If he does not give heed to my words and do what

I tell him to do, when he dies, he will become as I am." She smiled bitterly. "And after that, of course, he will probably come looking for you."

Holly went white. "This is impossible!" she whispered, her body beginning to tremble violently and her eyes darting madly around the dark room. "I must have lost my mind!

"Stand aside!" Lucy hissed.

"Holly," Malcolm said soothingly, "please. Please let her out. It's my only hope."

Holly gazed at him numbly as Lucy crouched and moved toward her with slow, deliberate steps. Holly's blank eyes shifted to the creature that seemed to be creeping toward her, and then in a burst of resolve Holly held the crucifix out in front of her and said, "No!"

Lucy Westenra's red eyes glowered at her, and then in an instant too brief for either Malcolm or Holly to prepare themselves for it, Lucy dropped to her hands and knees. Before her hands hit the floor, she was changed into a growling, salivating wolf. The wolf snarled and feinted a charge at the terrified woman. Holly screamed and instinctively jumped away, thus removing herself and her crucifix from the doorway of the crypt. The wolf ambled slowly and warily over to the door and rose up on its hind legs, changing once more into Lucy in conjunction with the movement. She smiled at the two people and said, in a voice dripping with mockery and amusement, "Thank you, my dear. Wait here for me, Malcolm. I shall return before dawn." She slipped out the doorway, seeming to drift like mist between the still-closed iron grates, and was gone.

Holly and Malcolm stood in silence and stared at the door for what seemed a long while, and then Holly turned to him and said, "Do you realize what you've done?"

"Yes," he sighed. "I realize what I've done. I've taken a risk in the interests of self-preservation."

"She's going to go out and infect someone, Malcolm! An innocent person!"

"And what am I guilty of?" he shouted at her. "What great sin did I commit to be stuck with this thing!"

"That's not the point—"

"It *is* the point, it *is* the point! I know what she's going to do, but if my theory is right, she's going to drink from someone, not make them drink from her. I mean, why should she? Why should she want to create more vampires?"

Holly buttoned her coat. "I'm getting out of here," she said, her trembling voice nonetheless somehow firm and determined. "I'm not going to stand around here, waiting for her to come back. I'm going back to the hotel and I'm going to call the police."

Malcolm began laughing, and his laughter was unkind and humorless.

"What's so goddamned funny!"

"You're leaving," Malcolm said, laughing. "You're going to walk out of here, walk out into a cemetery in the middle of the night, knowing that there's a vampire out there somewhere!"

"I'm not afraid of her!" Holly said defensively.

"Of course you are," he said, suddenly angry. "You'd be an idiot if you weren't. Hell, she can't do anything to me, can't give me any injury that I wasn't born with, and I'm still afraid of her." Malcolm took Holly by the hand, and she recoiled slightly from his touch. "Think, Holly, think. That creature was once a beautiful, kind, loving girl, just like you are. And what she is now is what you could end up as if you walk out of this crypt." He dropped her hand and walked back over toward Lucy's empty coffin. "You're not going anywhere."

Holly was silent for a moment. "Okay, then, I'll stay here until dawn, but then I'm going to the police."

He nodded approvingly. "Okay. Just make sure I have the address of the asylum before I leave England. That's where they'll stick you, of course."

Holly started to weep. "Malcolm, this is horrible! What are we going to do? We can't just leave her free to spread this! She'll create vampires, and then they'll create vampires, and so on and so forth until there will be thousands of them, millions of them."

"No." He shook his head. "I don't think so."

"You don't think so!" Holly exclaimed. "You don't think so! How can you take it upon yourself to take a chance like that?"

"Think about it, Holly," Malcolm said. "Dracula lived for centuries in the Carpathians, and he must have killed hundreds of thousands of people. And yet when Van Helsing killed the vampires in his castle, there were only three of them, only three."

"Wh...what do you...? I don't understand."

"And when he came to England, again there were only three people he infected, only Lucy, my great-grandmother, and the madman, Renfield. Maybe it's only three at a time. For all we know, maybe only Dracula can do it! Maybe Lucy can't create new vampires! Maybe the blood has to come directly from Dracula himself!"

"So everything's okay, then?" she asked bitterly. "So all she's going to do is run around at night killing innocent people, but it's okay because when they die they stay dead?"

He rubbed his eyes. "I don't know, I don't know. If she can help me, I'll worry about everything else later. I'm not worrying about moral implications right now."

"Well, maybe you should be! How can you—"

"Holly, be quiet," he said wearily. "I don't want to talk any more. What's done is done. Let's just wait for her to come back." He sat down upon the cold stone floor, and Holly, after a moment's hesitation, sat down beside him. He placed his arm around her shoulder and they sat there in silence as the hours passed slowly.

It was nearly dawn when she returned. The telltale glow of the rising sun was just barely skirting the edges of the horizon when they heard the cold voice say from outside the crypt, "Malcolm Harker! Come here."

He rose to his feet and walked to the doorway. "Why don't you come in. It's almost dawn, isn't it?"

"Yes," she said, laughing, "but I have time enough before I must sleep, and I'll not allow myself to be trapped in there. You come out to me, you and your friend with you."

Malcolm held his hand out to Holly and she took it as she stood up. She held the crucifix tightly as they stepped out into the dew-laden mist of early morning.

Lucy Westenra looked different. Her face was rosy and healthy, her eyes wide and clear, and her voice liquid and pleasing, though the underlying inhuman coldness had not departed. Malcolm moved the flashlight beam up and down the creature, noting how the flesh, which had such a short time ago been pale and cadaverous, was now pink and robust.

Holly noticed the difference also. "What's happened to her?" she whispered.

"She has fed," Malcolm replied evenly as he walked forward.

"Stop there, little Harker," Lucy said firmly, and then

smiled. "Tell me, do women in this age really wear such clothing as this?" She gestured downward at the faded dungarees, the dirty tennis shoes, the bulky, oversized sweatshirt. "Is this regarded as attractive?"

He ignored her question. "Where did you get the clothes?"

"They came with my meal," she said, laughing.

"My God," Holly said. "She's killed someone. You killed someone, didn't you!"

Lucy shrugged. "I haven't eaten since I don't know when! I suppose I made something of a glutton of myself," she chuckled.

"Jesus, Malcolm, Jesus!" Holly said, and turned away from the creature. She placed her hands over her eyes and wept.

"Will you answer my questions?" Malcolm asked, choosing to ignore what he knew had just happened.

"I shall," Lucy said, "out of the, ah, goodness of my heart, and because... well, Mina was my friend."

"In your state, you still have human emotions?" Malcolm asked. "You can still feel friendship?"

"I do not feel it, but I remember it." She glanced at the horizon. "Ask your questions, and be quick about them."

"Okay." He took a deep breath. "First question is this: How can I be sure that what you're going to say is reliable? What is your source of knowledge?"

"My source of knowledge!" she exclaimed. "Why, the same source as your own, though you are unable to use it."

He shook his head. "I don't understand."

"The blood, my dear, the blood! The blood speaks to me even as it speaks to you, but only dead ears can hear it. The blood tells me everything I need to know. It is instinct and education combined."

He took a moment to assimilate this idea, then he nodded. "Very well. Second question: Is there any truth to the idea that Dracula somehow altered his own body chemistry to create this condition?"

She frowned and shook her head. "I don't understand the question."

"Let me put it this way. What is there about the blood that makes the dead walk? What is the source of the blood's power?"

"Such easy questions, Malcolm!" She smiled. "It is obvious, is it not? The blood has power because of whose blood it is!"

"That's not an answer," he insisted. "You can't tell me that Dracula's blood has power because it is Dracula's blood. That just leads the question around in a circle."

"It is not Dracula's blood," Lucy said. "It is Satan's blood. It is the Devil's blood."

He stared at her for a moment. Then he said, "I need rational explanations, not supernatural nonsense. If I am to—"

Peals of laughter erupted from the creature and she drowned out his words. "After what you have seen and what you have done, after finding out what you *are*, you say that supernatural reality is nonsense? Oh, poor Mina, poor Jonathan, to have spawned a family line of idiots." Her laughter went on and on, then stopped abruptly. Her mirthful face clouded over with sudden anger. "Now hear me well, Malcolm. I will give you answers and share with you my knowledge, but I will not argue with you. I know what I am and I know why I am what I am. If you want to hear, I will speak. If not, I shall leave you." She glanced again at the horizon.

"Okay, okay," he said hurriedly. "Tell me how Dracula became a vampire."

"It was a pact, as in the old tale of Faust. Continued existence, century after century, a perpetual life in death, living on and feeding on the blood of the living, spreading terror and misery and sorrow and death. All of this pleases the Devil. The Count received the Devil's blood, the Devil filled his dead heart with it, and gave him his Undeath."

Malcolm thought this over. "I think I see. So when the stake is driven through the heart, the blood is released and the vampire is free of the curse. Correct?"

"Absolutely not, my dear Malcolm," she said impatiently. "You must think poetically, my boy, symbolically. Why was the master in his life called Vlad Tepes, Vlad the Impaler?"

He understood immediately. "Of course. He impaled people upon wooden stakes."

"Precisely. And you may have read that we cast no reflection in mirrors. Have you never wondered why?" She waited for an answer, and when none was forthcoming, she went on, "Who is the mirror image, the polar opposite as if were, of the Prince of Darkness?"

The answer became simple as soon as she had given him

the clue. "Yes, yes," he said, nodding. "The Prince of Light. Jesus Christ."

"Who was impaled upon a piece of wood," Lucy finished for him. "For these reasons, the wooden stake frees the vampire from the pact with the devil." She paused. "For the Count it was a pact. For all others, it is a curse."

"And yet you do not wish to be free from it."

She shrugged. "The dog grows to love the leash. The slave grows to love the lash."

"And what of the rest of the legend?"

Her eyebrows rose.

"The facts, then," he said quickly. "What about garlic?"

"It burns. The smell burns into our brains and makes us mad with agony."

"And the crucifix? The consecrated communion wafer, the consecrated wine?"

"Water quenches fire, little Harker. The sun dispels the moon, the light overcomes the darkness, life denies death."

"Opposites," he observed.

"Eternal enemies," she corrected him. "Before the infinite, everything finite falls. And even the devil himself is finite." She glanced again impatiently at the horizon. "Hurry with your questions. It is not more than thirty minutes before the sun breeches the darkness."

"Okay," he said. "Next question: Are there other vampires, other than you?"

She smiled wickedly. "Not yet!"

"But you can make more?"

"I *shall* make more."

"Three more?"

The precision and accuracy of his question seemed to startle her. "Yes, three. How did you know that?"

He allowed himself a smug grin. "Three women at the castle in Transylvania. Three people infected in England a century ago: you, my great-grandmother, and the lunatic Renfield."

She laughed. "Clever, but incorrect. The Count could make as many Undead as he chose. It is only we, his creations, who are limited. We can give forth enough of the devil's blood to make three others like ourselves. But Dracula's heart was like a bottomless, fathomless well that tapped the veins of Satan. He could give of it endlessly and remain undiminished."

"But now he is gone," Malcolm said. "So you alone are left as a vampire, and you can only create three others."

"Yes, I alone am left. I and you and your family, my dear Malcolm."

He shook his head. "I'm infected, but I'm not like you are. I'm still alive."

"At the moment," she said, smiling.

He ignored the remark. "What of the three you create, if you do create any? Can they then create others?"

"No," she said. "The farther removed from the source of the power, the weaker the blood. The Count sucked on Satan's teat. He could have created a multitude of vampires, had he so chosen. I can create but three, and my creations can create none."

"I don't understand," Malcolm said, frowning. "You say the blood's power weakens as it is removed from the source. Then why is it affecting me at all? I'm three generations removed from Mina Harker."

"You're not listening to me, you little idiot," she hissed. "The blood speaks to you when you are dead. It only influences you just slightly when you are yet living. Mina gave birth to a son and passed the blood on to him. It rested in him and fed on his blood every moment that it coursed through his veins. It still does. He passed the blood on to his son, and his son passed it on to you. It is only when you die that the power of the blood will assert itself."

He took a moment to think this over. "So my danger will come when I die. Now, while I live, it is still manageable."

"Yes."

"By regularly taking the sacrament."

"Yes."

"But it burned me. I mean, the last time I took communion, it burned my mouth and my stomach."

"Because you have allowed the blood's power to gain an advantage. You told me that you had stayed away from church for a long while. Anything wears off, even sanctity."

"And if I take communion regularly from now on...?"

"The pain will diminish and eventually disappear, and the power of the blood will be reduced."

"But not eliminated," he said.

"No," Lucy agreed. "Not eliminated. There will still be danger for you after you die."

Not with my veins filled with embalming fluid, he

thought a bit smugly. He did not share his thought with her. "And if I ever have children?"

"It will pass to them, through the generations." She looked nervously over at the rose-tinged horizon. "Quickly. I am being kind to you by giving you this much time, but you must hurry."

"Okay," he said. "One more question. I don't just want to control this, I want to end it. I want to lift this from myself and my family. Can it be done? Is there any way just to eliminate the power of the blood completely?"

"That, I cannot say for certain. But I have a feeling, an intuition, if you like. It speaks to me but unclearly."

"Tell me what you can," he said.

She paused for a moment. "The Devil is tied to the blood, and the blood is tied to the Count, and all three are tied to the soil of the Count's native land." She stopped speaking, as if this cryptic remark contained all the information he needed.

He waited for her to continue. When she did not, he said, "I don't understand what you mean. How is that supposed to help . . . ?"

"Think, little fool, think!" she spat angrily. "Do people lack brains in this century? As long as his remains rest in the soil of his native land, the blood he has given retains its potency. Remove him from his native soil, and the blood becomes merely blood."

"But he isn't buried anywhere," Malcolm protested. "I've read the account in the book. It says that he was killed on a roadside near the castle, that his body collapsed into dust after his heart was pierced."

"And does it say that he was alone?" she asked.

He thought for a moment. "No, there were Gypsies with him, servants."

"Ah," she said, smiling. "And what did they do after the Count was killed?"

"They ran away," he said, shrugging.

"And then?"

He stared at her. "Nothing else is mentioned of them. I imagine that they just kept running."

Lucy Westenra shook her head and laughed sadly. "Stupid boy, blind, stupid boy. They must have returned to gather up his dust. They must have taken it to the castle and placed it in his coffin. They *must* have! The dust of the Count must be there still, else his blood would have been powerless to rip me from my rest!"

Malcolm began to pace back and forth, attempting to formulate a coherent plan of action from all of this. "So if I go to his castle and take his dust away from his coffin—"

"Away from his native land," she corrected him. "If you scatter the dust in Transylvania, it will be as if you had done nothing at all. Bring it to England and scatter it here."

"Or to America," he mused.

She smiled. "As you wish."

"And if I do this, the power of the blood will be broken, in me and in my family, now and forever?"

"Yes."

He looked at her. "And you? What will happen to you if I do this?"

"Nothing," she said. "I am already risen, I am already cursed. All you will do is help yourself. My blood, the Devil's blood in me, will remain as ever." She looked at the rapidly increasing glow of the sun above the distant hills. "I have stayed long enough." She began to run off into the thick clusters of trees that stretched outward from the churchyard.

"Wait!" Malcolm called out. "Tell me why you've told me all of this! Tell me honestly, why have you cooperated with me?" The echoes of her cold laughter were the only answer she chose to give.

Malcolm turned back to Holly, who had remained close to the door of the crypt, clutching her crucifix, throughout the entire conversation. He could see in the dim morning light that she looked ill, pale and frightened, but he did not take the time to tend to her. He grabbed her by the hand and pulled her behind him as he began to walk toward the hotel. "Come on, we have to get to a telephone and we have to get packed."

She looked at the back of his head as he pulled her along, and somewhat dully she asked, "Wh . . . what? Are we going home?" She ran to catch up with him and she said eagerly, "Oh, Mal, I want to go home! I want to go home!"

"We aren't going home," he said. "We're going to Rumania."

She felt too weary and too drained to argue with him. Lack of sleep had combined with shock and terror to render her incapable of opposition. She walked along beside him, trying to keep up with his frantic pace. She entered the hotel right behind him, but he ran up the stairs toward their rooms while she trudged unhappily behind him. He was knocking on Jerry Herman's door when she reached the top of the stairs. "Jerry!" he was saying. "Wake up! We have to get packed! A lot has happened tonight. Jerry! Come on, will you?"

Holly came to Malcolm's side as Jerry's sleepy voice said, "All right, all right already!" from the other side of the door. Jerry pulled the door open, scratching his head and yawning loudly. "Goddamn it, Malcolm, do you know what time it is?" he asked irritably.

"Of course I do," Malcolm replied. "Listen, Jerry, we—"

"Don't you know enough not to wake somebody up until they've slept long enough not to get a hangover?" He placed his hands on the sides of his head. "God, I feel terrible!"

"Jerry, I'm not interested in how much you had to drink!" Malcolm said hotly. "I have something important to tell you!"

"Well, tell me more softly, will you?" Jerry said as he sank back onto his bed and moaned. "God, do I feel like shit! I haven't felt this lousy in years! What the hell do they make gin out of, anyway?" He rolled over on his side and continued moaning.

Malcolm glanced over at Holly. "Just what I need, an ally with a hangover." To Jerry he said, "It's going to take hours for you to be straight again, Jer, and I need your help right now. It takes hours for your body to metabolize every ounce of alcohol you drink, you know."

"Don't lecture me, Malcolm, okay?" Jerry whined. "I feel terrible."

"Just be quiet and listen to me," Malcolm said. "Holly and I—" He suddenly stopped speaking and stood staring at Jerry.

Holly came up beside him and asked, "What is it, Mal?" Then she saw it, too, and screamed.

"What's with her?" Jerry asked, scratching absent-mindedly at the two little wounds on his throat.

Chapter Ten

It was Rachel's turn to serve on the Altar Guild at church, and she was putting on her coat to leave when the phone rang. She huffed with annoyance, even though whatever delay the phone call might cause was of no particular importance. She could change the altar cloth and replace the candles anytime she wished that day, but she was a woman who tried to keep to a schedule, and Saturday morning was Altar Guild time on those days when it was her turn. Muttering under her breath, she draped her coat over a chair and went into the parlor to answer the phone. "Hello?"

"Rachel? Is that you?" her brother's foggy voice replied.

"Malcolm," she said without further salutation. "I can't hear you very well. We have a poor connection. Where are you?"

"In London."

"What? Speak up!"

"I'm in London," he said more loudly, "I'm still in London. What time is it there?"

"Nine in the morning," she replied. "Why are you calling? Is something wrong?"

He paused before replying. "You could say that, I guess."

"Are you ill?" Her concern for her brother transcended her annoyance with him, and she frowned as she held the phone more tightly to her face.

"No, no, I'm fine, we're all fine. Well, Jerry...has a little problem. But that's not why I'm calling you."

"Is he all right?" she asked, relieved that her brother was not ill, and caring despite herself about his friend.

"He's...well, he's been better. But listen, Rachel, I'm

140

calling because I need more money. You have to wire it to me at the American Express office near Victoria Station."

"Malcolm," she said testily in clipped tones, "I was all in favor of this little expedition of yours because I thought it might help you come to accept the truth, but I'm not inclined to subsidize a vacation for you and your friends to any greater extent. If you are out of money already, that means that this has cost us nearly three thousand dollars so far, and I just don't—"

"I resurrected Lucy Westenra."

It took a few moments for Rachel to absorb her brother's words. At last she stammered, "Y... you... you did what?"

She heard him sigh loudly on the other end of the line. "I resurrected Lucy Westenra. Holly and I went to her grave, removed the stake, washed her remains off with vinegar. And when I cut myself and poured some blood on her skull, she rose from the dead."

Rachel did not speak for a long while. She took the receiver from her face and held it in front of her, staring at it openmouthed and speechless. And then she screamed, "You did *what*? You did *what*!"

"Calm down, Rachel," Malcolm said quickly. "She gave me some information, some very valuable—"

"How could you *do* such a thing!" she screamed. "What in God's name is wrong with you? How could you *do* such a thing!"

"Rachel, will you please listen to me?" he shouted at her over the phone. "There's a way to get rid of the curse. Do you hear what I'm saying? There's a way to get rid of the curse!"

"Wh... what are you talking about?" she asked, trying to control her fury.

Her husband, Daniel, entered the room quickly as she spoke, followed a few moments later by old Quincy, who shuffled in at as rapid a pace as he could manage. Both of them had heard Rachel screaming.

"Listen," Malcolm was saying as her husband and grandfather came toward her. "I decided to try to raise Lucy so I could question her. I figured that she'd know more about this stuff than any of us do, right?"

"Oh, Malcolm!" she said, beginning to weep.

"Come on, Rachel, listen to me, damn it! I have to go to Rumania. That's why I need more money."

"Rachel, what's wrong?" Daniel asked.

"What's the boy done?" her grandfather added.

She waved them both silent with a curt, irritated gesture. "Why, Malcolm? Why do you have to go there?"

She listened carefully as Malcolm outlined for her the conversation he had had with the vampire the night before. He concluded by saying, "So if I can find his remains and get them out of Rumania, away from his native soil, and then scatter them, we'll all be safe. We'll all be okay. You, me, Gramps, and any children either of us may ever have." He paused. "I mean, I know about Daniel and everything, but I've been thinking... well, I mean I might... you know what I'm trying to say, Rachel. This is a solution, it's a way out of this for us. I have to go to Rumania. I *have* to go!"

She nodded, not approving of what he had done, but understanding it, and realizing that he had indeed found them a possible means of escape from their dark heritage. "Talk to your grandfather for a few minutes, Malcolm," she said. "I'm going to go into Daniel's office and use his private line to call Mr. Bruno at the bank. How much do you think you'll need?"

"I'm not sure. A thousand, I guess."

"Okay. Talk to Grandfather. I'll be back on the line as soon as I can."

"Rachel, what... ?" Quincy began, but she cut him off by handing him the receiver and then leaving the room.

Stopping at the edge of the parlor, she said, "Daniel, make sure Grandfather stays seated." I don't want him fainting or collapsing when Malcolm tells him what he has done, she thought as she went into Daniel's combination study and office.

Daniel, perplexed and annoyed, helped the old man into a chair and then stood back in silence, wondering just what was going on. Old Quincy's tearful and aghast reaction to whatever it was he was hearing on the phone did nothing to assuage his curiosity.

Rachel returned ten minutes later and took the receiver from her grandfather. The old man seemed to sink miserably into the cushions of the chair as he put his hands over his face and shook his head in sorrow.

"It's all arranged, Malcolm," Rachel said. "Bruno is taking care of it right now. He says that the money should be available to you within one hour."

"That's great, Sis. Thanks."

"Malcolm, just listen to me carefully," she said, her voice serious and just slightly tremulous. "I want you to be very, very careful. Promise me that you'll be careful."

"Of course I will, Rachel," he replied, "but there shouldn't be anything to worry about. Lucy told me what needs to be done, and I—"

"I'm not talking about that," she interrupted him. "I mean that going to Rumania is not like going to England. It's a communist country, a Russian satellite. Be very careful not to break any laws, or even call undue attention to yourself."

"Sure, Rachel, okay."

His tone of voice told her he was just agreeing to forestall a pointless discussion, so she added, "Promise me, Malcolm."

"I promise, Rachel, honest."

"And Malcolm . . . Malcolm?"

"I'm still here, Sis."

"Wear a crucifix when . . . well, just wear a crucifix."

His voice this time was serious. "I will, Rachel. Bye."

"Good-bye." She waited until she heard the line click dead, then she hung up the phone.

"Will someone please tell me what's going on here?" Daniel asked petulantly. "What has the boy done now?"

Rachel shook her head. "It's a long story, Daniel, and it's one that I probably should have told you years ago, but I just don't have the energy to go into it now."

"Well," he began, and then stopped. Having expected a more illuminating reply, he was now nonplussed. "Well," he repeated.

"You said you were going to see Harry Stevenson this afternoon, weren't you?" she asked as she once again picked up her coat and began to put it on.

"Yes. What of it?"

She sighed. "You'll be home by dinnertime, won't you?"

"I suppose so." Daniel frowned. "Now, see here, Rachel—"

"Later, Daniel. Later I'll explain everything." She went to the door of the house and pulled it open. "You have a right to know, I suppose."

"A right to know what?" he asked, but she had already shut the door behind her. Daniel Rowland turned to old Quincy and repeated, "A right to know what? What is she talking about, Grandfather?"

Quincy Harker seemed not to have heard the question. In any event, his response had nothing to do with it. "I don't feel too well, Daniel. Help me up to my room, would you please?"

"Certainly." Daniel helped the elderly man to his feet and lent him an arm for support as they made their way slowly toward the stairs.

"Just remember," Quincy said, panting slightly. "When I die, I want a simple funeral. No viewing, no expensive casket, none of that wasteful fuss."

"Yes, Grandfather."

"You make sure of it, Daniel, if Rachel and Malcolm forget."

"Yes, Grandfather."

As Quincy Harker was slowly mounting the stairs toward his bedroom, his granddaughter was walking around the corner and drawing close to St. Thomas's Episcopal Church. Rachel was, even at her lowest ebb, very well organized and very methodical. Having done all that she could do for the time being, she saw no reason not to proceed with her Saturday just as if her brother had not called her—just as if she did not know that Malcolm had unleashed a vampire upon an unsuspecting world, just as if she was not worried to the depths of her being about her brother's going to Rumania in search of the remains of the creature that had been the source of so much sorrow to her family.

She walked up the few steps that led to the large oaken doors at the entranceway of the Gothic-style church and leaned back as she held on to the brass door ring, using her weight as an aid in pulling it open. The church was never locked, though it had been burglarized a number of times and the church council was forever debating the issue. As a matter of security, either Father Henley or his assistant, Father Langstone, were always in the building during the day on Saturday, knowing that the ladies of the Altar Guild would be coming in to prepare for the next day's services.

Father Henley heard the heavy door close and got up from behind the desk in his office to see who had entered. He smiled at Rachel and said, "Good morning!" as he saw her walking forward down the aisle between the rows of pews.

"Father," she said, and nodded in response, hoping that he was not in a conversational mood.

He was. "Have you heard from Malcolm?"

"Yes," she replied, trying to mask her disquiet. "I've spoken to him on the phone."

"How is he enjoying England? Has he gone to the cathedral at Canterbury?"

"I don't believe so, Father, but he probably will before he leaves." He isn't there to sight-see, she thought to herself.

"Well, he certainly should go there while he's in England," Henley said, walking with Rachel back to the storage room where the candles and altar cloths were kept. "Travel can be such a broadening experience if you make a point of seeing the right things." He heard Rachel emit a curt, humorless laugh, and he looked at her closely, noticing for the first time that something seemed to be amiss. "Rachel?" he asked. "Is everything all right? You seem troubled."

She shook her head emphatically. "No, I'm fine, Father. Everything is just fine."

Henley was not persuaded. "You're worried about Malcolm, aren't you."

She grimaced. "Yes, I suppose I am."

He took her hand and patted it comfortingly. "Well, I don't think you should be. He's a good boy deep down. He'll turn out just fine, I'm sure of it."

"Yes, I know," she replied without conviction. She withdrew her hand from his and turned away.

"This isn't unusual, you know. We all have periods of doubt and temptation." Henley laughed softly. "I seem to recall that you had your moments yourself, when you were a teenager. Remember?"

"Yes, Father. I remember." Rachel gazed distractedly at the wall as she took the folded altar cloth from the shelf. I remember, Father Henley, she thought.

I remember how suffocated I felt in my grandfather's home. I remember how absolutely stifling the piety and the propriety seemed to me as I entered my teenage years.

And I remember how much in love I was with Billy Malone when I was fifteen. He was eighteen, practically a grown man, and he made me feel so special, so different, so grown up. A bad boy, Grandfather said. A bad influence. I remember that big argument the day I ran away from home, ran away with Billy, went to live in Manhattan with him and his friend . . . what was his name? Frank? Fred? . . .

I remember, Father Henley. I remember how delightfully wicked it all was, how exciting and Bohemian and romantic. I remember that bottle of chianti we drank up on the roof of that run-down tenement. I remember lying on my back on the warm, prickly tar, staring up at the moon as I gave myself to Billy and clutched his shuddering body tightly to mine.

A woman and free. Fifteen years old, and I felt myself a woman and free.

I remember.

And then I went home to confront Grandfather, to demand a recognition of my freedom and my womanhood. He wept so hard, so long, so bitterly, but I was adamant. I would not be moved.

And then he told me everything. And then I read Mina's diary.

And something died inside me, some glowing ember was extinguished, some flame flickered and was snuffed out. Perhaps it was the evil dying. Perhaps it was the blood sinking back into the cold darkness of oblivion.

Or perhaps what I felt was the cold steel of chains wrapping themselves around my soul, locking me up within the prison of fate, stripping away all happiness and all freedom.

Possibilities. That was what I had felt die in me, possibilities. It was the end of joy, the loss of hope, the death of dreams.

Yes, I remember.

Henley was speaking to her, and she turned abruptly in his direction. "I'm sorry, Father. What did you say?"

"I said that we all go through dangerous times in our youth, but we come through them, with God's help, just as you did. Your life could have turned in a tragic direction. But just look at you now."

"Yes," she muttered as she took the candles out of the cardboard box which rested on the shelf beneath the altar cloths. "Just look at me now." Henley seemed about to speak again, but her tone and demeanor had a cold finality about them and Henley felt himself somehow dismissed. He went back to his office, wondering what was bothering her.

Rachel went about the process of preparation with her customary efficiency, and soon the candles had been replaced, the citorium and chalice polished, and the cloths upon the altar, lectern and pulpit changed to the colors appropriate to the Sunday on the church calendar.

When she was finished she sat down in the front pew and

stared silently at the large golden crucifix upon the altar. Then she crossed herself, closed her eyes and began to pray.

"Lord, protect Malcolm," she whispered. She could feel the tears roll down her cheeks despite her attempt to prevent herself from crying. "Don't let anything happen to my little brother, Lord, don't let anything happen to my little brother..."

Father Henley stood at his office door, quiet and motionless, watching the weeping woman, listening to the soft and unintelligible sounds of her muttered prayer. His assistant, Father Terrence Langstone, came up beside him and whispered, "Matt, is something wrong? Mrs. Rowland seems very upset."

"It appears so, Terry," Henley said softly.

"Is it her brother again?"

"I thought so at first, but I get the feeling it's something else. I don't know. She doesn't seem to want to discuss it with me, and I don't want to intrude unless she brings her problem to me herself. She's communing with God, and He can be more help to her than I can." The two priests disappeared behind the office door and left Rachel Rowland to the privacy of her prayers and her fear.

"Be with him, Lord, be with Malcolm. Protect my little brother, Lord, don't let anything happen to my little brother..."

Chapter Eleven

... When I could see again, the driver was climbing into the caleche, and the wolves had disappeared. This was all so strange and uncanny that a dreadful fear came upon me, and I was afraid to speak or move. The time seemed interminable as we swept on our way, now in almost complete darkness, for the rolling clouds obscured the moon. We kept on ascending, with occasional periods of quick descent, but in the main always ascending. Suddenly I became conscious of the fact that the driver was in the act of pulling up the horses in the courtyard of a vast ruined castle, from whose tall black windows came no ray of light, and whose broken battlements showed a jagged line against the moonlit sky...

"I don't want to hear it anymore, man!" Jerry shouted, grabbing Malcolm's copy of *Dracula* from his friend's hands and throwing it on the floor. "I just don't want to hear it anymore!"

"Jerry," Holly said sympathetically, "try to calm down. Of course you're upset by all of this, but—"

"Upset!" he shouted. "Why the hell should I be upset? Lots of people get bitten by vampires!" He shook a closed fist at Malcolm and spat, "I swear to God, man, if we get out of this alive, I'm gonna kill you!"

Malcolm returned Jerry's furious glower with a steady, impassive, almost indifferent look of minor irritation. "If we're to be certain that we've come to the right place, Jerry, we have to check and review all of the references in the book.

I was only reading it aloud so as to invite your comments, that's all." He sniffed. "Sorry if it annoyed you!"

"You want a comment?" Jerry shouted. "Okay, here's a comment! How could you get the two of us involved in this thing? You stupid son of a bitch, don't you realize what's happened to me?"

Malcolm reached down and picked up the paperback book. "I've already apologized, Jerry," he said softly. "I don't know what else I can say."

"Apologized! What good does that do me?"

"All right," he said testily. "If you're so damn angry at me, why did you continue on with us? Why are you here in this hotel with us in Rumania? Why aren't you back in the United States?"

"Because this isn't a game anymore! I had to come with you to make sure you don't fuck anything up! I mean, we're talking about *my* life now!"

"And we were talking about my life before," Malcolm pointed out.

"The hell we were! We were talking about some nutty obsession of yours, some stupid story your crazy old grandfather told you! We weren't talking about anything real!"

"Yes, we were," Holly sighed. "We just didn't know it." She walked over to the window and pulled aside the drape that Malcolm had closed earlier to shield his eyes from the brilliant sun of the Carpathian summer. She did not open the drape but merely parted it slightly so that she could look out at the town square of the small Rumanian city of Oradea.

It had taken them a full week to get from London to Bucharest. The actual travel time, of course, was a mere five hours by plane, but the preparation for departure had taken six days. A two-hour wait in line at the Rumanian Tourist Bureau offices on Halsworth Road in London had been their introduction to the almost Byzantine complexity of the Rumanian bureaucratic labyrinth, made all the more frustrating by the fact that there were only two people ahead of them dealing with one apathetic, lethargic clerk. It had required another five days for Malcolm, Holly, and Jerry to obtain the necessary entrance visas, transit visas, exit visas, auto insurance card, and temporary driver's permit, to which was added the mandatory security checks, questionnaires, and itinerary verifications. Malcolm had made certain that the latter were left somewhat flexible, for he was not entirely certain at that point where they would be going. He knew that Bran Castle near Brasov and the Snagov Monastery were two places that they had to examine, but he was aware of the strong possibility that other areas might need to be visited if the remains of the Count were to be found.

He did not waste the week during which the Rumanian bureaucrats were processing their forms. While Jerry and Holly nervously watched the days and hours pass away, Malcolm spent half of each day sequestered in the stacks of books on geography and history at the British Library. He spent the other half teaching himself Rumanian—a task made less difficult by the facts that Rumanian is of Latin derivation (not Slavic like most of its neighbors); that Malcolm was already fluent in German and French, could sight-read Latin and ancient Greek, and thus had a demonstrable affinity for foreign languages; and that he had discovered a kosher restaurant not far from St. John's Wood in London which was run by a Rumanian Jew, with whom he was able to practice speaking and listening. By the end of the week he had developed a competency in the tongue. Though not fluent, to be sure, he felt secure in the hope that he would be able to get around in Rumania without too much difficulty, as long as he kept his grammar book and dictionary close at hand.

It was the other half of his daily study that he knew to be the more important, for to find Dracula's remains it would be necessary to find his grave. This promised to be no easy task. Malcolm made copious notes on his reading and research, and he realized after only a few days in Rumania that he had been correct in his careful attention to historical fact.

The three young Americans had departed from Heathrow Airport in London in the morning, arriving in Bucharest in the afternoon. The rest of that day was spent in checking and rechecking their visas and other documents, and they were unable to begin the search until the next day. By the end of that second day, Malcolm had begun to suspect that the sites visited by the so-called Dracula Tours organized by the government of Rumania were to be of no use to him; by the end of the fourth day, he was certain of it.

In the center of Lake Snagov, just outside of Bucharest, was an island upon which stood a monastery that had been endowed by Vlad the Impaler, and which was the traditional site of his burial place; but a few hours in the monastery, looking around and reading the literature available there, had made Malcolm and his friends realize that this tradition was without foundation. The long drive the next day took them from Bucharest in Wallachia to Brasov in Transylvania, just outside of which was Bran Castle, built by the Voivode Ion the Terrible in 1377 and briefly occupied by Vlad IV in 1462; hardly the "Castle Dracula" his great-grandfather had visited in 1889, the castle within which Van Helsing had destroyed the three female vampires and beneath the shadows of which Jonathan Harker and Quincey Morris had stabbed the monster to death later that same year.

None of this surprised Malcolm, for his own researches had led him to some conclusions derived from the careful comparison of facts and very careful reasoning.

There were many traditions regarding the death of Vlad IV, one of which was that he died fighting the Turks at the Battle of Oradea in 1476. Malcolm knew that though Vlad had been the Voivode of Wallachia, it was to a castle in Transylvania that his great-grandfather had been summoned a century before. Oradea was in Transylvania, and the original manuscript of the Stoker book had shown that Oradea was the site of the first journal entry by Jonathan Harker, not Bistritz as the printed version would have it. If Vlad IV did indeed die in the Battle of Oradea, that might explain his subsequent rise from death to undeath in Transylvania rather than his own province of Wallachia.

If Oradea was the city near the castle, then near there they would find the ruins of the vampire's medieval fortress. All of the nobles of medieval Rumania were related by marriage or blood, so it would not be unusual for Vlad to have had a personal residence in the province of a cousin voivode. The problem, of course, was that Rumania, like all European countries, had been picked to the archeological and historical bones years ago. If there were a ruin associated with Vlad Dracula near Oradea, the Rumanian Tourist Bureau would have been exploiting it already. Then he found a notation in an archeological guide that near the border—near Oradea but in Transylvania—was a site designated by the Rumanian government as a historical edifice not open to tourists. The exact words, expressed with the unintentional humor so characteristic of communist bureaucracies, were that the site was an "unauthorized ruin."

And so, after visiting Snagov Monastery and Bran Castle, just to be certain, just to be sure to leave no stone unturned,

Malcolm, Holly, and Jerry had driven to the small city near the Hungarian border, all believing that it was this "unauthorized ruin," this decaying castle, unmarked by scholars other than Balkan medievalists and unknown to the Western Dracula enthusiasts, that was the burial place of Vlad the Impaler.

It was this castle whose tumbledown towers and broken battlements, as Jonathan Harker had so accurately and evocatively described them, even now brooded over the little Rumanian city. The castle that Holly Larsen gazed at from the window of the hotel room with such unadulterated dread.

"All you have to do is gather up his remains, right?" she asked. "You don't need me to help do that, do you?"

"Hmmm?" Malcolm asked.

"I just can't go with you," she muttered. "I just couldn't take it if something else terrible happened."

Malcolm, who had resumed reading in the midst of Jerry's tirade, looked up from his book. "What did you say, Holly?"

She turned back to him. "I just can't go with you, up there to that place. I'm sorry, Mal, but I just can't. I don't think I'm ever going to forget what I saw in that crypt, and I just couldn't take it if anything like that happened again."

Malcolm nodded. "It's just as well. I don't think either of you should go with me. If the remains of the Count are connected to the power of my . . . of the blood . . . well, I don't know what kind of an effect it might have on me."

Holly blanched. "What do you mean?"

He rose from his seat to walk over and take her in his arms. "I'm just thinking of what happened when I was with Vanessa, that's all. There may be a risk, and I don't want you exposed to it. It's enough that you came here with me. Remember, I told you to wait for us in Bucharest."

"I know," she said, nodding. "I just couldn't let you go by yourself."

"Hey, thanks a lot," Jerry grumbled. "What am I, a suitcase?"

"You know what I meant, Jerry," she said kindly. "I'm worried about you, too." She looked back at Malcolm. "But I just can't go to that castle. I'm too scared."

"I understand completely," Malcolm said. "You're not the only one who's scared. So am I."

She shook her head. "You don't act it. You don't seem scared at all."

"Maybe 'apprehensive' is the better word," Malcolm conceded. "You know, it's funny, but now that I know the truth about myself and my family, now that I have some hope for a solution to the problem, everything seems to be . . . well, somehow more manageable. I'm worried, I'm nervous, I'm tense. But . . ." He paused, as if seeking the proper words with which to express his nebulous feelings. "This all seems right to me somehow. It seems like I'm doing what I'm supposed to do, what I was born to do. I know it sounds silly, but this all seems somehow predestined."

"Now he's talking about destiny," Jerry sighed. "Born to be a corpse collector. Why couldn't you be born to be a chiropractor or something?"

"Oh, Jerry, cut it out," Malcolm said irritably. "I'm not explaining this very well. All I mean is that I have to go up there, I'm *supposed* to go up there. You two aren't."

"Wait a minute, man," Jerry said. "I'm going there with you. I have too much riding on this to let you do it all by yourself. No offense, Malcolm, but this little European expedition of yours hasn't exactly been a smashing success so far."

Malcolm shook his head. "Jerry, I don't want Holly left here all alone."

"What do you mean, all alone?" he asked with exasperation. "We're in a hotel, for Christ's sake, not some bar in the South Bronx! Nothing's gonna happen to her in a fancy hotel." He paused. "Fancy for Rumania, anyway."

"Jerry, this is a provincial backwater in what is still really an underdeveloped country. We aren't in France or Sweden, you know. A young foreign woman alone is just not safe, and I'll be able to concentrate on what I'm doing a lot more easily if I'm not worried about her."

"What the hell are you worried about her for?" Jerry asked, raising his voice. "You and me are the ones in trouble, not her."

"Shh!" Holly said. "Stop yelling. The people who run this place might get mad."

"So let 'em get mad!" Jerry said even louder. "What are they gonna do, arrest me?"

"We're in a communist dictatorship, Jerry," Malcolm reminded him. "They can do anything to you they want." Jerry Herman lapsed into disgruntled silence as Malcolm walked over to the cheap old bureau. He poured a glass of the thick, syrupy white wine that the Intourist hotel manager had sent up to them as a courtesy. He handed it to Jerry, saying, "Look, Jer, I know that something horrible has happened to you, but don't lose your perspective on it."

"Don't lose my perspective," he grumbled. "I get bitten by a fucking hundred-year-old vampire, and he wants me to keep it in perspective."

"Yes," Malcolm said firmly. "You've read the book. You were bitten—"

"Used like a goddamned faucet!"

"—but she didn't force you to drink her blood. As long as nothing else happens to you, you'll be fine. It's just as if you'd been bitten by an animal, that's all. We got you some antibiotics in London, so you'll be fine."

"Easy for you to say," he muttered.

"He's right, Jerry," Holly said. "And to be honest, I'd rather not be here all by myself, waiting for you guys to come back."

Jerry looked back and forth from Holly to Malcolm and then muttered, "Oh, what the hell, okay." He sat down glumly in the reading chair near the window and gazed morosely at the inside of the closed drapes.

Malcolm looked back at the book and began to read it aloud once again, saying, " 'The blacksmith hammer which I took in the carriage from Veresti was useful; though the doors were open, I broke them off the rusty hinges, lest some ill chance or ill intent should close them . . .' "

"I can't listen to this shit anymore," Jerry said once again, springing to his feet. "I'm going down to the bar and have a drink. Or two or ten or twenty." He stormed out of the room in a state of intense agitation.

"Holly, why don't you go with him?" Malcolm suggested. "I think I've gotten as much information out of Stoker as I need. I'm going up there now."

"Do you know where to look?"

"I think so." Malcolm opened his suitcase and removed the imitation-gold jewelry case that he had purchased in London. "Both Van Helsing and my great-grandfather said that the graves, the coffins, were in the chapel. Most castle chapels were built along the south or eastern wall, depending upon the country. It should be somewhere along the south wall here in Rumania."

"Why the south wall?" she asked as she gathered up her

purse and traveler's checks in preparation for joining Jerry down at the bar.

"Medieval chapels were built in the part of the castle that was closest to Jerusalem," he explained. "In Spain or Italy, that would be the eastern wall. Here in Rumania, it would be the southern one." He checked the interior of the jewelry box to make certain, for the hundredth time, that it was free of holes or punctures, then checked the padlock that fitted through the latch loop, again for the hundredth time. He had purchased the box for the purpose of storing and shipping the dust of the ancient monster until such time as he could dump it in the Hudson River or bury it or scatter it or in some other way dispose of it far from Rumania. "I'm relatively certain that it won't be an interior room for that same reason. All I have to do is find the south wall and follow it along until I find the chapel."

"Wouldn't the crosses in a chapel . . . I mean, they would probably hide their caskets somewhere else, wouldn't they?"

Malcolm grinned as he opened the door. "You're thinking in terms of American funerals."

"What do you mean?" They walked out into the hallway and began to descend the stairs toward the lobby and the bar.

"Medieval nobles were buried in stone sarcophagi, not wooden boxes. The chapel would be where he was buried, and that would be where he would stay."

"But the crosses . . ."

He shrugged. "Doubtless removed centuries ago."

"But by whom?" she asked. "He couldn't very well do that himself!"

"Well," he said thoughtfully, "according to the book, vampires often have servants or slaves—people who do things for them during the daylight hours, people who have been infected and thus brought under their control, but who still aren't vampires themselves."

She nodded. "Like Renfield."

"Yes. Or my great-grandmother. Remember what the book says about her. On occasion she presented a danger to her husband and the others, until they killed the Count."

Malcolm and Holly reached the lobby and then turned to the right and entered the hotel bar, a room dimly lighted even in midday where the glow of the lamps reflected off the polished dark wood. Jerry Herman was sitting at the bar, glumly holding a tall glass of vodka and staring off into space. "I'm going now, Jer," Malcolm said.

Jerry looked over at him, his fear and anger still evident in his expression. "Good. Don't fuck it up." He looked away. Malcolm waited for a few moments, waited for Jerry to say something more, tried to think of something to say himself, and then he turned to leave. "Malcolm," Jerry said without turning to look at him.

He paused at the doorway. "What?"

"Be careful," he muttered.

Malcolm smiled, glad of his friend's grudging concern. "Thanks. I will. There's no danger anyway, I don't think." He continued on out of the hotel.

Holly sat down beside Jerry, and in an attempt to be light and casual, she grinned and said, "Hiya, sailor. Buy me a drink?"

Jerry laughed humorlessly. "Cute, Holly. Real cute."

Though the ruins of the castle were clearly visible from the city, it took Malcolm nearly an hour to reach them by car. The government of communist Rumania had made many reforms since wresting power from the hands of the corrupt and incompetent King Michael in the years after World War Two, and it had committed as many crimes as it had made reforms; but road construction had focused on linking the population centers, leaving areas such as the one in which Malcolm was driving in serious want of decent roadways. Thus it was that to get from Oradea to the "unauthorized ruin," he found himself maneuvering his rented Eastern European car over the same pitted dirt road that his great-grandfather had suffered a century before. The transmission of the Soviet-built automobile screeched and ground along the roller-coasterlike road.

Malcolm had expected to find the entrance to the ruin sealed, had expected perhaps even a barricade; he had not expected to find a bored and irritable guard sitting upon an uncomfortable-looking wooden chair not five hundred yards from the entranceway, reading a newspaper and yawning so loudly that Malcolm could hear him even over the sound of his engine.

Why the hell would they guard this place? he wondered. This isn't a museum with valuable exhibits; it doesn't contain anything anyone would want to steal. If it ever had, it was all stolen years ago, I'm sure. So why guard it?

He answered his own question nearly as soon as he had asked it. A country with Rumania's economic problems would, in a free-market society, have a serious unemployment problem, but no communist country allows unemployment to exist. Thus, jobs are found for all, even if there is no need for the job to be done. As Malcolm approached the bored middle-aged man, he realized that he was witnessing one small example of the kind of inefficiency that seemed endemic to this part of the world.

He climbed out of the car, leaving the engine running, and he smiled and waved as he walked toward the guard. *"Buna ziua,"* he called out. Good day.

"Buna seara," the guard replied, just a bit suspiciously. Good evening, he had said, even though it was still afternoon.

"Vorbitsi engleza?" Do you speak English, Malcolm had asked, just in the hopes that he might be able to avoid stumbling through Rumanian in his attempt to gain entrance into a sealed ruin.

The guard shook his head and replied without smiling, *"Nu."*

Damn, Malcolm thought, and then he said, *"Scuzati-ma, nu vorbesc romaneshte bune."* I'm sorry, I don't speak Rumanian well. He waved his hand at the ruin and asked, *"Cum se numeshte acest loc?"* What's this place called?

The guard glanced up at the ruin, following the sweep of Malcolm's hand rather than actually looking at the castle, and then he answered, *"Castelul pokol."*

A chill ran up Malcolm's spine, for the guard had told him that the ruin was called Hell Castle. *"Castelul pokol,"* he repeated, as if his curiosity had been piqued by the name. He nodded his head as if thinking it over and then said, *"Va rog, ash vrea intrare. Cit costa?"* I would like to go inside, please, he had said. What is the charge?

The guard shook his head and spoke so rapidly that Malcolm was unable to follow what he was saying. *"Vorbitrar, vorbitrar, va rog!"* Malcolm said quickly, asking the guard to slow down.

The guard heaved a burdened sigh and said, slowly though with obvious annoyance, *"Intrarea oprita, inteleg? Inchis, inchis!"* No entry, understand? Closed!

Malcolm pretended not to understand and decided to

take a risk by offering the guard money. It would be a bribe, of course, but Malcolm could maintain the fiction that he thought he was paying an entrance fee, while the guard's dignity would be protected by the possibility that the ignorant foreigner did not know he was bribing him. Malcolm had read in numerous places that nothing got done in any Eastern European country without payoffs, and he hoped that he had heard correctly. As he pulled a roll of American twenty-dollar bills from his pocket, he asked innocently, "*Pot plati cu acest?*"

The guard's eyes widened visibly at the sight of the green bills, and he gave Malcolm a sudden, knowing smile. "*Da, da, buna, buna!*" He held out his hand and Malcolm placed a twenty-dollar bill into it, then a second, and then, seeing the guard had not yet withdrawn his hand, a third. The guard stuffed the money into his pocket and still smiling, said, "*Intratsi, va rog.*" Please go on in. He returned his attention to the newspaper, grinning to himself, doubtless reveling in the unexpected windfall, doubtless doing some mental calculation as to how many Rumanian lei he could get for sixty American dollars on the black market currency exchange.

Malcolm said, "*Multumesc,*" thank you, as he got back into the car and began to drive up to the castle entrance. A curve in the dirt pathway took him out of sight of the guard. He had no wish to be seen carrying the jewelry box in or out of the ruin. He parked the car near the surprisingly small door, and carrying the box under his arm, he approached the entrance.

The ruined castle appeared to be roughly square in shape, with the front wall and the side wall close to a quarter of a mile in length. As was common with medieval fortresses, each corner of the square defensive wall was topped with a tower, though both of the towers in front had been obviously collapsing for centuries. Malcolm drew closer to the old, gray structure and nodded, smiling grimly as he saw the iron grating lying flat and partially buried in the earth before the door. Of course, he thought. The gates are not hanging from their hinges. Van Helsing knocked them off back in 1889 to preclude any possibility of his being trapped inside after sundown. The wind and the weather of the intervening century had caused the iron gates to sink slightly into the ground, and thus they lay only half-uncovered.

Malcolm entered the fortress and walked to the center of the cold, gray courtyard. Tufts of grass had forced their way up from between the heavy stones that formed the surface of the court. Birds were flitting back and forth from the thick vines hanging from the cracked and broken walls, which, though ravaged by time, still maintained some element of austere majesty.

Malcolm walked slowly through the courtyard toward the large main building of the castle, listening to the faint echoes of his footsteps against the stones. He felt nervous, frightened, but also grimly determined and a bit lonely. This was a dead building, a place not meant for living men. He knew that the castle had been inhabited continuously from the time of Vlad's death in the fifteenth century until just about a century ago; but not by living human beings. Not by the living.

"No need to be nervous," he muttered aloud. I'm not like Van Helsing, walking into this castle alone, knowing what lay sleeping within, knowing that three undead women rested in their coffins awaiting sundown, knowing that Count Dracula was somewhere near on his way home from England. Dust, just dust. That's all I'm here for, just the remains of the Beast. No danger. No danger.

He entered the building and found himself standing in the great hall. The huge room was totally empty, devoid of any sort of decoration or furnishing. The local people must have looted this place decades ago, he thought. Malcolm looked around and found a door on the southern side of the room. He headed for it, reasoning that even if the chapel did not lie off the great hall, it must nonetheless be somewhere in that general direction.

He glanced at his watch as he wandered down the dusty, dark corridors: two o'clock. "I'd hate to be here at night," he muttered. Nothing to be frightened of, really, but this place makes me uncomfortable enough now, with the sun streaming in through the broken windows and cracked walls. At night it would be terrible!

He walked for a half hour through the rooms and hallways before finding the chapel. It was, as he had suspected, along the south wall of the castle, but it was in a subterranean vault at the bottom of a long flight of uneven stone steps. He descended the stairs and stood in the midst of the chapel. It was just as Van Helsing had described it.

The large subterranean room had apparently doubled as place of worship and crypt. Unlike castle chapels in Western Europe, which contained a limited number of sarcophagi, there were dozens of stone coffins here, some of them small and plain, some ornate and majestic. He noticed that a few of them had lids just slightly ajar, and on an impulse he walked over to one such coffin and pushed the lid back.

A skeleton lay within the box, a stake protruding from its rib cage. The still-present long black hair and rotting yellow gown told him that it had been a woman. "One of his wives," he muttered. One of the three who attacked my great-grandfather. One of the ones killed by Van Helsing. He reached out and gently caressed the top of the stake, and he smiled. "You were a brave man, Professor," he said aloud.

He wandered around the chapel, reading the Latin titles that were carved so deeply upon the stone bases of the sarcophagi. Basarab the Grim. Mircea the Old. Nicholae the Unrelenting. Generation after generation of rulers, princes, voivodes, their wives and their children, their names and even their popular appellatives preserved in the cold, hard stone. The Grim, the Old, the Unrelenting. Where was the Impaler?

He turned and looked toward a recessed alcove off the rear of the crypt, and Van Helsing's written record drifted through his mind as he walked slowly toward it. "There was one great tomb more lordly than the rest," Van Helsing had written. "Huge it was and nobly proportioned. On it was but one word: DRACULA."

It was still there, still huge, still lordly. And the name was still carved deep upon the stone.

Malcolm approached the sarcophagus and reached out to touch the letters, his fear and misery almost forgotten in the horrible wonder of the moment. "Count Dracula," he muttered. This is where they buried him, five centuries ago. Vlad Tepes, Vlad the Impaler. This is the foul home from which he rose to spread pain through the hamlets and forests of the Carpathians.

Malcolm placed the jewelry box down upon the stone floor and placed his hands upon the coffin lid. He pushed up against it. The old lid hinges creaked and scraped against the rust, and the lid swung open with greater ease than he had expected.

He looked into the coffin, and he smiled. Lucy Westenra

was right, he thought. The Gypsies must have gathered up his remains after my ancestors and their friends left the scene, must have carefully collected the fragments of bone and dust and brought them back here for interment. They must have removed the consecrated host that Van Helsing had placed there as a barrier to the Count, and then they must have placed the remains in the coffin. A pile of bone and dust rested in the shape of a blunt cone in the center of the large coffin. It was obvious from the shape of the pile that it was not dust that had seeped in, borne by the air. The dust had been poured into the coffin. Bits of white and yellow protruded from the pile, bits of bone and teeth.

Malcolm looked closely and carefully at the pile, covering his nose with his hand so as not to breathe on the dust and scatter it. One very long tooth lay on the sloping side of the pile. He reached in and carefully took the tooth from the dust and then held it in the palm of his hand, examining it, reflecting that a hundred years before this very tooth had been embedded in his great-grandmother's throat.

He opened the jewelry box and placed it in the coffin beside the piled remains. Very carefully he reached in with both hands and scooped up some of the bone and dust and put it into the box. He began to repeat his motion, but his hands suddenly felt somehow odd and a bit numb. He flexed them, rubbed them together, but the numbness remained and grew, spread up his arms and toward his chest.

Malcolm began to hear voices, very soft and muted, but increasingly clear and distinct as the numbness continued to spread over his body. He fell back from the coffin and landed on the floor of the crypt as his now rubbery legs folded under him. Feeling rising panic, he tried to force himself to remain calm, to analyze what was happening to him. In an instant, he understood. The blood in his veins and the dust in the coffin were beckoning to each other, calling to each other.

He crawled away from the sarcophagus slowly as the numbness began to engulf him, trying to get as far away from the remains as he could. At last his body could no longer move, and he felt himself slipping into a state of semi-consciousness. He fought against it, struggled to remain awake.

And then words and voices, pictures and images, began to drift upward from the depths of his being into the forefront of his mind, and he began to feel himself seeing with another's eyes, hearing with another's ears, speaking with another's tongue.

It was the blood remembering what it was, remembering *whose* it was, stimulated by the proximity of the dust, awakening dreamlike memories from centuries gone by.

Malcolm shuddered. He felt as if he were falling headfirst into a bottomless pit, plummeting uncontrollably into the past.

III

VLAD THE IMPALER

And his eyes have all the seeming
of a demon's that is dreaming...
—from "The Raven"

Chapter Twelve

First there was mist and a sense of emptiness as if he were passing from one form of existence to another, and then the mist thinned out and allowed him to see. Malcolm had a sense of standing aside from his own being, watching himself, listening to himself, aware that he was no longer truly Malcolm Harker, but someone whom he did not know. That one small part of his consciousness, his Malcolm-being, remained isolated, observant, fascinated, and terrified.

He began to feel with someone else's body and think with someone else's mind, and the facts of the strange world and the situation into which the awakening blood had cast him became known to him through the mind and thoughts of the memories buried in the blood.

He looked down at his hands and found them surprisingly small, and then he realized that he was a child, a little boy. He looked around him at the opulent tapestries and the shiny marble floor, at the windows with their cupola shape and the high, vaulted ceiling. The delicate scent of flowers from the garden without drifted into the room through the oriental windows. He looked to his left and saw another small boy, younger than himself, wiping a tear from his eye and gazing with undisguised fear at the two men who stood before them.

And as the memories crystalized, he understood everything. He knew that it was the year 1440. He knew that the little boy whose hand he was holding was his little brother Radu, age five. He knew that the fat man with the silken robes and the insincere smile and the shiny, oil-smeared skin was the Beloved of Allah, Murad II, the master of the Ottoman Turks, the Sultan at whose name the Christian princes of the Balkans trembled. He knew that the other man, the tall, slender man with the easy smile and the flashing eyes, was his father, Vlad II, the Voivode of Wallachia, often called Dracul, the Dragon, by his adoring subjects.

And he knew that he was nine years old, that he was in the city of Smyrna near the Aegean coast, that he was his father's second son. His older brother Mircea would be Vlad II's heir, but it was to his second son that the voivode had bequeathed his own name. The boy was already being called Vlad the Little Dragon, Vlad Dracula, by the people of Wallachia and the members of the sultan's court.

His father knelt down before his two little sons and said smoothly, "Vlad and Radu, I want you to make me proud of you. Mircea and I are returning to Bucharest, but we have been able to get our sublime friend's permission for the two of you to remain here and represent us." The voivode smiled. "It is a great honor and a great responsibility, my boys. For as long as you are here in Smyrna, you will be representing me and our principality. You must behave yourselves and be good guests."

Radu nodded obediently. "Yes, Father."

Vlad nodded also, saying, "We shall be good, Father. And I trust that you will be faithful in your duties." He said this knowingly, without a hint of arrogance or disrespect.

The voivode's heart swelled with silent pride at the astuteness of his middle son. Unlike Radu, Vlad knew that the two children were not guests, but hostages.

All the realms of the Balkans were in flux in 1440. The primitive principality of Wallachia, a vassal state of the Kingdom of Hungary until a scant fifty years ago, was now a tributary dependency of the Ottoman Empire. Moldavia to the north had enjoyed a brief period of independence from the Hungarians, then had fallen under Lithuanian rule, and was now as closely tied to the Turks as was Wallachia. Of the Rumanian principalities, only Transylvania to the west was still firmly in Hungarian hands, and this fact particularly rankled, for it was in the little Transylvanian city of Sighisoara that Vlad Dracula had been born in 1431, the same city in which his father Vlad Dracul had been born three decades earlier.

But neither Voivode Vlad II nor his sons could spare much time lamenting the alien rule over their birthplace. The Carpathian lords followed rising stars, not setting ones, and it was clear that the Ottoman Turks were destined to be

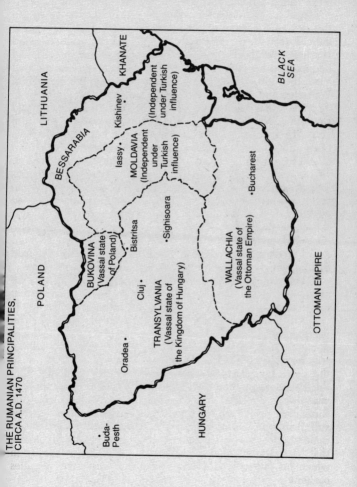

THE RUMANIAN PRINCIPALITIES, CIRCA A.D. 1470

LITHUANIA

KHANATE

BLACK SEA

Kishinev •

BESSARABIA

Iassy •

MOLDAVIA (Independent under Turkish influence)

(Independent under Turkish influence)

POLAND

BUKOVINA (Vassal state of Poland)

Bistritsa •

• Sighisoara

• Bucharest

Cluj •

WALLACHIA (Vassal state of the Ottoman Empire)

Oradea •

TRANSYLVANIA (Vassal state of the Kingdom of Hungary)

OTTOMAN EMPIRE

Buda-Pesth •

HUNGARY

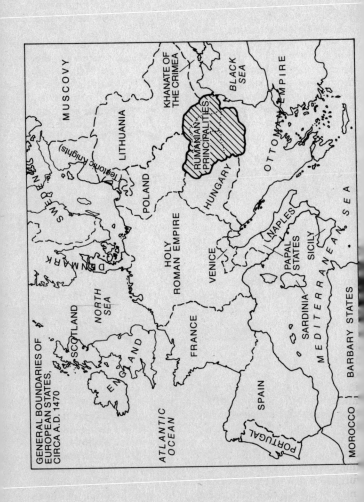

GENERAL BOUNDARIES OF EUROPEAN STATES, CIRCA A.D. 1470

the masters of the Balkans, if not all Europe. And so Vlad II had switched his allegiance from Budapest to the Ottomans. The Turks had been content, at first, to give their new vassal a long and loose leash.

That was before 1437, before the attempt on the part of Sultan Murad II to overrun Hungary was thwarted by the Magyar patriot John Hunyadi; that was before 1440, when the thrones of Hungary and Poland were united in the person of King Vladislav I and VI, of Hungary and Poland respectively. Now the destiny of the Ottoman dynasty seemed less than certain. Now it seemed wise to Murad to keep the children of his vassals close at hand, pledges of the continued loyalty of their fathers.

Little Vlad Dracula understood this, even if little Radu did not. And the Voivode Vlad II was pleased and proud at his son's intelligence.

"Either Mircea or I will return to Smyrna next spring to visit you," the voivode said. "Until then, be good boys, and obey our illustrious friend."

"Yes, Father," Vlad said quietly.

"Oh, please, you come, Father," Radu whined, "not Mircea! I hate Mircea! He calls me names and—" Vlad punched Radu in the side as covertly as possible.

"We shall await your return, Father," Vlad said, his voice a calm, guarded monotone. "Please tell our dear brother that we will remember you both in our prayers."

"Good, my boy, good," the voivode said, rising to his feet and then the surroundings seemed to fade away into the billowing mists. Malcolm realized that the memories were drifting to the surface selectively, as if those events and incidents that had made the deepest impression upon the mind of the long-dead Rumanian nobleman were the ones that emerged foremost and strongest, as the memories in the blood struggled to integrate themselves into a living mind.

Malcolm felt, briefly, the cold stone floor of the ruined castle press against his bruised cheek, but the mist carried him away again, and now he was standing in an ornately furnished private chamber, his trembling child's hands holding a small white kitten. He kept his eyes lowered, neither wishing nor daring to look up at the fat, oily sultan who stood before him, smiling malevolently.

"Do you like the kitten, Little Dragon?" Murad asked smoothly.

"Yes, Sublime One," Vlad muttered. "Thank you very much."

The sultan shrugged casually, dismissing the thanks. "It is a trifle, my dear one, a trifle. I have many gifts for you, many, many nice gifts." The chubby fingers of the sultan reached out and gently caressed Vlad's smooth, close-cropped black hair. "We are always kind and generous to people who are kind and generous to us, Little Dragon."

Vlad did not raise his eyes. "Yes, Sublime One," he repeated. The little boy gritted his teeth behind his tightly shut lips and attempted to maintain a stoic calm as the fat, scented arms enfolded him and drew him close to the hairy bovine belly of the lord of the Turks.

And then the mist descended again and rose again, as if the memory that had been awakened was one which was so painful that the disjointed yet stirring mind of the long-dead nobleman was fleeing from it. When the mist cleared, he found himself sitting in great discomfort, in great pain, upon a large cushion in the chambers that had been designated for him and his little brother. Radu was standing in front of him, his face a study in shock and fear. Vlad tasted something salty, then realized that a few unbidden tears were rolling down from his reddened eyes and dripping upon his lips.

"I would die!" Radu was saying in a hoarse whisper. "I would take my own life before I would allow—"

"You would not," Vlad spat, shifting his weight in an attempt to ease the pain upon which he sat. "You would do what you must, until Father can free us from these pig-eaters."

"No." Little Radu shook his head obstinately. "I would never let the sultan lay his hands upon me! Never!"

Vlad laughed grimly. "And do you think he will ask for your permission, you little idiot?" Radu began to protest again, and Vlad silenced him with a brusque, "Oh, Radu, get out of here. Leave me alone. Leave me in peace."

Radu's lower lip thrust out angrily and he spun about on his heels, leaving his older brother sitting in quiet solitude upon the cushion. Vlad made no sound and did not stir, and yet a burning rage was seething within him. A seed of violence and hatred had been planted in soil already made fertile by insecurity and fear, by abandonment and loneliness by the almost instinctive bravado of noble birth and the natural timidity of a frightened child.

Pig-eater, Vlad thought bitterly. You fat, disgusting ani

mal. I'll have my revenge upon you, someday, somehow, Turkish slime. I only pray to God that you live long enough for me to grow old enough to ... to ...

"To do what, Little Dragon?" a soft, intimate voice asked. "Tell me, what would you like to do to Murad?"

Vlad looked around the room, startled by the sudden intrusion, but he did not move from the soft cushion. "Radu?" he snapped. "Is that you?"

Gentle laughter seemed to float about his ears. "I am not Radu, Little Dragon."

"Who are you, then?" Vlad asked, frightened yet attempting to mask his fear. His blanching face and trembling hands belied his poise. "Show yourself this instant!"

"Ah, but I cannot show myself, Little Dragon," the voice said. "I am sorry, but I have no body to show."

Vlad leaned back upon the cushion, wincing as the cool silk rubbed against the sores. "What manner of trickery is this?" He allowed his eyes to move carefully over the interior of his private chamber. "Is this supposed to be an amusement? Are you Turks in such dire need of diversion that you resort to such silly games?"

Again the voice laughed. "I am not a Turk, Little Dragon. I am not a man."

Vlad repressed a smile. Having persuaded himself that this was all some pig-eater prank, he relaxed somewhat. "Not a man! You have not a woman's voice."

"Nor am I a woman," the gentle voice said. "I am merely your friend, Little Dragon."

"So great is my fortune," he said, laughing, "to have invisible friends." Suddenly serious, and attempting to infuse his voice with imperious hauteur, he snapped, "Now show yourself to me at once! I am not some little Bulgarian shepherd, to be impressed with your tricks! Present yourself, or begone!"

The voice seemed to lose some of its friendliness. "I shall be your companion and your ally, Little Dragon, but I shall not be your servant. If you desire my friendship, it is yours for the taking; but friendship with me is based upon service."

Vlad lay down upon the cushion, weary and growing annoyed. "Such impressive magic, Turk! Where are you? Behind the tapestry? Is there a hidden chamber behind the walls?"

There was a long stillness in the room, and then the

voice said, "You received a present this day from Murad the Sultan, did you not?"

"Yes," he said bitterly. "A gift from the goodness of his heart."

"Where is the cat?" the voice asked.

Vlad looked around irritably and saw the little white kitten sleeping peacefully upon Radu's mat near the large eastern window. "There," he said casually. "Over there."

"Watch the cat, Little Dragon," the voice said. "Watch it carefully."

Despite his irritation, Vlad looked at the small animal and noticed that it was suddenly awake and visibly discomforted. The kitten rubbed its face with its forepaws, trembled, whined, and then leaped in confusion and pain. It rushed over toward him, its little face contorted in terror. And then Vlad noticed that the face was not truly contorted; it was changing, shifting its shape, melting into a visage utterly unfeline. In a moment a miniature head of the sultan stared up at him from the shaking body of the little cat.

"Here is a token of my friendship, Little Dragon," the voice said. "I have other plans for our friend Murad, but for your pleasure I shall allow you to enjoy some small vengeance upon his image."

Vlad gulped and tried to speak, but no words issued forth from his mouth. He continued to stare at the monstrosity that sat upon the marble floor in front of him, the diminutive Turkish head perched atop the white kitten's frame. The Murad face moved its small lips but managed only to hiss a cry of uncomprehending terror.

At last Vlad was able to force himself to ask, "Are you God?"

The voice laughed. "No, Little Dragon, far from that. And yet He and I are associates of long standing."

"Are you an angel, or a saint?"

"Perhaps I should not have said 'associates,' Little Dragon. God and I are adversaries, we are enemies."

Vlad finally understood. "Ordogh!" he whispered, addressing the voice after the manner of his people. "Ordogh!" The Devil.

"At your service," the voice said. "Take my gift to you, Little Dragon. Let us be friends. Let us help each other. Take my gift."

Vlad stared back down at the misshapen creature, and it

seemed that the Murad face twisted its lips into a self-satisfied smile, gazing back up at him smugly. A wave of uncontrollable rage swept over the boy, and he grabbed the cat by the scruff of the neck and yanked it up into the air. His trembling hands closed around the neck of the creature, and he began to strangle it madly. The eyes of the Murad-face bugged out and the mouth opened in a silent cry of agony. Vlad relaxed his grip just slightly, then looked over to the ornamental spears that had been hung on either side of the doorway of his chamber. He kept the cat firmly in his grasp as he rose painfully from the cushion and stumbled over to the wall. He took one of the spears from its holder and held it tightly in his left hand, bracing the shaft in the crook of his armpit, pressing it tightly against his body. Then he put the cat creature on the floor, never releasing his tight grip upon the fatty neck folds, and placed the spear tip against the animal's abdomen.

Vlad smiled to himself, then thrust the spear into the creature's body. The sharp blade tore through the fur and the fat and the muscles, causing the animal to writhe in mute agony as Vlad lifted the spear upward toward the high ceiling of the chamber. The boy smiled as the Murad-face wept and screamed silently, as the blood began to pour from the Murad-mouth and the icy glaze of death spread over the Murad-eyes. The writhing body shuddered and then was still. The boy threw the spear away from him, watching as the dead animal slid across the marble floor upon a slick of its own blood.

He stared at the dead form as the Murad-face slowly shifted back to the face of a cat, and then he laughed softly. "I thank you, Ordogh. That was a great pleasure."

"It pleases me to please you, Little Dragon," the voice said.

"And what am I to give in exchange for your gift?"

The voice laughed again. "Only that which you will give of your own free will, Little Dragon. I have chosen you because I know you. You are like unto a dancing girl who strips away layer after layer of silk to reveal only more silk beneath. None can see the flesh that is masked by the garments, none but I. All others see you and know you not, but I see you and know you well. You shall serve me well, Little Dragon. You shall write your name in blood, and I shall give you pen and parchment for the writing."

Little Vlad did not respond immediately. When he did, he said carefully, "We are told that God loves us and forgives us our sins. We are told that God's victory over Ordogh is certain and preordained. Why then should I serve you?"

"Because it is your will to serve me, Little Dragon. You shall serve me because it shall please you to serve me. You shall serve me because I shall give you power for a time, and pleasure and wealth. You shall serve me because your heart is black and your soul is as predestined for damnation as I." The voice paused and then said, "Hear me well, Little Dragon. Never again shall you see your father or your brother Mircea. You shall be Voivode of Wallachia, and you shall inflict much suffering and shall in your turn suffer much. Your life shall be hard and bitter and brief, and yet shall you serve me with devotion. You shall experience ecstasy such as few ever experience, and such misery as few ever suffer, and yet shall you serve me."

Vlad shook his head. "I do not like your words, Ordogh. If you offer me a cup of sweet and bitter wine, why should I drink it? If you offer me a short life, uncertain rule, and suffering—"

"I do not offer these things to you," the voice said. "I tell what must be, what shall be, regardless. I do not control this world, Little Dragon, I can only influence it. But some things I can do. I can see to it that you become voivode, and not Radu. I can see to it that while you rule, however brief that may be, you will be able to use your power for your own pleasure. I can see to it that whatever anger you have, whatever bitterness or sorrow, whatever misery you suffer, will be balanced by as much pleasure, power, wealth, and renown. The former are your destiny, Little Dragon. The pleasure, power, wealth, and renown are mine to give."

Vlad gazed over at the mutilated body of the cat and thought for a moment. "I want you to give me Murad."

The voice did not respond.

"I want to kill him, myself, with my own hands. I want *him*, not a beast with his face. I want *him*!"

At last the voice spoke. "The lives of all men follow predestined courses, Little Dragon; but even the flow of the river can be diverted for a little time. The day of Murad's death is fixed and cannot be altered. But the manner of his death . . ."

The voice ceased to speak to him, and Vlad surmised

that Ordogh was thinking. He waited patiently, and after a long while the voice said, "It shall be as you wish, Little Dragon."

The mist descended upon the world and the years floated by him, scenes and incidents and events seeming to merge with one another as he grew from childhood to young manhood in the Ottoman court. As Malcolm Harker lay in cold paralysis upon the moist floor of the ruined castle, his mind's eye saw the events of that other life—buried deep in the polluted blood that coursed through his veins—drift past him. He saw the year 1447 come and go, watched himself, a thin but vigorous boy of sixteen being informed by Murad's vizier Khalil that the Hungarians had captured and beheaded his father and elder brother. He watched himself depart from Smyrna at the head of a small host of Turkish foot soldiers early the next year, the good wishes and promises of support from Sultan Murad following upon the heels of his small but well-trained army. He saw himself enter Bucharest with his sword drawn, easily overcoming the small force that the Hungarians had left to guard the provincial capital, saw himself proclaimed voivode by the aged Orthodox prelate, heard himself publicly avow his loyalty to the sultan, felt himself repress the urge to bite off his own tongue as he voiced the words of vassalage directed toward the man whom he hated with such passionate intensity.

He watched as the year 1448 drew to an end, as the Wallachian nobles rejected his claim to his father's throne. He saw himself defeated in a pitched battle against the proud boyars of his homeland. He saw himself flee for his life into the Carpathian hills.

It was 1453 when the mist lifted again.

He was sitting easily upon a low-cut tree stump, surveying the little domain which was all he had to call his own. He had spent the past five years as little better than a bandit, roaming the Balkans with his little band of marauders, looting without discrimination the settlements of Turks and Greeks, Bulgars and Serbs, Macedonians and Moldavians, Wallachians and Transylvanians. His host—how dare he call this assemblage of thieves and murderers a host?—consisted of a few hundred Gypsies and renegades, Turks who loved the fruit of the vine more than they loved Allah, Slavs fleeing from rapacious landlords, homeless Magyars, uprooted Jews, vengeful Greeks.

And in the midst of their ragged camp, bound with thick

ropes, lying naked, weeping, and trembling, was Murad II, onetime master of the Ottoman Empire. Now no better than a refugee himself, he had fallen by unhappy chance into the hands of his old friend Vlad.

Unhappy chance? Vlad thought. No, there is no chance involved here. It is Ordogh, keeping his word.

Vlad rose from the tree stump and walked slowly over to the fat old man who lay in misery upon the cold forest floor. "Sublime One," Vlad said easily. "I think that it is time we negotiate with one another."

Murad looked up as the tall, thin, young man approached him. He tried to ignore the circle of ruffians who giggled with anticipatory glee as they scratched their scarred faces through flea-infested beards and waited for the fun to begin. "Little Dragon. . . ." Murad said thickly, "we were friends . . . allies . . ."

"Yes, yes." Vlad nodded seriously. "How sad that fortune has so unjustly afflicted you, Sublime One."

"When I regain my throne, I shall give you all Dacia," Murad said desperately. "All of it, not just Wallachia. Moldavia as well, and your homeland, Transylvania."

Vlad nodded again as if impressed by the offer. "And what of Bukovina, Sublime One? Will you give me Bukovina as well?"

"Yes, yes, Bukovina as well!" Murad said quickly.

Vlad nodded once more, then shook his head sadly. "But you have no throne, Sublime One. There is another Sultan. Mohammed, he calls himself, Mohammed II."

"A usurper!" Murad screamed. "Allah will damn him for his treason!"

"That may be," Vlad agreed, sitting down upon the ground beside the onetime master of the east. He placed his hand sympathetically upon Murad's arm and said, "But the problem, Sublime One, is that this usurper happens to be ruling the Ottoman Empire right now, and you are merely the prisoner of a group of homeless bandits." He frowned as if in thought. "And yet, a sultan may bestow provinces."

"Yes, yes!" Murad agreed, the terror showing in his face. "When I have reclaimed the throne, I shall—"

"Oh, my dear old friend, I do not mean you!" Vlad said "Mohammed has been sultan for two years, ever since your overthrow. You have been a fugitive, powerless, now even out of gold to buy yourself supporters and protection." He leaned his face close to Murad's. "Haven't you heard, Sublime One

Even now Mohammed's cannons are pounding against the walls of Constantinople. He is the greatest power since Charlemagne, the greatest conqueror since Genghis Khan. If anyone can restore me to my rightful place in Wallachia, it is he, not you! If anyone can give me Moldavia and Transylvania, it is he!"

"Little Dragon..." the old man whimpered.

"No, I am sorry, Sublime One," Vlad said, rising to his feet. "I must buy myself into the good graces of Mohammed. I think that I must do two things in order to become his friend and ally. First, I must become a Moslem." He shrugged, dismissing the idea as a trivial matter. "And second, I must give him your head as a token of my devotion."

"No! You would not dare!" Murad sputtered. "Ransom me, at least! Yes, yes, Little Dragon, a ransom! I have friends, I have friends!"

Vlad rose to his feet, ignoring the pleading from the fallen sultan. "Janos, Anatoly, Kurza," he snapped. "Prepare him." Three members of Vlad's eclectic army rushed forward and grabbed hold of the sultan. One of them grabbed the old man's left leg, one other the right, and the third took the sultan's head in his hands and pulled open the eyelids, so as to force Murad to watch what was about to occur.

Vlad walked over to the edge of the small clearing, and Murad's eyes followed him as if mesmerized. The young man ran his fingers fondly up and down the smooth trunk of a small, straight tree, smiling to himself and muttering a few low, unintelligible words. Murad squinted to see the tree more clearly, then realized to his horror that it was not a tree at all. It was a long stake which had been sunk into a deep hole in the forest ground, a long stake with a menacingly sharpened tip.

Murad screamed and begged and wept as Vlad pulled the stake free from its foundation with a mighty heave, then carried it over toward the old man. He dropped it heavily upon the ground and stood over Murad, smiling as one of the Gypsies handed him a woodcutter's axe. Vlad nodded to another of his men, who ran forward and positioned the sharp tip of the stake against the entrance to Murad's anus.

"Sublime One," Vlad said gently, "do you remember, many years ago, when I was an honored guest in your house? Do you remember when you gave me a little gift, a little kitten?" He waited for a reply, but none was forthcoming.

"Do you remember why you gave me that kitten?" Again no reply, only whimpers and moans from the fat old man who lay upon his back, held immobile by Vlad's men. "I remember, Sublime One," Vlad said. "I remember well. I have never forgotten." He paused. "Do you know what it felt like, Sublime One? Do you know what that kind of pain feels like to a child?" He gazed into Murad's wild, pleading eyes. "Let me give you some idea of what it felt like, Beloved of Allah."

He swung the axe back to his right as his Gypsy lifted the bottom end of the stake slightly upward. Vlad paused for a moment, then brought the flat side of the axe head around in a wide arc, striking the blunt end of the stake with all his might.

The sharpened tip of the stake drove up through Murad's intestines, and his agonized scream was choked off by the blood which began to flow like a river from his open, shuddering lips. Vlad struck again, driving the stake deeper and deeper. He struck again and again, his face twisting into a mask of unrelieved rage and hatred. By the time the tip of the stake came thrusting out of Murad's body just below his neck, the old sultan had long since died.

Vlad stood over the bloody corpse, stared at it for a long while, then laughed loudly and long. "You keep your promises, Ordogh, and I keep mine!" His laughter rang through the dark forest as his men stood by and watched, rejoicing for their leader, fearful of him, confused by his strange words. After a few moments he turned to his man and said, "Behead him. Place the head in a cask of vinegar, then leave his body for the crows. Make ready to leave, my friends," he shouted, so that all would hear him. "We leave tomorrow for Constantinople! We seek an audience with Mohammed the Sultan!"

Vlad walked away from the grisly scene, leaving his men to tend to the beheading. He walked deep into the woods until he was a considerable distance from the camp, then said, "Ordogh! Are you here?"

After a few moments the voice came to him, speaking in his ear and saying, "I am here, Little Dragon. I am always here."

"My vengeance was years in the making, Ordogh, and it was sweeter for the long anticipation."

"As always, Little Dragon," the voice said. "I have long experience with the pleasures of vengeance."

Vlad sat down upon the cold earth. "And now? What will happen now?"

"I am not here to tell you details of your future, Little Dragon," the voice said. "But these next few years will be wondrous for you."

And the mist rolled over him and carried him forward through the years. The mist carried him to the opulent camp of Mohammed II before the broken walls of the plundered capital of what had until a few weeks before been the Byzantine Empire. The mist carried him on the campaigns of Mohammed the Conqueror for the next two years as a trusted and valuable lieutenant, and the mist carried him deep into the Carpathian forest for a secret conference with the king of Hungary.

He watched himself extract from the sultan a promise to help him overthrow the usurper who sat upon the throne in Bucharest, which was rightfully his, the usurper who had the effrontery to call himself Vlad III; he watched himself extract from the Hungarian king a pledge to allow passively the destruction of his vassal, whom he had placed upon the Wallachian throne after murdering Vlad's father and brother; and he saw himself thus become the ally of two enemies—a public ally of the Turks, whom he hated for the abuse he had suffered at their hands throughout the early years of his life, and a secret ally of the Hungarians, whom he hated for the execution of his family.

He watched himself scheme and plan, kill and plunder, lie and cheat and deceive, waiting for the day when the Turks would put him on the Wallachian throne, waiting for the day when he was strong enough to cast off the Ottoman yoke and declare his allegiance to Buda-Pesth; and hoping that there would be a day when he could cast off the Hungarian yoke as well and unite the Balkans beneath his scepter.

The mist carried him to Bucharest, to the year 1456, to the day when he became at long last the absolute master of his small Carpathian realm. The mist thinned slightly, and he saw himself seated upon a throne in the great hall of a large castle. Vlad IV, the Voivode of Wallachia. Vlad Tepes. Vlad the Impaler.

And then in an instant the mist was gone. As feeling flooded back into his cold, stiff body and as his own consciousness reasserted itself, Malcolm felt the damp stone floor of the ruined chapel pressing against his cheek. The overwhelming power of the deeply buried memories had receded as suddenly, and as startlingly, as it had emerged.

Malcolm rose painfully to his knees and then to his feet, trembling and breathing heavily, then he collapsed as his legs gave out from beneath him. My God! he thought. My God! Memories in the blood! *His* memories, that *thing's* memories, in my blood!

Stay calm! he ordered himself. Don't panic! You have to gather up the dust and get out of here and get home! Calm! Calm!

He took a deep breath and then got to his feet again, slowly and carefully, watching warily for any sign of weakness or fainting. He forced himself to stumble back over toward the open sarcophagus. The jewelry box was still resting beside the conical pile of dust and bone, and his still-befuddled mind tried to devise some way of removing the remains without touching them. Looking around the chapel crypt, he spied a short, thin piece of wood lying on the floor amid a pile of debris. He reached down and picked it up with his shaking hands.

He used the thin wood as a shovel, scooping and scraping as much of the dust as was possible and then pouring it into the jewelry box. He wiped his feverish brow with the sleeve of his trembling arm, and then, after checking the interior of the coffin one last time to make certain that no bits of bone or dust remained, he shut the lid of the jewelry box and locked it. He left the chapel hastily, and only when he was back in the great hall, heading for the doorway, did he take a moment to reflect upon the remarkable experience he had just had; one that he earnestly hoped never to repeat.

The power of the blood, Lucy had told him. She had said nothing of the power of the dust. But then perhaps she had not known.

The sun was setting as he walked back out into the courtyard, and he felt for no logical reason that he had best be far from the ruins before darkness covered them. He knew this was foolish. He knew that no vampires were left to emerge from the dark windows or to crawl down the cold gray stones. But he hurried into the car and sped away.

He had driven for about fifteen minutes when he pulled over to the side of the road and leaned his head against the steering wheel. He placed his hand upon his chest in an attempt somehow to calm his racing heart.

The blood and the dust, the blood and the dust.

It was as if the blood had a life of its own, a mind of its own, and for the first time since he had begun to believe the tale his grandfather had told him, he was aware of an alien power inhabiting his body. It made him feel polluted and dirty, and he prayed silently that he would be free of it when he cast the accursed remains to the wind on the far distant continent.

It was well past dark when he arrived back at the hotel in Oradea. He was tired, drained from his vision, sore and weary and worn. He parked the car in front of the hotel and walked groggily inside, past the desk and into the bar. Holly was sitting at a table alone, and only two other patrons, obviously locals, were in the room. Holly looked up at him as he entered, and a flood of relief washed over her face. "Oh, Malcolm, thank God! I was frantic!" She stood up and ran to him, grabbing him joyfully and hugging him to her. He was so tired that he could barely manage a halfhearted squeeze in return. "What happened? What kept you so long? Did you find it? Are you okay?" She stared apprehensively at the jewelry box.

"One thing at a time," he said. "Yes, I found it, and yes, I'm okay."

"You've been gone almost eight hours!"

"I know." He sat down heavily at the table. "Get me a drink, will you? I have a hell of a story to tell you."

She ran over to the bar and managed to explain to the bartender that she wanted a large glass of vodka. When she returned and gave it to Malcolm, she sat down and said, "Okay, so what happened?"

Malcolm looked around. "Where's Jerry? I don't think I could go through this story twice."

"Oh, that creep," she muttered. "He went upstairs about two hours ago. Said he wanted to get his cigarettes or something, and when he didn't come back, I went up to make sure he was okay. He picked up some girl somehow!"

Malcolm laughed softly despite his weariness and his unease at the day's events. "In the middle of all this, Jerry picked up a girl?"

"Yeah. Do you believe him?" Holly could not help but join in his laughter.

"Is she pretty at least?" he asked.

"I assume so," she replied, "though I doubt that it would

matter to him one way or the other, considering the mood he's been in. I didn't see her. I just went to his room and heard their voices, so I didn't intrude."

Malcolm poured the vodka down his throat and said, "Well, I'm not so polite. Let's go upstairs and get him. Like I said, I don't think I can tell this story twice."

They went upstairs and walked to Jerry's door. Malcolm heard the gentle sound of a woman's laughter from within, and he smiled at Holly with amusement. He held the jewelry box tightly to his side with one arm as he knocked on the door. "Jerry, it's me. Sorry if I'm interrupting anything, but I have to talk to you."

The woman's laughter rose and she sang out, "Come in!"

Malcolm went white and began to tremble. He recognized the voice.

He flung open the door and rushed into the room, then froze at the sight before him. Lucy Westenra was kneeling on Jerry's bed, her mad eyes dancing with her laughter. She was wearing a simple peasant blouse and skirt, but the blouse had been pulled down from her breasts. She was holding Jerry Herman's head by the hair as his body lay sloping upward in a cobralike manner. Her breasts were covered with blood, and she was pressing his face against them, and he was gurgling audibly as the blood poured into his mouth and down his throat.

"Welcome to the nursery, dear Malcolm." She laughed, then with a movement bespeaking contempt, pushed Jerry away from her. "I can't thank you enough for all you have done for me."

"You can't be here," Malcolm whispered, his voice cracking and his knees growing weak. "You can't be here!"

"Oh, but I have been with you every step of the way, little Harker," she purred. She glanced down at Jerry Herman, who was paralyzed with shock, his open mouth streaming with her blood. "I hope you don't mind my dropping in like this, but"—and she frowned in consternation—"no one in this bloody village speaks English!"

A sudden surge of anger gave Malcolm back his strength, and he dove at her, but she raised one hand and grabbed him by the throat, bringing him to an abrupt stop. "Don't be a fool, Malcolm," she hissed, "or at least don't be a bigger one than you already are." She grabbed the jewelry box from him, then pushed him away as easily as if he had been a small child. "Did you seriously believe that I had any interest in helping you eliminate the power of the blood? Little idiot! I needed the master's dust for my own protection, not for yours!"

"Then . . . then . . ." he muttered, "the curse . . . the blood . . ."

"It is yours, my dear," she said, smiling. "Make the most of it." She pulled her blouse up over her breasts and it clung to the wet blood that covered her. "The master's blood gives me my power. If his dust is scattered, you would indeed be free of your, ah, interesting family situation, but then I would cease to awaken with the sunset." She laughed. "Oh, you are so easy to trick, you modern men! Van Helsing would never have believed me. He wouldn't even have spoken to me!"

Malcolm was having a difficult time accepting what he was hearing. "Then . . . then the dust does have a connection . . ."

"Of course it does, idiot!" She laughed. "The blood, the soil, the body. The Devil, the World, and our Flesh!" She wagged a finger at him reprovingly. "You don't read your Bible, Malcolm!"

Malcolm struggled to control his rage as Holly stood at the doorway, gazing at Lucy with undisguised dread. "But why?" he demanded. "Why have you done this? I don't understand!"

"I could not find the castle myself, little fool," she said. "I could not waste precious time following the instincts of my blood. It was difficult enough for me to manage to follow you from England to Rumania. No, I had to allow you to find the dust and bring it to me. I must keep the master's remains safe, for if his dust is scattered, my blood will leave me, and I will die yet again."

"You're already dead!" he screamed.

"Yes, confusing, isn't it!" She looked at Holly and smiled. "Once again, my dear, you seem to be the only human being in the room." Lucy walked over to the window and flung it open. She turned back to Malcolm and said, in a suddenly serious, even tone, "We hate life, don't you understand? We hate everyone who lives and loves and laughs with happiness. No, perhaps you do not understand. But be assured, Malcolm, someday you shall. Someday you shall." She turned from them and made ready to leap from the window, but Malcolm called out to her, desperate to keep her there, desperate not to allow her to leave with the remains of her ancient master.

"Lucy, wait!" he cried. "There is something you don't know. There's something I have to tell you!"

Lucy Westenra turned back to him impatiently. "I doubt that, little Harker, but if you have something to say, be quick about it."

Malcolm looked madly about the room, seeking something, anything that he could use as a weapon against her. "It's . . . it's something that happened to me when I went to collect the remains . . ." he stammered. His eyes fell upon a table beside the bed. On the table was half of an orange that Jerry had apparently been eating earlier in the day. Resting upon the plate beside the pile of orange peels was a knife. "It was when . . . when I touched the dust . . ." He moved as casually as possible toward the knife.

"Let me guess, my dear Malcolm," Lucy said, smiling. "You found that the blood has memories, did you not?"

This startled him, and he stopped briefly in his slow movement toward the knife. He started moving almost immediately, however, and he said, "Why didn't you tell me about that, if you knew about it?"

She laughed. "Why on earth should I have? I owe you nothing, you little fool!"

He reached the table and turned his back to Lucy so that she did not see as he picked up the knife. "But how did you know?" he asked as he hid the blade behind his slightly cupped palm and then turned to face her.

"Do you think the blood speaks to you alone?" she asked. "Really, Malcolm! You are such a fool. But enough of this nonsense. Is that all you had to say?"

He walked toward her, and behind his back, he moved the knife from his palm into the grip of his right hand. "No," he said. "There is this as well." With a motion faster than he would have thought himself capable, he swung his arm around and slammed the knife into Lucy's chest, burying the blade deep into her undead flesh.

She staggered back on the window ledge and seemed for a moment to lose her footing, but she never released her hold on the jewelry box. In an instant she was once again standing securely upon the ledge, and her eyes blazed red with fury as she reached up and grasped the handle of the knife. "You little worm!" she hissed. She pulled on the knife and it popped out of her with a flat, sucking sound. Lucy leaped from the ledge back into the room and approached Malcolm menacingly. "How dare you!" She reached out at him with her one free hand, still clutching the box with the other, and grabbed him by the throat.

Holly had been standing aside, frozen in a paralysis induced by fear, but the sight of Lucy's hand upon Malcolm's throat seemed to break her free from it. She ripped the small silver crucifix from the chain around her neck and ran forward to thrust it between Lucy's face and Malcolm's. Lucy recoiled immediately, screaming and spitting.

Lucy Westenra jumped back up onto the window ledge and cried, "Soon, little idiots, very soon, you shall pay for your impertinence!" Then she jumped from the window and seemed almost to take wing as she disappeared into the darkness, still holding the jewelry box that contained the remains of the founder of her inhuman line.

Malcolm had fallen to the floor when Lucy had released him, and he now moved on his hands and knees over to the bed. As he pulled himself up onto it, he placed his hand upon his friend's arm and said, "Jerry?"

Jerry Herman's nervous system seemed to have overloaded. He had lain motionless—but for the incessant shuddering of his stiff body—during the confrontation between Malcolm and Lucy. His mouth seemed to have been frozen open, and his tongue darted in and out in a frenzied, serpentine fashion.

"Jerry?" Malcolm repeated.

Jerry turned his head very slowly in Malcolm's direction, stared at him for a moment, and then began to scream. He screamed without stopping, without pausing. He was still screaming when the hotel manager strode angrily into the room, he was still screaming when the doctor arrived and plunged the needle into his arm, and he screamed right up to the moment when the sedative cast him into a blissful forgetfulness.

But they who drink from narcotic Lethe have no permanent escape from evil memories, and he awakened screaming the next day.

Chapter Thirteen

As he sat with his friends on the edge of the large fountain that stood before the Hotel Bernini in Rome, Malcolm knew that he should have felt at least a bit lucky. The Rumanian authorities had not wanted to take any actions or generate any publicity that might adversely affect the American tourist trade, so they chose to disregard Jerry's behavior in the hotel and in the hospital the next day. The voluntary and immediate departure of Malcolm and his party from Rumania aboard the next available plane had been sufficient to smooth the ruffled official feathers.

And old Quincy Harker, informed of the situation by a frenzied phone call from his grandson, had promptly wired yet more money for the Alitalia flight from Bucharest to Rome.

Yeah, real lucky, Malcolm thought. Twenty-four hours since Lucy stole the jewelry box, and here we are with a great suite of rooms in a luxury hotel, with two days of rest and relaxation and sight-seeing before our flight from Da Vinci Airport takes us back to Kennedy in New York.

Lucky as hell.

The argument was not convincing. Neither Malcolm nor Holly felt particularly lucky, and Jerry felt positively cursed—which is precisely what he was.

Jerry Herman looked over at Malcolm and said, "Mal? What are we gonna do? There's gotta be something we can do, isn't there?" His voice was weak and tremulous, and his shaking hands fidgeted incessantly.

Malcolm sighed and shook his head. "I don't know, Jerry. I honest to God don't know what to do next."

"We have to go home," Holly said, her customarily

steady, even voice now a whine. "We have to forget about this whole horrible thing, put it all behind us, just forget it!"

"Easy for you to say," Jerry muttered. "How am I supposed to forget it? How can either of us, me or Mal, forget it? Right, Mal? We have to *do* something!" The emotional shock that Jerry had sustained had rendered him incapable of the petulant rage with which he had greeted the first of Lucy's assaults. He now clung to Malcolm with a submissive devotion, desperately depending upon his friend to help extricate him from his situation.

Malcolm nodded. "We have to find Lucy, we have to get the dust away from her, and we have to scatter it."

"And we have to kill her, right? We have to kill her, don't we, Mal?" Jerry said eagerly in his trembling voice. "We have to *kill* her, we have to *kill* her, we have to beat a fuckin' *stake* into her goddamn fuckin' *heart*!"

Holly grabbed Jerry's hand and squeezed it. "Jerry, try to stay calm. Don't lose your grip. Try hard, Jerry."

"Yeah, yeah." He nodded, wiping the sweat from his brow and trying to smile as he jerked his head up and down spasmodically. "I'm okay, I'm okay, I'm okay."

"I think," Malcolm said slowly, "that you should go back to the U.S. without us, Holly. You aren't infected, so you might still be in danger. I think Jer and I should go back to England and see if we can find her there."

"Okay, fine with me," Holly said quickly. She firmly believed in standing beside her man, but there were limits.

"Why England?" Jerry asked. "Why not Timbuktu or Peking or fuckin' New Zealand or something? She could go anywhere she wants to go. I mean, she followed us all the way to Rumania, didn't she? Why would she go back to England?"

"Because that's where her grave is," Malcolm replied thoughtfully. "Remember, her coming to Rumania was a matter of necessity for her. She had to get hold of the remains of the one who made her a vampire in the first place, just to insure her own survival. But that doesn't mean that she had any desire or intention of leaving England, not permanently." He paused and thought further. "I wish I could figure out how she managed to move about with such ease from one place to another. I mean, when Dracula moved from Transylvania to England a century ago, he took months of preparation to do it. Where did she sleep? How did she travel?"

"Maybe she turned into a bat and flew," Jerry said. Two weeks ago this would have been a joke. Now it was a serious suggestion.

"No, remember what it says in the book, what Van Helsing said about their powers and limitations. They can't move over water. They have to be carried, as Dracula was, by ship."

"Or by plane," Holly said.

Malcolm considered this. "A night flight from London to Bucharest? A suitcase full of earth from Hempstead? Find somewhere secluded to rest during the day? It's possible."

"But where would she get the money?" Holly asked.

He sighed. "The same place she got her clothes, I imagine. From someone she killed."

Holly shuddered.

Jerry stood up and began pacing up and down in front of them. "Okay, okay, so we get Holly on board a plane, and then we go back to England. If we find her, we kill her, right?"

"It won't be necessary to do that if we retrieve the dust and scatter it," Malcolm said, "but if we find her, we should kill her anyway—just to be safe."

"Yeah, yeah"—Jerry nodded obsessively—"just to be safe."

"When we go to the airport tomorrow night, we'll cancel our two tickets and get a couple of reservations on a flight to London. Holly, you'll go on to New York."

Jerry breathed deeply. "Look, I can't sit around here watching the clock and waiting to leave. I got to walk around for a while. I'll see you later on, okay?" He began to walk away from them.

"Jerry," Malcolm called after him, "you okay?"

"Yeah, yeah, I just want to use up some energy, that's all," he called over his shoulder. "I'll see you around dinnertime."

"Jerry," Holly shouted, "it's way past dinnertime! It's nearly eight o'clock!"

"Okay, so for midnight snacks, okay?"

"Where are you gonna go?" she shouted louder at the retreating figure.

"I don't know," he shouted back. "Go see Michelangelo's Moses or something."

"Church'll be closed," Malcolm muttered. "He isn't going to that church to see that statue anyway. He's just got to wander around, look at stuff, try not to think about everything."

The summer sun was sinking low in the sky over Rome, and Holly glanced up at it as she asked, "Will he be all right? I mean, what if Lucy..."

"Followed us to Italy?" Malcolm finished for her. "I doubt that very much. She's got what she wanted. Why jeopardize herself by coming to Italy when she'll be safe in England, in surroundings she knows?"

Holly nodded, wishing to agree with him and forcing herself to do so. "I'm hungry," she said after an interval of silence. "Are you hungry? I wish Jerry hadn't mentioned dinner!"

"Yeah, a little, I guess," he said. "Want to get something to eat?"

"Yeah, I do. And you need something to eat, Mal. You're gonna waste away to nothing, the way you've been just picking at your food." She realized as soon as she made the observation that she should have kept it to herself. They both knew the reason for the reduction in his appetite.

Four hours later they lay silently in the cool darkness of their hotel room, resting in each other's arms, each lost in private reveries. Holly was in a reasonably happy state of mind, considering the circumstances. At dinner Malcolm had eaten but little, but the quantities of wine that they had consumed during and after dinner had seemed to lift his spirits somewhat. It was as if he were a man with a serious illness who was cast into a deep depression for as long as the nature of the disease and the nature of its treatment remained unclear to him, but who, once diagnosis and prognosis had been pronounced, strove to remain cheerful and to avoid thinking of the operation to come. He smiled more frequently than he probably wished to and even ventured a few amusing remarks. Holly seized upon them as a starving woman would a hot meal, and her response to his limited conviviality inspired him to more.

Now, lying quietly in their room, the muted sounds of people and buses and automobiles on the street below reminding them of the potential for life and happiness, they were more content than either of them had been for many days. Holly ventured to roll over and kiss him, and when to her surprise his tongue insinuated itself between her lips, she responded enthusiastically.

Malcolm felt the familiar tingling in his loins, and his hands gently sought out her breasts beneath the soft silk of her blouse. The old Arab epigram drifted into his mind, that God invented silk so that women could be naked in clothes, and he squeezed her cool, soft breasts with careful intensity.

The Arabs... akin to the Turks in religion and culture... akin to Sultan Murad... STOP IT... STOP IT... NO SUCH THOUGHTS NOW...

"Oh, Malcolm," she sighed.

"Holly," he murmured, kissing her eyes and her cheeks and her lips, feeling her hand gently move to the thickening bulge between his legs and massage it slowly, causing his still-half-flaccid organ to become further engorged with blood, with sweet red blood, with hot, pulsing streams of blood...

NO... NO... NO SUCH THOUGHTS... STOP IT...

He drove the unwanted ideas from his mind and concentrated on the beautiful woman who was lying beside him. She unbuttoned her blouse and tossed it away as he reached behind her and unsnapped her bra. He buried his face between her breasts and kissed them and licked them and sucked on them... it was just like... just like...

JERRY AND LUCY... JERRY AND LUCY... NO ... NO... STOP...

She dropped her skirt to the floor and then opened his belt buckle. In a few moments they were naked, pressed together in an embrace of rapidly deepening passion, their hands running up and down each other's body, their tongues and lips exploring each other gently. Malcolm moved above her and began to kiss her as she spread her knees apart beneath him and closed her eyes in a brief spasm of anticipatory pleasure. He kissed her lips as she took his erect organ in her hands and began to guide it into her, and his kisses moved down from her lips to her chin and from her lips to her throat, to her throat, and his erection shriveled to nothing as he kissed her throat, as he tasted the sweet sweat on her throat, as he heard the blood pounding through the veins and the arteries in her throat—and her throat was white and long and rich and filled with blood. His blood called to him to taste her blood, to drink her rich, sweet, red blood, and his blood told him where to strike, and his blood cried out for more blood, for blood, for blood. She was cattle, she was food, she was redolent of blood, she was filled with blood, she was nothing to him but a cow with blood in her udder, a cow to be milked for her blood, for her life-giving blood. He grabbed her by the hair and pulled her head back, and it was as if he could see the blood coursing through the channels just beneath the skin of her throat; just there, just there, in that spot, the white spot, just there, and that was where he was to strike, that was where his teeth would sink into her warm, living flesh and suck out the warm, living blood. He wanted her blood, he needed her blood, and his own blood cried out to him to kill her, to kill her, to kill her...

Malcolm pushed Holly away from him as he jumped backward away from the bed and stared at her in abject terror and self-loathing. She returned his gaze with one of confusion. "Honey, what is it? What's wrong?" He grabbed his pants and shirt and pulled on his clothes and his shoes and ran for the door. "Malcolm!" she cried. "What is it? Malcolm? Malcolm!"

He slammed the door behind him.

Malcolm wandered the streets of Rome through the dark hours after midnight, terrified at the sounds and smells around him. Much as he fought against the sensation, each person whom he passed smelled like food, and the smell of food was the smell of blood, and the blood that ran through his own veins was calling out to him in a voice that he could not still.

It was the dust of the Count, he reasoned madly as he ran wildly down the Roman streets. My blood came into contact with the remains, and I've awakened the blood, I've awakened it! I came to Europe seeking to end this curse, this bastard inheritance, and all I've done is worsen it. I've delivered the only hope of my salvation into the hands of a creature more deeply cursed than I. Damn her, damn her!

The need was overpowering him, and the smell of blood was so thick around each person he passed that he was scarcely able to keep his hands from reaching out and grasping them by their necks. Their warm, rich flesh called out to him. The blood surging through the veins in their throats called out to him.

He ran and ran for what seemed to be hours, until at last he collapsed, exhausted and barely able to breathe. He crawled over to an alleyway and sat back against the hard stone wall of one of the buildings bordering on the alley. Malcolm began to weep and pray, sobbing incoherently. *All I had to do was just go to church and take the sacrament,* he thought in his misery. *That's all I had to do, just listen to my grandfather. And now I've awakened an evil within me; I've inflicted it upon my best friend and nearly killed the girl I love. I've released a murdering monster...*

Malcolm was so deeply lost in his self-recriminations that he did not hear the clicking of the high heels as they approached him. He looked up when he heard the soft, inviting voice addressing him in melodious Italian.

A girl of no more than twenty stood over him, smiling down at him and speaking words which he could not understand. She was dark haired and pale in the dim street lighting, long-legged and malnourished beneath her excessive makeup. She wore a very skimpy halter top through which the points of her nipples were clearly visible, and the tone of her voice and the smile of feigned lasciviousness told him that she was a streetwalker hoping to roll what she assumed to be a drunk.

He got to his feet, swaying slightly upon his tired, rubbery legs, and he inhaled deeply of the sweet smell of blood that she exuded. She continued to speak to him in her soft, seductive voice as she ran her fingers enticingly over his body, seeking his wallet. He ignored her hands, he ignored her voice. All he was aware of was the smell of the young woman, a smell of food. He gazed at her for a few moments as the predatory urge welled up in him with overpowering force. He fought against the urge. He resisted it. And then he surrendered to it.

And he felt himself swept up and away once again by the enveloping mists of time, and the sense of emptiness returned as he was cast into the black maelstrom of evil remembrance. Malcolm shook his head and rubbed his face, grateful that he had feeling and presence of mind; but then he noticed that his hair was much thicker and much longer than it should have been; that his upper lip was covered by a thick mustache; that he was wearing chain-mail armor over a caftan of purest silk; that he was standing alone in the dark, silent room, his left hand resting upon the hilt of the sword which hung from the leather belt that encircled his waist. He knew that it was the year 1459, and that he, Vlad Tepes, Voivode of Wallachia, was about to take a dangerous gamble, one which might lead to his death—or to more power than he had ever dreamed of possessing. If he failed, the sultan would have him skinned and raise his hide from a flagpole above the citadel at Stambul; if he succeeded, he would have the armies of the Hapsburgs and their European allies beside him in a war to destroy the Turks; and if *that* enterprise were to prosper, he, Vlad IV of Wallachia, might well become Vlad I, Emperor of a restored Byzantine realm.

"Ordogh," he whispered. "Come to me."

A few long moments passed, then the voice said, "I am here, Little Dragon."

"I need your advice, Ordogh," the Voivode said. "Do you know of my intentions?"

"They are obvious, Little Dragon. I see a great feast beginning in the courtyard of your fortress. I see fifty sharpened stakes implanted in a large circle around the tables. I see the banners of Corvinus, the Hungarian king, flying from the poles above the battlements, and I see no banners bearing the crescent of the Turks."

The Voivode laughed, but there was no amusement in his laughter. "I do not need you to tell me that which any ignorant peasant can surmise, Ordogh. I need you to tell me if the path I am turning toward will lead me to imperial purple or to a traitor's death. You can pierce the veil of the future, Ordogh, this I know. Tell me what is to be."

The voice seemed to sigh as it replied, "And have you been my servant for so long and yet do not understand, Little Dragon? I am no Gypsy fortune-teller. Turn down whatever path you choose. All paths of all men lead to the grave and the dust of death."

"Yes," the Voivode said irritably, "but one may die tomorrow or in fifty years. Time is meaningless to you, Ordogh, but not to me."

"And would you have it be meaningless to you also, Little Dragon?" the voice asked. "Would you like to be as unconcerned about the turning of the wheel of time as I?"

The Voivode frowned. "What are you talking about, Ordogh?"

The voice did not reply at first. After a long silence, it said, "No, Little Dragon, the time is not yet. Later, many years from now, we shall discuss this again."

"Many years from now?" the Voivode asked, smiling. "Then I shall triumph, shall I not, Ordogh?"

"That have I not said, Little Dragon," the voice replied. "But I can tell you that, win or lose, this risk will not lead to death."

The Voivode paused, reflecting upon this. "A man may risk all, knowing that death does not await him. Only death can make a man irresolute." He laughed. "I thank you, Ordogh, for your speech. I go now unto my allies and my enemies."

"You please me greatly, Little Dragon," the voice said, fading away even as it whispered in his ear. "I await the cries of agony and the howls of pain." And then the voice was gone.

The Voivode strode out of the dark, silent room and walked in contemplative silence through the corridors of the castle, making his way toward the huge oaken doors which led to the great courtyard without. *I shall not see death because of this*, he thought. *Then it is worth the risk.*

Final preparations for the feast had been finished as he stood in the empty room communing with the dark spirit, and his wives, Magda and Katarina, who had supervised the arrangements, curtsied to him as he walked out into the courtyard. He shot each a curt bow. They withdrew as soon as he entered the courtyard, for the feast was to be for men alone. He took his seat in the large chair upon the dais and nodded to his chamberlain.

As his servant went to summon the guests, the Voivode sat back and surveyed the scene before him. His soldiers, clad in full battle gear, stood in tightly packed lines against all four walls enclosing the courtyard. The long rectangular tables, some thirty in number, were set with golden plates and golden wine goblets, bowls of fruit and generous hunks of bread and cheese. The roasts would be brought in by the servants once his guests were seated. In the center of the courtyard, a fire was burning upon an iron platform designed for the purpose, and torches flickered from their holders along the walls.

And fluttering above the battlements of the castle were the banners bearing the crimson dragon that was the heraldic symbol of his house, and the two-headed eagle of the King of Hungary, Matthias Corvinus. The star and crescent of the Sultan Mohammed II, the Voivode's supposed master, were nowhere to be seen.

His guests, their retainers, and their pitiful handful of

personal guards entered the courtyard warily. Leading the entering procession was Kemal Pasha, the cousin of the Sultan. The pasha was a wiry, olive-skinned man with eyes of an oriental cast. His scarred face and slight limp proclaimed him a fearsome warrior, not a soft sycophant from Istanbul. With him was his youngest son, Mustafa, and behind them came his guards, each attired in Ottoman battle gear, each with his hand nervously clasping the hilt of his scimitar.

"Voivode!" Kemal Pasha shouted as he strode imperiously forward. "I demand a reply! I'll not feast and make merry with you until you declare yourself and remove those insulting banners!"

The Voivode rose and made an obsequious bow. "Beloved of Allah, I beg that you have patience! I did not know that the Magyar king would send his esteemed representatives to me at the same time that your illustrious self chose to honor me with your presence!"

"You lie, Voivode!" the pasha said bitterly. The soldiers glanced at each other with amusement, knowing that it was not safe to speak thus to the Voivode in his own fortress. "My eldest son, Orkhan, came to you two weeks ago and told you I would be here on this day!"

"And yet he did not arrive, Illustrious One," the Voivode replied, his voice dripping with honest concern. "Nor did any messengers from Corvinus! It was a surprise to me—a great honor, but a surprise—when you arrived in the morning and Duke Stephan arrived in the afternoon. My women have been all the day trying to make ready the . . . ah"—he paused—"here is Duke Stephan now." The Voivode bowed low to the Hungarian nobleman, the trusted adviser to King Matthias Corvinus the Just.

Duke Stephan was only slightly older than the Voivode, for Vlad had not yet reached thirty and Stephan had only recently passed it. Stephan could not accurately be described as a dandy—for no such creature would have survived life among the warrior aristocracy—but there was an air of precision about him. His beard was just a bit too carefully clipped, boot thongs just a bit too carefully tied, fingernails just slightly too long. Kemal Pasha despised him for his appearance, his nationality, and his religion; and he deeply resented the presence of an ally of Corvinus here in the fortress of a vassal of the sultan.

"Hail, Vlad, My Lord," Stephan said cheerfully as he

walked forward and clasped the Voivode's hand fraternally. He ignored Kemal completely.

"Your Grace," the Voivode said with equal good humor. "Allow me to present to you Kemal Pasha, trusted servant of His Islamic Majesty."

Duke Stephan and Kemal Pasha exchanged curt bows. The Turk then turned to the Voivode and said, "Enough of this, Voivode. I demand an answer and an explanation."

The Voivode raised his hand and said, "Please, Illustrious One! The amenities! We must dine. All will be made clear."

Kemal Pasha would have protested further, but everyone began to take seats at the tables. Amid the loud bustle of voices that ensued, he thought the better of it. He sat down disgruntledly at the table beside the Voivode, noticing with irritation that the Hungarian seated himself on the other side of the sultan's mercurial vassal.

Vlad made a few casual introductions of the people who were seated at his table upon the dais, then said to the pasha, "I don't believe I have met your aide, Illustrious One." He smiled amicably at the young Turk who had accompanied the pasha and his son, and who had thus far remained quietly attentive.

Kemal snorted. "This is my nephew, Torghuz."

"Torghuz Beg," the young man reminded him. He turned to the Voivode and inclined his head slightly. "You honor me with your hospitality, Beloved of the Sultan."

"And you do me honor with your presence, Torghuz Beg. Is this your first expedition to the Balkans?"

Torghuz laughed. "No, Voivode. I fought at the siege of Constantinople six years ago, and fought at the siege of Belgrade a few years later."

"Interesting," Duke Stephan interjected, leaning forward from his side of the table and looking over at the Turk. "I too was at Belgrade. My late master Hunyadi dealt you quite a blow at that battle, as I recall." The duke smiled as he spoke, but this reference to a major Turkish defeat was obviously designed to be provocative.

Torghuz Beg refused to be provoked. He laughed and replied, "Yes, the crows grew fat on the remains of both our armies. Empires rise and fall, and the only true victors are the birds."

The Voivode laughed. "And yet some empires last longer

than others, my dear Beg. You Ottomans have had an interesting century, but it may be that the tide has already turned against you."

Torghuz shrugged. "If that is Allah's will, then so be it. But I think not. We have Constantinople, we have taken the Morea and slaughtered Greeks by the tens of thousands. Soon enough we will advance again. Soon enough."

"It is ordained," Kemal Pasha said angrily. "We shall sweep away the corrupt and degenerate Christian kingdoms and establish Allah's rule in all the lands of the earth."

Torghuz Beg glanced over at the Voivode as the pasha was speaking, and the twinkle in his eye told the Voivode that he regarded his uncle as an ignorant fanatic. Vlad repressed the urge to smile as he returned the beg's amused glance. He formed the opinion that the Turk was as amoral and pragmatic as he, with no concern for divine destinies or spiritual imperatives.

The feast progressed into the night, and the odd mixture of Magyar and Turk under the watchful eye of Wallachian soldiers did not result in the violence that so volatile a combination might have been expected to engender. A huge suckling pig was provided for the Hungarians and Rumanians in attendance, and the Voivode offered the Moslems a spicy stew of uncertain contents that he assured his guests was not pork.

At last Kemal Pasha had reached the limits of his patience. As the torches began to flicker low in the cool night sky, the Turkish envoy turned to the Voivode and demanded, "We have had our meal, Vlad, and social propriety has been observed. Now I insist that you answer the question that I have been sent here to ask you."

"And what question is that?" Duke Stephan asked casually, sipping wine from a golden goblet.

"Be still, Magyar dog!" the pasha spat. Stephan smiled calmly at him.

"The problem, my dear Stephan," the Voivode said, "is that for some reason or other, the tribute that I send to the sultan each year has not yet arrived."

"It has not been sent, Voivode!" the pasha shouted. "My master is patient and long-suffering, but he will not await the payment of the tribute much longer!"

"Yes, yes," Vlad said seriously, nodding in concern and

frowning in consternation. "But that's the problem, you see, my dear Pasha. I have no intention of paying it."

Kemal began to grow red in the face. "You young idiot... you disloyal, ungrateful..." he sputtered. "What do you mean by this!"

Vlad heard Torghuz Beg laughing softly, and he said to him, "I believe that the beg knows. Why don't you explain it to your uncle?"

The younger Turk sighed and smiled. "It has been obvious since the moment we arrived, Uncle. The Voivode has turned from the sultan to the king of Hungary. He is making common cause with the Christian princes against us, and we here in this castle are all dead men."

Kemal Pasha stared at his nephew in astonishment. "We are the special emissaries of the sultan himself! Our persons are inviolate!"

Torghuz Beg nodded in agreement. "Yes, to be sure. That is the reason why we are to be killed. It will make the Voivode's point all the better."

"Excellently reasoned, Beg," the Voivode said, liking the Turk enormously. "But for someone facing death, you are quite calm and unconcerned!"

The beg shrugged. "If I am to die, then I am to die. Becoming upset would merely have interfered with enjoying my dinner."

"By God, you are a man, Torghuz Beg!" The Voivode laughed. "But apparently you did *not* enjoy your dinner. I watched, and you ate very little."

Torghuz Beg reached out and took a goblet of wine. He ignored his uncle's angry protests at his violation of Islamic law and drank deeply of the sweet Rumanian vintage. "It was the meat, Voivode. I disliked the taste."

"Enough of this!" Kemal Pasha shouted, jumping to his feet. His movement was emulated by the guards who had accompanied him, and they rose from their table and drew their swords. "Voivode, in the name of the Beloved of Allah, Mohammed II, I depose you!"

The Voivode snapped his fingers, and the hundreds of soldiers who had been standing silently along the walls throughout the night disarmed the handful of Turkish guards in a matter of minutes. The Voivode smiled at the pasha. "I think not, Illustrious One." He nodded at one of his officers, and a detachment of soldiers sprang up to the dais and dragged Kemal from his place. They grabbed Torghuz Beg as well, but the Voivode said sharply, "Not him. Leave him where he is."

A slight glimmer of relief flickered in the beg's eyes, but he masked it with amused bravado. "I trust that this reprieve may someday become a pardon, Voivode?"

"Indeed," Vlad replied, smiling. "I need someone to take a message to the sultan. I have chosen you to do so."

This time the relief was evident. "May Allah bless you, Voivode."

"Allah can keep his blessings," the Voivode said. "I cast off the Moslem faith with the Moslem yoke." He stepped down from the dais and approached the pasha, held by two burly Serbs. "I am sorry about this, my dear Pasha," he said, smiling with total insincerity. "But this is, after all, war."

"You will not dare to harm me!" the pasha screamed. "The sultan will avenge me! My sons will avenge me!"

"Your sons!" the Voivode replied. "But your youngest is here, and will die with you."

"My eldest, Orkhan . . . !"

"Ah, yes, Orkhan. Now that I think about it, he did indeed come here a short while ago."

The pasha blanched. "What . . . ? Where . . . ? What have you done to him? Where is he?"

The Voivode leaned forward, stared the pasha directly in the eyes, and smiled sweetly. "I put him in the stew. All I had to serve you for meat was that delicious pig, and I did not wish to offend your religious sensitivities." He turned and nodded curtly to one of his officers, and the executions began.

The feast continued for many hours, its background music the agonized screams of dozens of Turks, their mutilated bodies skewered upon dozens of long wooden stakes, their dripping blood making slick and shiny the cold gray stone of the courtyard. Kemal Pasha died the moment the rough-hewn tip was thrust into his aged frame, but many of his guards lingered on for hours.

Upon the dais, Voivode Vlad IV of Wallachia smiled. He had noticed the nauseated pallor that had spread over the face of Duke Stephan as the executions began, and he was slightly annoyed at the Hungarian's lack of fortitude. Torghuz Beg, on the other hand, seemed almost to be enjoying himself, though his cheer may very well have been a result of his presence upon a chair and not upon a stake.

"You will inform the sultan of the events of this night," the Voivode commanded.

"As you wish," the beg replied.

"And you, my dear Duke," he said, turning to the Hungarian, "make certain, if you please, that King Matthias knows that I have cemented my alliance with him with the blood of Turks."

"I shall do so, Voivode," Duke Stephan agreed. "And I shall tell him of the horror of your vengeance against your enemies."

The Voivode shrugged. "These poor men are not my enemies, Your Grace. They are pawns, nothing more. And this is not vengeance." He sat back upon his chair and smiled malevolently. "This is pleasure. . . ."

And the mist swept the scene away and the years passed in fluid silence. Images of battle and victory and defeat floated past Malcolm's consciousness. He watched as he, Vlad, knelt before a bearded Orthodox patriarch and repented of his apostasy. He heard the frenzied cheers of crowds of Carpathian nobles as they hailed him as their savior, as the man destined by God to restore the Byzantine Empire. He watched as the year 1462 arrived and he led a host across the Danube in an invasion of the territories held under the Ottoman scepter. He watched as the banners bearing the bloodred dragon rode into combat against the crescent and the star, and he saw his armies slaughtered by the Turkish hosts under the command of Torghuz Beg.

He saw himself fleeing once more, fleeing from Wallachia even as he had done after losing his throne the first time so many years before, fleeing to the presumed safety of the protection of the Hungarian king; and he saw himself betrayed by the Magyars, imprisoned by King Matthias Corvinus, imprisoned for his failure, for his barbarism, for his lust for death; imprisoned as a heretic, an apostate, a sorcerer, and most importantly, as a hostage, an expendable pawn in the ongoing chess game between the king of Hungary and the sultan of the Ottoman Empire. The king cared little for him one way or the other. The sultan wanted very much to torture him to death.

He was bitter and angry, and he was filled with frustration and hatred. He grew even colder than he had been, and his cruelty grew apace. And as the years passed he remained a prisoner of the Hungarians.

And then there was screaming and the sensation of a fist striking his cheek. Malcolm Harker found himself once again standing upon the cobblestones of the alleyway in Rome. He was confused and disoriented, but another blow to his face brought him back to awareness.

He found himself struggling violently with the young prostitute. He had nipped her on the throat, and he could taste the bittersweet blood upon his lips. The girl was screaming and beating his face with her fists. He relaxed his grip instantly, but the terrified girl continued to flail away at him.

Malcolm ran from the alleyway, pushing his way through the crowd that was gathering to investigate the cries. He ran on as fast as his legs could carry him, without direction, without looking back to see if he was being pursued. He ran for block after block, as if he were attempting to escape from himself.

Christ help me! he thought as he ran. Christ help me! I can't control it! The memories, the power of the blood—I can't control either of them! The dust is hundreds of miles away from here, but that doesn't matter, because the blood is awake! The blood is awake! He felt filthy and polluted and diseased.

He ran until he came to a small church—one of the thousands of small churches that proliferate in Rome, dwarfed by the basilicas and largely unfrequented by tourists. He stopped suddenly in front of the church, panting and breathing hard. He heard one weak voice chanting within, and his nostrils detected the faint aroma of incense.

Mass! he thought. They are saying mass!

It was true, what Lucy Westenra had told him. His body was polluted with unholy blood, and only the regular infusion of the exact opposite could hold the power of the blood in check. He remembered the excruciating pain he had experienced when he went to communion a short while before, back home in Forest Hills, and he braced himself for what he knew he had to do.

I have to burn this pollution away. I don't care about the pain, I don't care about the agony. Only the blood of Christ can help me. Only the blood of Christ . . .

Malcolm knew that he was not thinking clearly, but he also knew that what he planned to do was necessary. He noticed as he entered the dimly lighted church that no one was in attendance other than an old priest and a rather tired-looking altar boy. Roman Catholic doctrine taught that the mass is more than a worship service; it is an ongoing sacrifice and must be held even if only the priest is present.

Malcolm strode with a mad, intense determination up the central aisle of the little church. The priest saw him coming and he smiled, assuming that Malcolm had come in to receive the sacrament.

The priest's smile faded into a look of anger, then confusion, then fear, as Malcolm ran up the steps, past the altar railing, and into the very chancel itself. He pushed the priest away from the altar and sent the altar boy running from the church with a sharp kick to the rump. Malcolm grabbed the chalice of consecrated wine from the altar and drained it with one draught, pouring the sacred liquid down his throat. It burned like fire, it ate into him, but he did not care, he welcomed the pain as a wounded man might welcome the cauterizing pain of the hot iron. He dropped the chalice to the floor and then grabbed the host from the small silver plate upon which it lay, and he stuffed it into his mouth, muttering, "Heal me, save me, forgive me..." and then screamed at the agony. He grabbed the small silver vessel in which additional wine was held for the Eucharist and he raised it to his lips. "Jesus, help me, help me!" he cried, then poured the wine into his mouth. The pain so intense that he doubled over, he reached out mindlessly to grab anything that he might hold on to. His hands grasped the crucifix which stood upon the altar, and the last thing he noticed before sinking into unconsciousness was the smell of the flesh of his hands sizzling.

Dawn found him stumbling past the fountain in the piazza before his hotel. The old priest, a man of care and compassion, had not summoned the police but had rather attempted to minister to the obviously disturbed young man as best he could. He had hugged Malcolm to him soothingly as the young man wept, saying words of comfort. Malcolm, still racked with pain, had stumbled out of the church and wandered aimlessly around the city, coming at last to the door of his hotel as the sun began its ascent.

He ignored the desk clerks and the porters as he made his way up to the room he and Holly had taken for the two days they would be in Rome, and he put his key into the latch with scarred, trembling hands.

Holly awaited him within, her face a study in sorrow and concern. "Are you all right?" she asked softly.

He shook his head slowly. "Last night... last night..."

"Don't think about last night," she said, not realizing the heinous act to which he was referring. "It doesn't matter. Just tell me if you're all right."

"I burned myself," he rasped through his scalded, blistering throat. "At a church... communion..."

She nodded, understanding what he was trying to tell her. "Do you want to go to a hospital?"

He shook his head. "No help... no help... Holly, I..."

"Stop, Mal," she said, her voice quite serious and even. "As long as you're not injured seriously, then I have something to say." She seemed to take a deep breath. "I'm going home, today, if I can arrange it, and when I'm home, I don't think we should see each other anymore. It's just too much, Mal, it's just too much. I feel guilty, like I'm leaving you in a lurch or something, but I'm sorry, I just—" She seemed to be struggling against herself not to cry.

"Holly..." he said miserably.

"No, Malcolm, please don't say anything. I just can't take it anymore, I just can't."

"Holly..." he repeated, and was then interrupted by a knock on the door. He opened it and a bellboy bowed slightly to him as he handed him a folded piece of paper. Malcolm closed the door, forgetting the tip that the bellboy so obviously expected to receive, then unfolded the paper and read it silently. He began to shake his head and mutter, "Stupid, stupid ass! My God, he can't mean it!"

Holly walked over to him. "What is it, Malcolm?"

He handed the paper to her and then sat down on the bed, weeping and pressing his clenched fists to his forehead. Holly looked at the paper, allowing her eyes to drop down to the scrawled signature before reading the body of the message. It was a note from Jerry Herman, which began without a salutation and was obviously written in haste:

> She found me last night near the Colosseum. She's
> been following us, she's been with us all along. I
> have to help her, I don't have any choice. I'm sorry,
> I don't have any choice. She wants to ship English

and Rumanian dirt to New York, she wants to go to America, I have to help her get there, I don't have any choice. She says that if I help her, she'll release me, let me go, take her blood out of me somehow. It's my only hope, don't you see? I'm sorry, I don't have any choice.

Holly sighed. "Poor Jerry." She looked over at Malcolm. "She isn't telling him the truth, is she."

"Of course not," he said. "She's enslaved him, and she'll keep control of him until he dies, and then he'll become like her, he'll become like *us*!"

She frowned. "What do you mean, like us?"

"You see what she's doing, don't you? It's my family, me and my sister and my grandfather. *They're* in New York, *they're* the ones he wants!"

"The ones he wants?" she echoed with confusion. "The ones who wants? Jerry?"

"Dracula!" he shouted. "He still exists, in Lucy Westenra, and in me and my grandfather and my sister! He's reaching out from beyond his own death to avenge himself on my family, to take revenge upon my great-grandparents." He fell suddenly silent, and as he stared down at the burns upon his hands, his face grew suddenly strong and determined.

Holly stared at him apprehensively, and at last she asked, "Malcolm? What are you thinking?"

"Then that's what it shall be," he whispered to himself, not hearing her question. "I know where she's going, and why. I know where his blood is leading her, and I know why it is leading her there." He began to walk to the door. "My great-grandparents and their friends destroyed him once. He *can* be beaten! He *can* be beaten!"

"Where are you going?" she asked.

"To church," he replied, "to any church. I'm going to take the sacrament all day, all night, too, if need be. In a city like Rome there must be hundreds of churches, and they must say thousands of masses each day. I'm going to take communion until the pain stops, until I've purged myself, until I've brought this damn thing under control. Lucy is going to America, and I have to be ready for her. I have to be ready for *him*."

He closed the hotel door behind him, leaving the sad, frightened young woman in the room alone. He did not ask her to come with him. He did not want her to come with him. The image of the woman he had attacked was burned into his memory, and he wanted to pose no threat to Holly.

She did not understand this, of course. As she sat and stared morosely at the closed door, she thought, poor Malcolm. I wish I could help him. I wish I could love him.

She sighed inwardly. But I just can't take any more of this.

Chapter Fourteen

The taxi ride from Kennedy Airport in south Queens back to Forest Hills was as strained and as void of conversation as had been the long transatlantic flight from Europe. Holly had made her decision, and much as it grieved him, Malcolm understood. They were not wed; no vows had been exchanged; marital obligations of support in all things "for better or worse" did not bind her. And even if they had, Malcolm would have understood her reluctance. This was not a matter of conventional disease or the normal vicissitudes of fortune; thanks to Malcolm's misdirected efforts, a blood-thirsty monster was probably trailing them at this very moment. And Holly was of course aware of the fact that any children whom Malcolm might someday beget would inherit the same terrible legacy with which he was afflicted.

Thus he did not attempt to win her back or woo her with soft words and sweet promises. He did not tell her what he had done that night in Rome, but neither did he attempt to minimize the severity of his problem. They spoke but little all the way from Da Vinci Airport to Kennedy, and in the taxi that took them back to Forest Hills, they spoke not at all.

As they drew near Continental Avenue, Malcolm coughed and said, "I think maybe my grandfather would like to see you, say hello, something like that, if you don't mind. I'll walk you back to your apartment afterward."

"Sure, Mal," she said quietly. "Your grandfather's a kind old man. I'd like to say hello to him, too." Malcolm leaned forward to give a brief instruction to the cabdriver, and they turned toward Granville Place. It was early evening, and the streetlamps had just switched on as the sun disappeared behind the horizon. Malcolm noticed what he thought was chill in the air, unusual for midsummer; but then upon reflection he realized that it was he, not the air, that was cold.

The realization unnerved him. He was certain that the pain he had suffered that last day in Rome, when he had consumed the consecrated host hour after hour in church after church until at last the pain receded and then ceased, had restored to him the dominance of his own humanity over the pollution in his veins. But he was still weak beneath the sunshine and vigorous beneath the moon. He still felt no great hunger pangs when he should have, still had to force himself to eat food. The chill in his bones was unnatural and threatening.

The cab pulled to the curb before Malcolm's home, and he and Holly went quietly up to the front door. The driver walked behind them, carrying the two suitcases, assuming that anyone living in Forest Hills Gardens would likely be a big tipper. He was not mistaken, for Malcolm absentmindedly handed him a twenty-dollar bill and then turned to unlock the door, ignoring the driver's instinctive motion to make change.

Malcolm and Holly entered the oddly silent foyer of the large house. This early in the evening old Quincy should have been sitting in the den, watching the news, but there were no sounds whatsoever. They walked into the sitting room and found Malcolm's sister slumped down in a large easy chair, staring pensively off into space. Rachel turned as she heard their footsteps, and she rose as they entered.

Malcolm came up to her and looked closely at her face, at the tear-reddened eyes, the lined, sorrowfully downturned mouth. He had spared but little time for thought about Rachel over the past few weeks, and he felt now as if he were seeing her for the first time. All these years, while he was growing up in blissful ignorance, she had borne the burden of their terrible secret. She had guarded him, fretted over him, and loved him, all the while he had indulged in adolescent rebelliousness and insensitivity. As he looked into her eyes now, he felt an emotion combining guilt and love and understanding, and he knew that he needed her as much as she needed him. They were bound together by the curse, heirs of the selfsame plague, siblings of unnatural descent.

Something seemed to break in Malcolm's throat as he tried to speak, and he was unable to restrain himself from weeping. Rachel took him in her arms and hugged him tightly, stroking his head as she pressed it down upon her shoulder, whispering to him through her own tears.

Holly stood aside quietly and respectfully. Feeling the tears welling up in her own eyes, she fought them down. After a few moments Rachel looked over at her and smiled sadly. "Hello, Miss Larsen," she said. "I'm sorry you had to become involved in this."

"I know," Holly replied softly. "And I'm very, very sorry, too, Rachel. I'm sorry for the things I said to you."

"Where's Gramps?" Malcolm sniffed. "Where's Daniel?"

Rachel sighed. "Grandfather is in his room, resting. He's very ill, Malcolm. I think that the worry and tension ever since you left has, well, weakened him beyond recovery."

Malcolm sank down into a chair and shook his head, thinking, he's going to die. And it will be my fault.

As if sensing his thoughts, Rachel added, "He's a very old man, Malcolm. You mustn't reproach yourself. This time would have come eventually anyway."

Malcolm nodded, not wishing to argue about it. "And Daniel?"

Rachel sat down also. "He's gone. Left me. Walked out." Her face was a stoic mask, and only her brother could have seen the hurt and anger that she hid behind it.

"But why?" Holly asked. "You and he seemed so . . . well, so good together."

Rachel laughed bitterly. "You know most of the truth about our family, Miss Larsen, so you might as well know it all. I resolved early in my life that I would never have children, never pass this . . . this *disease* on to anyone else. I had an operation years ago, a tubal ligation, so that there would be no chance of my becoming pregnant. I met Daniel at church, and as we got to know each other, I learned that he didn't want children. Perfect for me, in other words. I married him because I wanted companionship. He married me because I'm affluent and come from a respectable family." She laughed again, softly. "A respectable family!" She shook her head, amused at the irony, then continued, "We never loved each other, not in the way that . . . well, not in the conventional sense. Ours was a marriage of convenience on both sides."

"But why did he leave you?" Malcolm asked.

"Why do you think?" she replied bitterly. "After you called us and told us what had happened with Lucy Westenra, I decided that Daniel best be told the whole truth. I expected him to be shocked and disturbed, but he was furious, outraged. We argued terribly, and he said some absolutely horrible things to me. And then he packed his bags and left."

"So much for the 'better or worse' stuff," Malcolm muttered.

Holly felt herself growing angry for Rachel. "That bastard!" she said.

"Yes," Rachel agreed. "We've been married for ten years. I expected better of him than this."

Malcolm closed his eyes and sighed. "I'm sorry, truly I am. This is my fault, too. It's all my fault." He pounded his fist angrily onto the arm of the chair.

Rachel reached over and placed her hand on his arm. "Malcolm," she said kindly, "stop all this nonsense. None of it is your fault. It's all that monster's fault, that damned beast's fault!" Her voice became suddenly tremulous. "I pray that God tortures him for all eternity!"

"Rachel, please," Malcolm said quickly. "We can't afford to get upset, not now. We have to be calm, rational." He was attempting to be strong, though his own anger and sorrow were overwhelming. "We have another problem."

Rachel looked at him, surprised. "Another problem? You mean, besides our condition?"

He nodded. "Before we left England, Lucy bit my friend Jerry. She trailed us to Rumania, and she made him drink her blood."

Rachel recoiled from the words and sank back into her chair. "Lord, have mercy!"

"She followed us to Rome. I told Gramps on the phone that she took Dracula's remains from me. You knew about that, right?" His sister nodded numbly. "Well, when we were in Rome, she forced Jerry to help her come here, to the United States. She promised him that she would free him if he helped her."

"And he believed her?"

"Yes."

Rachel shook her head. "The fool. The poor fool."

"Rachel," he said slowly, "I don't think you're following me. Dracula's remains are here in our country." She stared at him blankly. "Don't you see? She's after us, *he's* after us, after you and me and Gramps. Do you remember what he told our great-grandmother, Mina? He said that he spread his revenge out over centuries. That's what this is all about. He's been gone for a century, but he's still after us."

Holly coughed softly, breaking into what had become a private conversation. "Excuse me. I think I'll go upstairs and visit Mr. Harker, if you don't mind. I think the two of you should discuss this alone."

"Certainly," Rachel said. "His room is the first one at the top of the stairs." As Holly turned and began to ascend the steps, Rachel turned to her brother and said, "You cannot marry that girl, Malcolm."

He nodded. "I know. We've already broken up. I just brought her home tonight because I thought Gramps might want to say hi to her."

"That's good," Rachel muttered. "This has to stop with us. It has to end with our generation. There can't be any others. Do what I did, Malcolm, at least use the same idea. Find yourself a girl who doesn't want children, or one who can't have any. Get yourself sterilized—"

"Rachel," he interrupted, "listen to me. There's more." He outlined the effects that close proximity to the remains had engendered, told her of the dreamlike visions he had been experiencing. He did not mention the girl in Rome. "It's as if the blood itself were a living entity," he concluded, "something with its own life, its own existence separate from me. Do you understand what I'm trying to say?"

She frowned. "I'm not sure."

"That's why Lucy came to the United States! That's the real reason she stole the remains from me. She wants to bring the blood to full, I don't know, full wakefulness, full consciousness, something like that. If she can, then you and I and Gramps will be like robot arms of that dead creature. Dracula will continue to exist, in us, through us."

Rachel seemed to grow angry and frightened simultaneously. "That's unspeakable! That's horrible!"

"Yes, it is," he agreed, "and we have to be ready for it and be prepared to fight it. We have to find Jerry, that's the first step. As soon as I take Holly home, I'm going to go out looking for him. We have to get him to tell us where Lucy is sleeping during the day, where she's hidden the dust of the Count. We have to find her, kill her, then scatter the remains. Once we've done all this, then the only danger remaining will be the blood in our veins. And when we die, it will die with us. But we have to be careful, we have to be ready."

Rachel absorbed all of this in silence, reflected upon it, and then nodded. "What do you want me to do?"

"You have to make the house vampire-proof. Crosses and garlic on all the doors and windows. If you can get holy water from Father Henley, get some. If you can steal some consecrated wafers and consecrated wine, steal it."

"Malcolm!"

"Rachel, we can't worry about offending religious ethics, not now. God will forgive us for any sacrilege, I'm sure He will. It's Satan we're fighting here, remember."

She seemed unconvinced, but she did not press the point. "And you? What will you do?"

"As I said, I'm going out to look for Jerry. I think he left Rome the day before Holly and I did. That means that he and Lucy have had enough time to find her a resting place where she'll be safe during the daytime. They haven't had enough time to do anything else. You have to see to the security of the house immediately, before she tries to get in; and remember, she can't enter unless someone invites her in. That's one of the barriers against them that we can exploit to our advantage."

"Where will you look for him?" Rachel asked.

"I'll start at the Strand, the bar where he and I work." Malcolm paused. "Used to work, probably. We extended our vacation so long that we've probably both been fired. If he isn't there, drowning his sorrows, I'll check his apartment, his mother's apartment, the other places where he hangs out. I can think of dozens of places to check."

"Well." Rachel rose to her feet in her customary businesslike manner. "We'd best be about it, then. Go up and visit with Grandfather for a while, Malcolm. I'm going to the vegetable store and buy some garlic."

As Rachel left the house, Malcolm walked up the stairs toward his grandfather's bedroom. If I'd only left everything alone, he thought as he pushed open the bedroom door. If only I hadn't been so damned sure of myself, so damned cocky. Jerry wouldn't be in trouble, Lucy wouldn't be here, wouldn't even be "undead" again. Gramps probably wouldn't be ill, Daniel wouldn't have left Rachel, and Holly wouldn't have left me. Great job, Malcolm. Real good work.

He entered to find Holly sitting on the side of the old man's bed, whispering to him softly. He heard Quincy's feeble voice mutter something so low as to be unintelligible, and Holly responded to the words with a soft ripple of laughter. Malcolm felt almost as if he were intruding upon something private, but he knew that much as his grandfather liked Holly, and much as she might like the old man in return, there was no future for Holly and Malcolm, no future for Malcolm and anyone.

He walked forward and sat down on the other side of the bed. "Hiya, Gramps," he said, feigning cheer.

Quincy took his hand and squeezed it weakly. "Hello, boy. I'm glad you returned in one piece."

"Just barely," he said, laughing. "How are you feeling?"

Quincy replied with a very slight shrug. "I've lived a long life. I have no complaints."

"Oh, don't talk like that, Mr. Harker," Holly said. "You're going to be fine."

"Of course you are," Malcolm hastened to agree. "My stupid little escapade has just upset you, that's all. I'm very sorry about that."

Quincy smiled and nodded, not in agreement but in dismissal. "I have to rest awhile, boy. You take your girl home, and come back to visit with me later. All right?"

"Sure, Gramps. You get some sleep. I'll see you later." Malcolm led Holly from the room and closed the door behind them. As they descended the stairs, he asked, "How do you think he is?"

She shook her head. "I wouldn't admit it to him, but he's right, Mal. I think he's reached the end of his time. My grandmother died of old age when I was a little kid, and she looked and sounded like he does now."

Malcolm shook his head. "My fault, like everything."

"Not everything," she said. "It's really Dracula's fault, just as Rachel said."

They left the house silently. Malcolm locked the door behind him. As they walked from Granville Place toward Austin Street, they did not touch. They were no longer a couple, and each self-consciously observed the proprieties of their new situation. As they drew closer to Burns Street, Holly said, "I could use a drink, Mal. How about you?"

"Sure," he said, switching her suitcase from his right hand to his left. "I was going to go to the Strand after I took you home anyway."

"Looking for Jerry?"

"Yeah. Gotta start somewhere."

"Well," she said, "I'd like a drink, whether he's there or not."

They continued on down Ascan Avenue past Burns Street and lapsed once again into silence.

When they entered the Strand, they saw Jerry Herman sitting at the end of the still-uncrowded bar, staring morosely into a half-empty glass of beer. Malcolm and Holly walked over to him and seated themselves on either side of him. He turned his head slowly from Malcolm to Holly and back again, and then he started to cry. "I'm sorry."

Malcolm nodded, placing his hand on Jerry's shoulder. "I know, Jer. I understand."

"She said she would take her blood out of me. She promised."

"Of course she did, Jerry," Holly said. "And you know she wasn't telling the truth, don't you?"

He nodded, allowing his head to sink downward toward the bartop, seeming almost to double over in his misery. "She laughed at me. After I got her here, I asked her to keep her end of the bargain, and she just laughed at me."

Malcolm sighed. "Jerry, what has happened to you is my fault, not yours. Don't reproach yourself. You can't trust these creatures. We've all learned that the hard way."

Jerry Herman grabbed Malcolm's arm and held it hard, gripped it with an intensity born of fear. "What am I gonna do, Mal? What am I gonna do?"

"The first thing we're all going to do is have a drink," Malcolm said, motioning toward the bartender—his replacement, in all likelihood, he thought glumly—who stood near the cash register. "Bourbon for me and my friend, and another beer for him. Give me a beer, too." He glanced over at Holly. "Wine?" he asked.

"Scotch on the rocks," she told the bartender. "A double shot, please."

Jerry wiped away a tear and said, "Holly, I'm sorry I left you guys like that. I mean—"

"Jerry, forget it," Holly said. "You don't owe me an apology. I'm . . . well, I'm not involved in all this anymore, anyway."

Jerry glanced from Holly to Malcolm, started to comment, thought the better of it, then turned back to the beer glass he clutched in his hand.

After a few moments, Malcolm asked, "How did she get here? I mean, how did you manage it?"

"Well," Jerry began, "it wasn't all that difficult. It was

just something that she couldn't do by herself, because she realized that she didn't understand what was involved. She knew she needed a passport—"

"Sure she knew," Malcolm commented. "They used passports in the nineteenth century, too."

"—and so she got one from somebody she killed. She hung around in nightclubs and places like that around Rome, listening for American accents. Eventually she picked someone out who looked a little like her, knocked her off, and took her passport."

"Jesus, don't they check those things out?" Holly asked. "I mean, if somebody gets killed and someone with the same name shows up at the airport with a passport picture that doesn't look like them, wouldn't the police—"

"Holly," Malcolm said patiently, "do you realize how many people fly in and out of Rome every day? It's got to be tens of thousands. And they check passport photos and stuff like that much more carefully when you're entering a country than when you're leaving it."

"Well, then," she protested, "at Kennedy—"

"She didn't go through customs," Jerry said.

"Of course not." Malcolm nodded. "What did she do? Turn into mist?"

"I don't know. All I know is that she disappeared when we got off the plane and was waiting for me when I went to get the luggage."

"And the jewelry box with the remains in it?"

"With the luggage." Jerry sighed. "God knows where the boxes of dirt are."

Malcolm frowned. "For something as important to her as she seemed to think it was, she didn't seem to take any precautions. That's odd."

"No, it isn't," Jerry said. "You don't know her, Mal. She's, I don't know, like a little kid somehow. She doesn't think too clearly, not the way a...a normal person would. I don't think it ever occurred to her that she had to guard the dust from anyone, as long as you were still in Rome."

"And where is it now?" Malcolm asked. "And where is she?"

Jerry sighed and shook his head. "I don't know. As soon as we got out of the airport, she took the jewelry box from me and started laughing at me, calling me a stupid fool and telling me that I'd never be free of her." He started to cry.

again. "She just left me standing there. I didn't know what to do, where to go. I didn't want to go back to my apartment. I just wandered around for hours, and then I came here. I've been here ever since."

Malcolm considered everything Jerry had said. "So we can make a few assumptions. The two of you got here at night. About what time?"

"Oh, two in the morning, maybe. Something like that."

"Okay, so she had to find a safe resting place immediately. She didn't have time to do anything else."

"Anything else?" Jerry asked. "What else? What do you mean?"

"I'll explain later," Malcolm replied. "The point is, if Rachel has seen to the security of the house, then we're safe from her, safe from the remains."

"Wait a minute," Holly said. "How can she find a place to sleep? Doesn't she have to sleep in her own grave, or something like that?"

"In her native soil," Jerry answered her. "She brought a knapsack filled with dirt with her. Brought it all the way from England to Rumania, before shipping the English and Rumanian dirt to New York."

Holly frowned and shook her head. "This doesn't make sense. If she could get from England to Rumania all by herself, why did she need you to get to America? And why would she need Rumanian soil?"

"We can't be all that certain of our facts," Malcolm replied. "We don't know for sure that she did get from England to Rumania all alone. Maybe she had another... maybe she did to someone else what she did to Jerry. Maybe she only needed him because of the luggage, because of the dust of the Count. And as for the Rumanian dirt..." He paused for a moment. "I don't know. Maybe the remains have to rest in their native soil for the blood in Lucy's body to remain potent. I just don't know."

"Mal, what are we gonna do?" Jerry whined.

Malcolm took hold of his friend's hands and squeezed them tightly. "We're going to find her and kill her, and then we're going to find the remains of the Count and scatter them. And then we'll be safe, all of us."

"But how can we find her?" Jerry asked. "We don't have any idea where she is!"

Malcolm nodded in agreement. "I know, but we also

know that she's going to come after us, you, me, Gramps, and Rachel. We're going to have to be extremely careful and wait for her to make the first move, give us some clue as to where she's hiding. If we can find that out, we can find her during the daytime, and we can kill her."

"And the remains?"

"They won't be far from her. If we find her, we find them." Malcolm turned his attention to his drink, and his two companions did the same. There seemed, for the present at least, to be little else to say.

An hour later, Malcolm Harker and Holly Larsen stood in uneasy silence at the door to her co-op apartment. Neither of them knew what to say. This was, each knew, in all likelihood the last time they would see each other. Each loved the other, each wished that circumstances were different, and each knew that a parting of the ways was necessary, inevitable.

Malcolm coughed. "I'd better get back outside. Jerry'll be getting impatient."

"Yes," she said, and nodded.

A long silence ensued. Then Malcolm said, "I'm sorry, Holly. I'm sorry for everything."

"So am I, Mal." She unlocked her door and stepped inside, wanting to end the conversation quickly. "Good-bye."

"Good-bye." He watched the door swing shut, heard the lock click softly into place, and then he turned and walked toward the elevator.

Inside, Holly listened for the sound of the closing elevator door. As soon as she heard it, she went over to the window and looked out at the street below. Jerry Herman was standing beneath a light pole, nervously smoking a cigarette. She watched as he paced back and forth, watched as Malcolm came up to him, watched as they conversed briefly in words she could not hear, and watched as they walked away.

And so, good-bye, Malcolm, she thought sadly.

Holly turned sorrowfully away from the window and went into her bedroom. She sat down before her vanity and stared at her tired face in the mirror. Back to work tomorrow, she thought. Back to the singles' bars tomorrow night. Back to being alone, back to trying to separate the decent guys from the jerks. Back to the superficial conversations and the pathetic, posturing games. Back to wondering if there will ever be a good man, a decent man, someone to be trusted and admired and loved.

Someone other than dear, sweet, poor Malcolm.

Sighing, Holly removed her earrings and her necklace and then set about the task of removing her makeup. She was wiping off her mascara when she thought she heard a sound from the other room.

Lucy...

She felt a brief surge of panic, then realized that, no, it couldn't be Lucy, it's impossible. Vampires can't enter a house unless they're invited in first, and I certainly never invited her in. Imagination. All my imagination.

She was rubbing cold cream on her face when a thought occurred to her. This isn't a house, this is an apartment. And isn't an apartment just like a room in a building? When Dracula wanted to get at Mina Harker, he induced the lunatic Renfield to invite him into the asylum, and then he was able to go from room to room in the same building. And couldn't Lucy somehow get someone to invite her into the apartment building, a janitor, the superintendent, some old man who would hold the door for her and say, please, after you, or something like that. *Couldn't she get in here if she wanted to?*

A moment later she heard soft laughter close to her ear and she glanced up into the mirror. The only reflection she saw was her own. In that split second before Holly could turn her head, Lucy Westenra was upon her.

Chapter Fifteen

As Malcolm approached the front door of his home, the pungent aroma of freshly sliced garlic assailed his nostrils, and he smiled slightly as he examined the garlic bulbs that hung from the doorknob. Anyone else, he for example, might simply have tied the plants to any convenient protuberance without concern for appearance or regularity, but not Rachel. She had split each garlic bulb neatly in half, peeled them, and tied red string carefully about each one. Three split bulbs dangled from the doorknob. Three others hung from the windows on either side of the door, and Malcolm could see that the acrid plant had been placed both within and without the house. Shaking his head with amusement at Rachel's orderliness under even these circumstances, he unlocked the front door and entered.

He found his sister in the kitchen where she was washing off the long kitchen knife she had used to prepare the garlic bulbs. She turned as she heard him enter and said, without any further formal greeting, "I've put garlic on all the windows, inside and out, and on all the doors, including the interior doors to our bedrooms. I've also managed to rummage up more crucifixes from Mother's trunks in the basement. I've put them at strategic points about the house."

"Good." Malcolm nodded. "We're safe now, anyway. The sun has been up for at least twenty minutes."

"And so then, we wait." She smoothed her apron. "I've been up all night, waiting for you, tending to Grandfather, and getting the house prepared for our defense. I'm going to go and check on him now, and then I think I'll lie down for a few hours. I'm exhausted."

"Me, too." Malcolm yawned. "I've got bad jet lag. Jerry's going to come over later on this afternoon, so we'd better set

218

some alarm clocks to wake us up. The way I feel right now, I'd sleep through the doorbell and almost anything else."

"Well, I wouldn't," Rachel said. "Don't worry, Malcolm. I'll wake you when he arrives." She frowned slightly. "I thought you had no idea where he was?"

"We found him at the Strand, Holly and I," Malcolm said as he began to walk toward the staircase. "He has no idea where Lucy is, no idea where the remains of the Count are."

"Well, then, what...?"

"Remember in the book, the Stoker book, how Van Helsing used the psychic link between the Count and our great-grandmother to track him down? Well, we're going to try the same thing." He began to mount the stairs, and Rachel followed close behind him. "It isn't a sure thing, but it's the only thing I can think of doing."

She nodded approvingly. "It's a good idea. It might work."

"If it doesn't, I don't know what we'll do. We'll never be free of this thing until we've killed Lucy and scattered the remains of the Count."

"Trust in God, Malcolm," his sister said as she reached the door of their grandfather's room. "This is an old battle for Him. We have a potent ally." She closed the door of old Quincy's room behind her.

Malcolm gazed at the shut door for a moment, then continued on down to his bedroom. He was trying not to think about Holly.

He dropped down upon his bed and folded his hands behind his head. So beautiful, he mused as his eyelids grew heavy and a yawn forced its way from his chest. She is so beautiful, so warm, so kind, so beautiful.

"She is still a child, of course," the Gypsy said, "but you can tell, My Lord, that she will be ravishing when she comes of age."

He nodded, stroking his mustache and leering at the little girl who stood trembling before him. He dropped down upon one knee and smiled. "What is your name, little one?"

"S... Simone," the child mumbled.

"Simone," the Voivode repeated softly. "That is a lovely name. Have you a last name, child, a family name?" The little girl shook her head. "Well, tell me, Simone," he went on, "would you like to live in a big house and have lots of food and dogs to play with and servants to wait on you?" The child, terrified and confused, did not answer. The Voivode stood up and gathered his collar tight around his neck against the damp, cool wind of the Hungarian autumn. "Where is she from?" he asked the Gypsy.

. . . What is happening here? Malcolm wondered. I am in my bed, but it is cold, it is cold . . .

"She is from France, My Lord," the Gypsy replied. "From the city of Aachen."

"But that is Germany, surely!" the Voivode said.

The Gypsy shrugged. "As you wish, My Lord. Borders mean but little to us."

"A little Frank," the Voivode mused, gazing down at the little blond-haired girl. "A little Teuton. How much do you want for her?"

The Gypsy pretended to do some mental calculation before stating the price he had long ago decided upon. "I think that five pieces of silver would be a fair price."

The Voivode laughed. "Yes, it would indeed be a fair price, if you were selling ten mature women! For this child I shall give you one silver piece, and you can account yourself lucky with that." He cast a nod at the servant who stood in obsequious silence behind him, then turned and walked back into the villa. He would not bargain with the Gypsy, and the Gypsy would not refuse the one piece of silver. This was known and understood by all. The servant handed the Gypsy the coin and then took the little girl by the hand. He led her toward the servants' quarters.

The Voivode walked through the opened doors to his villa, paying not the slightest attention to the servants who closed the doors behind him. He returned to the large dining room and sat down at the end of the table opposite his guest. "I'm sorry for the delay, Your Majesty. Local business, private business. You were saying?"

"I was watching you out the window, Little Dragon," Matthias Corvinus, the king of Hungary, replied, laughing. "Your confidence astounds me! That child will not be grown for ten years! How can you be so certain that ten years from now your head will still be sitting upon your shoulders?"

The Voivode shrugged. "Nothing is certain, Your Majesty, not life and not even death."

Corvinus drank from a wine goblet. "Death is the only certainty, Voivode."

"Perhaps," he agreed. "But the day of its coming is not.

Perhaps I shall die tomorrow. Perhaps I shall still live twenty years from now. Who is to say?"

"I am to say," Corvinus reminded him. "Make no mistake, Little Dragon. The sultan still wants your head, and if it ever serves my purposes to do so, I shall give it to him."

"Of course, My Lord." The Voivode smiled sweetly, hating the man who sat before him, hating him with every fiber of his hate-filled being. "But you know as well as I that your purposes will be better served if I can present you with the sultan's head."

Corvinus laughed. "Indeed it would, Little Dragon! But your recent attempt to do so was not, shall we say, designed to inspire my confidence in your abilities."

Son of a maggot, the Voivode thought as he smiled again and replied, "I made an error, Your Majesty. I should have seen to my defenses before invading the territory of the Turk. And it was not so recent, if I may be so bold as to remind you. I have been your guest for over four years now."

King Matthias Corvinus laughed and nodded at the shared bit of humor. When the Voivode had fled into Hungarian territory after his disastrous defeat by the forces of the sultan under Torghuz Beg in 1462, he had expected to be protected, rearmed, and sent back to do battle. Instead he had been imprisoned by the Magyar king, kept in chains for over a year. True, the past three years had not been unplesant. He had been provided with a large villa on the outskirts of Buda-Pesth, he had servants, he had a stipend, he had his two wives—and now this little girl, who would be serviceable in a few years—but he was still a prisoner, still under guard. And he was still far from Wallachia, his rightful domain, still far from Transylvania, his birthplace, still far from Constantinople and the Byzantine crown, which he regarded as his destiny.

"And you shall remain my guest indefinitely, Voivode, until such time as it shall please me either to unleash you against the sultan or buy the sultan's friendship with your death."

The Voivode nodded slightly. "I am in all things Your Majesty's humble servant."

"Indeed you are." Corvinus laughed, knowing full well how much the Voivode hated him. "But servants such as you can ruin the reputation of a prince. Not a month goes by without someone telling me of some action of yours while you were Voivode of Wallachia—"

"I am *still* Voivode of Wallachia," he pointed out, trying to repress his anger.

"Your younger brother, Radu, might disagree with you. It is he who now does the sultan's bidding in Bucharest."

"Radu is a weakling, a sycophant," the Voivode muttered.

"Oh, I am sure he is," Corvinus said, nodding. "But still, he is there, and you are here. But no matter. As I was saying, reports keep reaching me of things you did while you were ruling. I find it difficult to believe some of them, I must admit." He drank again from his wine. "Tell me, Little Dragon, is it true that you attempted to rid your principality of beggars and cripples by killing them all?"

"Yes, and orphans and useless old men and women also," the Voivode agreed, "but it sounds inhumane as you phrase it, if I may be so bold."

"Ha!" Corvinus chuckled. "Then, please tell me how it can be more humanely phrased!"

"You have read of the Spartans, have you not, Your Majesty? The great warriors of ancient Greece?"

"Of course I have, and I have read of their systematic elimination of the unfit. But that was two thousand years ago, Little Dragon!"

"Two thousand years ago or last month, it makes no difference. A prince must make his nation strong, and to do that he must make his people strong. You and I have both sent men off to fight and die in battle, have we not, My Lord? It is the same thing. Some lives must be sacrificed so that the nation may grow stronger and more secure. It was necessary."

"And then you fed their bodies to the bears and the wolves that you kept as pets, did you not?"

The Voivode sighed. "Mine is a poor country, Your Majesty. Should I have wasted so much meat?"

"Certainly not, certainly not." Corvinus laughed. "The point is that you are a terror to your own people, Little Dragon! A prince must be loved, not hated."

"A prince must be feared and respected!" the Voivode said heatedly. "Do not forget that while I ruled in Wallachia, there was very little crime. My people feared my justice! Why, in the town square in Bucharest, I placed a golden goblet upon the public well so that passersby could refresh themselves with it. The goblet was pure gold, unchained, unguarded, and yet it remained there for four years! No one dared to steal it for fear of my justice."

"For fear of your wooden stakes, more likely." Corvinus grinned.

"Punishments must be strict so that law will be respected."

"Strict? Strict!" Corvinus shook his head, suddenly serious. "I pride myself on maintaining an orderly realm, Little Dragon, but I have never impaled pregnant women through their birth canals or held feasts in the midst of hundreds of impaled prisoners! I have torture chambers for the use of my judges, as all rulers must, but I have none for my own use, my own amusement."

"My Lord," the Voivode said, seething beneath the surface, "pray allow me to remind you of a few things. When we were about to begin our campaign against the sultan, Torghuz Beg invited me to a parley at Giurgiu, on the Danube. A weaker man might have taken him at his word, a less intelligent man might have walked into his trap. But I am not weak, and I am not foolish, and so I sent my cavalry through the forests to fall upon the Turks by surprise before they even reached Giurgiu."

"Yes, I remember," Corvinus said. "You captured many of them."

"Twenty thousand of them!" the Voivode shouted. "Twenty thousand prisoners."

"Whom you then impaled upon twenty thousand stakes."

"Their fate was well deserved," he muttered, sitting back in his chair. "Torghuz Beg escaped, of course, as always."

"As always," Corvinus agreed, amused by the Voivode's passion.

"And remember, My Lord, that when the sultan arrived at Giurgiu and found the twenty thousand bodies, or what the crows had left of them, he stopped his invasion of Wallachia and returned to Constantinople. And then, when I invaded Bulgaria and freed the Bulgars from the Turkish yoke, the people sang hymns of praise to me, and the bells of the churches rang in celebration!"

"Ah, yes, but the Bulgars did not know you, Vlad the Impaler. They knew only the sultan. They had no reason to suppose that they had traded one whip for another."

The Voivode poured himself some wine from the pewter pitcher. "What matter what the peasants know or do not know? The point is this, My Lord: The Turk points his sword at all Europe. Yesterday he took Constantinople. Tomorrow, he may take Buda-Pesth." He sipped from his goblet. "You need my sword arm more than you need give my head to the sultan."

"Maybe, maybe," Corvinus said, nodding. "But if—and I say *if*, my dear Vlad, not when—if I choose to unleash you against the sultan, I must be assured that your violence is, shall we say, surgical, not general."

The Voivode laughed disparagingly. "Does the blood of peasants and prisoners trouble My Lord?"

"No," Corvinus answered. "Blood and I are old companions. But a dead peasant is one who cannot harvest wheat, and a dead prisoner is one who cannot be ransomed." He leaned forward. "That is the difference between you and me, Vlad. I kill when I must, as often as I must, but no more than I must. I kill without regret, but without passion. You, Voivode, you are in love with violence. You are in love with pain. You are in love with blood."

Vlad the Impaler smiled.

Malcolm sat up in bed.

He was shaking, frightened. I just slipped into the memories, he thought, no transition, no awareness of its happening, not the slightest feeling that anything was wrong.

It's getting stronger! The blood is getting stronger!

He leaped from the bed and began to pace about his bedroom. There must be an explanation for this, he thought desperately. I've taken the sacrament, I've purged myself, I've beaten the blood back down, and yet the memories still rise to the surface. How can this be happening?

He sat back down upon the bed, feeling his chest contracting painfully from his labored, panicky breathing. "Lord Jesus, help me," he whispered as he folded his hands and pressed them against his forehead. "Help me, Lord, help me, help me, help me!"

"Do you renounce your adherence to the excommunicate in Constantinople?" the archbishop asked.

"Yes, yes," Malcolm replied. "Help me, Lord, help me."

"Do you make obeisance to the Vicar of Christ in Rome?" the archbishop asked. "Do you bind yourself to the one holy Catholic Church and to the successor of Saint Peter, who is its lawful master upon this world?"

"Yes," the Voivode replied.

"Will you live as a faithful son of the holy Mother Church, defending her against her enemies, and putting your sword at her disposal?"

"Yes," the Voivode said.

The archbishop turned toward Matthias Corvinus and nodded as he said, "Rise, then, Vlad of Wallachia, Voivode, vassal of His Majesty the King of Hungary."

Vlad the Impaler rose slowly from his knees and then leaned forward to kiss the proffered ring of the archbishop of Buda-Pesth. He bowed slightly as the prelate said, "The Lord be with you, Prince," then turned to leave.

King Matthias smiled at the Voivode and said, "And so now you are Catholic, Little Dragon, and thus an acceptable tool in my war upon the sultan."

"Yes, Catholic indeed." The Voivode laughed. "A true and devout son of the Church." The king shared his laughter. Each knew the depth of the Voivode's devotion. "And now to my army," the Voivode said, "and back to my principality."

Corvinus began to walk toward the exit from the chapel, and the Voivode followed him slowly. "Your army, I am afraid, will consist only of whatever mercenaries you can recruit," Corvinus said.

"It is no matter," the Voivode replied. "My brother, Radu, has the military skill of a little girl, and his army is commanded by inexperienced fools. I shall topple him in a day, and after I have reorganized his army—*my* army, I should say—then I shall meet the Turk."

Corvinus paused before speaking. "We have received word that the sultan has sent Torghuz Beg to occupy Wallachia in anticipation of my sending you against your brother. I am afraid, Little Dragon, that you will have to deal with Torghuz Beg before you deal with Radu, not after."

The Voivode was not pleased with this news. He thought for a few moments and then nodded grimly. "It will be difficult, but I shall choose my own ground. Torghuz Beg wants my head, and he will pursue me in order to get it."

"What will you do?" the king asked, pausing at the door of the chapel.

The Voivode placed his hands upon his hips and arched his back, which was a bit stiff from the lengthy genuflection he had just been obliged to undertake. "As you know, my cousin Bassarab is the Voivode of Transylvania."

"Yes, my faithful vassal," Corvinus said, nodding, "unlike your other cousins, the Voivodes of Moldavia and Bukovina."

The Voivode shrugged. "Mircea and Nicholae live hemmed in by the Turks, the Poles, and the Muscovites. They have little choice in the matter of alignment. But as I was saying, Bassarab and I long ago extended to each other the courtesy of a private residence in each other's principality. I have maintained a fortress near Oradea for many years. Even during my stay as your honored guest"—he smiled mirthlessly at the king—"Bassarab has not confiscated it."

"And so you shall tempt Torghuz Beg into Transylvania?"

"Yes, by returning to my castle near Oradea. Strategic necessity will impel him to invade, for the longer he waits, the stronger I shall grow. His army is at peak strength, it cannot become stronger, not with so many of the sultan's troops tied down on the Polish border."

Corvinus nodded. "Clever. You realize, do you not, that you are attempting to draw the Turks into an invasion of Hungarian territory?"

The Voivode smiled. "Of course I do."

"And you must also be aware that I have no intention of meeting such an invasion myself under these circumstances?"

The Voivode's smile did not fade, but anger shone in his eyes. "I did not expect you to."

"Good," Corvinus replied. "Remember, Little Dragon, that I am using you for my own purposes. I will not be used by you. If you fall before Torghuz Beg, I shall assert that you acted without my knowledge or support, and he will evacuate Transylvania so as to avoid a war with me."

"He will know that you are lying."

"Of course he will, but that is an irrelevant point. Diplomatic niceties and the complexities of negotiation rarely have anything to do with truth and honesty."

The Voivode nodded. "I agree, Your Majesty. And I understand full well my position."

"My prayers go with you into battle, of course, but if you are defeated—"

"Then at least I will be buried in the castle crypt near Oradea, with my father, my older brother, and my ancestors. Your illustrious predecessor Hunyadi allowed my father and brother to be buried there after he killed them."

Corvinus ignored the subtle rebuke, replying merely, "Vlad II and Mircea were executed because they lied to everyone, betrayed everyone, Turk and Magyar alike. Do not follow in their footsteps, Little Dragon."

"I shall strive to avoid them," he muttered.

"Yes. Well." The king stepped out of the chapel into the

warm air of the Hungarian summer. "I must meet with the Venetian ambassador. You may join us, if you wish."

"Not quite yet," the Voivode said. "I wish to remain here and pray for a while."

"Pray!" The king laughed. "By God, I think you mean it!" Still laughing, Matthias Corvinus left the chapel, allowing the heavy oaken door to close behind him.

The Voivode stood motionless for a moment and then whispered, "Ordogh! Ordogh! The time has come, has it not?"

There was only silence for a short while, and then the voice from the Pit said softly, "The time has come, Little Dragon. My time has come, and your time has come."

"I shall triumph, shall I not? I shall sit again upon the throne of Wallachia, shall I not?"

"Are you not the Voivode?" the voice asked ambiguously.

"And I shall triumph over the Turk, shall I not?"

The voice did not reply.

"I shall triumph, shall I not?" the Voivode repeated.

"Must I tell you again that I am no Gypsy fortune-teller, Little Dragon?" Ordogh asked. "You shall triumph in ways you do not know, over men not yet born. Your name shall be heralded far and wide for reasons you cannot as yet comprehend. But as for the Turk, the outcome of that battle is not yet for you to know."

The Voivode stood in contemplative silence, his graying mustache drooping with the frown of his face. There was a scream that rent the silence, but the Voivode did not hear it.

The woman screamed again, and Malcolm jumped up. "Rachel!" he shouted, "Rachel! What is it?" He ran from his bedroom and threw open the door to his sister's room. Malcolm shook his head to clear it as the words of the dark spirit echoed in his ears.

Rachel was sitting upon the edge of her bed, pallid and trembling, her eyes darting insanely back and forth. "Malcolm!" he screamed when she saw him. She pushed herself up onto her feet and seemed almost to collapse forward into his arms.

"What happened?" he asked. "Why are you screaming? What the hell happened?"

"I was dreaming...I was...I was someone else...I was him! I was him! I was dreaming, but my dreams were his memories!"

"Wh...? Rachel, that can't be." Malcolm led her back to

the bed and seated her upon it, sitting down beside her. "I have these . . . I don't know, these visions because I was in close proximity to the remains. But you . . ." His face went white. A terrible idea had occurred to him.

"I was speaking to a . . . to a *thing*, a demon," she wept. "Malcolm, he had a plan, he had a trick he was playing. I don't know what it was, but there's something, something!"

"Rachel," Malcolm said urgently, "the evening I returned from Europe, did you let anyone in the house, anyone you didn't know, didn't recognize?"

"The thing laughed at me, it laughed at all of us," she babbled on, not hearing him. "It kept saying that things were not as they seemed to be, that we were all fools, that he would triumph."

"Rachel, damn it, listen to me!" Malcolm shouted. "Did you let anyone . . ." His question was interrupted by the sounds of crazed laughter coming from down the hall. He cocked his head to listen, and Rachel, hearing it also, took her breath in sharply. It was their grandfather.

Malcolm ran from the room with his sister close behind him. They burst into old Quincy's bedroom to find the old man standing unsteadily beside his sickbed, his aged frame trembling and swaying, his eyes wide and mad, his quivering lips turned upward in a frightening grimace as the bizarre laughter continued to erupt in short, feeble bursts from his creaky lungs.

Malcolm rushed forward and grabbed the old man by the shoulders. "Gramps!" he said. "What are you doing? Are you okay?"

"Fools, stupid fools!" old Quincy said, and laughed. "You think to baffle me, you with your pale faces all in a row, like sheep in a butcher's."

"Grandfather!" Rachel whispered. "What are you saying?"

"You shall be sorry yet," the old man said, still laughing. "My revenge is just begun! I spread it over centuries!"

Malcolm shook his grandfather gently. "Gramps, wake up, wake up! You're dreaming. Wake up!"

The mad aspect of the old man's eyes suddenly faded into a confused normalcy. "M . . . Malcolm," he said weakly, then fell forward into his grandson's arms. Quincy wheezed and pressed his hands spasmodically to his chest as he muttered unintelligible sounds of fear and pain. Malcolm continued to hold his grandfather as Rachel ran to the phone to call an ambulance.

Chapter Sixteen

Hours later, Jerry Herman pressed the doorbell of the Harker home for the fifth time. He tapped his foot with irritation, cursed under his breath, and was just about to turn and walk away when the cab pulled up and Malcolm and Rachel climbed out. Malcolm put his arm around his sister, and together they walked slowly toward the front door. As they drew closer, Jerry did his best to muster up a smile as he said, "Where were you two? I was just about to..." He stopped as he realized from the looks on their faces that something was amiss. "Hey, what's wrong?"

"It's Gramps," Malcolm sighed. "He's in the hospital."

"Oh, shit, Mal, that's too bad. Is he going to be okay?"

"He's going to die," Rachel muttered as she walked past him and entered the house.

Jerry looked at Malcolm, and Malcolm shook his head. "He had a memory, like I've been having, a memory from the blood. Rachel had one, too, but Gramps is just too old and too weak to be able to handle it." He laughed without humor. "God, I don't know if _I_ can handle it."

"But how...I mean, I thought...how could they be having these dreams like you've been having?"

Malcolm entered the house and Jerry followed. As Malcolm poured himself a glass of bourbon at the bar in the sitting room, he said, "Early last evening, before Holly and I got home, Lucy must have killed a nun and stolen her clothes. Maybe she did it in England, I don't know. She came here to the house, pretending to be a new worker at our parish church, sent over to visit with Gramps."

Jerry sighed, knowing what Malcolm was about to say. "And so Rachel invited her in."

"Yes," Malcolm said, nodding. "Rachel thought she was a nun and invited her in. She was carrying a large shoulder bag, and the jewelry box must have been in it. She must have hidden it somewhere in the house."

Jerry shook his head and frowned. "I don't understand it, Mal. I just don't understand it. What's the purpose of all this? Why is she doing this to us, to you and me and your family? It just doesn't make any sense."

Malcolm poured a glass of bourbon for Jerry and handed it to him. "It makes perfect sense. At least I can think of a scenario that explains it all."

"Well, let me in on it," Jerry said, seating himself in Quincy's plush chair. "I do have a personal interest in all this, you know."

Malcolm sat on the sofa and drank deeply from the fiery liquor. He shuddered slightly as the bourbon burned its way down his throat, then he said, "Dracula vowed revenge on his enemies, and whenever he vowed revenge, he somehow managed to take revenge. The Turks found that out, I think."

"The Turks? What—"

"Imagine this," Malcolm went on. "Imagine that the Count knew that Van Helsing and my grandparents and the others posed a threat to him. Imagine that he forced my great-grandmother to drink his blood so that just in case— just in case, mind you—he was destroyed, some part of him would live on in Mina Harker and her descendants. His being, his blood, would be ever present and always influential, though largely dormant. Imagine that he reasoned that someday, maybe in a hundred years or in five hundred years, the blood would awaken, might somehow lead the person whose veins held the blood, lead him to Dracula's dust. The proximity of the dust would awaken the blood, and Dracula could live again in the form of the Harker descendant."

"Doesn't make sense," Jerry said quickly. "If you hadn't decided to go to England to check this all out, if you hadn't come up with your fucked-up idea to resurrect Lucy, you would never have gone to Rumania. Just too many ifs."

"I know, but remember that the threat my ancestors and their friends posed to him was in England while he himself was in England. He may have made the assumption that if they ever caught and killed him it would have been in England, so that his remains and my ancestors would have been in the same country, probably in the same region."

Jerry absorbed this. "Possible. Possible. But then what about me? What do I have to do with all of this?"

Malcolm sighed. "Innocent bystander. Lucy needed you, that's all." He did not bother to apologize once again. "The point is that Lucy is following the commands of the blood. It's in her, too, don't forget. She followed me back here, with your help"—Jerry's jaw clenched at these words—"and managed to hide the remains of the Count somewhere here in the house. There are only three people who inherited the blood, only three who are still alive, anyway. Me, Gramps, and Rachel. Lucy must have hidden the remains somewhere in the house in the hopes of giving the blood enough . . . I don't know, enough time, enough of an impetus, something like that, to take over the three of us."

Jerry sighed. "Gets worse and worse."

"No, better and better," Malcolm said. "At least we know where the remains are. We have to search the house, tear it apart if need be, and find those remains. She wouldn't take any chances with them, wouldn't just dump them somewhere or sweep them under a rug. She'd keep them in the jewelry box or put them in some other container. The only time Rachel wasn't with her was when Lucy was upstairs, so they have to be up there somewhere."

"Is it safe for you to be in the house with the remains? I mean, is it safe for either of you?"

"No," Malcolm replied. "It isn't. But we have no choice. I assume that the power of the blood is greatest at night . . . though now that I think about it, I've had visions during daytime. But at least we have to take the precaution of not being here after sundown. Rachel and I will have to stay elsewhere, your place maybe."

"Lucy knows where I live, remember," Jerry sighed. "She knows everything there is to know about me."

"I'll have to . . . I'll have to call Holly, ask her if we can stay with her."

"She'll say no, Mal. She's a sweet kid and all that, but I don't think she wants anything to do with any of this ever again."

"I know, I know. But I have to try. No one else would understand." Malcolm emptied his glass into his mouth and then stood up. "Let's get going."

"Going where?"

"To search the house. We have to . . ." He paused, placing his hand upon his forehead. He was suddenly dizzy, and he heard the distant echoes of laughter and the clash of swords. He shook his head, and the unbidden sounds faded. "We have to find that box and get the remains out of it and then scatter them. That's our first priority. Once we've done that, Rachel, Gramps, and I should be free of the visions. It's still daytime, so let's not waste any of it."

He and Jerry went to search Malcolm's and Quincy's rooms respectively while Rachel began a thorough examination of her own. Hours passed, and they redoubled their efforts, expanding their search to include the entire upstairs and then the ground floor and the dark, unfinished basement. They searched every corner, every closet, under every stick of furniture, and when they had finished, they searched again in the same places. They moved from room to room, from level to level, seeking the hiding place of the small box, and, failing to find it, looking in every possible container into which the dust might conceivably have been poured. The box was nowhere to be seen, and the dust was nowhere to be found.

But Malcolm knew it was somewhere in the house, he knew that the remains of the Count were continuing to awaken the memories buried deep in the unholy blood, for another vision hit him as he took a break from his efforts to pour himself a glass of sherry. He found suddenly that the glass had become a pewter tankard, that a broadsword hung from the belt around his waist, and that he was surveying a room filled with loud, drunken rabble. He blinked and shook his head, then remembered who he was, where he was, when he was. My army, he thought. My gutter rats, making merry on the eve of battle.

The feast was progressing with a licentious revelry made even greater and driven to even more frenzied heights by the unspoken knowledge that the Turks were pressing close to the borders. Fear ran as an undercurrent beneath the laughter and the wenching and the drinking and the swordplay. It was fear that drove the drunken rabble who composed the better part of his army to even greater depths of indulgence. It was fear that made them fight and whore and drink as if this were the last feast they would ever enjoy.

But he was not afraid. He was never afraid. He had never been afraid, not once in his entire life. His life had been spent with the threat of death his constant companion, from the moment in his childhood when his father had left him a hostage with the sultan.

He looked out over the revelry, allowing his eyes to drift lazily from one side of the great hall to the other. Here, two dogs were fighting viciously over a cast-off lamb bone; there, two of his scum were slashing at each other with swords; here a young peasant girl was being taken, brutally, against her will by a few of the Mongol mercenaries, her cries of fear and misery inciting laughter and applause; there, a few drunken foot soldiers were vomiting copiously into an empty wine jug.

The Voivode smiled grimly. And have I been reduced to this? he thought. I, who once sat beside Corvinus, the Magyar king, and drank from his own golden chalice; I, who once slept upon silken sheets in the private quarters of the sultan himself; I, whose word was law and whose will was life or death for hundreds of thousands of my subjects; I am now the lord of rabble, the leader of mercenaries, the most glorious master of earth's most murderous scum.

When the battle comes, will they stand by me? Do they fear me more than they fear the Turks? I pray that they do.

He did not pray to God, of course. He had no faith in God, no love for God, no need for God, and he hoped heartily that the sentiment was reciprocated. Throughout his long and tortuous career he had adopted and discarded religions as another man might change his cloak. He had abandoned his ancestral Orthodox Christianity while living at the sultan's court, and his conversion to Islam had been one reason why the Turks had helped him gain control of Wallachia twenty years before. And when he had felt strong enough to withhold the annual tribute to the sultan and declare himself an independent prince, he resumed his Orthodoxy as if he had never rejected it. And when the God-cursed Hungarians abandoned him and cast him into prison, he once more cast off his allegiance to the Orthodox Church and made submission to the Roman pope.

Here he was now, the supposedly Catholic ruler of an Orthodox people under Moslem attack. If he was to win the battle that the morrow portended, he would again cast off this most recent religious cloak, reaffirm his Orthodoxy, and thus bind the peasants to him with bonds of icons and Slavonic chants.

Catholic, Orthodox, Moslem—it made no difference. He

would become a Hussite or a Jew if policy necessitated it. He had no interest in God.

Ordogh, he prayed silently, put iron into the backbones of this rabble army of mine. I will need each one of them tomorrow against Torghuz Beg.

He moved his eyes toward the center of the room and he smiled again, not grimly this time, but in anticipation. I shall give this scum some entertainment, he thought, entertainment that will amuse them and that will drive home to them how terrible an enemy I can be when angered. You must fear me more than you fear the Turks, my children.

In the center of the great hall, two tall oak stakes thrust fifteen feet up toward the high ceiling. Many years ago—long before his most recent imprisonment—the Voivode had ordered that circular holes be carved into the stone floor of this fortress to give the stakes a permanent resting place.

Tonight two terrified peasants sat on the floor, hands tied behind their backs and ankles bound together. Their simple faces were contorted by the frequent beatings they had received in recent days as they stared upward with abject fear at the sharpened tips of the wooden stakes.

The Voivode gazed down at the two peasants impassively. One of them felt the Voivode's eyes upon him, and he glanced over at the austere figure upon the dais, then immediately averted his gaze. The peasant knew that he was about to die to provide a brief amusement for his lord the Impaler, but to look into the devil's evil eyes would be to endanger his immortal soul. He looked at his own knees with a fervid concentration, silently muttering prayers to Christ and His Mother.

The Voivode smiled. Fear me, peasant animal, he thought. Your fear may be infectious, and I need my scum to fear me. He turned and nodded curtly at his chamberlain, who immediately walked briskly forward and cried out in a loud voice, "Be still! Be still! Be still and attend! Be still and attend! The Voivode speaks! The Voivode speaks!" Then he stepped back to his position beside the throne and froze in place. The clamor subsided almost immediately.

The Voivode rose slowly to his feet and stood smiling, his pearly-white teeth clearly visible beneath his thick gray mustache. "Is all to your liking, my children?" he asked loudly.

Shouts of praise and approbation arose from the rabble who packed the great hall, shouts of devotion to their Voivode.

He raised his hands, and again the noise subsided. "Where are Jagatuik the Mongol and Yaroslav the Serb?"

Two intoxicated ruffians stumbled forward and saluted.

"It was you who captured these two miserable peasants hunting deer on my estate. I have sentenced them to death in the usual manner, a manner entirely appropriate for thieves and rebels. For your loyalty and service, I shall allow you to see to their punishment. Choose two comrades each, and attend to it immediately." He resumed his seat and smiled as the hall was suddenly filled with cheers and laughter.

The Mongol and the Serb pulled a few other drunken revelers from the ranks, and they stumbled over to the two terrified peasants. The cries of fear and pleas for mercy were lost in the din of the great hall, and the Voivode smiled as the execution commenced.

The two peasants were stripped and carried by the soldiers up the long ladders that leaned against the stakes. In their drunken lack of coordination they dropped one of the peasants, who fell the fifteen feet to floor and landed on his side. But the soldiers carried him up again, then held his legs apart as they positioned the pointed end of the stake against the pucker of his anus. The other soldiers had positioned the second peasant in the same manner, and after looking at each other so as to coordinate their actions, they counted, "ONE . . . TWO . . . THREE . . ." and shoved the peasants down. The sharp wood thrust up through their intestines and into their stomachs, to the general glee and delight of the assembled soldiery. The first peasant died immediately. The second lingered on for a few minutes, writhing upon the impalement post, his eyes bugging out and blood pouring from his mouth.

The Voivode smiled, satisfied. Peasants may not kill my deer, he thought. There must be order.

He gestured to his chamberlain, who came forward and nodded obediently at the whispered instructions. The chamberlain scurried out of the hall as the Voivode rose again from his throne and said, "We are honored tonight, my children, by the arrival of envoys from our dear friend Torghuz Beg." The soldiers shouted obscenities and curses at the mention of the name. He quieted them with a wave of his hand. "I shall confer with the Turks here and now. Let us all listen politely to their message." A ripple of laughter floated over the assembly. They knew full well how carefully their Voivode would listen.

The chamberlain returned a moment later and stood by the door to announce the envoys, who strode past him with rapid arrogance as he cried out, "The representatives of Torghuz Beg, the sultan's commander."

The Turks walked up to the foot of the throne. Two of them bowed curtly but did not remove their hats in the presence of the Voivode; the third, a younger man less aware of the significance of omissions and irregularities in diplomatic behavior, removed his plumed fez but did not bow. He looked around nervously at the drunken rabble that surrounded him.

The leader of the Turkish mission evidenced no signs of unease. He brushed a few specks of dust from his flowing silk blouse and did not even look at the Voivode as he said, "My sublime and illustrious master, Torghuz Beg, beloved of Allah and friend of the sultan, demands your immediate surrender. In his magnanimous generosity my master has condescended to allow you this opportunity to save your life and spare your people bloodshed." He then looked at the Voivode impassively, his face a study in boredom and disdain.

The Voivode smiled malevolently. "Have you Turkish pig-eaters no manners? Have you never been told that you must remove your hats in the presence of your superiors?"

The Turkish spokesman emitted an exaggerated yawn. "There is no voivode here, only a usurper who has attempted to steal a throne from his brother, the true voivode of Wallachia. The true voivode has sworn allegiance to the sultan. The usurper, whose mother, as I understand it, was an Albanian whore, is being generously offered a chance to avoid being fed to my master's dogs. My master suggests that he avail himself of it."

The Voivode laughed darkly. "My children, these pig-eaters seem determined to keep their hats on in our presence. Well, let us be good hosts. Seize them, and nail their hats to their heads."

The two Turks who had not removed their hats sputtered stunned protests as the laughing rabble grabbed them and forced them down upon their knees. Their incredulous faces bespoke their arrogant assumption that, as envoys of Torghuz Beg, their persons were inviolate.

But of course, no one's person was inviolate to the Voivode. They realized this in their last moments of life before those who held them drove the nails into their brains.

The Voivode motioned the third Turk forward. The young man was green with fear and nausea, and he approached with trembling steps. "You have manners, little Turk," the Voivode said. "That speaks well of your upbringing." His voice was kind and melodious.

"Th... thank you, Lord," the young man stammered.

"I do, however, detect a hint of arrogance in your eyes as you look at me," he went on, his voice growing increasingly cold with each successive word. "Do you look upon me with scorn, Turkish sheep lover?"

"N... no, My Lord! I..."

The Voivode nodded pensively. "Ah, but you do, I think you do indeed. I think that a lesson in manners is called for." He snapped his fingers and the young man was immediately seized by four men. The Voivode took a dagger from the sheath that hung from his leather belt and tested the blade's tip with his forefinger. A drop of blood oozed up from the prick, and the Voivode licked it off. "Now listen to me, lover of little boys, and deliver this message to the whoremonger whose ass you lick. Tell him that we shall water our crops with the blood of Turks, and that the bellies of our dogs will swell with the meat from your bodies. Tell Torghuz Beg that I shall piss on his corpse and then leave his body for the crows. Tell him all this, if you can see your way back to the Turkish camp." Then he grabbed the young man by the hair and sliced through his scalp from ear to ear around the back of his head. The Voivode reached back and grabbed the torn edge of the scalp just above the nape of the neck and wrenched it forward, pulling it over the crown of his head and down over his face. The young man screamed in pain and the soldiers cheered with delight.

The bleeding Turk stumbled from the hall as the Voivode said to his army, "Feast and enjoy yourselves. I go now to my women. Tomorrow we shall crush these Turkish insects beneath our boots and grind them into the mud." He left the hall to a cacophony of cheers and cries of loyalty.

He walked alone up the winding staircase to his private chambers, listening as the sounds of revelry faded behind him. He opened the heavy wooden door and walked into the large, silent room. It was dimly lighted by one small oil lamp, and all three of his wives were sleeping upon the wide, canopied bed. He walked over quietly, considered awakening them, but then decided to allow them to sleep a bit longer.

There would be time enough for the delights of the flesh later, before sleep overtook him, if indeed he could sleep at all. He rarely slept on the eve of battle.

He looked down at them one by one, and he smiled, enjoying their beauty, secure in their slavish, frightened devotion to him. Magda, his first and only wife recognized by the unbendable Orthodox Church, had given him his little heir, the boy Nicholae, asleep elsewhere in the castle. The second, Katarina, was a whore of such enthusiasm and expertise that he had kept her and married her, the priest's objections notwithstanding. The first priest to object to the polygamous marriage had been impaled upon a stake; likewise the second. The third had performed the ceremony willingly. Finally, Simone, the blond one, the little Frankish girl he had purchased as a slave from some Gypsies a decade ago. He had taken great pleasure with her.

None of his wives objected to the presence of the others, of course. None of them would have dared to object. There were many trees in Wallachia which could be sharpened into stakes, after all, and these women were not fools.

Taking the oil lamp with him, he left the room and descended the staircase. He did not reenter the great hall but rather continued to descend until he reached the subterranean room which served as both crypt and chapel for the castle. He placed the oil lamp into the small alcove near the doorway and walked into the dark, damp room.

The child that he had left here earlier was still in the same place, bound hand and foot and lying in trembling fear upon the surface of the coffin lid of one of the earlier voivodes. He smiled coldly at the little boy and then drew forth his dagger, still wet and red with the blood of the Turk. He placed his hand over the child's mouth and then plunged the blade into his stomach. The child died almost instantly, for which the Voivode was grateful. The wailing and sobbing of children always annoyed him.

He turned from the corpse and whispered, "Ordogh! I am here! I have given you a gift! Come to me!"

He waited for a few moments, and then the voice said, "Your gift pleases me, Little Dragon."

"For that I am happy, Ordogh," the Voivode said.

"Why do you wish to speak to me?" the voice asked. "Do you tremble upon the eve of battle?"

"I tremble before nothing and no one," the Voivode replied evenly. "You know that, Ordogh."

"Yes, I know." The voice came from nowhere and everywhere at once—an invisible tongue, noncorporeal, formless, but present nonetheless. "Why then have you called upon me? Do you desire to know more secrets of the alchemists?"

"No, Ordogh," the Voivode said. "Tomorrow I join battle with Torghuz Beg."

"This I know."

"I have five thousand soldiers: drunken ruffians, mercenaries, and peasants. Torghuz Beg has ten thousand soldiers, seasoned veterans. His generals fought at Vaslui last year."

"This also I know."

The Voivode paused. "I may not win the battle."

"You shall not win the battle."

"I may die."

"You shall die."

The Voivode began to pace back and forth and spoke contemplatively. "If I win, I shall be the greatest of my race, and I shall unite all Dacia beneath my scepter."

"Beneath your whip," the voice corrected him.

"If I lose, then my land is lost to the Turk, and my life is lost to Torghuz Beg." He shook his head. "If I lose," he mused, "but you say *when* I lose. Can you tell what will transpire, Ordogh? Are you omniscient?"

"No," the voice replied, "but I can count, Little Dragon. And even I, who have never needed to wield a sword or hurl a spear, know the difference between an experienced soldier and the scum you have hired to fill your depleted ranks."

"So you make a judgment," the Voivode said. "You may be wrong."

"I may be wrong," the voice agreed.

"I may win."

"The pope may become sultan," the voice said. "The king of Hungary may become a Moor, and the king of France a Hussite."

The Voivode laughed bitterly. "I shall not win the battle, and I shall die."

"Yes, horribly, at the hands of Torghuz Beg."

The Voivode began to pace up and down in the silent crypt. "It cannot end thus. I must have an alternative. I must go into battle knowing that even in defeat I shall triumph."

The voice did not respond for a long while. Then it said,

"There is a way, Little Dragon, but it will entail a special damnation."

The Voivode laughed. "Do you think I fear damnation, Ordogh? I am damned already!"

"Yes," the voice agreed, "but for as long as you live, you have the option of repentance."

He spat a bitter laugh. "Sooner will the raven walk or the wolf fly."

"I know," the voice said. "You bring great joy to me, Little Dragon. You have always brought great joy to me."

"Then tell me of this way, Ordogh. Tell me how I can triumph over Torghuz Beg, even in defeat."

"If you choose the way, you will be serving me and pleasing me long after the name of Torghuz Beg is forgotten, and long after the stones of this fortress have been reduced to dust by the wind and the rain. If you choose the way, your service to me will not end with death."

"Tell me, Ordogh. What is the alternative which I have?"

The voice seemed to whisper in his ear. It whispered of strange powers, of great joy in the midst of misery and great suffering in the midst of exquisite pleasure. It spoke of life and death, of life in death and death in life, of terror and ecstasy and pain.

When the voice had finished its whispering, the Voivode stood motionless and silent. "I had not dreamed of such a thing," he muttered.

"That is the offer I make to you, Little Dragon. It is yours to accept or reject, but know that you are damned regardless."

The Voivode nodded. "But I must think, Ordogh, I must consider this carefully. Must I answer now?"

"Call upon me unto the point of death. For as long as you live and breathe, you can choose to accept my offer. But remember, Little Dragon, that you are damned regardless; know that you will lose the battle; know that whether you accept or reject the way I have described to you, your land is fated to be ground beneath the heels of the Turk for many years."

The Voivode thought about this. "And if I accept, then I shall be here to rule again when the Turks are gone?"

"You will be here, but you will not care about kingdoms and castles and power and glory. The centuries will change you greatly, Voivode. *I* shall change you greatly."

He nodded again. "I shall call upon you again, Ordogh, and give you my answer, when the outcome of tomorrow's contest has been decided."

"I await your summons, Little Dragon," the voice said, and then there was silence.

The Voivode was deep in thought as he mounted the stairs that led from the crypt to the main floor of the fortress. He ignored the salutes of the guards as he continued back up to his private chambers.

Is vengeance and victory worth such a fate? he asked himself. Yes, it is. He smiled. If the battle is lost, if I am to die at the hands of Torghuz Beg, then it will be worth such a fate to see him die in terror and pain.

He entered his chambers once again and sat down on the side of the huge bed beside the sleeping figure of Simone, the Frankish girl. He stroked her hair absently and admired her naked form, draped by her golden tresses. "Simone," he whispered.

The girl opened her eyes groggily and gazed up at him with confusion. Then, seeing who had awakened her, she became instantly alert, and she smiled at him. Her smile was both loving and wary, for this was a hard man to please, and a dangerous man to displease. "My Lord!" she said softly. "I am glad of your presence."

"Are you indeed," he said, and smiled. "Tell me, my little Teuton, do you fear death?"

Her eyes went wide with apprehension. Such questions, when asked by the Voivode, were rarely rhetorical. "I . . . I am but eighteen, My Lord. I pray that death will spare me for many years."

"Tomorrow I battle the Turk, Simone. If I am victorious, then all will be well. But if I am defeated, if the Turk takes this fortress, then death may be something that you welcome."

She shook her head, relieved that his question was not a prelude to something more immediately frightening. "You shall win, My Lord. Of that I have no doubt."

He smiled at her with what passed for affection. "Do you want to live forever, little Simone?"

"My Lord?" she asked, not understanding his words.

"Would you live forever, if you could?"

She shrugged slightly. "Of course I would, My Lord."

"And if it meant death and misery for others? Would you still choose to live forever?"

"Why do you ask me this, My Lord?"

But he did not hear her response. He was stroking her firm young thigh absentmindedly as he stared off at nothing. "I would still choose it," he muttered. "What do the deaths of others mean to me? What is their misery beside my desires?"

"My Lord?"

He smiled at the girl. "Go back to sleep, Simone."

"Do you wish to take pleasure with me, My Lord?"

"No," he sighed, lying back on the bed and putting his arm around her. "I save my strength for Torghuz Beg. Sleep, little German." She leaned her head down and rested it upon his chest, listening to his heartbeat and wondering what his odd discourse portended. In a few minutes she was sleeping.

To triumph over my enemies, he thought. To reach out from beyond the grave and destroy them, make them beg and plead and whimper. What was it Genghis Khan said? Life has four great joys: killing your enemies, torturing their sons, raping their daughters, and making their widows weep.

You were wrong, Mongol. He smiled. There is a fifth pleasure, one so horrible that even you could never have dreamed of it.

He dozed lightly for a few hours, and as the sun rose slowly over the mountaintops he was awakened by the sounds of bustle and voices in the great hall and out in the courtyard. A knocking on his door was followed by a nervous voice from without saying, "My Lord! The Turkish forces have been sighted near Dobresti!"

"Assemble my host!" the Voivode said as he sprang from the bed. "Tell Yaroslav to bring me my armor. Tell my generals to meet me in the great hall in fifteen minutes."

"Yes, Lord," the chamberlain said, and then hurried away from the door, shouting out the orders of his master.

"Malcolm!" he heard a distant voice saying.

The Voivode walked over to the window and looked out at the mountains.

"Malcolm! Wake up!"

Sunrise, he thought. By sunset, either I will be victorious or I will be in chains. If victorious, then tomorrow's sunrise will see me on the way to becoming lord of all Dacia. And if in chains, then I shall see no more sunrises.

Even if I accept Ordogh's offer, even if I exist for centuries to come, never again shall I see the light of day.

He gazed out the window for a few more moments.

Then, as he turned to leave the room and go out to meet the Turk, a resounding slap landed on his cheek.

"Malcolm, wake up, goddamn it!" Jerry said.

"J . . . Jerry," he said weakly. "Wh . . . what . . . ?"

"Are you okay?" Jerry asked.

"Yes . . . another dream . . ."

"Shit," his friend muttered. "Why don't you sit down for a minute?"

It was only when Jerry made this suggestion that Malcolm realized that he was standing motionless, an untouched glass of sherry in his hand. He stared at it for a few moments and then impulsively poured the entire glass down his throat. The phone began ringing as he placed the glass down upon the table, and he stumbled over to it, "H . . . hello?"

"Malcolm?"

Her voice was like a ray of sunlight. "Holly! I . . . I was going to call you."

"I have to see you, Malcolm. Can you come over right away?"

"Yes, yes, I want to come over. An awful lot has happened, and—"

"You can tell me about it when you get here. I'm home, in my apartment. Can you come over now?"

"Sure I can," he said, smiling and relieved.

"Good. Come alone."

"Holly, I'm so happy that—" But there was dead air on the other end of the line. She had hung up. Malcolm turned to Jerry and said, "Tell Rachel that I'm going over to see Holly. Either I'll be back in a little while or I'll call you from her place." He rushed out the door, without waiting for a response.

It was just after sundown.

Chapter Seventeen

Malcolm coughed nervously as he stood before the door of Holly Larsen's co-op apartment. He was alone in the narrow, dimly lighted hallway, and he glanced to his right and to his left to make certain that there were no witnesses to his unease and discomfort. How can I ask her to put us up, after everything that has happened? How can I try to impose on her? But he knew that he had to impose on her. And he knew that she would agree, knew that her decision to end their relationship had been a rational one that ran contrary to her emotions. He told himself that he knew this. In reality, he merely hoped it.

Malcolm coughed again, took a deep breath, and rang the buzzer. A long moment passed and then he heard Holly's voice say, "Come in, Malcolm." Her voice sounded somehow odd.

Malcolm found to his surprise that the door was not locked, and as he pushed it open and leaned his head into the apartment, he noticed first that all of the lights were out and all of the shades were drawn. Then an odor reached his nostrils, and he crinkled his nose against the sickeningly sweet smell. "Holly?" he said into the darkness of the interior.

"Come in, Malcolm," she said again.

He stepped into the dark room, leaving the door open behind him. Attempting a bit of humor, he said, "I guess you didn't clean out your refrigerator before we left for England, right? Whew! There's one hell of a stink in here. This place i ripe!"

"Close the door behind you," she said. "Don't turn on the lights."

Malcolm pushed the door shut and then stood there

allowing his eyes to adjust to the darkness before walking forward. "Holly, what are you doing sitting in the dark?"

"Find a chair, Malcolm," she said softly. "We have some things to discuss."

He groped around in the general vicinity of where he remembered a chair as being, then sat down in it. "Holly, I can barely see you. Why do you have the lights out?"

"I'll explain in a moment. Just be quiet and listen to me."

"Sure, Holly, but first I have a favor to ask of you. I think that Lucy managed to hide the remains in my house somewhere, and we haven't been able to find them yet. I don't think that Rachel and I should stay there at night, and Lucy knows where Jerry lives, so would you be able to let us stay here tonight?"

"No."

Her answer was unambiguous and immediate. Malcolm was slightly nonplussed and managed only to say, "But . . . I mean, I know that we . . . I mean, you and I . . ."

Holly laughed, and there was a quality to her laugh that caused the hair on Malcolm's nape to bristle. "I'm afraid that I can't really give you any help, Malcolm. And I really think that it would be best for all concerned if you and Rachel stayed at home."

Malcolm peered through the darkness at his ex-girlfriend. His eyes had adjusted to the darkness as much as they were able, and still he could barely see her. He was able to see her teeth very dimly as she smiled, and the whiteness of her skin was very, very slightly visible in what little light insinuated its way through the slats of the blinds from the streetlamp. "Holly, I don't think you understand what I'm saying. If I stay in the house—"

"Stay in the house, Malcolm," she interrupted. "Don't fight it anymore. There are things happening here that you don't understand, that you can't even guess at. Just stay in the house. Give up."

"Give up!" he exclaimed, growing angry. "After what we've been through? After what I've done, after what might happen? Are you serious!" He paused as he reached out toward the table beside the chair and felt around in the darkness for the lamp. "Holly, I don't understand why you're—" He stopped speaking the moment after he switched on the light. He remained motionless, speechless, stunned, staring at Holly Larsen. She sat across from him on the sofa, her right leg crossed over her left, her hands folded demurely in her lap; but only the studied poise of her position was the same as the Holly he had known. Her skin, once so delicate and rosy, now had the aspect of marble—cold, hard, and lifeless. Her face, once so warm and expressive and loving, was a drawn, pallid mask of inhuman amusement. Her smile, once sincere, was now sardonic, and her once hazel eyes now burned with a reddish glow.

"Lucy visited me last evening," she explained simply. "She killed me, you see."

Malcolm shuddered and felt a sob rising up from his throat. "Oh, Holly," he moaned. "Holly, Holly!"

"I understand everything now, Mal," she said, rising to her feet and approaching him. "You have to understand everything, too. You can't win, Malcolm. You can't beat him, you can't defeat him. Just give up, Malcolm. Give up, give in, let the final memory arise in the blood, and then you can rest. You can rest forever."

Malcolm leaped from the chair and backed away from her. He stared at her as he stammered, "D...don't you touch her," loving her, hating her, fearing her, pitying her, hating himself for what he had caused to happen to her.

Holly laughed cruelly, baring her fangs as her dead mouth curled in a sadistic smile. "Oh, Malcolm, you really are so pathetic. Do you really think you can fight us? Do you really think you can fight *him*?"

"Where's Lucy?" he demanded. "Holly, it's too late for you, and maybe it's too late for me and Rachel, but think about Jerry for just one minute. He was your friend, Holly, he was our friend. Just try to remember what you were, who you were. Think about Jerry. Think about all the other poor people who may become victims of this terrible thing."

The red glow in her eyes dimmed for an instant, but then she said, "Stop it, Malcolm. I know who I was and what I was, but I'm someone else now, I'm some*thing* else now." He had backed up against the wall, and she reached up to wrap her arms around his neck as she drew him close to her. Her soft breasts pressed against his chest, and they were cold, so cold. "You have to remember everything, Malcolm. You have to let the blood remember and understand everything, as I understand everything, as Lucy understood everything ever since that first night in the crypt in England. The blood mube fully awakened for the circle to be closed." She smiled at him, a lascivious, vulgar smile. "A final vision, my dear love. A final memory, and then everything will be set right again."

"Set right for whom?" he spat, consciously ordering himself not to want her, not to return her embrace, not to love the walking corpse whose inviting lips he knew were as cold as the grave. "Set right for you, for Lucy, for *him*?" He grabbed her wrists and attempted to throw her arms away from him, but she seemed molded of iron, unmovable and fixed.

His hands were still grasping her wrists as she moved her palms up and placed them on his feverish temples. "Awaken," she whispered. "Awaken, remember." The dancing fire in her eyes aroused the memories that were struggling to emerge from the dark depths of the past, memories of that fateful day when Vlad the Impaler last trod the earth as a human being, memories of that dark night when he first stepped undead from his grave.

The red glow seemed to suck him deep into its depths, and the ruddy fire transformed itself into thick billows of mist. The one small part of his consciousness that was still Malcolm Harker knew that he was still standing on his feet in an apartment in Forest Hills, New York, but the rest of his mind was cast back over the centuries to the year 1476, to the field of battle.

He found himself seated upon a strong white stallion that bucked and snorted with excitement. The cacophonous din of the rabble host that surrounded him assaulted his ears, and the frenzied beating of swords upon shields filled him with eagerness for the taste of battle. His soldiers responded to his words with the age-old sound of martial approbation, the clangor of blade upon armor.

His own sword was drawn and raised high above his head as he shouted to his host, "Leave not one alive, my children! The blood of the Turk is as perfume to me, and I command you to sweeten the air with the smell!" His soldiers smote their shields and cried words of praise for their Voivode. "A silver piece for each of you for each Turkish head! A golden piece for each of you for each Turkish noble!"

Spear points and sword tips thrust upward at the sky from the assembled host, and they screamed horrible threats against the Ottoman enemy. The Voivode's heart beat fast with excitement and the lust for blood, and he sat high up in his saddle as he raised his shield up beside his sword and cried out in a voice loud enough for all to hear, "Forward to Oradea, my children! Forward to spill their blood and slice their bodies into food for our dogs! Death to Torghuz Beg!"

"Death to Torghuz Beg!" the host shouted, their war cry a deafening onslaught of sound.

"Death to the Turk!" he cried.

"Death to the Turk!" they shouted.

"Freedom for all Dacia!" The last cry he made was lost in the overwhelming din of their voices as they shouted imprecations and curses to their enemies, and then he moved his stallion into a gallop and led his frenzied army down from the high ground to meet the Turkish invaders on the plain of Oradea.

The mist thickened and then thinned, and he found himself in the midst of a pitched battle, his sword singing out as it struck shield and armor, whizzing through the air as it sought human flesh and bone and blood, lopping off heads, slicing through arms, ripping through stomachs and chests. The screams of the dying and the mutilated echoed in his ears like music, and he grinned and his black eyes burned with animal lust and savage pleasure and he reveled in the destruction and the death. The field was red with blood, the field stank of blood, his bright silver sword dripped with blood. He smiled and charged again and again and again.

He saw the Turkish standards in the distance, the banner of the commander of the enemy army, and he sliced his way through the multitude atop his bleeding horse, killing his own men as indiscriminately as he killed the enemy in his eagerness to get to Torghuz Beg. The Turk saw his white stallion approaching, laughed, and shouted something that he could not hear over the din of the battle. As he drew closer, the voice of the Turk rose over the battle cries and the screams of pain and reached his ears. "A good day, is it not, Little Dragon?"

He charged through the mass of foot soldiers and swung his sword at the beg. The Turk raised his shield and deflected the blow. "A good day for us," he shouted in reply. "It will not end well for you."

The Turk's sword sliced the air and crashed against his own, and then they were locked in a personal combat of muscle against muscle, iron against iron. Any one of the foot soldiers who surrounded them could easily have thrust up a spear and killed the enemy commander, but that would have been unthinkable, and fatally dangerous. This was a combat of lord against lord, and neither lord would accept aid or interference. Any Turk who dared attack the Wallachian at this moment would have been tortured to death by his own beg; and any Wallachian who robbed his lord of the pleasure of the kill would have been executed in the customary manner. It was not for nothing that he was called Vlad the Impaler, this Little Dragon, this Dracula.

The beg's shield thudded against his and he almost fell from his saddle, but he was able to rein back and retreat a few steps from his enemy. He righted himself and charged again, crying, "Go back to your tents and your little boys, son of a whore!"

Torghuz Beg laughed and landed a mighty blow upon his shield and then took one upon his own. "You are weak today, Little Dragon! Did you not drink your god's blood before battle, Christian cannibal?"

He laughed also, enjoying the combat and the insults immensely. "No, I did not, but I shall drink yours by nightfall, lover of sheep!"

"You shall drink my water, Little Dragon!" The beg laughed again, then charged. Back and forth the combat went, and the battle lasted long and the screams of the dying mingled with the terrified shrieks of the horses and blood innundated the fields of Oradea.

And the mist thickened and he was no longer in the battle, and all was quiet and calm. He was cold, and he was in pain.

He looked up through the thinning mist at the shackles that stretched up from his raised arms, binding him to the cold, damp wall. He heard the scratching of the rats in the dark shadows of the dungeon, and he spat a bitter curse at the defeat of his army. He had been captured on the field and chained in the dungeon of his own castle.

The door of the cell swung open and Torghuz Beg entered. Two retainers followed him, the one holding a lighted torch and the other a bottle of thick wine. The torch burned brightly in the darkness and sent billows of sooty smoke upward to bounce silently from the stone ceiling of the dungeon. "Little Dragon!" the beg said in mock surprise. "What a state you are in!"

He knew that he was at this man's mercy, and he also

knew that the beg was as merciless as he. He saw no reason
to grovel. Instead he smiled and said, "Welcome, eater of
pigs."

Torghuz Beg laughed heartily. "Oh, Little Dragon, how
alike we are! I shall miss you, I shall indeed!"

"Have you come to see me weep and hear me plead, you
pox-ridden whoremonger? If so, your time were better spent
elsewhere, for you will find no pleasure in me."

"You offend me, my dear Vlad," the beg said. "I have
come to share a glass of wine with an old friend."

He glanced up at the chains and smiled. "I am sorry, but
I appear to be indisposed."

The Turk snapped his fingers at one of the guards. In a
moment the defeated Voivode was freed from the cold iron,
and he rubbed his wrists as he walked toward his enemy.

"We shall drink from the same bottle," the beg said. "A
final gesture of friendship." The Turk took the bottle from his
retainer and poured a generous quantity down his throat. He
handed it to the Voivode, who took an even larger portion.

As he wiped his mouth the Voivode said, "Be careful,
Turk. Your god of sheep lovers hates the fruit of the vine."

"Allah is merciful, and understanding," the beg replied.
"I have this day delivered all Wallachia into his hands. He
will forgive me this slight immorality."

"Today you have triumphed, but it will not always be so.
My people will cast you out, wipe you as cow dung from the
soles of their boots."

"Perhaps, perhaps." The beg smiled, taking the bottle
and drinking again. "But I think not. We are the conquering
race, Voivode. Twenty years ago we captured Constantinople,
and today we are overrunning the Balkans. Soon will come
Budapest, then Vienna, and then Warsaw and Prague, and—
who knows?—eventually Paris and London."

The Voivode shook his head slowly, smiling maliciously at
his enemy. "Never. We shall drive you out, those of you
whom we do not behead."

"Perhaps," the Turk repeated, "but I am afraid you
cannot say 'we,' Voivode. You will die, quite painfully, I am
afraid, at dawn." He handed over the bottle again.

The Voivode shrugged, a gesture of casual acceptance,
and swallowed another draught. "What of my wife and children?"

"Your wife?" The beg laughed. "Surely you do not mean

to pretend piety with me, Little Dragon! Your wives you mean, surely!"

He smiled. "The ladies, then, of concern to me."

"Dead, I am afraid," the beg said sadly, his eyes twinkling. "But do not be upset, Voivode. I took my pleasure with each of them before I slew them, and they died happy."

He clenched his teeth through his smile. "And my children?"

"Ah, I am afraid that they are nowhere to be found. I have heard a rumor that my hunting dogs are unusually lacking in hunger tonight, but why I cannot say."

The Voivode did not respond, but his black eyes blazed with hatred.

The beg laughed. "Come, Voivode, no anger! Ask yourself this question: Had you won the battle, what would have been the fate of my wives and my sons? What would you have done to them, and to me, Vlad the Impaler? How many stakes would you have thrust into them, skewering them from anus to ear and laughing over their agony?"

He smiled at the Turk calmly. "Truly, you and I are much alike."

"Truly we are," Torghuz Beg agreed, slapping him on the shoulder. "You should have been born a Turk, Little Dragon. We would have been formidable allies, you and I!"

"We were allies," he reminded him.

"Ah, but that was always your problem, Voivode!" the Turk replied. "Alliance with you was like marriage to a whore. We never knew whose bed you were crawling into when our backs were turned."

"I did only that which I thought was best for my people," he said simply.

Torghuz Beg laughed loudly. "Save the legends for posterity, Little Dragon. You did whatever satisfied yourself. Your people were sheep to you, pawns, nothing more. Whom do you think your people hate more, you or me?" He grinned. "It would be a close contest, Impaler!"

The Voivode drank again from the bottle, finishing it. The thick red wine warmed his cold and empty stomach. "I ask a favor of you, Torghuz Beg."

"Ah, do you now beg for your life? You disappoint me, Little Dragon."

"No, I do not," he replied. "After you have killed me, take my body and the bodies of my women and give them to

my people, that I may be buried according to custom." He
paused. "I would have done no less for you, were I the victor
this day."

The Turk slapped him again on the shoulder. "Consider
it done! I can be magnanimous in victory, Voivode."

He laughed quietly. "And is your victory certain, licker of
the sultan's hole? Do not be smug. Much else may happen,
and soon."

"Perhaps, Little Dragon, perhaps. But I am afraid that
you will not be there to see it."

He smiled again and then the mist descended and
obscured the cell around him. When the mist dissipated
sufficiently for him to be able to see, he was still in the
dungeon cell, but he was alone, and the darkness outside the
small window near the ceiling was beginning to be displaced
by the light of dawn, the dawn of his death.

"Ordogh," he whispered. "Come to me!"

He waited for what seemed a long while, and then the
infernal voice spoke to him. "I am here, Little Dragon. I am
here."

"Tell me again, Ordogh," the Voivode asked. "Explain it
all to me again, as you did before this last battle."

"Do you accept, Little Dragon?"

"I want to hear it again, all of it, Ordogh. What you ask
of me is no small thing."

"And what I offer you is no small thing."

The Voivode gazed into the still, deep darkness of the
dungeon cell. "Life in death and death in life," he whispered,
remembering the words of the dark spirit. "If I accept,
Ordogh . . . if I accept, I will become . . . I will become . . ."
He stopped speaking, as if frightened of the very word.

"Nosferatu," the spirit finished for him. "You will become nosferatu."

He shook his head and muttered, "I had always thought
such stories were but to frighten children."

The voice seemed almost to laugh as it replied, "The fear
of children holds much wisdom, Little Dragon, even as the
wisdom of man holds much folly."

The Voivode clenched his teeth and swallowed hard as
he contemplated the implications of the pact being offered to
him. "And in that form, in that state of existence, I shall
triumph over my enemies?"

"I have told you this, Little Dragon, that you shall

triumph over generations of men not yet born. You shall be free to kill and torture at will, on through the centuries."

"Centuries..." the Voivode whispered. "Centuries..."

"You shall drink the blood of the living and be a harbinger of death and terror, immune to the weapons of the mortals whom you destroy. The sword, the musketball, poison, fire, all shall leave you unharmed. And you shall be as a mirror image of my Enemy, Little Dragon, and so the looking glass will not hold your reflection, and in all things shall you be to Him as a dark twin."

The Voivode waited and then said, "More, Ordogh. I wish to hear more. I, a dark twin to Christ?"

"Yes, Little Dragon. As He rose from the dead at sunrise, so shall you rise from the dead at sunset. As He walked upon water, so shall you be unable to cross water unaided. As He died impaled upon wood, and as you have delighted in impaling others upon wood, so shall your destruction be possible only by the wooden stake. As He gave His blood to others on that last night before His crucifixion, when He shared bread and wine with His disciples, so shall you share your blood with others and curse them with your own undeath. As He was transfigured on the night when He met with Moses and Elijah, so shall you transfigure yourself at will and become bat and wolf and rat and mist and wind. And as He shed His blood for others, so shall others shed their blood for you." The voice paused. "I shall take you beneath my wings, Little Dragon, and you shall be my son."

The Voivode drank in the words as he heard them whispered into his ears by that intimate, seductive voice, the voice that had once spoken to Eve beneath the tree of forbidden fruit, the voice that had once bargained for the soul of Job, the voice that had once urged the young man from Nazareth to turn stones into bread. The Voivode listened and thought. "Nosferatu," he muttered.

"Nosferatu," the voice echoed.

"And I shall live on as nosferatu through the centuries," he mused.

"Through the hundreds of years and the thousands of years, until the sun itself grows cold."

The Voivode nodded. "Ordogh, I agree. I accept."

"Of your own free will?"

"Yes, of my own free will."

"Do you know what fate awaits you upon the Day of Judgment?"

He laughed bitterly. "That fate awaits me regardless. It is my hatred of my enemies that impels me to this pact, not any hope for special consideration."

"No, Little Dragon, it is not hatred of your enemies," the voice whispered. "Your enemies are not the Turks, they are not the Magyars. You hate life, Little Dragon. Life is your enemy. Mankind is your enemy, as mankind is my enemy. You are filled with hatred and bitterness and the lust for blood."

The Voivode contemplated this for a few moments, and then he nodded. "Yes, Ordogh, your words are true."

"I know, Little Dragon."

"And you have always known, have you not?"

"I have always known, Little Dragon, and for the sake of your hatred and your bitterness and your lust, I have loved you more than any mortal whom I have known. And I am old, Little Dragon. I am old."

The Voivode nodded again. "So I shall be the mirror image of your Enemy, Ordogh, the mirror image of the Prince of Light."

"The Prince of Darkness," the voice agreed. "Nosferatu."

"Nosferatu." The Voivode laughed. "Nosferatu! Nosferatu!" He laughed louder and the echoes of his laughter resounded throughout the dungeon. "Yes, I shall be nosferatu! I shall be walking Death! I shall be Hell embodied, incarnate!" His laughter was mad and shrill. "I accept, Ordogh. I accept, I accept!"

"You shall join me in Hell, Little Dragon," the voice warned.

"I look forward to it!" the Voivode shouted.

There was a long pause, a deep silence in the cell. And then the voice whispered, "It is done, Little Dragon. It is done."

The cell door swung open and five Turkish guards entered the dungeon cell. The Voivode looked up at the small window near the ceiling. "Daylight," he muttered. "Dawn. The sun was darkened when He died, and it shines for me. But when the sun sets . . ."

One of the guards unfolded a piece of parchment and began to read from it. "Vlad Vladescu," the guard began with words which denied him his title, which called him simply

Vlad the son of Vlad, "you have been condemned to death for the crimes of treason, usurpation, and rebellion. The order for your execution bears the seals of Torghuz Beg and Voivode Radu I of Wallachia." The guard looked up. "Have you anything to say?"

The Voivode smiled. "I have much to say," he muttered. "But I shall speak later, after sunset." He was still smiling as the guards led him from the cell and the mist once again descended upon him...

...and the dark mist became darker, and only sporadic images were able to pierce through the thick blackness...

...the grinning face of Torghuz Beg as the Voivode was tied to the stone slab...

...the excruciating agony as the execution began...

...the death of a thousand cuts...

...the right forefinger, joint by joint...the right middle finger, joint by joint...the right thumb, joint by joint...

Ordogh! They are severing my body to bits!

It will mean nothing, Little Dragon.

When I am nosferatu, will my body be whole?

It will, Little Dragon.

...the left forefinger, joint by joint...the left middle finger, joint by joint...

Ordogh! Ordogh!

I am here, Little Dragon. Wait, my son, wait. All will be well. All will be well.

...the wrists...the ankles...the elbows...the knees...

The pain! Ordogh, the pain!

Yes, Little Dragon, yes! Let the pain feed your hatred!

...the thighs...the arms...

Kill me, Ordogh, kill me, please, please, let me die! How can I still be alive? How can I live through such pain?

Pain is your mother, Little Dragon. Pain is your lover. Pain is your bride.

...the tongue...the eyes...the testicles...the penis...

Soon, my son, soon, soon.

...the head...

And then all was darkness.

And in the darkness the mutilated body rested in the stone coffin in the chapel crypt near Oradea in Transylvania.

And in the darkness the raped and ruined and gutted bodies of Magda and Katarina and Simone gave festival to the insects and the worms.

And in the darkness the bits and pieces of the bloody flesh and the severed bone of the Voivode grew together.

And in the darkness a soft, infernal voice whispered, *Yes, Little Dragon, yes! Nosferatu! Nosferatu!*

The darkness was deep and lasted for an eternity. The darkness was emptiness and nothingness, a horrid, barren void, without life, without thought, without being. The darkness and the emptiness was all.

And time had ceased. And life had ceased.

He was dead.

He was dead.

Death was an eternal nonexistence, black and silent.

And then, into that silence, that darkness, that barren nothingness of death, a sudden infusion of horrible power struck his corpse with such force that his dead limbs pushed upward and threw the stone lid from his coffin.

He stepped out of death, but not into life. From death there was no true return, not at least by the power of the Lord of the Damned; only the Creator, from Whose mouth the words of creation had once come, could restore life to the dead. But Ordogh, the Devil, the Master of Hell, could bestow Undeath. And so the Little Dragon stepped Undead from his sarcophagus and stood in the midst of the dark and silent crypt in the lower level of his once proud castle. His nostrils smelled the smoke of the campfires of the Turks, and he smiled. *Torghuz Beg,* he thought, *the game goes on. The last move is mine.*

He raised his hands before his eyes and gazed at them appraisingly. They were as white as marble, bloodless, cold, dead hands. He placed one finger in his mouth and felt the sharp tips of the long fangs which now extended downward from his upper jaw, and then he closed his eyes and listened to his blood. The blood was Satan's foul gift to him, and the blood taught him all he needed to know. In a moment, the lesson was learned.

He walked slowly over to the three sarcophagi which he knew contained the bodies of his dead wives. He opened one and looked down at the corpse. "Magda," he whispered, and then plunged one of his long razorlike fingernails into his wrist. The thick purple blood flowed like a river, an endless river, and he drenched the mouth and face of his dead woman with the accursed flood.

Her eyes opened and the blood spoke to her as well. She

reached up and grabbed his wrist and sucked on it greedily, like a child at her mother's breast. And then she climbed out of her coffin.

He walked over to another sarcophagus and threw the lid back with disdain for its weight. "Katarina," he whispered, and then poured the elixir of Undeath into her dead mouth. "Simone, my little Frank," he said, smiling at the third dead woman in the third casket as he inflicted his curse upon her.

The three women and the man stood in silent communication with one another. There was no need to speak, for the blood spoke to them all. They each knew precisely what powers they now had, and each knew precisely what was now to be done. Silently, like hungry serpents creeping unseen and unheard through high grass, they left the chapel crypt, shielding their eyes from the crosses and crucifixes as they mounted the steps. Four pairs of eyes glowed red like hellfire in the darkness, and four tongues slavered hungrily over four pairs of fangs.

The mist descended upon him, then drifted away, and he was standing over the sleeping form of the Turkish chief. Smiling malevolently, the Voivode reached down and shook him gently by the shoulder. "Awaken, old ally," he whispered. "It is my move in the game."

The Turk's eyes opened slowly and gazed blearily up at the figure that loomed over him. "What?" he muttered. "What is wrong? Why have you . . . ?" Then he focused on the face of his enemy, and he smiled thoughtlessly as he attempted to think of an insulting quip. His smile faded as he remembered that he had killed his enemy earlier that day.

The Voivode grabbed the Turk by the throat and lifted him up into the air with astonishing ease. His strength was so great that the large Turk felt no heavier than a twig, and he laughed heartily as he threw the man down upon the ground.

Torghuz Beg tried to rise to his feet and run, but the Voivode leaped upon him and pressed him down upon the cold stone floor. His red orbs burned into the terrified eyes of the beg, and he whispered malevolently, "Last move of the game, my old ally, and I am the victor." Then he sank his fangs into the beg's throat and began to drain the blood from him.

The Turk hovered between life and death when the Voivode stood up and gazed down upon him with contempt. He turned to the three shrouded women who were waiting near the doorway and issued a silent command. They responded instantly. They leaped upon Torghuz Beg in a frenzy of hunger and anger and vindictiveness, and in the eagerness of their newfound drives, they tore him to pieces.

Terror and death descended upon the occupied castle and the camp of the Turks as the hours passed, and the screams of horror and pain drifted upward into the night sky. They killed and killed and killed, impervious to the knives and arrows and swords, reveling in the death and the terror. This, thought the Voivode, this is better than battle! It is better than torturing peasants, better than impaling enemies, better than nailing Turkish hats to Turkish heads! This is magnificently wondrous! The screams, the fear, the misery, the power, and the blood, the blood!

The mist swept over him and carried him through century after century of inhuman horror. He saw the terrified faces of women as he bore down upon them, the pleading eyes of men as he ripped through their throats with his great fangs, heard the delightful wails of infants as he tasted their sweet new blood. He and his wives ran joyfully through the Carpathian woods in the form of wolves; they flew upon their leathery wings through the windows of taverns and palaces and peasant huts; they floated invisible in the fog amid the ignorant evening merrymakers. They drank and they killed and they mocked the stupid, foolish cattle.

And each dawn they pulled shut the lids of their coffins, and they slept a sleep like unto death.

And each twilight they felt the same inhuman power course through them, filling them with cruelty and the lust for blood.

And they hovered like angels of death above the terrified peasants of the Carpathians.

The mist thinned and the centuries ceased their lightning passage, and he knew that the peasants had learned how to protect themselves. They covered their windows with garlands of garlic and placed crosses and crucifixes upon themselves and their doors. Priests armed with consecrated hosts and holy water and wooden stakes searched for them, never finding them, but inspiring the peasants to seek refuge from the demon in the symbols and sacraments of the Orthodox Church.

And he grew hungry and restless as the decades passed into centuries.

He pulled open the great door of the castle and stood motionless inside the great hall, smiling at the clear-eyed young man who waited politely without. He made no movement toward the young man, did nothing to impel him forward, for no one may be forced to pass through the gates of Hell. "Welcome to my house!" he said, and smiled. "Enter freely and of your own will!" As the young man stepped over the threshold he grabbed his hand and shook it firmly, thinking, little fool, little fool! Such easy prey you and your kind will be, you proper English with your ignorance and your skepticism and your reliance upon reason and your pathetic faith in science! "Welcome to my house," he repeated. "Come freely. Go safely; and leave something of the happiness you bring."

The young man returned the smile and the handshake but was apparently uncertain whom he was addressing. "Count Dracula?"

He bowed and said, "I am Dracula; and I bid you welcome, Mr. Harker, to my house..."

The mists swept him away and carried him along. Time seemed to be compressed into snatched and fleeting moments, scenes blending into scenes, people and places indistinguishable from each other. And then he found himself standing upon the deck of a ship, drawing closer to a deserted beach on the English coast. He stood motionless, impervious to the biting, rain-drenched wind, unshaken even as the dead ship drifted closer to shore and then impaled itself upon the jagged reef which bordered the harbor at Whitby, the reef which would have been so easy for a navigator to avoid if only the ship were piloted by a living man. But this was a ship of the dead, the dead captain's hands bound to the wheel, the mates and crew all dead.

England, he thought. A new land, filled with new cattle, running with new blood. His eyes blazed in the tornadic darkness. England...

He felt himself again swept along by the mists of memory, saw himself as if from a distance running upon four padded feet and flying upon two taloned wings; and then he was in human form, floating in midair outside a barred window, looking in at the feverish face of a madman.

Renfield wrapped his scabby fingers around the bars and drew his pallid face close to the apparition that floated before him. "I know what you are," he whispered. "I know what you want. You want me to invite you in, don't you." The apparition did not reply, and Renfield went on, "Why should I? Why should I invite you in, bloodsucker?"

He smiled. Fly-eater, he thought. Spider-eater. Invite me into your cell, and the entire mansion will then be open to me. He swept his hand out behind him, and Renfield looked down at the dark mass that was spreading over the grass. Renfield's eyes went wide as the vampire whispered, "Rats, rats, rats! Hundreds, thousands, millions of them; and dogs, and cats. All lives! All red blood, with years of life in it! Not little buzzing flies, but millions and millions of rats!"

Renfield licked his lips and drooled as the tidal wave of rodents rolled over the grass and surrounded the Victorian mansion which served as St. Anselm's Asylum. "All these lives will I give you," the creature said, "aye, and many more and greater, through countless ages, if you will fall down and worship me."

Renfield's eyes were those of a child before a candy shop window as he stepped back from the bars and whispered, "Come in, Lord and Master!"

He changed into mist and floated into the cell. After resuming human form he looked at Renfield and commanded, "Kneel, servant. Kneel to your lord." The madman fell to his knees and looked up at his master worshipfully. The vampire plunged a sharp fingernail into his wrist and held it out, saying, "Take, drink. This is the new covenant in my blood, which will bind you to my service . . ." The madman fastened his lips upon the bleeding wrist and drank long and deep.

The cell dissolved before his eyes, and then he was standing upon a balcony on the east wing of St. Anselm's Asylum, the building he could now enter at will as a result of the lunatic's invitation. He smoothed his gray mustache and quietly opened the window door to the bedroom. All was silent in the stately Victorian mansion; all were sleeping. He crept into the room.

Lucy Westenra lay upon her bed, lost in sweet dreams of her fiancé, Arthur Wellesley, the heir to the Wellington title and its attendant fortune. She was a lovely young woman, rosy-cheeked and healthy, filled with delicious young blood. As he gazed down at her, he smiled at the sight of her long blond hair as it lay in delightful dishevelment upon her pillow. How like Simone you are, sweet Lucy!

He walked quietly over to her bedside and leaned over

her, allowing the inviting aroma of her person to drift upward
to his flaring nostrils as his tongue flicked eagerly upon the
pointed tips of his fangs. Then he leaned closer and gently
pressed the tips against her throat.

She started and moaned as he punctured her soft skin,
but she did not awaken. Centuries of experience had given
him the skill with which to drink without detection. He
sucked the blood greedily from her white throat, leaving no
stain upon her linen pillowcase when he withdrew from her.
Then he whispered, "Lucy!"

She opened her eyes slowly and languidly. He captured
her gaze with his own in the instant between awakening and
wakefulness, and she was drawn deep into their burning red
depths. She was immobile but at his command, unconscious
of her actions, still asleep though awake. "Lucy!" he repeated
in the same serpentine whisper. "You thirst, do you not?"

"Yes," she whispered. "I'm very thirsty."

He plunged one of his sharp teeth into his own wrist and
then pressed it against her lips. "Drink, sweet Lucy. Drink of
my elixir. It is warm and sweet, is it not?" Lucy Westenra
swallowed the tainted blood and with it drank her own
destruction.

The mist surrounded him again, swept him away from
the dark bedroom, and he found himself standing before the
Westenra crypt in Hempstead, awaiting her emergence. It
was long past sundown, but she had not yet come forth from
her grave. He pushed open the door of the mausoleum and
entered, expecting to find her there, but seeing nothing.

He noticed a repugnant odor, however, and a strange,
unpleasant heat. He walked over to her casket and lifted the
lid, then recoiled in disgust from the overpowering stench of
garlic. He forced himself to look into the coffin, and his lips
curled in a furious snarl at the sight of the stake that
protruded from her chest, at the severed head and the open
mouth stuffed with the foul plant. The communion wafer that
rested upon her stomach was the source of the bitter heat,
and it prevented him from drawing close enough to the coffin
to remove the stake and the garlic and bathe the corpse in his
blood. Outraged, he ran from the tomb. "Van Helsing," he
muttered angrily. "Van Helsing and his society of meddling
fools!"

He drifted again through time and memory, until he was
once more a wave of mist seeping into Renfield's cell, the

only entranceway into the asylum that had not been barred to him by garlic and crosses. But as the mist resolved itself into undead flesh, the madman attacked him, grabbed him with his powerful hands, crying, "No, you shall not, you shall not! She is kind and gentle to me! You shall not take her life, you shall not drink her blood!"

He was simultaneously angered at the presumption and amused at the futile rebellion. He freed himself easily from Renfield's grasp and then spun him around, breaking the madman's back with one mighty blow from his fist. He picked Renfield up, threw him down hard, and with his heel ground his face on the cold stone floor. The vampire left the lunatic paralyzed and dying in a pool of blood as he set out to avenge himself upon the miserable cattle who had dared to oppose him...

...And he laughed as he pressed Mina Harker's terrified face to his bleeding chest, laughed at her idiot husband who lay unconscious upon the bed near the window...

"Flesh of my flesh," he murmured to the woman, "blood of my blood, kin of my kin..."

And then suddenly there was darkness and bumpy, jostling motion, and he felt the rough interior walls of a wooden box scraping against his hands as he passed from his deep sleep of death to undead wakefulness, and in an instant he knew that he was back in his homeland, that his Gypsy servants were rushing to bring him back to the ruins of his castle, that he was being pursued by Jonathan Harker and Quincey Morris and the Duke of Wellington.

And he knew that a choice needed to be made, a risk needed to be taken.

He felt the box being pushed by eager, frenzied hands, heard the sounds of gunfire and the shouting of voices, felt the wooden box being shoved roughly from the wagon to the ground, squinted against the dying rays of the sun as the lid was ripped away and the faces of Jonathan Harker and Quincey Morris bore down upon him. He made his decision in an instant.

"Ordogh!" he muttered as the knives of Harker and Morris plunged into his throat and chest.

Malcolm screamed. In the instant between the last moment of Dracula's memory and the first revival of his own consciousness, he felt the cold blades tear into him and felt the incredible agony of disintegration as flesh began to collapse into dust. And then he was again in Holly's apartment, lying on the floor in the empty room. Holly was gone.

He jumped slightly as the harsh ringing of Holly's telephone shattered the silence. He crawled over to the small end table upon which the phone rested and picked up the receiver. "H . . . hello?" he said, his breathless voice trembling and weak.

"Mal?" he heard Jerry Herman say. "Malcolm? Is that you?"

"Jerry," he said desperately. "She's dead. Holly's dead, worse than dead. Lucy got to her, killed her, turned her into . . . turned her into . . ." He could not bring himself to say the words.

Jerry took a moment to react. "Christ!" he whispered. "It can't be!"

"It is," Malcolm said, his voice breaking. "She called me to come over here so that she could help wake up the blood."

"Mal," Jerry interrupted him, "you can tell me about it when you get here . . . I mean, I *want* you to tell me about it, everything about it, but you have to get over here right away."

"Over where? Where are you?"

"I'm at the hospital with Rachel. Your grandfather is sinking fast. The doctor says he won't last the night."

Malcolm dropped the phone and ran to the door. He was motivated by two desires, the one being a frantic hope to be able to be with the old man when the time came for him to leave this world. But there was another motive, a motive more urgent and more compelling.

Rachel had glimpsed part of the truth, and Malcolm had also been aware, dimly, that there was indeed a plan, a plot, a terribly significant fact which was as yet not understood. In the moment of dissolution, as the immortal body of Dracula succumbed to mortality beneath the attack of Morris and Harker, Malcolm's blood memory had detected a smug satisfaction in the mind of the Count. He did not know what it was for, what plan had been set into motion on the cold Carpathian road a century before. But he knew that it had something to do with the blood. It all, always, had something to do with the blood.

If old Quincy Harker died before sunrise, he had to be here to keep the blood from asserting its power over the dead man's flesh.

Malcolm burst out of the apartment building and began running toward St. John's Hospital. The silent laughter of Dracula echoed in his ears as he ran, the vindictive, triumphant laughter which had been the last thought of the evil mind at the moment of destruction a hundred years before.

IV

DRACULA

You think to baffle me, you—with your pale faces all in a row, like sheep in a butcher's! You shall be sorry yet, each one of you! You think you have left me without a place to rest; but I have more. My revenge is just begun! I spread it over centuries, and time is on my side. Your girls that you all love are mine already; and through them you and others shall yet be mine, my creatures to do my bidding and to be my jackals when I want to feed...

—from Dr. Seward's diary, in
Dracula by Bram Stoker

Chapter Eighteen

Panting, trembling, almost faint from his exertions, Malcolm pushed open the door to the lobby of St. John's Hospital and ran over to the admitting desk. "Harker, Quincy Harker," he said in a loud, demanding voice. "What room?"

The desk nurse peered at him over the rim of her glasses and asked, "I beg your pardon?" in an irritated tone.

"My grandfather, Quincy Harker," he repeated. "I got a call that he's getting worse, that he may die. What room is he in?"

"Oh, yes, I'm sorry," she replied, suddenly all business. She ran her forefinger down the patient list on the clipboard in front of her and then said, "Room four eighteen. You follow the blue line from this corridor to the...," but Malcolm had already run from the desk and was heading toward the stairs.

When he reached the fourth floor, he looked around wildly, seeking some directional sign. When he found it, a yellow arrow on a blue field pointing the way to rooms 400 to 432, he walked at a somewhat slower but still brisk pace in the proper direction. Finding room 418, he took a deep breath, then entered.

The old man was lying on the bed semiconscious, tubes entering his arms and his nostrils. The room was redolent of the ubiquitous institutional disinfectant that so ironically seems associated with disease and death, and the silence was broken only by the irregular beeping of the heart monitor. Rachel sat at the edge of the bed beside her grandfather. Jerry stood off to the side, his hands folded in front of him in an oddly, and uncharacteristically, respectful manner. On the opposite edge of the bed, facing Rachel, sat Father Henley, who was speaking to old Quincy Harker in a low, soothing voice. Malcolm noticed that the priest's portable communion kit was opened and resting upon the chair beside the bed. Malcolm sighed, realizing that the priest had been administering the last rites to the old man.

Hang on, Gramps, Malcolm thought to himself as he glanced at the clock on the wall. It's still night. It's going to be hours before dawn. If you die after daybreak, we can have the blood out of you and the embalming fluid in your veins before the blood can awaken you.

"Don't die yet, Gramps," he whispered. "Hang on. Don't die yet."

Father Henley heard the whispered plea and looked up from his aged and dying parishioner. Misunderstanding Malcolm's words entirely, the priest rose from the bedside and walked over to take Malcolm by the hand. "We all come to our appointed ends someday, Malcolm," he said gently. "Your grandfather has had a long and full life, and his end is blessed and peaceful." He looked back at the deathbed. "Go and speak to him, Malcolm. I don't know if he can hear you, but he may be able to. It may be a comfort to him."

Malcolm nodded as he walked over to the bed and sat down on the edge. He and his sister looked at each other, their eyes communicating a shared but unspoken thought, a hope that their grandfather would not die before dawn. Malcolm took his grandfather's hand and said, "Gramps? Can you hear me? It's Malcolm, Gramps." He leaned forward, putting his lips close to his grandfather's ear. "Hang on, Gramps, hang on. Can you hear me, Gramps? It's night, it's still night. Hang on until daybreak." He thought for a moment that he could feel his grandfather's hand squeeze his own slightly, that he could see the aged eyelids flutter. "You've beaten him all your life, Gramps. Don't let him win now. Fight, Gramps, fight. Don't die now, don't die yet. Hang on until dawn."

Rachel rose from the bed and stepped back to where Jerry was standing. "Come out into the hall," she muttered. He followed her out of the room, and after closing the door behind them, she said, "Malcolm is right in what he's been saying to Grandfather. The remains are somewhere in our house, and their presence has stirred the blood in our grandfather. If he dies now, before sunrise, he may rise undead."

Jerry nodded. "I know. I understand."

"I have to stay here. I have to be with him, I *want* to be with him."

He nodded again. "What do you want me to do?"

She sighed. "Go out to the dumpster behind the hospital. Find some wood, a board, a stick, anything we can use as a stake if he..." She stopped, shaking her head. "You know what I'm saying. We can't let another creature like Lucy Westenra loose in the city. One is bad enough."

"Two," Jerry said softly. "I couldn't tell you before, with the priest in the room with us, but Malcolm told me on the phone that Lucy killed Holly. She's one of them now."

Rachel pressed her fingers to her eyes. "The poor child. The poor, poor child."

"Yeah," Jerry muttered. "I'll go and find something."

Rachel watched him go before she turned and went back into the room. And you also, you poor man, she thought. Our curse is your curse as well. We are like carriers of a plague, spreading our foulness and our filth everywhere we go.

She sat back down upon the edge of the bed and took her grandfather's other hand in hers, listening as Malcolm continued his soft exhortations.

The door opened and a doctor entered. This young man, to all appearances a Pakistani or an Indian, like so many of the health workers in New York City, said with a clipped and precise accent, "Good evening. Has the patient stirred at all?"

"No," Father Henley said. "He's been motionless."

The doctor shook his head as he walked over to the bed. Rachel moved aside so that he could examine the old man. Malcolm continued to speak to his grandfather in low, soft tones as the doctor made a superficial and, Rachel assumed, perfunctory examination. After a few canned comments of hope and comfort, he left.

Malcolm looked up at the clock. One o'clock. A good five hours until sunrise. "Hang on, Gramps," he whispered urgently. "Hang on!"

The hours passed slowly. Two o'clock, two-thirty, three. Jerry Herman returned and winked at Rachel. He held his left arm stiffly at his side, and he turned his hand slightly to the side so that she could see the edge of the piece of wood that he had hidden along his arm beneath the sleeve of his shirt. She nodded, then turned her attention back to her grandfather. They remained motionless in the room as the hours moved slowly past, Rachel on one side of the bed, Malcolm on the other, Jerry standing near the door, Father Henley standing off to the side, praying silently. Only the beep of the heart monitor and Malcolm's urgent whispers intruded upon the still deathwatch.

The beeping ceased at four A.M.

"Damn!" Malcolm muttered. He began to tremble as he rose from the bed and looked at his sister. "Rachel, we have to . . ."

"I know what we have to do," she said softly. She turned to Jerry. "You do it, Mr. Herman. I can't."

Jerry nodded as he drew the wooden stake forth from his sleeve. "Long enough?" he asked. "It's all I could find. I think it's part of a fruit crate from the hospital kitchen."

"It's long enough," Rachel replied. "It will pierce the heart. That's all that we need to do."

Father Henley stepped forward, his furrowed brow expressing his perplexity. "Rachel, what are you talking about?" His mouth fell open as Jerry walked forward and placed the tip of the wood against the motionless chest of the old man's body. The jagged edges of the hastily fashioned stake pressed down upon the clean white hospital gown. Henley rushed over and grabbed Jerry's hand. "What in God's name do you think you're doing!"

"Don't interfere, Father," Malcolm said as he took the priest's hand away from Jerry's with a firm yet somehow gentle grip. "He's doing what has to be done. He's doing what needs to be done."

"Malcolm, I don't understand," Father Henley said. "What is the meaning of this? What's going on here?"

Malcolm brushed away a tear. "It's a long, long story, Father, and I doubt that you'd believe it."

"Jerry," Rachel said with quiet urgency, "hurry up. There no time to delay."

"What should I use for a hammer?" Jerry asked. "I didn't have time to find one."

"You don't need a hammer," she replied. "Put your weight behind it and stab it in."

"Just a moment here!" Henley said in a loud voice.

"What kind of nonsense is this! You, get away from there! Get away from him!" As he spoke, the priest disengaged his hand from Malcolm's and grabbed the wood from Jerry.

"Father Henley, do not interfere!" Rachel snapped. "This is hard enough for us. Please, just leave."

"I'll do nothing of the kind!" Henley shouted. "What is wrong with you people?"

Malcolm grabbed hold of the wood and pulled it roughly from the priest's hands. "I'll try to explain later, Father. Just stand back."

"Malcolm, for the love of God!"

Malcolm handed the stake to Jerry, saying, "Rachel's right, Jer. I don't think I can do it either. You'll have to."

Father Henley once again grabbed hold of the piece of wood, but this time Jerry kept his grip tight and refused to allow the stake to be taken from him. "Stop this nonsense immediately!" the priest demanded. He stood on one side of the bed and Jerry stood on the other, their hands stretched out over the corpse, their eyes locked as they engaged in a motionless contest for possession of the wood.

A third hand reached up and entered the contest. Quincy Harker's dead eyes snapped open and a low chuckle rumbled forth from his lips as he ripped the stake from their hands and threw it across the room. He sat up in bed and allowed his eyes to drift lazily from face to face as they all gazed at him in silence, Henley with shock, Jerry with fear, Malcolm and Rachel with sorrowful regret.

Father Henley placed his hand upon Quincy's shoulder and said softly, "Mr. Harker! Please lie down and rest!" He smiled. "We thought for a moment that we had lost you."

Quincy laughed, his eyes flashing red in the muted light of the hospital room. "I appreciate your concern, Father." Then he grabbed Henley by his white Roman collar and pulled him forward. The clerical ring tore free from around the priest's neck, and in that instant, as the old man lost his grip on the priest, Malcolm lunged forward and pulled Father Henley back from the bed, causing him to fall roughly into a corner of the room.

Quincy Harker leaped up from the deathbed, and the speed and agility of his motion was so out of keeping with the weak, shuffling old man they had all known that they were momentarily stunned. Their brief immobility was sufficient to allow Quincy to reach Father Henley, grab him by the shoulders, pull him forward and bury his teeth in the priest's throat.

Malcolm and Rachel tried in vain to pull the creature that had been their grandfather away from the priest, but Quincy seemed as heavy as granite and as strong as iron. Henley dangled from Quincy's grasp as if he were a rag doll, his legs kicking and jerking spasmodically as Quincy sucked the life from him. When at last the blood had been drained from the priest, Quincy allowed him to drop onto the floor, where he lay white and motionless. Quincy took the hands of his grandchildren in his and cast them easily from him, then stepped back and faced them. "Go home and go to sleep," he said, smiling darkly. "Sleep and dream and rest."

Malcolm sighed and shook his head. "Oh, Gramps," he muttered. "Why couldn't you hold on until dawn."

"Grandfather..." Rachel began, and then stopped. She had nothing to say, and this creature was not truly her grandfather. Quincy began to move toward the door and Rachel stepped in front of him. "No," she said. "You may not leave."

"I may not!" He laughed. "I must wait until the sun rises and then allow it to destroy me, I suppose?"

"I'm sorry, Gramps," Malcolm said, moving to his sister's side. "You must understand. There must be a part of you, the real Quincy Harker, who understands. We can't let you leave here."

"And you two will stop me?" he asked, his voice dripping with amusement. "You two, and that cowardly little fool over there in the corner?" He shot Jerry a disparaging glance. "You say that I must understand, Malcolm? No. It is *you* who must understand. It is pointless to resist. You cannot win."

Rachel shook her head. "We are on the side of God. We cannot lose." Her face was an impassive mask, and only the single tear that ran down her cheek bespoke her emotional turmoil.

"God's side!" Quincy laughed. "God's side! I see, my dear. You are more religious, a better Christian, more beloved of God than I was!" He began to move toward his grandchildren. "How comforting that must be for you!"

Malcolm reached out to hold Quincy back, but the old man pushed him away, sending him thudding against a wall. He kicked open the door and ran out into the corridor, laughing insanely as he shoved a bewildered orderly aside and made for the stairs. Malcolm and Rachel, followed by a shaking and hesitant Jerry, ran after him.

Quincy seemed almost to fly down the stairs. He was through the main entrance of the hospital before his three pursuers had reached the bottom of the stairwell. Malcolm rushed out onto the street, tensed and ready for a continued chase, but as he looked up and down Queens Boulevard, east and west, he could find no sign of his grandfather. Malcolm did not know whether Quincy had used his inhuman speed to run so fast or used his vampiric powers to disappear into mist or change his shape and flee as an animal. In any event, he was gone.

Malcolm, Rachel, and Jerry stood silent and motionless upon the dark early-morning sidewalk. In a very few moments they heard the sound of a police siren.

Detective Mario De La Vega sat pensively behind his desk at the 110th Precinct police station, tapping his pen softly on the desktop, staring at the three people who sat in front of him on the hard wooden chairs. At last he sighed and said, "Well, I really don't quite know what to say to all this, folks."

"It's just like we described it to you, Officer," Malcolm said, "and we can't explain it any better than you can."

"Honest to God," Jerry agreed. "That's what happened." Rachel said nothing.

De La Vega nodded, not in agreement or approval but merely as an acknowledgment of what had been said. "I've seen people do all sorts of crazy things when they're on the brink of death," he said. "I could understand it if all that happened here was that your grandfather got up and ran out of the hospital. It's awfully hard to imagine a dying man in his nineties doing something like that, let alone outrunning you"—and he looked at Malcolm—"but stranger things have happened." He tossed his pen down and shook his head as he brushed his mustache away from his lip with the back of his left forefinger. "But there has to be some other explanation of what happened to the clergyman. It's hard to believe that your grandfather could have killed him at all, but when the coroner tells me that the cause of death was exsanguination . . ." He shook his head again.

"We can't change the facts, Detective," Rachel said,

adding in her thoughts, and we don't have to tell them all to you either.

"And no one else entered or left the room, other than the three of you, your grandfather, and Father Henley?" De La Vega asked for the tenth time.

"No one," Malcolm said, "except the doctor an hour or so before."

"And you have no idea what that piece of wood was doing in there, or why the coroner found splinters in the priest's hand?" They all shook their heads, and De La Vega sighed again. "Listen to me very carefully. We're not in court right now, and we aren't talking about perjury or anything, but providing the police with false information is a serious crime. If you—"

"We are not lying to you, Detective," Rachel said, attempting to project offended hauteur at his suggestion of deceit, and feeling guilty for the fact that they were indeed deceiving him by leaving certain truths unspoken. "Everything we have told you is true. Our grandfather got up from the bed, and attacked us. He bit Father Henley, escaped from the room, and by the time we got downstairs, he was nowhere to be found."

De La Vega nodded again, but his pursed lips and narrowing eyes told them that he was growing angry. "I want you to try to listen to yourselves, try to understand what this all sounds like to me, to someone else just hearing it from you. You tell me that your grandfather, a man in his late nineties, drinks the blood of a priest and leaves him dead on the floor. He runs out of the hospital—*runs out*, mind you, a man who was in the hospital to die, in all likelihood—and disappears. We find what looks to us like a wooden stake in the room with the body, with evidence that the priest was holding the stake before he was killed." He paused and allowed his eyes to drift from one of the faces before him to the others. "Do you understand what I'm saying here? I mean, do you think that I or anyone else on the force is stupid enough to believe this? Do you think that I intend to file a report that states this horror story of yours is factual?" He leaned forward and his voice became stern and demanding. "Now, one last time: What the hell happened last night?"

"Are we under arrest, Detective?" Rachel asked.

"No." The policeman shook his head. "Not yet, at least. But I want some answers to—"

"Then I would think that we are free to leave," she interrupted him. "If not, then perhaps we had better call our attorney, Peter Gierer. Perhaps you've heard of him?"

De La Vega frowned at the question. He had, of course, heard of the high-priced lawyer whose services were available to so many of the wealthy families in New York City. Gierer was no featherweight, and De La Vega had no desire to have to deal with Gierer and his battery of lawyers until and unless it was absolutely necessary. "You are free to leave, of course," he said carefully, "though I would have to ask you all to hold yourselves available for further questioning, until this matter is settled."

"Like in the movies," Jerry muttered.

"I beg your pardon?"

"'Don't leave town,'" he said.

"Our grandfather ran off at about four in the morning," Rachel commented, ignoring Jerry. "We have been here talking to you and other officers since five. It is now ten o'clock, and I for one would like to get some sleep, if it's all the same to you." Her voice was infuriatingly imperious.

"And if it's all the same to you," De La Vega said heatedly, "I would like to get a few believable answers to a few simple—" The ringing of the telephone on his desk interrupted his sentence, and as he picked it up and spoke to the caller, Rachel looked over at Malcolm. Only one who knew her as well as he did could have detected the nervous concern which was hiding just behind the cool, impassive expression. Malcolm winked at her, and she gave him a very slight, very sad smile.

De La Vega replaced the phone and then said, "Well, your grandfather has been found."

"He's been found!" Rachel exclaimed. "What do you mean he's been found?" It's daytime, she thought. He couldn't be out in the sunlight, it's impossible! "You mean that he's alive?"

"No, I'm sorry, I didn't say that," the detective added quickly. "I should have said that his body has been found. I'm afraid that one of you will have to come with me to the morgue and identify him. It's a legal formality. There's no doubt that it's your grandfather."

"Where was he found?" Malcolm asked.

De La Vega looked at him hard, ready to observe and

gauge his reaction. "Another priest at Father Henley's church found him a little while ago."

"At our church?" Rachel asked, astonished. "He was in a *church*?"

"Not in the church, no. The priest, Father Lang-something . . ."

"Father Langstone," Malcolm muttered.

"Yes, Langstone. He found your grandfather's body in the church's cemetery. Apparently he was trying to dig down into the ground when he died."

There was no need for Malcolm, Rachel, and Jerry to compare interpretations of this, for each realized what had happened. After old Quincy escaped from the hospital, he had gone to the graveyard, attempting to gain entrance into the burial ground before the sun rose. He must have been too late. As soon as the dawn broke, the sunlight had rendered him helpless, and so he had been found. Like all the members of his breed, he needed to be buried in sanctified earth. Malcolm recalled Van Helsing's words: In soil barren of holy memories, the vampire cannot rest. This was the reason the satanic creatures returned daily to hallowed ground for their deathlike sleep.

"I'll take you over there, whichever of you wants to make the identification," De La Vega said.

"We'll all go," Rachel replied quickly, then turned to her brother. "But if you don't mind, I'll let you identify him, Malcolm. I . . ." She paused and seemed to bite her lip slightly. "I'd rather not have to see him."

"Me either," Jerry muttered, more to himself than to anyone else.

"There is going to have to be an autopsy, I'm afraid," De La Vega said, rising from behind his desk. "In fact, that call was from an officer at the one hundred and twelfth, and he told me that the medical examiner put your grandfather on the top of the list, because of the homicide involved here. Father Henley, I mean." He glanced at his watch. "We should be able to get to the morgue just about as they're finishing with him." He looked at Rachel and Malcolm for a moment. "Look, there are a lot of unanswered questions about this whole thing, but that doesn't stop me from sympathizing with you over your loss. I'm very sorry."

"Thank you, Detective," Rachel said as she got to her feet. She, Malcolm, and Jerry followed De La Vega out of the police station and sat in silence in the unmarked police car as he drove them to the morgue. Malcolm sat in the back with his sister, and Jerry sat in front beside the policeman, who made a few halfhearted attempts at conversation.

They drove to the Grand Central Parkway and cruised along it until they reached the Parsons Boulevard exit. A few hundred yards along the service road brought them to the turn that took them to the Queens Hospital Center, a large, sprawling complex of buildings at the rear of which was the county morgue. De La Vega pulled to a stop at the side of the old red-brick building, turned off the ignition, and left the car. Malcolm followed him, and together they entered the morgue. Like so many of the municipal buildings in New York City, this one was old and impersonal, dingy and poorly lighted, sorely in need of fresh paint and new flooring. The high, yellowed ceilings echoed sounds with hollow tones, and Malcolm felt depression descending upon him, overwhelming his fear and regret.

He listened as De La Vega told the desk clerk why they were there, and Malcolm wordlessly signed the forms that were thrust in front of him. The preliminary death certificate listed heart failure as the cause of death, an analysis that would probably have been quite accurate if his grandfather had been truly dead.

De La Vega led him into a small, dark, dirty room that was designated VIEWING ROOM AND CHAPEL by a black sign with white lettering on the door. Nothing about the room reminded Malcolm of a chapel. There was a square wooden table and a few chairs in one corner and dilapidated sofa against the opposite wall. At the center of the rear wall was a large rectangular window some five feet long by four feet high, covered with a heavy white vinyl curtain. The attendant left Malcolm and De La Vega alone for a moment to wait in uneasy silence. He returned a few moments later and without preamble or preparation pulled back the white curtain. Malcolm moved forward and looked through the window.

Quincy Harker's body lay upon a narrow, wheeled table. Only his face was visible. A white sheet covered his body from the chin down, and a smaller white cloth had been draped over his head from just above his eyebrows back, tucked in to cover the sides of his head. Malcolm understood why, of course. The autopsy had already been performed by the medical examiners. His grandfather's head had been sawed open, his chest had been slit, his internal organs removed and weighed, tissue samples taken, chemical tests performed. He had then been put back together and sewn up, but respect for the feelings of the bereaved and a concern for their emotional state led the officials to hide the incisions. For purposes of identification, the face was generally enough.

Malcolm stared at Quincy's pale, white, motionless face. He could read the emotions etched into the ancient features. Rage and desperation had been frozen onto his features as the first rays of the morning sun had struck his undead corpse.

"Is that him?" the attendant asked softly. Malcolm nodded, then turned away as the white curtain was dropped to cover the window.

He walked quietly out of the room and left the building, the detective following close behind him. Rachel and Jerry were standing beside the car, waiting for him, and as he approached, Rachel asked, "Are you all right, Malcolm?"

"Yes, I'm okay," he replied, wiping his brow. He turned to Detective De La Vega and asked, "What do we do now?"

"Well," he said, "you'll have to make arrangements for burial, get in touch with a funeral home. They'll come and pick up the body. From that point on, you just work out a funeral schedule with them."

"Arrangements have already been made," Rachel said.

Malcolm looked at her with surprise. "When did you do that?"

"I didn't," she replied. "Grandfather did. Remember how he always feared that you and I would give him a big funeral?"

"Yes. What about it?"

"Well, when he started to feel ill last week, he called up the Simonsen Funeral Home and ordered his own funeral to his own specifications. When he started to fail last night . . . before he . . . before he . . ." She neither spoke nor finished the thought. "I called them from the hospital and asked them to get things ready. If they can get the grave at Maple Grove open today, he can be buried this afternoon."

Malcolm smiled sadly. "I guess he didn't trust us to do what he wanted."

She returned his smile with one equally sad. "I suppose not."

And then as they looked into each other's eyes, the grief that their fear and worry had suppressed burst through. Their grandfather was dead. The kindly old man who had bounced both of them on his knee, who had loved them and cared for them since the day each of them was born, was gone now, leaving Rachel and Malcolm the last living members of the Harker family. Rachel and Malcolm hugged each other impulsively and held on tightly as each released a flood of tears. Jerry Herman and Detective De La Vega looked away respectfully, leaving them to their grief, trying not to look at the trembling bodies of the brother and sister as they clung to each other in their overwhelming sorrow.

Chapter Nineteen

It was later that same day that Malcolm Harker stood by the window of Jerry Herman's apartment on 110th Street in the middle-class section of Forest Hills, watching as the late-afternoon sun began to disappear behind the distant skyscrapers of Manhattan. Jerry sat at a cheap formica table, nursing a shot of bourbon, lost in his own thoughts. Rachel sat upon the aged, faded sofa, trying not to look at the two enormous breasts that seemed to be shouting at her from the cover of a girlie magazine that lay upon the stained coffee table.

No one was speaking, and Jerry was growing uncomfortable in the silence. At last, for lack of anything else to say, he commented, "That was a nice ceremony."

"It was as he would have wanted it," Rachel agreed, sighing and rubbing her eyes. "Very simple and very small. Just the two . . . I mean, the three of us, and Father Langstone. A few prayers, then burial. It's exactly as Grandfather would have wanted it."

"Yes," Malcolm agreed, turning from the window and walking over to the table where Jerry was seated. "And we can be relieved that it's all over for him. He's at peace now." He sat down beside his friend and asked, "Can I have a shot of that?"

"Oh, sure, Mal." Jerry went to the cupboard and got another shot glass, one of the many he had stolen from the Strand while he was working there. As he filled the glass for Malcolm, he reflected for the first time since returning from Europe that he was now unemployed and had best start looking for a job bright and early the next day. Unless, of course, more important responsibilities interfered, as he suspected they might. It was with this in mind that he asked, "What do we do now?"

"Well," Malcolm sighed, sipping from the glass of bourbon, "we have to find them, Lucy and Holly, and we have to find the remains of the Count."

"I think you should get some sleep before we do anything," his sister said. "You look terrible, Malcolm. When was the last time you got any rest?"

"Real rest? Real sleep?" He shook his head. "It's been days."

"Well, you won't be able to accomplish anything if you don't get some sleep."

"I can't sleep, Rachel. I'm afraid to sleep, for one thing. I'm afraid of those damned visions coming back. And it's getting dark out. Even though I think I've brought the blood under control by taking the sacrament so much in Rome, it's still having an effect on me. I still feel energetic at nighttime. I couldn't sleep now, even if I wanted to." He put the glass to his lips again and drained it. "No, we have to think and plan." He reached for the bourbon and refilled the shot glass.

"You won't be able to think and plan anything if you fuddle your mind with that liquor," Rachel pointed out.

"I know my limits, Rachel," he muttered, unkind in his distraction.

"Well," Rachel sighed, "no matter what we do, at least we know that Grandfather is at peace."

"Yeah," Jerry said, and nodded. "It's a good thing he didn't get into the ground before the sunlight hit him. That solved one problem for us, anyway."

Malcolm shook his head. "You've seen too many horror movies, Jer, and you didn't read the Stoker book carefully enough."

Jerry frowned, confused. "What do you mean?"

"Sunlight doesn't destroy a vampire," Malcolm said, sipping again of the bourbon. "That's a Hollywood idea. All that the book says is that they are helpless and largely unconscious during the daytime." He looked around the cluttered living room of the small apartment. "Where's your copy of *Dracula*?"

"Over here," Jerry answered as he reached over to a stereo speaker and took the tattered volume from atop the imitation wood. He tossed it to Malcolm, who flipped through the pages until he found the place that would verify his words.

"This is the section of our great-grandmother's diary where she records what Van Helsing told them about the powers of the vampire, and his weaknesses also. Listen: 'His power ceases, as does that of all evil things, at the coming of the day.'" He closed the book and tossed it onto the table. "That's all it says, Jer. The idea that vampires disintegrate or die when the sunlight hits them is pure cinema."

Jerry shook his head. "I don't understand it, then. How can you be sure that your grandfather is...well, you know..."

"For the same reason that we know our father and great-grandmother are at peace," Malcolm answered. "The curse is in the blood, and if the blood is removed from the body, the curse is removed as well. All that is in Gramps's veins right now is embalming fluid."

Jerry nodded. "I get it. You had him embalmed?"

Malcolm glanced at his friend. "Of course he was embalmed. He was buried by a funeral home, wasn't he?"

Jerry looked at Malcolm for a moment, his face expressionless. "You got the bill from the funeral home?"

"I have it," Rachel said, picking up her purse and taking a long white envelope from it. She handed it to Jerry, and as he opened it up and began to examine it, she asked, "Why do you ask?"

Jerry looked up and down the itemized bill and then he sighed heavily. "I don't know how to tell you this," he began.

Malcolm was suddenly very attentive. "Tell us what?"

"You remember that I handled my dad's funeral a couple of years ago, and my aunt's funeral last year?"

"Yes. So?"

"Well, you know how my dad wasn't religious...I mean, a totally nonpracticing Jew...and my aunt Carmen was a Catholic...she wasn't really my aunt, she just married my uncle Dave..."

"Jerry, will you get to the point?"

"Yeah, right. The point is that in Jewish funerals, the bodies don't get embalmed, but in gentile funerals, they do. And both my dad and my aunt Carmen had gentile funerals, and I was the one who had to make all the arrangements for both of them."

"Okay. So what?"

"Well, there are a couple of things I learned about the

funeral business from those experiences. It's all part of consumer protection and all that stuff."

"Jerry," Malcolm said heatedly, "what the hell are you talking about?"

"Funeral homes only embalm people in this state if the family specifically requests it," Jerry explained, handing the bill to Malcolm. "Look. No embalming charge."

Malcolm looked at the bill and then jumped to his feet. "Holy shit!" he screamed. "Those stupid assholes!"

"Malcolm, it's the law," Jerry said quickly. "Your grandfather arranged his own burial in advance. He probably didn't want to spend the money on embalming, and since it was a closed casket anyway, the funeral home never even mentioned the option to you."

Rachel's face had lost every bit of its color. "Then he . . . then Grandfather . . ."

"'Fraid so," Jerry said. "Damn it, I thought the sunlight had taken care of him. It never occurred to me—"

"Christ Almighty!" Malcolm shouted. "It's almost night! He's going to come back, he's going to come back!"

"He won't come here," Jerry said, trying to calm his friend. "He doesn't know where I live."

"Sure, and Lucy didn't know what hotel we were staying in over in England, but she found you and attacked you, didn't she? Do you think that was a coincidence?" he shouted. "And that's not the point, anyway! He's going to kill people tonight, and we have to stop him!"

"Yes," Rachel said, strangely calm. "We have to get to the cemetery before the sun is down—"

"The goddamned sun is setting right now!" Malcolm said.

"Then we have to leave right now," Rachel said, getting to her feet. "I have a crucifix in my purse. We can buy some garlic at a fruit stand along the way. All we have to do is contain him, just for tonight, and then we can . . . well, I don't know, but whatever we can do, we'll do tomorrow."

"Wait a minute, wait a minute!" Jerry said as Malcolm and Rachel grabbed their coats and went to the door. "You don't go vampire hunting after dark! That's nuts!"

"We don't have any choice, Jerry," Malcolm said. "Are you coming with us?"

Jerry paused. He had no desire to go to the cemetery and wait in the darkness for the emergence of the undead, but neither did he relish the thought of waiting alone in his apartment with the knowledge that the vampires might know where he was.

"Come on, Jerry, make up your mind, will you?" Malcolm said urgently.

"Yeah, yeah, okay, okay, I'll come," he said miserably, following them out the door of the apartment. This is wonderful, he thought. This is just great.

Rachel had parked her BMW on the street outside Jerry's apartment building, and after unlocking the passenger door, she handed the keys to her brother, indicating that she wanted him to drive. Malcolm drove off even before Jerry had pulled the car door completely shut.

It took a scant two minutes for Rachel to run into a fruit stand and buy some garlic while Malcolm double-parked outside the store, and they drove up Queens Boulevard toward Kew Gardens at breakneck speed. As they reached the still-open gates of Maple Grove Memorial Park, the last rays of the sun were fading behind the already glowing skyline of Manhattan. Malcolm parked the car just inside.

The sign on the driveway gate warned all visitors that the cemetery was locked up daily at sunset, as is customary, and that meant that they would have to get to Quincy's freshly dug grave quickly, hoping that the caretaker and the security patrol would not see them before they were able to place the garlic and crucifix onto the mound of earth. They were not certain that this would keep their grandfather imprisoned beneath the ground, but they had to try.

"Let's go this way," Malcolm said, leaving the paved road and walking up onto a grassy knoll to the left of the entrance. "We'll be less likely to be seen if we aren't on the road."

"Good idea," Rachel said, following him. The entire expedition seemed like a bad idea to Jerry, but he trailed behind her in disgruntled silence. He stopped when Rachel stopped. "Malcolm," she said softly.

"What?" he asked in the same hushed tone, turning to her.

"Look"—she pointed into the distance—"over there."

He followed the direction of her finger with his eyes. "What are you pointing at? I don't see anything."

"Over there, near Grandfather's grave. It's all foggy."

Malcolm looked again. He could see the oblong mound of freshly turned dirt where Quincy Harker had been buried earlier that day, and it was in fact quite misty there. He shrugged. "So what? The weather is always weird in cemeteries. It doesn't mean anything."

"Except that vampires can turn themselves into mist," Rachel pointed out. "I've read the Stoker book also, you know, long before you did."

Malcolm looked hard at the distant fog. He clutched the garlic tightly in his hand and took a deep breath. "Well, let's go see." He walked ahead. Rachel followed him and Jerry walked beside her, not wishing to be isolated in the rear.

They reached their grandfather's grave site and stood for a moment as the fog swirled about them. Then Malcolm stepped over and placed the fresh, acrid plant onto the mound of dirt. Rachel placed the crucifix upon the mound also. They turned and looked at Jerry, who was holding his portion of the garlic close to his chest, and Malcolm said, "Come on, Jerry."

Jerry shook his head. "No way, man. I've got this stuff with me, and I'm keeping it!"

"Jerry—" Malcolm began.

"Forget it, Mal," Jerry said, his voice trembling. "I'm not letting go of this stuff until I'm back in the car."

Malcolm opened his mouth to speak, but the soft sound of laughter, coming at once from everywhere and from nowhere, silenced him. He looked around and saw to his great discomfort that the fog was growing rapidly thicker. His sister and his friend drew close to him, and they stood together as if in an oasis of clarity in a desert of mist.

"Malcolm!" Rachel said, her voice filled with fear. "What's happening here? Is it . . . is Grandfather . . . ?"

"Mal, let's get out of here, okay?" Jerry begged, his voice as tremulous as his hands. "Let's just go home or to the strand or someplace else, *anyplace* else!"

"There is nowhere you can go," Quincy Harker said as he stepped out of the fog. He smiled kindly at his grandchildren and their friend. "Just go home, Malcolm. Go home, Rachel—and Jerry, go with them. Go home and rest. We will come for you at the appointed time."

The three living humans stood in frightened, wary silence, looking at the undead creature. Quincy was wearing a dark black suit, the style of which matched nothing in his wardrobe, and the depth of the blackness accentuated the pallor of his flesh and the demonic glow in his eyes. Malcolm was gazing in wonder and fear at the walking corpse when Jerry tugged on his sleeve and said, "Mal! Look! Over there!"

He turned to see the fog parting as Holly Larsen and Lucy Westenra emerged into the oasis of clarity, each dressed in soft, flowing, transparent white gowns through which their nipples showed black as night; and as Malcolm gazed at them, and as if in response to his observation, the women's nipples grew suddenly red as blood. "Hello, honey," Holly said sweetly. "It's *so* good to see you again."

Malcolm held Rachel tightly to his side and Jerry tried to huddle in between them. "You can't win," Rachel said, trying to sound brave.

"We've already won," Lucy responded, her long blond hair seeming to blow in the absent wind. "And in any event, you have no idea what we are planning to do."

"We'll track you down," Malcolm said.

"Hide and seek," Holly said, and laughed. "We'll be waiting for you."

"Waiting for what?" Rachel asked bitterly. "Waiting to destroy us? Well, here we are. What's stopping you? It's three to three, and you are all the stronger for its being night. Why don't you attack us now?"

Lucy stepped forward and shook her head as if with patient and amused exasperation. "Attack you! Destroy you! Why, my dear, you misunderstand us. Your destruction is the *last* thing we want!"

"You want us to join you, to be as you are," Rachel said. "Well, I—"

"Nor that," Lucy interrupted. "Your grandfather's joining our little company was an accident, and certainly not one which I had anticipated... not that he isn't welcome, of course." Quincy Harker laughed quietly as Lucy continued. "I needed our sweet Holly for a variety of reasons, which I don't believe I will share with you just yet, and I needed that little fool"—she nodded at Jerry—"as an assistant for a time. She grinned. "Travel can present some difficulties for us, you see. But I certainly have no desire to see either of you become like we are, my dear Harkers."

"Of course not," Malcolm said to Rachel without taking his eyes from the creatures. "They want to awaken the blood in us so that their creator can live on in us, live on *through* us."

"Oh, Malcolm!" Lucy said. "You are such a little dolt. That's not my intention either!"

"But it must be!" Malcolm protested. "What else could you want? If that isn't it, then why are you here? Why did you follow me back to America? If you don't want us to be like you and you don't want the Count to exist in us, then what the hell *do* you want?"

Lucy laughed loudly and withdrew into the fog. "Hide and seek, little Harker, hide and seek!"

The fog enveloped her, and Quincy Harker along with her, leaving only Holly Larsen remaining. She very slowly and seductively ran her hands over her body from breast to belly as she whispered, "I'll see you soon, Malcolm, darling. And when I do, I'm going to just love you to death." Then the fog enveloped her as well, and she was gone.

The fog dissipated suddenly. It did not blow away, it did not thin out, it seemed merely to vanish. Malcolm, Rachel, and Jerry stood alone before the fresh, empty grave of Quincy Harker, and none of them spoke for what seemed a long while. Then Malcolm sighed, "Oh, Holly."

"Very well," Rachel said firmly. "So the worst has come."

Malcolm shook his head. "They haven't killed us yet, Rachel, and for all we know they're out creating more vampires at this very moment. We're nowhere near the worst yet."

Rachel smoothed back her hair and straightened her skirt. "Think like a defeatist and you'll be defeated, Malcolm. We still have to find them and kill them while they are helpless during the day, just as we had planned to do before. The only difference is that now there are three of them, not two of them."

"One," Malcolm said quietly. "There's only one. There has always been only one."

She nodded, understanding. "Yes. And it is his power that we must destroy, by destroying them. Our grandfather is dead, Malcolm. So is Miss Larsen. And so is that other poor creature. They are already dead, and we must steel ourselves to the task of freeing them from undeath."

"Uh, I hate to be a wet blanket here," Jerry said, his voice still quivering, "but we have absolutely no idea where to look for them."

"Three of them," Malcolm muttered pensively.

"Yes, and who knows how many more before—" Rachel began.

"No, no, you're missing the point," Malcolm interrupted. "Three of them, three of us."

Rachel and Jerry considered this for a moment, but neither was able to see where Malcolm's observation was leading. "Yeah, okay, three to three," Jerry said at last. "So what? Even odds? Is that what you mean?"

"No"—Malcolm frowned—"the odds are never even. If it were one vampire against a hundred of us, at night the odds would be in the vampire's favor. And if there were only one of us against a hundred vampires, we'd have the advantage during the day." He paused. "Of course, she killed Holly before she knew what would happen to Gramps, so maybe it's just a coincidence that it's three to three. Maybe she just needed at least one other."

"Malcolm, get to the point," Rachel demanded.

"Hey, can we finish this conversation back in the car?" Jerry asked. "I *really* want to get the hell out of here."

"Sure, Jerry," Malcolm agreed. As they walked back toward the cemetery gate, garlic and crosses at the ready, he went on, "Lucy said that she needed Holly for something. What could she need her for?"

"As an ally?" Jerry suggested.

"Of course, as an ally," Rachel snapped. "Malcolm's question is, as an ally for what?"

"If she were dealing with us all by herself, would she need an ally? Wouldn't she be able to escape from us if we went after her?"

"Most likely yes," Rachel answered without hesitation, "unless we had crosses or consecrated hosts and managed to corner her in a sealed room at sunrise."

"Which would probably be real easy for her to avoid," Jerry said.

"Right." Malcolm nodded, then lapsed into thoughtful silence as they reached the car. Malcolm started the engine and drove out through the cemetery gate just as the grounds keeper was preparing to shut and lock it. They were driving back down Queens Boulevard before Malcolm said, "I think she needs the three of us all together, all at once, in the same place."

"She just *had* all three of us together in the same place," Jerry pointed out.

"Yes, but we were ready for her, we were in control. I think she needs to get all three of us together when *she's* in control."

"Why, Malcolm?" Rachel asked. "I don't follow your reasoning at all."

"It's simple. Remember what Stewart wrote in his diary about the night when Dracula attacked our great-grandmother. He immobilized our great-grandfather Jonathan and then attacked Mina. But when Stewart and Van Helsing broke into the room—"

"Dracula fled," Rachel finished for him. "So?"

"So why would Lucy need an ally unless she anticipated having to control more than two people at one time? If Dracula didn't feel confident in a situation like that, Lucy certainly wouldn't. And also, remember that these creatures don't feel the same need for companionship that living beings feel. Whenever they intentionally create another vampire, there's always some sort of logical reason for doing it. Maybe I'm wrong, but I can't help but think that whatever she's planning to do involves having the three of us at her mercy simultaneously."

"But why?" Jerry asked. "If she wants to get rid of us or make us like they are, why not do it one at a time?"

"She just told us she didn't want to do either of those things, Jer. If she wanted to kill me, she could have done it in Rumania. If she wanted to kill you, she could have done it right after you helped her get into the country. She could have followed me to the hospital the night Gramps died and gotten any one of us when we left the hospital room. Think about it, Jerry. Have we three ever been together without some sort of weapon we could use to protect ourselves against her? The answer is no. Whatever she wants to do has to be done to all three of us at once, not one at a time, with Lucy in control of the situation."

"Assuming what you say is true," Rachel said, sighing wearily, "what does it mean for us? How can it help us plan?"

"Yeah, right," Jerry added. "If Lucy's waiting for me to be unprotected, she's gonna have one hell of a long wait. I mean, I ain't goin' nowhere without garlic for the rest of my life! Hell, I'm even gonna wear a cross, and I'm Jewish!"

"What it means," Malcolm said slowly, "is that we have to separate."

"What?" they asked in unison.

"Yes, separate." Malcolm's hands clenched the steering wheel tightly. "Look, we can't beat them by doing what we've been doing. We'll never get the upper hand on them at this rate. I think we're safer apart than together."

Rachel shook her head angrily. "Malcolm, that's ridiculous. We have to search for them, and when we've found them, destroy them. It would be foolish to separate."

"Is it?" he asked. "We can't find them and destroy them because we don't know where they're sleeping during the day, and New York City is just too big a place to look for them. We can't do anything to them at night because when they're conscious they're too powerful and too shrewd. All we can do for the time being is wait for them to make the next move, keep ourselves protected at night, and keep away from each other so that they can't trap us all together. I don't know what Lucy's plans are, and neither do you. So we separate, we protect ourselves, and we wait."

"We wait!" Jerry said. "We wait for what?"

"We wait for them to do something," Malcolm replied. "We wait for something to happen so that we can try to figure out what to do. We stay away from each other until they act, and then, and only then, we'll rejoin and face them."

They sat in silence for a long while. Malcolm was waiting for them either to agree or to argue further, but when Rachel and Jerry continued their silence, he said, "We have to figure out a way to keep in touch without letting each other know where we are."

"We could keep in touch by phone," Rachel suggested, her suggestion implying agreement with her brother's idea.

"No," Malcolm said. "Remember how Van Helsing tracked Dracula down? Mina Harker was tied to him by the blood, and by hypnotizing Mina, Van Helsing was able to get sense impressions from the mind of the Count. We're tied together by the blood, we three. We can't let each other know where we're staying, what our phone numbers are, anything at all that might provide a clue to our whereabouts. If one of us is captured, the other two could be found the same way Van Helsing found Dracula." He paused and thought. "How about this. We each go . . . wherever we're going, and then find phone booths somewhere near enough for us to get to them, but not near enough to give our locations away. Then we call the Strand and leave the numbers with . . . what's her name, the girl who works the Saturday afternoon shift?"

"Jennifer," Jerry replied.

"Right. We leave the numbers with Jennifer, and then call each other daily at around noon."

Rachel nodded.

Jerry, seeing her gesture, shrugged. "Well, okay. If you two want to separate, I don't have any choice. I think it's dangerous, but. . ." and he shrugged again.

"It is dangerous, Jer," Malcolm agreed. "It's very dangerous, because I could be completely wrong in this. But let's face it, we've passed beyond the point of being able to avoid danger."

Rachel gave her brother a sad but affectionate smile. "You're getting rather good at this, Malcolm," she said softly. "Very farsighted and very logical."

"Yes," he sighed, returning her smile. "I wonder if I'm finally developing a marketable skill!"

Chapter Twenty

June passed into July, and July approached August, and neither Malcolm nor Rachel nor Jerry detected any occurrence that could be attributed to the vampires. They followed Malcolm's plans and spoke with each other daily at noon, when the sun was at its zenith, when they were most safe from Lucy Westenra and Holly Larsen and Quincy Harker. Rachel called Malcolm at eleven forty-five, Malcolm called Jerry at twelve, and Jerry called Rachel at twelve-fifteen. On a few occasions a phone would be out of order or would be being used by someone else, and the delays caused tension and anxiety; but always, eventually, somehow, the link was maintained. Daily reports in guarded phraseology, careful conversations in furtive, conspiratorial tones, were all that kept them together. No hint of their whereabouts was allowed into their phone calls, and no hints as to the activities of the vampires presented themselves at all.

Jerry Herman went to live with his aunt Lucille in Commack, Long Island. They had never gotten along well, and Jerry somewhat callously reasoned that, if there were to be danger, he would rather endanger her than anyone else he knew. He concocted a tale of fleeing from a loan shark's enforcer, and Lucille had a low enough opinion of her nephew almost to believe him. She generously allowed herself to be guided by the old family adage that home is where, when you have to go there, they have to take you in.

They do not have to lend you their cars, however; and each day at ten-thirty Jerry hopped on a bicycle and began to peddle along Indian Head Road toward Kings Park and the public telephone in the train station.

Malcolm looked up Tom Meloun, an old friend from

New York University. Meloun was an avant garde sculptor who was eking out a living doing window displays in department stores while creating what he regarded as his real work in a large loft studio in New Haven, Connecticut, just across the Long Island Sound from New York. People came and went with bohemian abandon in Meloun's circle of friends, and one more mattress spread out against one more wall went virtually unnoticed. And the telephone booth in Campisi's deli was generally unoccupied.

Rachel chose the most secure of hiding places. The Episcopal Archdiocese of New York maintained a combination convent/secular retreat in Dutchess County, a place where the few remaining Episcopalian nuns in the United States could provide a place of meditation, introspection, and devotion to those women of the Anglican communion who sought an at-least-temporary refuge from the troubles of the world. Crosses, crucifixes, holy water, and consecrated elements abounded in this rural stronghold of the ancient faith, and Rachel felt so securely buttressed that she used the convent phone as her connecting link with her brother and his friend.

July came and went, and late in August Malcolm stood in front of the pay phone at Campisi's deli, glancing nervously at the clock that hung on the wall. Rachel was late, very late. Malcolm considered calling Jerry but forced himself to wait. The clock's minute hand moved from twelve to twelve-fifteen, and when the phone rang at twelve-twenty, he grabbed it possessively. "Hello?"

"Malcolm?"

It was not Rachel, and it took the startled young man a few moments to recognize the voice. "D . . . Daniel? Is that you?"

"Yes," his brother-in-law replied. Then he sighed heavily. "Come home, Malcolm. Come home before sunset, before any of them wake up."

"Where's Rachel?" he demanded.

"They have her, Malcolm, they have her," Daniel paused before adding, "And we have them!"

In less than a minute Malcolm was talking to Jerry Herman on the phone, and less than a minute after that he was speeding toward the ferry that would take him from New Haven to Port Jefferson, New York.

They have Rachel. Daniel's words echoed in his mind. *And we have them.*

*   *   *

Malcolm clenched his teeth as he patted the black athletic bag that he kept with him always, the bag containing the crosses and the garlic and the consecrated wafers and the consecrated wine that he had stolen from a church in New Haven. "This is it," he muttered. "One way or the other, this is it."

"Where do they get their clothes?" Jerry asked.

"What?" Malcolm was only half-listening to his friend. He was tapping his fingers impatiently on the steering wheel, wondering what was causing the stop-and-go, bumper-to-bumper traffic on the Long Island Expressway. They were driving west at two o'clock in the afternoon, and the traffic should have been light. Probably an accident, Malcolm thought, or construction or something.

"I said, where do they get their clothes?" Jerry repeated.

"Clothes. Whose clothes? What are you talking about?" Malcolm's voice was brusque and irritable.

Jerry understood why Malcolm was being so curt. He knew that his friend was worried about his sister, and he was making conversation in the hopes of making the time pass. "The vampires," he went on. "Where do they get their clothes?"

"The Vlad Boutique," Malcolm muttered. "How the hell should I know? Who cares where they get their clothes. From their victims, probably, like Lucy did in England."

"That's not what I mean," Jerry said, lighting a cigarette and offering one to his friend. Malcolm declined with a curt shake of his head, so Jerry went on, "Remember that night in the cemetery? They took the form of fog, right, like the book says they can, right? So when they took human form again, where did they get their clothes?"

Malcolm gave him an angry glance. "Jer, you wonder about the damnedest things!"

"Do their clothes turn into fog, too? Do they, I don't know, knit clothes out of fog or something? Where'd your grandfather get that suit? He was in a hospital gown when he died, right? So where'd he get that suit?"

"You can't look for logic in stuff like this," Malcolm said, accelerating slightly, moving forward a few yards and then stopping again. "In the book, Dracula turns himself into fog and into animals, but he's always fully clothed when he reconstitutes himself. And Lucy turned into a wolf soon after

I . . ." He paused, not wishing to remind himself of what he had done. "Anyway, when she changed back into her own form she was still wearing what was left of the dress she had been buried in."

Jerry frowned, considering this, and then said, "How can this thing get passed on from a man?"

"From a man? What are you talking about?"

"Well, Mina gave birth to Quincy, and her blood was flowing through his body for nine months, so it makes sense that she could pass it on to him. But how could he pass it on to your father or your father to you? I mean, how much blood can there be in a couple of sperm cells?"

Malcolm glanced over at him tiredly. "Enough, apparently."

Jerry nodded. "Yeah, I guess. Most of this doesn't really make any sense anyway." He paused. "What about AIDS?"

"What?"

"AIDS. They drink blood, so what if they attack somebody who—"

"For Christ's sake, Jerry," Malcolm shouted. "They're already dead! How the hell can they get AIDS?"

"Hey, don't get so upset! I was just wondering."

"Well, cut it out, will you? I have enough on my mind right now without having to answer all these stupid fucking questions!"

"Okay, okay," Jerry sniffed. "Jeez!" He drummed his fingers absentmindedly on the dashboard and then looked down at the black athletic bag. As he distractedly pulled open the zipper, he asked, "You don't think Rachel's dead, do you?"

"I don't know," Malcolm sighed. "When Daniel said that the vampires had her, I just assumed they'd kidnapped her. I hope he didn't mean that she'd become one of them. I mean, if they killed her, that's what would have happened."

Jerry peered into the bag. "Whatcha got in here, Mal?"

"Weapons," Malcolm replied. "That is a homemade antivampire kit."

"No kidding?" Jerry began to rummage through the contents of the bag. "Great, great," he muttered. "Stakes, garlic, crosses, hammers . . ." Malcolm was rubbing his tired eyes as Jerry took a large silver flask from the case and unscrewed the lid. He placed it to his nose and sniffed it, and then, smiling, he placed it to his lips and took a healthy swallow. "Hey, this is good!"

"Hmmm?" Malcolm asked, still rubbing his eyes.

Jerry took another long swallow. "Spicy, though." He put the flask back to his lips and drained it. "What is this, spiced rum or something? God, this stuff gives me heartburn!"

"What are you . . . ?" Malcolm began, stopping when he saw the flask in Jerry's hand. "Oh, shit! Damn it, Jerry!"

Jerry Herman's eyes were bulging. He grasped his throat with one hand and his stomach with the other and began screaming, "God Almighty! God Almighty!"

Whatever had been holding up the flow of traffic ended just as Jerry began to thrash back and forth wildly. Malcolm was able to move from the center lane to the right and then off onto the shoulder of the road. After turning off the ignition, he reached over and grabbed Jerry, holding him tightly. "I know it hurts, Jer, it hurts like hell. But it'll pass soon, believe me. I know exactly how it feels, but you'll be okay in a minute. Just try to stay calm." He knew from personal experience that the horrible burning would soon subside into a localized pain, and then into just a general, feverish discomfort.

A half hour passed before Jerry was able to formulate a coherent sentence. "What the hell . . . what the hell . . . what was that stuff!"

"That was consecrated wine, Jerry. If you accept the teachings of the High Anglicans, the Catholics, and a few other churches, the blood of Christ was in that flask."

"But . . . but I'm Jewish!"

"It doesn't make any difference what you are," Malcolm said. "Consecrated wine is consecrated wine." Malcolm started the car and drove back onto the expressway. "It's the same thing that happened to me that day when I went to church with Holly and Gramps, before I understood any of this. And it happened to me again in Rome, a number of times, but then it was intentional."

"Intentional!" Jerry gasped, wiping the perspiration from his brow. "You did this to yourself on purpose? Are you nuts?"

"Not at all," Malcolm replied, accelerating to sixty and speeding across the border between Suffolk and Nassau. "Gramps explained it to me the night he told me the story of my ancestry. The sacrament is a counteragent to the blood I inherited from my great-grandmother."

"Why didn't you tell me, Malcolm?" Jerry demanded angrily. "I mean, good grief!"

"I didn't expect you to drink it, you know!" Malcolm shot back. Now that Jerry was over the worst of the effects, Malcolm's annoyance at him was coming to the fore. "I hope you realize that you just wasted a very valuable weapon in a very limited arsenal. Look at the effect it had on you, and you're only slightly polluted. Lucy, Holly, and Gramps are nothing *but* pollution. Think what we could have done with that wine! Poured it on them, thrown it at them..." He sniffed. "Damn it, Jerry!"

Malcolm's anger made Jerry angry himself. "Well, excuse me all to hell, Malcolm! You could have let me in on it, you know!"

"You didn't have to drink the wine!"

"You didn't have to keep it such a big secret, either! I mean, shit! I see some wine, I drink it. What the hell did you expect me to do, pour it in the goddamned gas tank?"

"Didn't you stop to wonder why I had a flask of wine in there with crosses and garlic and stakes? Are you really that stupid?"

"Stupid! Me, stupid? Who was stupid enough to bring Lucy back from the dead? Who was stupid enough to get his best friend mixed up in this crazy thing? Who was stupid enough to get his girlfriend killed and his sister kidnapped or worse?"

Malcolm's jaw clenched and he gripped the steering wheel more tightly, not looking at his friend.

Jerry immediately regretted his last remarks, and he fidgeted silently for a long while. They were passing the exit sign for New Hyde Park when he said, "Mal, I'm sorry. I didn't mean that. I'm really sorry."

Malcolm nodded curtly. "Skip it." He glanced over at Jerry, thinking, he's as scared as I am. He's not only my ally, he's my best friend. He didn't mean what he said.

Even though what he said was true.

"You okay now, Jer?" Malcolm asked.

Jerry accepted the question as a gesture of peace. "Yeah, sure, I'm better. It still hurts, though."

"I know. It'll stop hurting in a few minutes, believe me."

"Yeah."

Malcolm paused. "Hey, Jerry, you see the silver cache in the bag?"

"Yeah. What about it?"

"There are two consecrated communion wafers in there.

Don't eat 'em." He smiled over at Jerry, and Jerry slowly returned the smile. "In fact, give them to me. I think I'll feel safer if I keep them in my shirt pocket."

Jerry took the cache from the bag gingerly and passed it to Malcolm. "Here. Take them out yourself. I don't even want to touch them, not after what happened with the wine."

"They're weapons, Jer, not dangers. They're a little warm to the touch for people like you and me, but as long as you keep them away from your face, they can't cause any pain."

"Good, then you keep them. I'll stick to the garlic and the crosses." He shook his head. "Communion wine, crucifixes... You know, my great-grandfather was a rabbi, back in Poland. He must be turning over in his grave."

Malcolm laughed grimly. "Not the best expression to use under the circumstances, Jerry."

It was two forty-five, a good four and a half hours before sunset, when they pulled into the driveway of the Harker home in Forest Hills Gardens. Daniel Rowland was sitting on the steps of the side porch, his elbows resting on his knees, his face buried in his hands. He looked up when he heard the approaching car, then walked over to greet Malcolm and Jerry as they climbed out. "Hello, Malcolm," he said softly.

"Dan," Malcolm responded, shifting the black bag from his right hand to his left and then shaking hands with his brother-in-law. "You remember Jerry Herman."

Daniel nodded at Jerry. "Mr. Herman."

"Jerry," was the reply. "I think that since we're all in this together, Dan, we shouldn't be so formal."

"As you wish, Mr. Herman," Daniel replied coldly, and then ignored him, turning to enter the house.

Hey, fuck you too! Jerry thought.

"Where's Rachel?" Malcolm asked as he followed Daniel up the steps to the door.

"In the basement. They're all in the basement."

"All of them?" Malcolm's voice was filled with sudden hope, and then equally sudden despair. "You mean that... you mean that Rachel...?"

"She's in one of the coffins in the basement," Daniel said sadly, his few words answering all of Malcolm's unvoiced questions. He felt tears beginning to well up in his eyes at the thought of what must have happened to his sister, but he fought them back. Not now. I'll mourn for her later. I'll griev when she's at peace, when Holly is at peace, when Gramps is at peace. And Lucy, too. I'll weep for her as well. Later. Not now. Later.

"Tell me the whole story, Dan," Malcolm said as he and Jerry followed Daniel down the stairs to the basement. "How long have they been here? For that matter, how did they get *in* here? Rachel and I had garlic and crosses all over the—"

"Not now, Malcolm," Daniel sighed. "Let's do what needs to be done first. We'll have lots of time for conversation afterwards."

Daniel flicked on the ceiling lamp when they reached the bottom of the stairs, and Malcolm and Jerry gasped at what they saw. The basement was filled with coffins, most of them old and fragile, rotting wood joined to rusted metal, but one of them apparently brand-new. Malcolm counted them quickly. "Seven! Daniel, seven? They made four more like themselves?"

"Rachel, and three others," Daniel said quietly. He turned to Malcolm and said, "I have some stakes ready, over in the corner. I called you because . . . because of Rachel. I just couldn't . . . I couldn't . . ." He began to weep.

This was the first time in the many years that Malcolm had known Daniel that his brother-in-law had displayed any emotion other than self-satisfaction, and he smiled at him warmly. "I understand, Dan. I'll do it. I'll be freeing her, sending her to God. She'd do the same for me."

"Let's get at it," Jerry said eagerly. "Lucy first, okay? And I want to do it." His face was determined, grim, eager.

Malcolm walked over to the corner and picked up the stakes. He handed one to Jerry and one to Daniel, saying, "I have some hammers in the bag, Dan. Get them out, will you?" Malcolm walked over to the new coffin as Jerry went to one of the old ones, and then, as with one motion, they lifted the respective lids.

Jerry frowned. "Hey, Malcolm! There's nothing in here but bones!"

Malcolm did not reply. He was looking into the coffin at his sister Rachel, bound, gagged, only semiconscious but unquestionably alive. He was about to turn to Daniel to demand an explanation when he heard the dull thud of the gun butt as it struck the back of Jerry's head, and the subsequent moan as his friend fell to the floor.

He turned to see Daniel Rowland level the revolver at him. "You son of a bitch!" Malcolm shouted, his fists clenching.

"Don't," Daniel said. "Don't try anything, Malcolm, please. I'd have to shoot you, and if you die now, you know what your blood will do to you at sunset."

Malcolm's body was shaking as his reason told him to remain motionless and his emotions told him to attack Daniel Rowland. "You son of a bitch!" he repeated.

Daniel shook his head. "I'm sorry, Malcolm, but I don't have any choice."

It was only when Daniel spoke these words that Malcolm realized why his brother-in-law was wearing a turtleneck sweater. "That sweater hiding the wounds on your throat?" he asked in a furious, trembling voice.

"Yes." Daniel nodded.

Malcolm stared at him, his anger unabated, feeling no pity for Daniel even though he was yet another victim of the Harkers' ancestral curse. "How long?"

"Lucy took me two months ago. She wants you alive, Malcolm, but she told me to kill you if I had to, and if I have to, I will." He took a pair of handcuffs from his pants pocket and nodded in the direction of the stairs. "Go sit on the bottom step and put your hands on either side of the newel post." Malcolm did not move to comply, and Daniel cocked the hammer of the pistol. "Now, Malcolm."

His eyes blazed with anger as he moved to the base of the stairway and sat down slowly, his eyes shifting back and forth from Daniel's face to the revolver to the handcuffs. He put his right hand between the final banister spoke and the thick newel post that served as the terminus of the banister, placing his left hand on the other side of the post. *I can't let him kill me. If I die now, I'll be undead in a few hours. Delay, think, calm down, plan.* He gritted his teeth. *Plan! Plan to do what? She's beaten me, she's won.*

He's won. That bastard has won.

Daniel Rowland kept the barrel of the gun pointed right at Malcolm's forehead as he slapped the cuffs shut on his wrists. And when Malcolm heard the snap that bound him to the thick wooden post that he knew was sunk into cement, he had to fight to repress his panic.

After checking to make sure that Malcolm was securely locked onto the banister, Daniel proceeded to tie Jerry's hands behind his back and then bind his feet and knees

When he was finished, he stood up and sighed. "Now we wait until sunset." He looked at Malcolm. "I'm sorry, I truly am. But I'm like Renfield was. I have to obey."

"Like Renfield," Malcolm muttered. "I assume then that you've read Stoker's book."

"Yes," he said softly. "I've read Stoker's book."

"Renfield rebelled," Malcolm said. "When Mina Harker was endangered, Renfield rebelled." He awaited the response, which was not forthcoming, then asked bitterly, "How did they find Rachel?"

"Oh, Lucy knew where all of you were. You couldn't hide from her for long."

He frowned. "But how...?"

Daniel sighed. "It's the blood, Malcolm, the blood that ties all of you"—he paused—"all of us together. When she wants to, she can hear your thoughts over a great distance."

"Damn it!" Malcolm said. "I thought she'd have to actually physically have one of us with her to do that, like Van Helsing had Mina with him."

"She isn't Van Helsing," Daniel said softly. "Van Helsing was a human being." He turned from Malcolm, sat down in a chair against the wall, and closed his eyes wearily. Malcolm looked around the basement, seeking something, anything that might help extricate him from his situation. There was nothing.

A few desultory moans were all that came from Jerry Herman and Rachel Harker. Neither of them awakened as the hours passed in slow silence, as Malcolm wept softly and the sun sank down toward the horizon. He was trapped, defeated, hopeless. He was a dead man.

Worse than a dead man.

Chapter Twenty-one

"My goodness, it's warm in here!" Lucy Westenra said conversationally from the top of the stairs. Malcolm snapped his head around, startled at her sudden appearance behind him. He had been watching the coffins with trepidation ever since sunset, waiting for the lids to open and the undead to emerge; but the lids had remained motionless, and the silence in the basement had remained undisturbed.

"How... I didn't see..." he stammered.

"You didn't see me get out of the coffin?" she finished for him amicably. "Of course not, little Harker. I wasn't *in* one of these coffins."

"But then, what...?"

She ignored his unfinished question. "Why is it so warm?" She frowned, perplexed, and then smiled, the point of her fangs glistening in the lamplight. "Oh, of course. Consecrated host! You really are such a clever boy, Malcolm." She swung her legs over the banister gracefully and seemed to float down to the basement floor below. "Not clever enough, of course, but clever, nonetheless."

"Hi, Mal, honey," Holly Larsen said from above him. He looked up to see her floating slowly along the ceiling of the basement, moving from the door at the top of the stairs to the center of the room before descending to the floor. Malcolm's attention was drawn by movement to his side, and he turned to see Quincy Harker crawling along the wall like a spider. His grandfather passed by him and then hopped down to stand beside Holly.

"Our dear Malcolm has some consecrated host with him," Lucy said calmly. "He thinks that it will protect him from us."

302

"And it would," Holly nodded, smiling, "if he could get his hands on it." Her cadaverous mouth smiled with amusement. "In your shirt pocket, is it? Well, fine. Let's just leave it there, shall we?"

Malcolm looked from creature to creature, simultaneously terrified and infuriated. They were just as they had been in the cemetery a few months before, the women in the same diaphanous gowns, the old man in the same black suit. Their faces wore the same mocking, sardonic smiles, and their voices had the same cruel, sadistic tone. The dead flesh was chalky white, and the inhuman eyes glowed in the dimly lit basement. Malcolm did not speak to them, for he had nothing to say. To plead and beg would only be to invite ridicule, and to attempt to reason with them would be futile. All he could hope for now was a death that was permanent, and he had little cause to hope for even that.

Quincy walked over to the open coffin and lifted Rachel from it easily, almost as if she were weightless. He took the gag from her mouth and then slapped her face gently a few times. She rose slowly to consciousness. "Rise and shine," her grandfather whispered.

All of the successive emotions that Rachel experienced as she gathered her wits about her were mirrored in her eyes. Confusion as she awakened; pain and discomfort from her bonds; confusion again as she stared into her grandfather's malevolent face, confusion turning to pity and anger and panic; fear as she looked around; hope followed by despair when she saw her brother handcuffed to the banister, "Malcolm," she said hoarsely.

"I'm sorry, Rachel," he whispered. "They tricked me."

"Yes, and it was oh, so difficult to do." Lucy laughed. "Almost as difficult as enlisting the unwilling aid of this fat fool in getting you all here." Daniel stood nervously in the corner, his eyes downcast, terrified and ashamed.

Quincy Harker tore the ropes from Rachel's arms and ankles and then pushed her toward Holly Larsen. Holly caught her and held her fast by the wrists. Rachel tried to break free of the cold hands that held her, but Holly's supernatural strength was not even remotely challenged by the mortal's struggle. As Rachel collapsed to her knees in front of Holly, Quincy walked over to the stairway and ripped the handcuffs from Malcolm's wrists. The instant his hands were free, Malcolm made a quick gesture toward his pocket, hoping to be able to grab one of the consecrated wafers; but Quincy grasped his grandson's hands before Malcolm even came close. "Not so fast, boy," Quincy said, smiling. "You heard what Holly said. Let's just leave them where they are for the time being." He looked at Lucy. "What about Herman?"

"We'll wait until after," she said. "I'm not hungry yet." Lucy looked around the basement and frowned with mock distaste. "My goodness, but it's filthy down here!" She took a broom from the closet and began to sweep the floor in a hideous parody of Victorian domesticity.

Malcolm felt rage rise up in him as he sought in vain to escape from the two dead hands that were like vises on his wrists. "God damn you!" he shouted at Lucy. "God damn you to hell!"

She laughed. "He very well may. Or He may not. This is all the Master's doing, you know. It really isn't any one of us who is responsible." She walked toward him and leaned forward, smiling into his face. He could smell her fetid breath as she said, "We're dead, after all. And the bargain between the Master and the Devil was struck five hundred years ago. We made no bargain, *he* did." She stood up and walked to the center of the room, chuckling. "Contemplate the theological implications, my dears. Sin without guilt, transgression without culpability, crime without punishment. Why, it's enough to turn a prelate's miter!"

"God's justice will come in its own time, in its own way," Rachel said coldly.

"It will, no doubt," Lucy agreed. "At the Day of Judgment, the Master will have much to answer for. But right now, the judgments of our lord . . . *our* lord, not yours . . . are the only ones that matter." She lay the broom against one of the coffins and then turned toward Jerry Herman, who was beginning to stir. "And another player enters the stage."

Jerry, lying against the wall, moaned loudly and then opened his eyes. When he tried to sit up, he became aware of his bonds. He struggled to a sitting position, and the tableau before him told him everything he needed to know. Daniel, silent and servile; Malcolm and Rachel, captive; Lucy and Quincy and Holly, triumphant. "Shit!" he muttered, trembling with fear.

"Good evening, lover." Lucy smiled. "You've awakened just in time for the best part of the evening. But where was I?" She paused and pretended to think. "Oh, yes. We were talking about how poor Malcolm just isn't clever enough, weren't we?"

Malcolm's face was red with frustration and anger. "Lucy, I swear... I swear I'll—"

"Oh, don't be pompous!" she snapped, as if he were an irritating child. "We've all reached the end of the charted course, Malcolm. You'll do nothing but bleed."

"What do you mean, 'charted course'?" he demanded.

"Why, surely you know that this has all been carefully planned," she answered. "I needed to gather up the Master's dust, and so I sent you to Rumania. I needed to get into the United States, and so I, shall we say, conscripted Jerry. I needed at least one assistant of my own kind for this evening's endeavor, and so I invited Holly into our rather restricted company. I could have completed what I had already begun with Jerry, but he was already on guard against me, and so Holly was the next-best choice. I needed a few months to make a few other preparations without your interference, and so I sent you three in different directions. And when I needed to gather you all together, I used Daniel."

"Bullshit," Malcolm said. "I made some stupid mistakes, but mostly you were just lucky, that's all. This plan of yours would have unraveled any one of a number of times if I had made the right decisions, drawn the right conclusions. You wouldn't have been resurrected in the first place if I hadn't made mistakes."

Lucy shook her head and smiled sadly. "Oh, my dear, I think I was wrong. You aren't the slightest bit clever. You're really rather stupid. Why, you haven't even figured this all out yet, have you! You still think that the plan was mine, that I arranged everything. It wasn't my plan at all. It was the Master's."

"What are you talking about?" Rachel demanded.

"It's all so simple," Lucy said, turning to her. "I'm not all that surprised at Malcolm's obtuseness, but I had expected better from you."

"What are you talking about?" Rachel repeated, trying again to pull herself free of Holly's iron grasp. "You said you didn't want to destroy us, didn't want to make us like you, didn't want the Count to live on within us. So what in God's name are you talking about?"

Lucy turned back to Malcolm. "I'm talking about Malcolm's stupidity. Your basic problem, Malcolm, my dear, is that you aren't observant, you don't think, you don't remember things! You don't remember what a vampire's powers are, you don't remember how we can be killed and how we can *not* be killed. You don't even remember how to bring us from death to undeath, even though you did it once yourself."

"Don't be ridiculous," Malcolm said. "Of course I remember that. I did it to you . . ." His eyes went wide with the shock of realization.

Holly Larsen's rippling laugh floated through the basement. "Getting the picture, sugar?"

"We have the Master's dust," Lucy went on. "All we need now is a generous helping of his blood, and he will rise again, just as I rose again." She looked from Malcolm to Rachel, smiling wickedly. "And guess who has been keeping his blood safe all these years?"

Rachel closed her eyes. "Sweet Jesus," she muttered.

Quincy laughed softly. "There were three of us, but I inconveniently died. You and I were here in America, Rachel, while Malcolm was in Europe. She couldn't use his veins to nourish the Master's dust while we were still free to figure out what had happened. That's why she had to bring the remains here before restoring the Count."

"My own blood is useless for such a purpose, of course," Lucy said. "I can visit the curse upon a mortal, but only such a mortal can nurture and nourish the blood that can restore the undead. The blood in the Master's veins can do it also, of course, but his blood is more potent than mine."

"And so you needed us," Rachel said softly, shaking her head sadly.

"Oh, I could have done it in Rumania with just Malcolm, I suppose, but it would have been unwise. The Master values security and caution. He might have returned no better off than he had gone, with his existence known and his enemies aware of it. Besides, the blood had to awaken fully before its power could be raised to its greatest level." She smiled. "That's why you had all of your delightful dreams, dear Malcolm. The Master's blood was waking up after a century of slumber."

"Where are the remains?" Rachel asked, her voice shaking.

Lucy pointed to the pile of dirt that she had just swept up on the basement floor. "Behold the lord," she said with genuine reverence.

As Malcolm gazed at the dirt he was so astounded that

he almost laughed. "On the floor? You dumped his remains on the *floor!*"

"Of course," Lucy replied. "When you were searching for the dust, did it occur to you to look on the dirty floor of a musty basement?"

Malcolm shook his head slowly.

"Even so," Lucy said with satisfaction. "Really, Malcolm, you are so terribly dense."

"But... but it could have been swept up and thrown out, stuck to the soles of our shoes when we walked on it..."

"Yes," Lucy agreed, "and it could have been blown away by the wind a hundred years ago after the Master was stabbed. It doesn't take much of a wind to move dust, after all." She smiled. "But it did not blow away, and it could not be swept up, and walking on it would not disturb it in the least, because it is, shall we say, a particular, special kind of dust."

Malcolm looked up from the pile of dust and stared into Lucy's flaming eyes. "This doesn't change anything. You were still lucky. Okay, maybe I was stupid, maybe I couldn't see my hand in front of my face, but you were still lucky. If I hadn't made the mistakes I made, you wouldn't—"

"Oh, Malcolm," Lucy sighed wearily. "You just don't understand, do you." She turned to Daniel Rowland. "Daniel. Give me Holly's copy of that silly book." Daniel took the dog-eared paperback from his pocket as he scurried over to Lucy and handed it to her. "Where is it, Holly?" Lucy asked.

"Two pages before the end," Holly Larsen replied.

Lucy thumbed through to the back of the book and then said, "Ah. Here it is. Listen carefully." She began to read from the final scene of Bram Stoker's *Dracula.* "'But, on the instant, came the sweep and flash of Jonathan's great knife. I shrieked as I saw it shear through the throat; whilst at the same moment Mr. Morris's bowie knife plunged into the heart. It was like a miracle; but before our very eyes, almost in the drawing of a breath, the whole body crumbled into dust and passed from our sight.'" She looked up. "Understand?"

Malcolm glared at her. "Understand what?" He waited for the reply, which did not come, and then he shouted. "Stop this goddamned cat-and-mouse game! We're here, we're in your power, and you've won, okay? So what the hell are you trying to say?"

Lucy shook her head and then held the opened book in

front of Malcolm's eyes. "Read it for yourself, and then think about it, little Harker."

Malcolm struggled to ignore her condescension and repress his own fear as he read the passage over and over again, seeking some clue that would make sense of what the vampire had been saying. He read and he thought and he read and he thought, and he saw nothing, nothing...

...Wait a minute...

Malcolm's brow furrowed.

...Wait a minute...

"'...on the instant, came the sweep and flash of Jonathan's great knife...'"

...But no...no, that's not...

"'...Mr. Morris's bowie knife plunged into the heart...'"

Malcolm Harker slammed his head furiously against the wooden newel post. "My God!" he shouted. "My God, my God!"

"Malcolm, what is it?" Rachel screamed.

"You never noticed, did you?" Holly asked. "When I was alive, I never noticed. That book was published a hundred years ago, and no one ever noticed."

Rachel looked from Holly back to her brother. "Malcolm, what is she saying? Malcolm? *Malcolm!*"

Tears were running down Malcolm Harker's face as he turned to his sister. "Don't you see, Rachel? You can't kill a vampire with a knife!"

Rachel's mouth hung open for a moment. "But...no, wait, Malcolm, no. We've read the original manuscript, the original documents. We both know what happened when Quincey Morris and our great-grandfather killed the Count—"

"Oh, Christ, Rachel, that's just the point!" Malcolm cried. "They *didn't* kill Dracula! You can't kill a vampire with a knife!"

"The knives were blessed, they must have been!" she countered. "Van Helsing must have poured holy water on them or—"

"St. Peter himself could have wept on the blades, and it would have made no difference," Lucy said lightly. "Malcolm has figured out part of the truth, my dear."

"No," Rachel said again, shaking her head. "They killed him. I know they killed him."

"Rachel, you know how these things work as well as

do," Malcolm insisted. "Face it! *You can't kill a vampire with a knife!*"

"They saw him die, Malcolm!" Rachel shouted. "Jonathan ripped through his throat and Quincey stabbed him in the heart, and his body rotted away. He had been dead for four hundred years, and what would have been four centuries of decay struck him in an instant." She looked at Lucy, her tear-filled eyes narrow and hateful. "You're lying to us. You're trying to heap humiliation onto our sorrow, you damned filthy bitch!"

Malcolm clung to his sister's words with pathetic desperation. "That's right, damn it, that's right! They saw him disintegrate. They must have killed him, they *must* have killed him!"

Lucy smiled at Holly. "What's the page, dear?"

"Two fifty-three," Holly replied, returning her smile.

Lucy flipped the pages until she found the section she was looking for. "Mina Harker's Journal," she said softly. "How poignant!" Looking at Malcolm, she went on, "This is your brave and wise Professor Van Helsing explaining our powers to his little band of vampire hunters." She cleared her throat and read, "'He can transform himself to wolf, as we gather from his ship arrival at Whitby, when he tear open the dog; he can be as bat, as Madam Mina saw him on the window. He can come on mist which he create, he can come on moonlight rays as elemental dust, he can become small, he can see in the dark...'" She paused. "That's enough, I think. Do you understand now, Malcolm?"

Malcolm did not respond, for at last he understood everything. He understood exactly what had happened and exactly why it had happened. He realized that he had not only lost: he had never had a chance to win.

He can turn himself into dust.

The words reverberated in Malcolm's mind as if they were the denouement of a black comedy.

He can turn himself into dust.

That was the risk, that was the chance, that was the gamble which the Voivode of Wallachia had taken on that Carpathian road a hundred years ago. He was being pursued, his enemies had reached him just as the sun was setting, armed with their puny knives and foolish rifles. He could have killed them all then and there; but his identity was known, and his castle's location was known. He had no way of

knowing who else knew about him, who else might have been
waiting until the next sunrise before stealing into his crypt
and pounding a wooden stake into his heart.

But there were some things that he did know. He knew
that his blood flowed in the body of a young woman, recently
married, likely to have children. He knew that as long as his
blood lived, he could not be truly dead. He knew that his
demonic consciousness, transcending life and death and form
and being and time itself, would continue to exist for as long
as his infernal blood continued to flow in Mina Harker and in
her descendants down through the ages. But the mind of the
Voivode was not tied to his blood; it was tied to his unnatural
physical body, and it would be in his body that his mind
would live on.

No matter what form his body took!

It was indeed a gamble, for he would have to surrender
his Satanic blood to the air and the earth, surrender his
physical form in so extreme a manner that even he would not
be able to reconstitute it at will. But he took the risk, for only
by providing an unquestionable and absolute semblance of
his own destruction could he be confident of his survival.

Malcolm looked at his sister, and as their eyes met, each
knew that the other was being struck by the same numbing
realizations. It was as if the scales had fallen and they could
see clearly, understand fully, for the first time in months.

He was a gambler, this Vlad the Impaler, he had always
been a gambler. He had gambled against the Turks, he had
gambled against the Hungarians, he had gambled against his
own Wallachian subjects; and he had dared to hope that in
this last, final game, the Devil would load the dice.

And thus it was that at that cold Carpathian twilight of
1889, as Jonathan Harker stabbed impotently at his throat
and Quincey Morris stabbed impotently at his heart, the
Voivode of Wallachia turned himself into dust, gave them the
illusion, the false belief that they had destroyed him.

And then he waited as the years passed into decades and
the decades passed into a century, his being trapped in a pile
of dust and bone in a silent coffin in a ruined castle in the
mountains of Transylvania. He waited, and he listened to
the distant sounds that echoed to him through the blood, the
sounds that drifted to him over the thousands of miles and
the long years. He sent out the tendrils of his mind and he
and touched and knew the hearts and minds and souls

those whose veins carried his foul legacy. He was looking for weakness, for the absence of God's grace. He sensed it first in little Quincy Harker a scant seven years later, and he sent the little boy to seek out the grave of Lucy Westenra; but Abraham Van Helsing was wise enough to figure out at least a part of the truth, enough to protect the child and frustrate the plan for a time. He sensed it next in Malcolm's father, who died before he could be used, and then he sensed it again in Malcolm, Malcolm the intellectual, Malcolm the rationalist, to whom the undead vampire and the resurrected Christ were but two sides of the same myth, rather than two sides of the same reality.

And then the Voivode of Wallachia threw his ancient powers behind the plan which he had been contemplating through all the long years of imprisonment in his own dust.

Malcolm did not know whether to laugh or cry. He felt an alien mentality alive in his own body, a mentality now so certain of victory that it had removed the few remaining barriers to Malcolm's ability to understand what had happened to him.

Such a fool, he thought. I've been such a fool.

From the very beginning, from the absolute very beginning, he had been manipulated. His ideas, his intentions, his reasoning, had not been his own. He had been nothing more than a puppet of that patient, powerful, evil undead mind.

There had never been any need to go to England. Jerry and Holly had told him that, and they had also told him that pouring his blood on Lucy Westenra's skeleton was an absurd idea. But the Impaler needed his Lucy resurrected to further the plan, and so Malcolm had gone to England and had restored her to undeath.

Malcolm felt tears trickling from his eyes as he remembered the sudden change that had come over Lucy while he was speaking to her in the sepulcher, the sudden blankness of her expression, her sudden willingness to help him. It had been at that moment that her ancient lord had spoken to her through her blood and had told her what needed to be done.

And everything had proceeded according to plan.

He went to Rumania, gathered up the dust, brought it back to America where Rachel Rowland and Quincy Harker were waiting like innocent lambs in a slaughterhouse pen; and not once did Malcolm or his sister or his grandfather make the simple, logical connection between the dust and their own blood. Not once did they see that Lucy intended to mingle their blood with the remains of her lord and thus restore him as Malcolm had restored her. And why did they never realize this? Because the mentality that was connected to them through their blood would not *allow* them to realize it.

And Jerry Herman had drunk the same tainted blood from Lucy Westenra's breast, and so he, too, was being manipulated. He, too, never drew the simple, obvious, logical conclusion from the facts. And Holly and Quincy had been taken over to the other side and thus were being more than manipulated.

And while all of this was happening, the demonic mentality resting in the dust in the silent coffin was slowly awakening his own slumbering blood, readying it for the hellish reunion that would restore him to prey upon an unsuspecting world.

"Do you finally understand, my little marionettes?" Lucy asked with a cold smile. "Do you finally feel the puppet master's strings?"

"I've been such a fool," Malcolm said, shaking his head sadly, "such a fool."

"Don't be too hard on yourself, boy," Quincy said. "The Master won this game long ago."

Malcolm looked at Lucy. "I stabbed you in the chest with a knife," he said miserably, "and you just pulled it out and tossed it away, and I never made the connection."

"No, you didn't," Lucy agreed. "You see, it is just as I told you on that very same night. Van Helsing wouldn't have believed the things I had told you. He wouldn't even have spoken to me."

"Of course not," Malcolm sighed. "He wasn't cursed with the blood."

"Not yet, anyway," Lucy added, laughing dreadfully.

Malcolm looked up. "What do you mean?"

"Look around you, foolish boy!" Lucy replied. "What do you think we've been doing for the past few months—Holly, Quincy, and I, with Daniel's kind assistance? What do you think would happen if the Master were to spill his blood on the remains of the truly dead? What do you think these coffins are here for?"

"Daniel . . . Daniel said . . ." Malcolm stammered.

"Oh, I know what Daniel said," Lucy interrupted. "And

you believed him, just as you believed me. Oh, Malcolm, you're disappointing me again."

Malcolm's eyes moved from old rotten casket to old rotten casket. "Van Helsing?" he whispered, horrified at the thought.

"Yes," Lucy said, and nodded. "And Mina Harker and Jonathan Harker and Quincey Morris and John Stewart and Arthur Wellesley. The new coffin, of course, we have procured for the Master himself. We've already covered the interior with Rumanian earth. He shall be resurrected, and then my old friends shall drink of the Master's blood, and then we shall have a reunion!" Her mocking voice grew suddenly dark and malevolent. "Many years ago, the Master told these people that he spreads his vengeance over centuries. He intends to prove it to them."

Malcolm swallowed hard. "He's going to... he's..."

"Precisely," Lucy said. "A rather definitive victory, don't you think?"

Malcolm looked at her, shocked and disgusted. "Arthur Wellesley loved you so much, and you're going to help that monster do this to him?"

The red glow in Lucy's eyes dimmed for an instant and something vaguely human infused her features, just as it had months before in the crypt in Hempstead, England; but now as then, the instant passed almost immediately. "You never learn, little Malcolm, you never learn. I am not Lucy Westenra, any more than that is Holly Larsen over there with Rachel, any more than it is your grandfather holding your wrists. We are vampires, we are the undead, we are nosferatu. We do not love, we do not pity. We hate and we curse and we kill." Lucy paused and then said, "But we've waited long enough." She nodded to Quincy and Holly. "Now," she whispered.

Quincy Harker was still holding his grandson's wrists, keeping his hands well away from the shirt pocket that contained the consecrated host, and at Lucy's nod he dragged Malcolm toward the pile of dust on the floor in the center of the room. Holly did the same with Rachel, and when they met by the dust they took the right hands of their respective captives and brought them to their mouths. Quincy bit deeply into Malcolm's wrist as Holly's fangs sank into Rachel's. The two mortals cried out from the pain of the bites, but their cries were drowned out by the laughter of the vampires as the blood began to spurt from the torn flesh and fall onto the dust.

The vampires held the bleeding wrists out over the pile, and the dust was becoming thick and muddy as it absorbed the blood. "Enough," Lucy said at last, walking forward and wrapping strips of cloth first around Rachel's wrist and then around Malcolm's. "We don't want you to die, not yet." She smiled. "During the reunion, before dawn, but not now. I think we'll have Mina and Jonathan do the honors. That would be rather poetic, don't you think?"

Quincy dragged Malcolm back toward the base of the stairs as Holly pulled Rachel back to the corner. Jerry Herman was still sitting up against the wall in mute terror, and Daniel Rowland stood quietly aside, hands folded in front of him, looking down at his feet. He alone was not staring at red mud in the center of the room. Six pairs of eyes were riveted on the blood-soaked remains, three of them glowing red with anticipation, and three of them filled with despair and dread.

A few long, silent moments passed.

And then, just as months before in the crypt in England, a fine red mist began to seep up from the remains; but as Malcolm watched the mud churn and move and begin to boil, he felt a charge in the atmosphere, an invisible power moving through the dark and silent basement. This had not happened when he restored Lucy Westenra. There had not been the sensation of invisible presence, the feeling of an unearthly intelligence moving around them, upon them, within them. Malcolm's skin tingled and he felt something brush his face.

The red mud churned and hissed and changed, and then it began to glow so brightly that it was painful to watch. Licks of black fire began to shoot upward from the mud, and then the fire became bloodred and at last a blinding yellow. The mortals squinted their eyes against the flaming light, and from the midst of the brilliance came peals of ear-rending, screaming laughter as the flames shot upward and became a virtual pillar of fire. A crack of deafening thunder smote the walls of the basement as the flames flew outward in all directions and then dissipated with a startling immediacy that left Malcolm momentarily blinded.

He was still blinking his eyes as he heard the shuffling of feet and then Daniel screaming, "No...no...you promised...," as he heard Lucy's unearthly laughter mingle with a hungry, inhuman snarl from the center of the room. When his vision returned, he saw Daniel Rowland's throat being ripped open by the tall man who was embracing him. He watched the greedy, frenzied attack, watched as blood and vein and artery were torn out and devoured to quench the thirst and appease the hunger which had been growing for a hundred years.

Malcolm's gaze followed Daniel's corpse as it dropped heavily to the floor, and then he looked up into the mad eyes which were blazing with cold triumph.

Here was no black-caped caricature, no Hollywood villain, no cinema monster. Here was Vlad the Impaler, the Voivode of Wallachia, a medieval warrior prince, caftan-clad and bedecked with jewels, his long black hair slightly white at the temples, his drooping mustache as gray as iron, his skin as pale as death itself, his eyes as red as Hell.

He ignored the others in the room with him, for he had been brooding about his enemies for a hundred years, and he began to take his revenge upon them as soon as his maddening hunger had been assuaged. He went from aged coffin to aged coffin, ripping open the lids with his mighty hands, laughing loudly and vindictively, plunging his sharp teeth into his own wrists and pouring his infernal blood upon the piles of dust and bones and decaying cloth. He paid no attention to the three other vampires or the three captive mortals as the red mists began to fill the basement and the boiling, churning, hissing sounds arose from each trembling casket.

Then he turned his eyes to the others. He walked forward to Lucy Westenra and kissed her hand lightly, needing to say nothing, for they had been communicating with each other for months. Holly Larsen and Quincy Harker bowed their heads when he looked at them, and with a curt nod he acknowledged them as his creatures and accepted them as his own. He glanced at Rachel and Jerry with cold amusement, and then he looked over at Malcolm.

The lord of the vampires walked slowly over to the base of the stairway. He placed his balled fists upon his hips imperiously, and then he smiled.

"Malcolm Harker, my dear boy," Dracula said. "At last we meet."

Chapter Twenty-two

He stood at the foyer window of the Harker house on Granville Place in Forest Hills Gardens, looking out at this strange new world into which he had awakened an hour before. He pressed his rough tongue against the tip of one of his fangs, and then he closed his eyes and whispered in his ancient Balkan tongue, "Ordogh! Come to me!"

There was silence for a moment, and then the soft voice answered him, the voice that he had known for so many centuries, that had kept him company through the long years of imprisonment in his own dust. "I am here, Little Dragon."

"How many people, Ordogh? How many did you say?"

"Legion, Little Dragon, legion. Millions upon millions in this city alone, hundreds of millions in this country, billions upon the face of the earth in this time."

The Voivode laughed. "Truly, Ordogh, this is a pleasant awakening."

"Yes, Little Dragon."

"And I am not known in this time?"

"Ah, but you are famous, Little Dragon. Yours is one of the most famous names in all the world. Every detail of your conflict in England a century ago is known."

A smug smile curled upon the Voivode's dead lips. "And it is all mythology."

"Yes, Little Dragon."

"And I am a hobgoblin, a fairy tale with which to frighten children."

"Yes, Little Dragon."

"And the nosferatu is dismissed as nonsense."

"Less than nonsense, Little Dragon. This is an age where men hide their deepest fears and instincts behind a mask

316

rationality. Mankind has become a herd of sheep which does not believe in the existence of wolves."

The Voivode laughed louder. "A wonderful age for one such as I, Ordogh."

"Yes, Little Dragon," the voice said. "Even Christians who believe in my Enemy and in Heaven tend not to believe in me or in Hell. And it is a violent age, Little Dragon. Men slaughter each other by the tens of million in wars and in death camps and upon city streets, and they have weapons so destructive that by comparison a cannon is but a stone knife."

The Voivode gazed again out at the street. "So I can kill as I please, torture as I choose, and no one will suspect."

"As I have said, it is a violent age, Little Dragon. It is not likely that anyone will notice."

He smiled, again flicking his tongue against his sharp teeth. "In this as in all things, you have been a faithful ally, Ordogh. I thank you."

The soft voice seemed almost to laugh as it said, "I assure you, Little Dragon, that the pleasure is all mine."

The voice faded away into nothing, and then Vlad Dracula turned and went back to the stairs that led down to the basement.

They were all still there, just as he had left them a short time before when he went to commune with his dark mentor. Quincy Harker stood at the foot of the stairs, holding his grandson Malcolm by the wrists. Jerry Herman was on the floor, sitting up against the wall, and Holly Larsen stood beside him, Rachel Harker firmly in her grasp. Lucy Westenra stood in the center of the room, near the spot where the pile of dust had once lain. All around her were open coffins.

Open, empty coffins.

Lucy was conversing in low, amicable tones with her three onetime suitors: John Stewart, Quincey Morris, and Arthur Wellesley. Wilhelmina Harker was standing beside her husband, Jonathan, their fangs dinting their lower lips as they smiled at their great-grandchildren in a perverse parody of familial affection, their eyes alive with appetite and the lust for blood. Professor Abraham Van Helsing was staring down at Jerry Herman, his pudgy dead fingers stroking his beard contemplatively. His aged eyes, though as red as those of the other nosferatu, burned as much with curiosity as hunger. But the hunger was there, too, and Jerry was shaking violently in his terror.

The Voivode descended the stairs and laughed softly as he said in thickly accented English, "And so, my old friends. Together again, after all these years." The six creatures whose dust and bones he had soaked with his own demonic blood an hour before now echoed his laughter. They had lost and the Voivode had won; but his greatest victory, his most exquisite triumph, was that they now were beings like himself, that they thus were joyful in their own horrible fates.

The Voivode walked over to Van Helsing and said, "You have caused me no end of trouble, my dear Professor, I must admit; but you had certain qualities I admired during our, ah, earlier acquaintance. I have long anticipated the pleasure of hunting with you. We will have an interesting association in the centuries to come."

"I have hunger, Count," Van Helsing said hoarsely, his accent different from the Voivode's, but equally thick. "Why can I not have this boy?"

"Oh, come now, Professor!" the Voivode exclaimed. "After all that he and Lucy have meant to each other, that would hardly be fair. No, we shall all go hunting together shortly" —and he allowed his cruel eyes to drift from Jerry to Rache to Malcolm—"after we have finished here."

Malcolm's hands were beginning to get numb from Quincy's tight grip, and he made yet another unsuccessful attempt to pull away as he said, "You haven't beaten them Count. Sure, you tricked them and escaped from them, and you beat us, but they lived and died natural deaths while you were trapped in your own remains. These poor things aren't Van Helsing or my ancestors or the others. They're just walking dust."

The Voivode approached Malcolm. "Everyone is but walking dust, my boy. Don't you read your Bible? Ah, no you don't, that's right." He smiled. "And how fortunate that was for me."

Malcolm knew that death and its unspeakable consequence awaited him, and he refused to allow himself to be killed without first making the Voivode see how empty was his victory. "Go to any graveyard and dig up any bone Count. Pour your blood on them and you'll have creatures just like these, and you won't have accomplished anything beyond what you've accomplished here. You failed, Count and even though you survived that attack a hundred years ago, they still won, Van Helsing and Mina and Jonathan an the rest. You wanted Mina to be yours while she lived, and she wasn't. You wanted to kill the men who were protecting her, and you couldn't do it." Malcolm snorted arrogantly. "Why, you couldn't even get back into your castle before they caught up with you."

The Voivode shook his head sadly. "Oh, Malcolm, Malcolm. So poor an attempt to offend me."

"You've beaten me," Malcolm repeated, "but they defeated you. In the ways that matter to you most, they *defeated* you!"

"Oh, yes, in a sense they most certainly did," the Voivode said calmly. "They did better against me than you did, at least."

He turned when he heard Rachel Harker's derisive laugh. "Don't try to minimize what Malcolm is saying," she insisted, squirming against Holly's powerful grasp. "With all the powers you have and all your centuries of experience, you should be ashamed of how close they came to destroying you."

The Voivode raised his thick eyebrows. "I am impressed, my dear Rachel. You and your brother are about to face death and undeath, and yet you do not cringe, you do not beg, you do not plead." He turned back to Malcolm and leaned slightly forward, baring his fangs as he smiled. "Even though I cannot admire your limited intelligence, I do admire your courage. I have always admired brave men, even when I hated them, even when they were my enemies. Yes, Malcolm, I admire you and your sister, even though I am unmoved by your pathetic attempts to insult me."

"Really? Well, let's give this a try," Malcolm said, and then spat in the Voivode's face.

The rage that erupted in the eyes of the vampire lord was awesome in its intensity, but it subsided in an instant. "It is true that condemned men dare much," he muttered. "You know what is about to happen to you, and you know you have no means of escape, and so your petty pride attempts to incite my wrath. But think on this, little Harker; I know that you carry the consecrated host in your pocket. I had intended to remove your shirt before I gave you to your great-grandmother, but now I shall not. You shall awaken to undeath with the agony of that wafer burning into your flesh. I shall remove your shirt before it burns down to your heart, and I shall let you heal, and then I shall inflict it upon you again and again. I know the pain you suffered from the sacrament in recent months. I assure you that it shall be as a pinprick when compared with what awaits you."

Malcolm shook his head. "That's all just bravado, Count. You can't touch the consecrated host, and we both know it."

"I don't have to touch the host, you little fool. All I have to do is touch the shirt."

Malcolm thought back on the agony he had experienced. He tried to imagine it magnified a thousandfold, and his already pale face grew whiter.

"And there is more," the Voivode went on. "You do not know—yet—the pain of needing to feed and being kept from feeding. But you shall know this pain, Malcolm Harker, for I shall starve you. And unlike the living, we cannot starve to death, for we are already dead; and your starvation shall torment you to a madness that will have no end." He drew himself up haughtily. "You are a peasant, little Harker, and you must learn your place. Were this five hundred years ago, there would already be a stake pushing its way out from your mouth." Malcolm lapsed into silence, and the Voivode looked over at Rachel. "And you guard your tongue, madam, lest I rip it out while you yet live."

Jerry Herman coughed softly. "Uh, excuse me . . . ?" He seemed to shrink from the burning eyes that snapped in his direction, but he continued to speak with his trembling voice. "Look, sir. I really don't have anything to do with any of this . . . I kinda got mixed up in this by accident, you know? . . . I'm not a member of the Harker family, and I promise that I won't tell anybody anything if . . ." His words trailed off into silence.

The Voivode stared at Jerry as one might gaze at an insect, and then, without even bothering to respond, he turned to Lucy and said, "Kill him."

Jerry screamed and tried to escape from Lucy as she began to walk toward him, but this was impossible with his hands tied behind his back and his legs tied together. All he managed to do was to push himself along the floor of the basement. "Let's not be troublesome, darling," Lucy said as she grabbed him by the collar and pulled him to his feet. "We have reached our rendezvous with destiny, as they say."

"Don't . . ." Jerry pleaded. The dead mouth came closer and the fetid breath assaulted his nostrils. "No, please don't . . . please don't . . ."

Lucy licked her lips as she pulled Jerry's head back, and

he cried out when she pressed her mouth against his throat. She drove her fangs into his flesh and began to suck greedily of the river of his blood. Jerry blinked and swayed and seemed to be growing weaker as she drained the life from him; but he was still conscious when he felt the fangs withdraw from his throat, and he heard an annoyed Lucy say, "And what is so amusing, Malcolm, if I may ask?"

Jerry looked over at Malcolm, and he realized that his friend was laughing, laughing loudly and deeply, laughing so hard that his entire body was quaking with the violence of his laughter. Quincy Harker maintained his relentless hold on his grandson's wrists, but the old man's face bespoke his confusion at Malcolm's behavior.

"What is the meaning of this?" Lucy demanded.

"You said that I'm stupid, that I don't remember things." His laughter was so overwhelming that it was a few moments before he could speak again. "I remember basic biology. I remember how long it takes the human body to metabolize and eliminate alcohol. I remember that the more you drink, the longer it takes." He collapsed into peals of laughter.

Lucy turned to her master. "What's wrong with him?"

"He is raving," the Voivode replied. "It has all been too much for him. His mind has snapped."

"Well, no matter," Lucy said, and shrugged. "He'll be one of us soon enough." But then she paused. She frowned and placed her hand upon her forehead.

"Lucy? Is something wrong?" the Voivode asked.

Lucy's eyes went wide with pain and shock and her pallid face grew suddenly very flushed. "No!" her voice rattled. "No!"

"Yes!" Malcolm shouted through his laughter. "Yes, Lucy, *my dear!*"

Lucy lost her hold on her victim, and Jerry fell to the floor as she stumbled backward, her eyes darting madly around the room. He managed to push himself over to Malcolm's feet, saying, "Mal, what... what...?" And then he suddenly realized why Malcolm was laughing so hard, and he began to laugh along with him, crying, "That's right! That's right!"

The Voivode looked angrily from the two young men to Lucy Westenra. He grabbed her by her quivering shoulders and said, "Lucy! What...?" but then he hissed and jumped back. Lucy's flesh had burned his hands.

"Consecrated wine!" Malcolm shouted, still laughing. "Not six hours ago Jerry drank an entire flask filled with consecrated wine, and it's still in his bloodstream. You just drank the blood of Christ, Lucy! You've just taken communion! You've"—and his laughter overwhelmed him again—"you've just gone to mass!"

Lucy Westenra clutched madly at her stomach and at her chest, opening her mouth to scream, but no sound issued forth save a low, gurgling moan.

"Remember, all of you, remember?" Malcolm laughed. "Remember, Mina, when Van Helsing touched your forehead with the consecrated host a hundred years ago? It *burned* you, it *burned* you, just like it burned me in the churches here and in Rome, just like the consecrated wine burned Jerry this afternoon!" His hate-filled eyes turned to Lucy. "And we were just polluted. But you, Lucy, you are *pollution!*"

Lucy backed up against the wall of the basement, shaking her head, her eyes wild and frenzied, her body racked by unspeakable agony. Liquidy postules began to swell upon her face; her skin grew bright red and began to blister; the fluids in her body began to boil.

"Burn, damn you!" Malcolm shouted. "Burn!"

She did not burn.

She exploded.

The roaring blast of her intense and instantaneous internal combustion shook the very foundations of the house. Bits and pieces of her body flew out in all directions, bloody chunks of inhuman meat that splattered against the walls and the ceiling, then turned into delicate bits of dust before they reached the floor.

And at the moment of the explosion, Malcolm, tensed and eager, was waiting with the motionless potential energy of a coiled spring.

For an instant, just an instant, Quincy Harker was startled by Lucy's sudden destruction, and he relaxed his grip on his grandson's wrists. But that instant was all Malcolm needed to pull his right hand free, plunge it into his shirt pocket, and grab hold of the two pieces of consecrated host; and he needed only to hold it up in front of his grandfather to cause Quincy Harker to run screaming from the bottom of the stairs.

Malcolm took one wafer in his left hand and tossed the other at Rachel with his right. Holly shrieked and fell back from what might as well have been a flaming missile, and in her panic she let go of Rachel, who picked up the wafer and then scurried over to Malcolm and Jerry.

It had all taken less than five seconds; but now the mortals were free, they were armed, and they were facing one less opponent. Rachel began to undo Jerry's bonds as best she could with one hand as Malcolm smiled at the Voivode. "Well, well, well," he said softly. "Changes things a bit, doesn't it!"

The Voivode stared at him angrily. "All it means is that you may be able to escape your fates this night. You have bought yourselves a little more time, little Harker, a bit more life, that is all."

"Escape!" Malcolm exclaimed. "What makes you think we want to escape? We're going to keep you here until sunrise, Count, and then we're going to destroy you all. And don't try any of that shape-changing stuff to try to scare us away. I don't care if you're a wolf or a bat or a mouse, you still can't get by me as long as I have this." And he held the wafer up confidently.

The vampires all laughed as the Voivode shook his head. "Even now, such ignorant arrogance. How do you propose to hold us prisoner, Malcolm Harker? How do you expect to keep us from becoming mist and seeping out through window spaces, for example?" Malcolm clenched his jaw and did not reply. "I see that you discern my drift. This is a temporary stalemate. It does not even begin to approach victory."

Malcolm did not respond. Instead he walked cautiously over to the black athletic bag that he had left in the corner earlier that day, holding the wafer in front of him as he moved. The undead fell back from the hated element and stared at Malcolm with undisguised fury—all but Van Helsing, who remained motionless, staring at the wafer. Malcolm picked up the bag and then went back to Rachel and Jerry at the foot of the stairs. He did not lower his eyes as he joined his free hand with Rachel's and finished untying Jerry's wrists. Rachel removed the crosses and the garlic from the bag as Jerry began to work on the ropes around his legs. When he had untied them, he took a cross and some garlic from Rachel and then stood up between her and his friend. Only then did Malcolm say, "It isn't victory yet, but it's a start. We were supposed to be undead tonight, but we're going to walk out of here at dawn. That's one failure you have to swallow. You can't get at us, Count, not with the shields we have. That's another failure. And even though he didn't plan to do it, Jerry destroyed Lucy. That makes three."

The Voivode dismissed this last statement with a wave of his long, thin hand. "Lucy will be back with me long before this evening is over. Can you truly be so foolish, Malcolm? Her dust is here, in this room, and the blood which has resurrected her twice already still runs in my veins. No, Malcolm Harker, you have not won, you have not even injured me. You may live past dawn, but eventually I shall find you and your sister and your friend."

"We'll be ready for you," Rachel said firmly.

"Good! Good!" the Voivode said. "Make your preparations! Lay your plans, build your defenses! Live another fifty years if you can! It will mean nothing, for as long as I live, my blood lives on in you, and when you die, you shall join our company."

"We'll make sure that we're embalmed," Rachel insisted. "We'll see to it that your damned blood is pumped out of us and thrown in the gutter!"

"Do so," the Voivode said, "by all means! And then I shall dig up your bodies and bathe them with my blood. And if you have your bodies burned, I shall resurrect you from your ashes. And if you leave orders for your ashes to be scattered, I shall countermand the orders. But it will not come to that, for I shall have gained control of you long before."

Malcolm and Rachel exchanged looks. The beast was right, and they both knew it. They had managed to avoid death and undeath that night by sheer accident, and nothing had really changed. They were still cursed, and the author of their misery was standing arrogantly before them.

"It is as true tonight as it was a hundred years ago and five hundred years ago," the Voivode said darkly. "I spread my revenge over centuries, and time is on my side."

"Don't be so sure, Count," Malcolm insisted. "A lot can still happen."

The Voivode laughed. "Oh, and it certainly shall, Malcolm Harker, it certainly shall." He glanced over at Van Helsing. "Professor, take that broom and sweep up Lucy's dust. I will restore her now. I want her back with me."

Van Helsing seemed not to have heard the order. He was still standing in the same spot, still gazing at the consecrated wafer in Malcolm's hand, swaying slowly from side to side, staring at the host as if transfixed. Malcolm looked at Van Helsing carefully, wondering what the oddly human expression on the old Professor's face portended. And as Malcolm studied Van Helsing's face, he saw the red glow of his vampire eyes dim almost imperceptibly.

It's the same as when Lucy's eyes seemed human for a moment, he thought. When I mentioned Arthur tonight, and when I referred to him back in England, it seemed as if for an instant something of her mortal being was still living in her undead body.

He remembered trying to arouse in Holly some small element of pity for Jerry. Didn't her eyes seem human, alive, just briefly as he spoke to her? *I'm someone else now,* Holly had replied on that horrible first night of her undeath, *I'm something else now.*

Maybe you aren't... maybe not... maybe not...

Malcolm felt a slight surge of excitement.

In life Lucy Westenra had loved Arthur Wellesley, the Duke of Wellington, and her love for him had been the all-consuming center of her existence. What if some small vestige of that love had remained, buried deep within the monstrous, undead mind? Might that love not have been a connecting link between the creature she had become and the human being she had once been?

Malcolm continued to stare at Van Helsing as Van Helsing continued to stare at the consecrated wafer.

And what had been Van Helsing's all-consuming passion? He had loved knowledge, to be sure, he had loved truth and wisdom and learning, but what had he been truly devoted to? What had been the central, structuring influence on the long life of Abraham Xavier Klemens Van Helsing? What had been his great love?

Malcolm knew the answer to his own question. He licked his lips nervously as he held the host in front of him and began to walk toward the professor. Jerry and Rachel looked at him quizzically but said nothing as he swung the host slowly from right to left, forcing the vampires to move aside and allow him to advance. As he drew closer to Van Helsing, he saw the professor begin to shrink back in fear, and he said quickly, "No, Professor Van Helsing, no. Don't retreat from the host. You have a dispensation, remember?"

"A... dispensation?"

"Yes, don't you remember? You are a faithful and loyal son of the Roman Catholic Church. Your faith is so strong and your devotion to the Church so deep and abiding that your archbishop gave you a dispensation so that you could carry the consecrated host with you when you went to England. Don't you remember, Professor?"

He shook his head sadly. "That was... that was before."

"Before or now, what difference does it make? You are still Abraham Van Helsing! You are still a Christian."

The Voivode laughed at this. "A Christian vampire! Oh, Malcolm, you are growing desperate! We are the mirror images of Christ. His enemies, not His servants!"

"*You* are, Count, you, not Van Helsing and the others," Malcolm shouted, and then looked back at the pathetic yearning in Van Helsing's face as the dimming red eyes again gazed longingly at the wafer. "Say the creed, Professor, say it along with me. 'I believe in God the Father Almighty, maker of heaven and earth, and of all things visible and invisible'... Professor, don't you remember the words? It's the Nicene creed! Say it with me. You said it a thousand times while you were alive, and you believed it. You must still believe it, you must! 'I believe in God the Father Almighty, maker of heaven and earth, and of all things visible and invisible...'"

"'And...'" Van Helsing murmured, "'and... in... Jesus... Christ... His only son... our... our Lord...'"

"Stop this at once!" the Voivode commanded. He took a step forward, but Malcolm swung the host in his direction and he fell back again, snarling angrily.

Rachel's heart skipped a beat when she realized what her brother was trying to do, and she embraced his attempt with an enthusiasm born of desperation. Yes, she thought, yes! They all lived in an age of faith, an age of Victorian devotion. Religion was a vibrant reality to them all, not a social custom or a cultural heritage, not something to be thought about only on Sunday mornings, if at all. It structured their lives, it was central to their lives. "Go on, Professor, go on," Rachel said. "'God of God, light of light, true God of true God...'"

"'Begotten of His Father before all worlds,'" Malcolm prompted, "'begotten, not made'... say the words, Professor, say the words!... 'being of one substance with the Father, through Whom all things were made...'"

"'Who for us men and for our salvation,'" Van Helsing

whispered, "'was incarnate by the Holy Ghost of the Virgin Mary...'" He sighed. "'By the Virgin Mary...'"

"'And was made man,'" said another voice softly. Malcolm looked for the source of the words, and he trembled with hope when he found it.

Mina Harker.

Rachel left Jerry at the foot of the stairs and went toward her great-grandmother. "Yes, Mina," she whispered eagerly. "You were a devout Christian, too! Remember, Mina. Remember." She turned to her great-grandfather. "And you, Jonathan, you were a pious man. All of you were—Dr. Stewart, Mr. Morris, Your Lordship, all of you were! Remember the words, say the words, remember who you were, what you were!" She walked forward and stood in front of her grandfather, Quincy Harker, and held the protective host behind her back. "Oh, Grandfather, please try."

Quincy looked at her oddly, knowing that her body shielded him from the consecrated wafer, knowing he could whip out one powerful arm and sweep her head from her body. He gazed at her and the dead flesh quivered on his face. "'And...and...was...made...man,'" he rasped.

The cracked dead lips of the other nosferatu began to move haltingly. Holly Larsen ran to the Voivode and hid behind him, clutching a sleeve of his caftan and looking at the other undead with confusion and fear.

"I say you will stop this at once!" the Voivode shouted.

They ignored him. "'He suffered under Pontius Pilate... was crucified, died and was buried...'"

"'... on the third day He rose again from the dead...'"

"'... He ascended into heaven...'"

"'... and sitteth at the right hand of God the Father...'"

"'... from whence He shall come to judge the living...'"

"'...and the dead...'"

"YOU TORE ME FROM MY REST!" Van Helsing screamed.

The blazing eyes of the Voivode fixed on the face of the old Professor. "You are undead, you fool, you are as I am! You serve Ordogh now, you serve the powers of Hell! Stop this foolishness! We shall go from this place, and we shall feed, and—"

"YOU TORE ME FROM MY REST!" Van Helsing repeated, his fists clenching at his sides as he moved threateningly toward the Impaler.

"Van Helsing, be silent!" the Voivode shouted. "Be silent and obey!"

The flames in the Professor's eyes flickered, and then they died.

"YOU . . . TORE . . . ME . . . FROM . . . MY . . . *REST!*" Van Helsing screamed again, and grabbing the Voivode roughly under the arms, he threw him against the wall.

Holly gasped at the unexpected and incomprehensible assault, and she fell back from the enraged Van Helsing. All the certitudes that the demonic blood had taught her had suddenly been cast into doubt. In her life she had been a child of a godless age, and no vestige of faith remained in her to give her strength against the dark forces which moved her dead limbs. A wave of panic washed over her, a desperate need to get away, away from Van Helsing, away from the horrible words the other nosferatu were speaking, out and away from this basement madhouse.

She began to run past Malcolm toward Rachel and Jerry, preparing to fly over them and get to the door at the top of the stairs, but Malcolm reached out his left arm and wrapped it around her waist as she passed him. Her strength was so great that she could have ripped his arm from its socket had she had the chance; but she did not have the chance. Before she could dislodge his grasp, Malcolm's right hand pressed the consecrated host against her throat.

"I love you, Holly," he whispered as he bore her down with him onto the floor, ignoring her shrieks of agony, ignoring the blood which burst from her throat as the host burned its way down into her undead flesh. She threw him away from her and then began to dig with frantic, desperate fingers into the fiery tunnel which the small bit of sanctity was creating. The host burned through her, and then the wound spread upon her throat in all directions. As Holly made a futile effort to rise to her feet, the flames consumed what remained of her neck, and her head fell from her shoulders onto the floor. Her body quivered spasmodically and then fell motionless. In an instant her body began to decompose, and the basement was filled with the stench of putrid flesh.

The Voivode pushed Van Helsing back and began to advance on Malcolm, who was no longer holding the protective wafer. "You shall pay, little Harker, you shall pay!" he said furiously through clenched teeth.

Jerry threw a bulb of garlic at the Voivode, momentarily

distracting him. It was time enough for Malcolm to retreat to the safety of Rachel and the other piece of consecrated host. He took a cross from the bag and held it in front of him. The three mortals huddled together at the foot of the stairs, hugging each other tightly, shaking with terror and anger and hope.

Van Helsing's body was trembling violently from his massive internal struggle as he held his hands out to Mina and Jonathan, saying, "Pray with me, Madam Mina, friend Jonathan, pray with me. Old friend Jack, Arthur, Quincey Morris, and Quincy, my dear boy Quincy, pray with me, pray with me!" Mina and Jonathan reached out and clasped his hands.

The expression on the Voivode's face was like that of a rabid animal as he looked from the shielded mortals to the rebellious nosferatu. "You will obey me!" he shouted. "You are mine, you are mine, *and you will obey me!*"

"'Our Father, which art in heaven,'" Van Helsing began.

"'Hallowed be Thy name,'" they said in unison.

"Stop this!" the Voivode screamed furiously.

"'Thy kingdom come, Thy will be done, on earth as it is in heaven . . .'"

The Voivode grabbed Mina Harker's arm and pulled her away from Van Helsing. "You are mine! You will obey me!"

"'Give us this day our daily bread, and forgive us our trespasses, as we forgive those who trespass against us . . .'"

"You cannot do this!" Vlad Dracula screamed. "You cannot pray, you cannot remember your old lives, you cannot! You are nosferatu, you are nosferatu!"

"'And lead us not into temptation, but deliver us from evil' . . . but deliver us from evil . . . *but deliver us from evil . . . !*"

They repeated the phrase over and over again in their frenzied, angry voices, a mad litany chanted by undead tongues. They moved slowly forward and began to surround the Voivode.

"*But deliver us from evil . . . !*" said Jonathan Harker and John Stewart as they grabbed him by the arms and held him in a grip as inhumanly powerful as his own.

"*But deliver us from evil . . . !*" said Abraham Van Helsing as he took hold of the wooden chair near the wall and tore off one of the narrow legs. "*But deliver us from evil . . . !*" he said again and again as he took the jagged piece of wood in both hands and began to approach the Impaler.

"No! Stop!" the Voivode shouted. "I command you!"

Their strength was his strength, their power was his power. He could take whatever form he wished, and they could assume the same shape and pursue him. He could become a mist pursued by mist, a bat attacked by bats, a wolf ravaged by wolves. He was trapped, a general facing a revolt of his own troops, a king confronting his own revolutionary subjects.

"*But deliver us from evil . . . !*" they cried as Van Helsing raised the stake above his head. "*But deliver us from evil . . . but deliver us from evil . . . BUT DELIVER US FROM EVIL . . . !*"

"Ordogh!" the Voivode screamed. "Ordogh! *Ordogh!*"

"*BUT DELIVER US FROM EVIL . . . !*"

"NO!" he screamed. "NO! NO!"

"*BUT DELIVER US FROM EVIL . . . BUT DELIVER US FROM EVIL . . . !*"

Van Helsing summoned every bit of his inhuman strength, and, a cry of rage bursting from his undead lips, he thrust the stake deep into the monster's heart.

The Voivode shrieked and fell to the floor as a jet of blue-black blood burst from his chest. He grabbed hold of the stake and tried to pull it out, but Quincey Morris grabbed one hand and Quincy Harker grabbed the other, and they held him fast as the unholy liquid poured out of him in a torrential flood.

"NO!" he screamed again. "NO! ORDOGH! ORDOGH!"

The room was suddenly filled with a blinding white light which burst outward from the tip of the stake as a freezing whirlwind whipped suddenly through the room and the shrieks of the Voivode grew deafening and echoed madly against the walls. A swirling cloud of red smoke coalesced above the glowing stake, and the screaming vampire arched his back as his dark soul was sucked up into the cloud, through the breech in the barrier between time and eternity. The cold wind blasted the faces of the onlookers, and as the agonized screams themselves grew agonizing in their intensity, the mortals shut their eyes against the light and covered their ears against the piercing sound.

And then there was a startling stillness and a sudden darkness in the quiet basement.

He was gone.

The stake lay on the floor amid a long pile of dust, and the vampires looked down at it, suddenly silent in their victory. Van Helsing shattered the silence by crying, "Free! We are free!" And then he began to decompose.

The three mortals watched in mute fascination as the undead flesh began to harden and crack and fall from the vampires' bodies in large, thick flakes. The creatures screamed in pain, but mingled with their screams were cries of joy as eye sockets grew empty and teeth were bared in fleshless skulls, as bony fingers trembled and naked ribs quivered from the dissolution. In the blinking of an eye six skeletons stood before them; and then the rotten bones collapsed to the floor with a clattering crash, and the air of the basement was filled with floating wisps of dust.

Quincy Harker's face was growing dark and liquidy, and chunks of rotten flesh broke free and fell off, landing with loud, wet splatters as he tried to smile at his grandchildren. Then he pitched forward onto his face and like Holly Larsen, began to emit noxious gases as his body, dead these three months, began to putrify.

As with one motion, Malcolm, Rachel, and Jerry sat down heavily on the stairs and surveyed the scene before them. Against one wall was Daniel Rowland's dead, mutilated body. The rotting corpses of Holly and old Quincy lay in the center of the room.

And everywhere else was only dust and bone.

Epilogue

The cold November wind whipped about his feet, blowing brown leaves against the gravestone. He had brought no flowers, for he remembered that she had never really cared for them. He looked up at the gray sky and then back down to the marble stone. "I'm sorry, Holly," he sighed, shaking his head sadly. "I'm so sorry."

"Mal?" Jerry Herman said softly, kindly, from a few feet away. "Let's go, okay? It's a long drive back."

"Yeah, okay." He turned from Holly Larsen's grave and followed Jerry back to the car parked on the cemetery road.

He had only been out of bed for a few days, and he was still too shaky to drive, so he got into the front seat beside Rachel as she started the engine. Jerry got into the back and closed the door. "Mal, you feeling all right?"

"I'm okay, Jerry," Malcolm said quietly.

"It's over, Malcolm," his sister said. "We all have to put it behind us and go on with our lives."

Malcolm glanced back at the grave as the car pulled away from the roadside. "Those of us who still have lives."

"She's at rest, Malcolm." Rachel's voice was gentle and comforting. "They're all at rest now."

He nodded a dismissive agreement, then fell silent.

They had driven up to the little town of Skaneateles, New York, for the sole purpose of visiting Holly's grave. It had taken them six hours to drive up and would take another six to drive back, and only Malcolm's insistence had impelled Rachel to agree to the journey. Jerry was taking turns with her in the driving, but it was still a long trip, and to Rachel and Jerry, an unnecessary one.

But though they did not relish the long drive, th

understood why Malcolm wanted to go, and so they had driven him up and were driving him back. He felt responsible for everything that had happened. Logically, he and they knew that the responsibility lay elsewhere; but when feelings and logic collide, logic rarely emerges victorious.

"They don't believe us, you know," Malcolm muttered.

"Hm?" Rachel responded. "Who doesn't believe us?"

"The police. De La Vega and the other detectives. They think we lied to them."

Rachel laughed grimly. "We *did* lie to them. We had to lie to them. If we'd told them the truth, we'd all have ended up in padded cells." She immediately regretted her thoughtless comment, for Malcolm's collapse from nervous exhaustion, while not quite a breakdown, had been close enough to make Rachel feel she should choose her words carefully. "Malcolm . . ." she began.

"Take it easy, Sis. I know what you meant." He smiled sadly. "I feel a little silly about it myself."

"Well, you shouldn't, you know," Jerry said. "With everything that happened and everything we went through, it's surprising we didn't all flip out."

"You didn't, though," Malcolm said, "neither of you. Just me."

"Yeah, well, Rachel's too strong and I'm too simple." Jerry smiled, and Rachel and Malcolm laughed. Then they fell silent again.

They were passing the Albany exit on the New York State Thruway when Malcolm said, "They're probably going to watch us, keep an eye on us."

"Who is?" Rachel asked.

"The cops. They think we killed Daniel and Holly and other Henley. They think we robbed all those graves."

"Let them think whatever they want to think," Rachel said. "They can't disprove that cock-and-bull story you two came up with about a Satanist cult. Daniel, Miss Larsen, and other Henley are just three more open cases to them, and they can't prove we did anything." She paused. "Which we didn't. And as for those coffins, all three of us can prove where we were when the graves were robbed. So let them watch us all they want." She rubbed her eyes. "Besides, grandfather's grave wasn't even really robbed. There was an empty coffin in it when they dug it up. As far as they know, the funeral home was at fault."

Malcolm listened and then asked gently, "Do you miss him?"

"Grandfather? Of course I do."

"No, Daniel."

She did not reply at first. Then she said, "Sometimes. Not often."

"He was a victim, too, you know."

"He wasn't a victim when he walked out on me," Rachel said. "When I told him our family history and what we were facing, he should have been supportive. He wasn't. He should have wanted to help. He didn't."

"I guess he was no Van Helsing," Jerry said.

Rachel harrumphed. "He wasn't even much of a Renfield. At least that poor lunatic rebelled when Mina was endangered." They were silent again for a while, and then Rachel said, "Malcolm, you're still young and you're still healthy, and the curse has been lifted from us all. You should marry, become a father. Not soon, of course. I know that wounds heal slowly, but—"

"No," Malcolm interrupted. "Marry, maybe, someday. But kids?" He shook his head. "Never."

"There's no reason why you shouldn't," Rachel said. "The power of the blood has been broken. There isn't any danger anymore."

Malcolm's laugh was humorless and grim. "We don't know that, Sis."

Rachel glanced at him. "Of course we do. We saw what happened when the Count was killed."

"Sure, Mal," Jerry said. "No more Dracula, no more vampires, no more curse. He dies, and the blood becomes nothing but blood."

Malcolm shook his head and repeated, "We don't know that. Sure, we know what we saw. We know that he's dead, really dead this time. A wooden stake is foolproof. But beyond that, we aren't sure of anything. We may still have the . . . the infection in our systems, and if we do, I'm sure as hell not going to pass it on to anyone else."

"Malcolm, you're being silly," Rachel insisted.

"Maybe I am," he conceded, "but I'm not taking any chances. Think about it. How do we know that the other vampires disintegrated just because Van Helsing killed the Count? I told you about the demon in my visions, the one who made the pact with Dracula. Maybe he destroyed them just to throw us off our guard. Don't forget, Dracula's di was swept up along with all the others, and it's all in an evidence locker in some police warehouse somewhere. Maybe the demon is waiting for us to die so he can try this all over again. Maybe there's someone else somewhere who has the Count's blood in his system. Maybe—"

"Maybe you should get a dictionary and look up the word 'paranoia,'" Jerry suggested. "Sure, the cops swept his dust up with all the other dust, and it's all mixed up together. How could anyone tell what's left of Dracula from what's left of Van Helsing and all the others?"

"It isn't normal dust," Malcolm countered. "Remember, it didn't blow away in the wind a hundred years ago on that road in Transylvania, but it should have if it were just ordinary remains. Why should we assume that the demon can't separate Dracula's dust from everyone else's when and if he wants to?"

"Malcolm," Rachel said gently, "I know you've been through a lot. We all have."

"No shit," Jerry muttered.

"But don't fall prey to foolish fears. We know that Dracula only forced three living people to drink his blood: Lucy Westenra, Mina Harker, and Renfield. If he had done it to anyone else, there would have been lots of legitimate reports of vampirism over the years, and there haven't been. We know that Lucy never had children. We know that Renfield was a young, unmarried, childless madman who was killed in Stewart's asylum and embalmed before burial. And Mina's descendants—"

"Still have Mina's blood in their veins," Malcolm finished for her. "You're right, I know, about Lucy and Renfield. And I know that there aren't any other vampires, at least none of Dracula's bloodline. But damn it, Rachel, I'm not going to take any chances. No kids for me. The sacrament every week. Embalming when I die." He paused. "And you two should do the same things, just to be safe."

"Is kosher wine on the Sabbath good enough?" Jerry asked.

Malcolm turned to see the grin spreading over his friend's face, and he laughed despite his depression. "Jerry, you're such a jerk."

"Hey, come on, I can't handle all this flattery."

Malcolm smiled at him warmly. "And you're a good friend."

"So are you, Mal," Jerry said. "But hey, with friends like you . . ."

They both laughed and then continued the drive in silence. Malcolm looked out the window at the sunset. *Night's coming,* he thought. *I wonder how long it will be before dusk stops making me nervous? If ever.*

I know they're right, he thought. *Dracula is dead, the bloodline ends with us, the dust is just dust and can never be separated from all the other dust. It's all over. We're safe now, all of us—me, Jerry, Rachel, the human race, all of us. We're safe. We're free.*

Malcolm struggled to convince himself.

He could not.

Three thousand miles away, in London, England, Dr. Michael Thorpe was greeting Dr. Edward Fitzgibbon with a handshake and a gesture inviting him into his office. "I'm so grateful that you were able to get away like this, Teddy. I have to admit that I'm a bit out of my depths with this child."

"I find that very hard to believe, Michael," Fitzgibbon said as he seated himself in the chair in front of Thorpe's desk. "You're one of the finest child psychologists I know. You're certainly as skilled as I am."

"I may have skill, but I don't have your insight," Thorpe said. "I haven't been able to make any progress with her whatsoever."

Fitzgibbon pulled a pipe and a tobacco pouch from his pocket. As he filled the pipe, he asked, "Dogs, was it?"

"Cats," Thorpe corrected him. "Kittens, actually. It was the headmistress of her school who contacted me."

"And her parents?"

"Her father is the only parent. Mother died a few years ago."

"Killing and eating cats," Fitzgibbon mused. "Bizarre aberration, what?"

"It seems to be a bizarre family," Thorpe said as he opened the file folder that lay on the desk. "Let me review the case with you..."

"Wait, Michael. I'd like to see the child first. I prefer having a face to hang the facts on before I start working on a case."

"Oh, certainly," Thorpe said. "She's in the playroom right now. It's this way."

He led Fitzgibbon out into the corridor, and as they

walked from the office to the playroom, Fitzgibbon asked, "What's your child-to-orderly ratio?"

"Ten to one."

"And child-to-doctor?"

"Fifty to one."

Fitzgibbon shook his head. "That's much too high, Michael, much too high."

"I agree, Teddy, but try telling that to the government. Whenever I petition for more funds, all I get are pep talks about retrenchment and lower taxes."

"And the children get lost in the red tape."

"Yes," he replied, then added: "Oh, we do a good job with most of them, because few of their problems are complicated. Child abuse is the most common source of the emotional distress, and we and the police together can deal with that. But in cases like this... yes, you're right, she needs more attention than I can give her. That's why I'm especially happy you could work this into your schedule."

"And I suppose I should forward the bill for my consultation fee to the prime minister?" Fitzgibbon grinned.

"Best of luck to you in that," he said, and laughed. They reached the playroom and Thorpe held the door open for his colleague. He entered to see a dozen little children, not one of them over the age of six, playing with blocks and wagons and coloring books, all under the watchful eye of a disinterested middle-aged woman dressed in white. "That's her, over there," Thorpe said softly, pointing to the far corner.

She was sitting by herself, hugging a doll tightly to her chest, rocking back and forth on her haunches, staring off at nothing. The faded dress she wore did not fit well, leading Fitzgibbon to conclude that the institution had provided her with the clothing. Her stringy hair was light brown, her skin was sallow, her large, sad eyes dark and sunken. Fitzgibbon turned to Thorpe and whispered, "Autistic?"

"No," came the quiet reply. "She's responsive enough. Rather observant and quick, actually."

Fitzgibbon nodded, looked again at the child, and then said, "Let's go back to your office. Tell me everything you know."

As the door closed behind them and they walked back down the corridor, Thorpe said, "Her name is Constance Sheldon, five years of age. Her father is Thomas Sheldon, unemployed stevedore. Her mother's name was Bridget Duffy."

"You said the mother was killed?"

"Yes, murdered four years ago, when Constance was still an infant."

"And she's lived alone with her father since then?"

"Yes."

Fitzgibbon nodded contemplatively. "Any indication of child abuse?"

"None. Her father isn't what I'd call a dutiful parent, but there's nothing out of the ordinary about him."

"When did the behavior pattern first become evident?"

"Last year. Her teacher saw her and a few other children catching insects and eating them."

"Not uncommon among four-year-olds," Fitzgibbon pointed out, "even if it's a bit unappetizing."

"That was the teacher's reaction," Thorpe agreed. "She reprimanded the children, frightened them with all manner of horror stories about illness, and that should have been the end of it."

"But it wasn't," Fitzgibbon said.

"Not for Constance, no. She continued to eat insects, then was found in the playground eating bits of flesh from a cat which had been hit by a car."

Fitzgibbon shook his head. "No chance that we're dealing with simple malnutrition here, is there?"

"No, none. The teacher reported the incident to the headmistress, and before any action was taken, the child had drowned two stray kittens and had started to eat them. That's when the father was called in, and he agreed to place her here for observation. That was six months ago, and . . . well, Teddy, I'm stumped. Her behavior doesn't fit any of the patterns."

"You've interviewed her, of course."

"Of course. She insists that she was following orders she received from the bogeyman."

Fitzgibbon nodded understandingly. "Guilt displacement."

"Of course." They returned to Thorpe's office and resumed their seats. Thorpe opened the file and said, "Let me give you the family background first."

"You just told me—"

"I just mentioned the parents, but there seems to be a pattern of family pathology here. I obtained most of this information from her father, and the rest of it from the police records. Her mother seems to have been a part-time prostitute, and she was killed by one of her clients. The child's grandfather was in and out of prison for most of his life. Her grandfather was also illegitimate, by the way."

"Hm," Fitzgibbon mused. "Illegitimate children sometimes grow into maladjusted adults and create life patterns for themselves that affect their children."

"And through the children, the grandchildren," Thorpe agreed. "I know. I suppose that Hitler's father is the best clinical example of that syndrome."

"Any details on the circumstances of her grandfather's birth?"

"A few," Thorpe replied. "I imposed upon my cousin at Scotland Yard to dig up the old records, and he found some interesting things."

"Scotland Yard! Michael, pregnancy out of wedlock isn't a crime. It never was."

"No, but the woman involved, Mary McCormick, Constance Sheldon's great-grandmother, reported a crime and filed a lawsuit."

"Against the father?"

"No, against St. Anselm's Asylum in Whitby, Yorkshire, and against a man named"—he glanced at the papers in front of him—"named Dr. John Stewart, the physician in residence. She was employed as a chambermaid at the asylum, and she claimed that her pregnancy was Stewart's fault."

"But she didn't claim he was the father?"

"No. The lawsuit was dropped and the complaint listed as a false police report. The woman must have gotten pregnant by a lover, panicked, and then tried to shift responsibility onto someone else."

"But if she didn't maintain that Stewart was the father, why did she try to sue him?"

"Because he was in charge of the asylum, and was therefore presumably responsible for the safety of the staff. She claimed that while she was working for Stewart at St. Anselm's, she was"—he glanced again at the papers—"ah, here it is. She claimed she was raped by an inmate named Renfield."

Constance watched the ant laboring to carry a tiny crumb of cookie back to the crack in the baseboard of the wall. She looked over at Mrs. Griffin to make sure the woman's attention was elsewhere, then she grabbed the ant and popped it into her mouth.

"Hello, Constance," said the soft voice which spoke to her from inside her head.

"Hello, Bogey Man," she whispered. She knew that she had to whisper, because she was the only one who could hear the Bogey Man, and their conversations were very, very secret.

"You've been such a good girl, Constance," the voice said. "You've made me so happy."

"I don't like this place, Bogey Man," she whispered sadly. "I want to go home."

"Yes, you must go home very soon, my dear child," the voice agreed. "I told you to eat the insects and the animals just to see if you were a good, obedient little girl, and you've proven to me that you are. So now you must not do those things again. You must do whatever the doctors and the nurses tell you to do, and soon they will let you go home."

"You said you were going to give me presents, Bogey Man."

"Oh, and I shall, my dear Constance, I shall. As soon as you leave this place and go home, I shall begin to give you gifts such as you cannot even begin to imagine."

"I want a puppy," Constance whispered, "but I don't want to have to eat him."

"You shall have your puppy," the soft, seductive voice said. "You shall have whatever you want. You shall have nice clothes, and lots of rings and bracelets, and you shall travel all over the world to do favors for me."

"Can Bonnie come with me?" Bonnie was her best friend.

"Of course Bonnie can come with you," the voice agreed. "And maybe, if I find that I like her, Bonnie can be my friend, too. And when time has passed, and you are all grown up into a fine lady, and you have gone all the places I tell you to go and have done all the things I tell you to do, then I shall give you the greatest gift of all, a gift of which most little girls only dream."

"What, Bogey Man?" she asked eagerly. "Tell me, please!"

The child was too young and innocent to detect the subtle hint of malevolence. "You, my dear sweet Constance," the soft voice answered, "shall be the bride of a prince. . . ."

ABOUT THE AUTHOR

JEFFREY SACKETT was born in Brooklyn in 1949, and counts himself fortunate to have made it home from the hospital unscathed. After studying briefly for the ministry, he chose to pursue an academic career—this being preferable at the time to his alternative, which was a year in the Mekong Delta as a guest of the government.

He obtained graduate degrees in history from Queens College and New York University, and also studied classical Greek, Latin, and several modern languages. Being thus possessed of a vast fund of fascinating but unmarketable information, he became a teacher of history and English, which he has remained until this day.

He explored other career alternatives at various times. He worked for a while as a bank guard (during which time the bank was robbed) and as a finder of missing persons (most of whom had disappeared by choice, and threatened him with all manner of violent reprisals when he found them). He decided that on the whole, teaching was his safest bet.

He has had three novels published by Bantam: *Stolen Souls*, *Candlemas Eve*, and now *Blood of the Impaler*. His fourth novel is about werewolves and will be out in spring 1990.

Sackett lives in a ridiculously overpriced house in Tanglewood Hills, New York, with his wife Paulette, an artist; their daughter Victoria Simonetta, an infant; their dog Paddington, a cocker spaniel; and their lizard Horatio, a seven-foot iguana. Theirs is the only house in the neighborhood with a sign saying Beware of Reptile on the fence.

John Saul is "a writer with the touch for
raising gooseflesh."
—Detroit News

John Saul has produced one bestseller after another:
masterful tales of terror and psychological suspense. Each
of his works is as shocking, as intense and as stunningly
real as those that preceded it.

☐	27261	THE UNLOVED	$4.50
☐	26657	THE UNWANTED	$4.50
☐	25864	HELLFIRE	$4.50
☐	26552	BRAINCHILD	$4.50
☐	26258	THE GOD PROJECT	$4.50
☐	26264	NATHANIEL	$4.50

Look for them at your bookstore or use the page to order: